Sto

STORM

JACK DRUMMOND

SPHERE

First published in Great Britain as a paperback
original in 2009 by Sphere

A CIP catalogue record for this book
is available from the British Library.

ISBN 978-0-7515-3909-7

Typeset in Bembo by Palimpsest Book Production Limited,
Grangemouth, Stirlingshire
Printed and bound in Great Britain by Clays Ltd, St Ives plc

Papers used by Sphere are natural, renewable and recyclable products
sourced from well-managed forests and certified in accordance with
the rules of the Forest Stewardship Council.

Mixed Sources
Product group from well-managed
forests and other controlled sources
www.fsc.org Cert no. SGS-COC-004081
© 1996 Forest Stewardship Council

Sphere
An imprint of
Little, Brown Book Group
100 Victoria Embankment
London EC4Y 0DY

An Hachette UK Company
www.hachette.co.uk

www.littlebrown.co.uk

For F,
My brave, beautiful wife

Part One

'Near sixty miles from the coast and abutting the Silver Hills, the Hanish and the Susqua streams form the head-waters of the Susquahanish River. Separated by a heavily forested ridge line, these two valleys offer rough, steep and inspirational country, a landscape of high, terraced lakes and deep, narrow canyons much favoured by trappers and loggers, though care and wise preparation should always be taken in any approach to these valleys . . .'

Shaws' Travelling Companion to the
Northern Pacific States, 1923

The plastic should have blown. A single, moulded charge as round and as thick as a deep-dish pizza puttied round the top of a pipeline flow-control. Rigged with a timer for 1:30 a.m. A safe ten-minute window to scramble back up the slope, start the truck and wait for the blow.

That was the plan. That's what they'd done.

Mort Johannesen glanced at his watch, its luminous second hand moving past contact time. Nothing. Not a whisper, save a cool night breeze scampering across the flats below them. Placement, wiring, connections, timer – he'd checked it all himself. On site. Last man away. It should have blown. But it hadn't.

Mort cursed softly – 'Shit' – but loud enough to be heard by his three companions.

'Shoulda blowed by now,' whispered Gene, lying beside him, belly down in the dirt.

Forty metres away the elevated section of pipe threw a dim star-shadow over the sage scrub. It looked like a giant looping spigot rising out of the ground – three steel wheels set into its trunk, one for each of the three pipes that lay buried two metres below ground. Blow that flow-control and the pipe pressure would send the oil fifty feet into the air. A hundred maybe. It wouldn't stop production for long, Mort knew, but it would send out a clear message to those land-thieving bastards who were raping this land.

We don't like what you're doing. Stop now. Or else.

There were four of them on the job. Mort, Gene and two local activists. They'd spent a couple of months scoping the site, watching from the hills when the first shovellers went in, tyres higher than a two-storey building, scraping off the top level of bush and root and rock. In the first week the rigs had cleared a brown scab forty acres wide on God's own country, pretty much no different now from when the State was a territory and the Cheyenne and Teton Sioux ranged across these high plains. Another week, it was ninety acres and the diggers and drillers arrived, levelling down to suck out that oil and pump it through to the railhead. Just a week earlier, the first sweet crude had started down these pipes.

And that's where they were right now, under a bright starlit sky, four miles from the main site, six from the railhead, enough margin to give them a good start when the charge blew.

Except it hadn't.

The other side of Gene, one of the locals who'd come along for the party stirred restlessly. Mort glanced across Gene's back. The guy was shaking his head. Mort knew who it was. Fucking Beardie, right on cue. Johnny something or other, the younger of the two locals, with the red whiskers and an 82nd Airborne tattoo on his forearm. Wore his sleeves rolled up so you couldn't miss it. Ever since Mort and Gene had come into town, it was Beardie who had the loudest voice. Always coming up with something. Some little twist to the plan. Some fucking refinement.

4

There was always one, Mort reflected. And this was theirs. His and Gene's. A pain in the fucking butt.

'It's just that damn timer,' said Beardie, in a croaking whisper. 'I said it was loose when I saw you set it. I seen it a million times,' he told them, and scrambled to his feet.

Beside him Mort sensed Gene about to move, to say something, to stop the guy. He reached out a hand swift as a spooked rattler and squeezed his fingers into Gene's upper arm. The message was clear and his old buddy settled back in the dirt.

Like Gene, Mort knew you never go back to the charge site in a timer situation. Not if you want to live. You send in Disposal, you choose another site, or you squeeze off a couple of rounds. Target practice. Anyone from the 82nd Airborne would have known that. But there were a lot of guys out here in the boondocks liked you to think they'd done their share. Over there in Afghanistan or I-raq. Sometimes they worked those lines so long – 'I did this', 'I saw that' – they let it damn well go right to their heads, ended up believing all that shit. Like Beardie there. Some piss-head thirty-year-old country poke who wouldn't have known a field latrine from a cocktail shaker. Probably never made it out of the motor pool.

By now said Beardie had slithered down the slope, reached the flat and was loping across open ground. Mort watched him every step of the way. Bent double he was, but still a wide-open target, the sage brush scraping againt his combat pants. He might as well have been banging a drum. Some para.

Mort shook his head, looked at his watch again.

Right about now, he reckoned, and worked his fingers into his ears.

The charge blew with Beardie no more than twenty feet distant. One second he was there, bent double and loping towards the control junction, the next he was off his feet, splayed out, and then gone. Eaten up by a white flash of ten-weight Plexi-Lye-60 that turned in a split second into a rolling orange ball, gulped up by a boiling black cloud that wiped away a thick column of stars.

A blast of hot air raced up the ridge and slapped across their cheeks.

'Holy shit,' said Mort. 'Did you see that?'

1

It would have surprised no-one to learn that the house
at the top of South Bluff Drive had been built by architects and was the home of architects. If anyone had been
able to see it, that is. From the road there was nothing
save a dead-end turning circle in a stand of spindly red
firs, with stone and mortar pillars bracketing tall timber
gates. A hundred metres beyond these gates the firs
thinned and the sloping land levelled to a chip-wood
parking area set against a final rising ridge. At first glance
this low bank of land would have looked like a meadow
of shifting grass and nodding wildflowers had it not been
for a set of double redwood doors built into it, the
meadow above nothing less than the roof of the house.

Because of the steep slope to the sea a hundred metres
below, the house was stepped, its topmost floor on a level
with the driveway, the three levels below it following
the line of the seaward slope. Like its entrance gates and
front doors, the house was built of local redwood, the

7

wide weathered planks cut on all four levels by sheets of tempered glass and solar panels that rose in a series of slanting squares from terraced decks to wildflower eaves.

Although the house occupied a headland above Melville there was no view of the old whaling town from the house, the northern edges of the property screened by the wind-break stand of firs that shaded South Bluff Drive. Instead, the only prospect from its glass-walled living rooms, bedrooms and bathrooms, its terraces, infinity pool and hot tub, and the lawns that sloped away from it, was a diminishing perspective of wooded coastline north and south and, as far as the eye could see, the ocean.

With nothing between her and the vast Pacific save a floor-to-ceiling sheet of glass, Dasha Pearse watched the swells roll into Melville Bay as she rinsed her crop of honey-blonde hair in the shower. Already she could see a couple of surfboards coming round the left-hand side of the curling breaks, much the same course she'd taken with her husband Zan when, twenty years earlier, the summer she'd started college, she'd finally summoned the nerve and the skill – nerve, most of all – to follow him out and take on one of the West Coast's more daunting and exhilarating rides.

Turning off the shower, Dasha stepped from the glass-panelled wet room, pulled a towel from the rail and went through to the bedroom. Towelling herself dry, she watched the first boarder come in from the left and start stroking fast. Beyond the board a curling swell rose from the ocean, clean and glassy green, reaching out in a long glittering arc that seemed to build and build until the surfer was lost in its toppling fury. Dasha stopped towelling and held her breath. If the surfer didn't ride that first break and come out of the pocket in one piece, he or she would end up on the headland rocks with more cuts and bruises than a pint of mercurochrome and a tub of arnica could stretch to. Or be held down in one of Melville's treacherous reef trenches praying that a gasped lungful of air would be enough to last through the following wave. Or two. Or three. They called it the hold-down. Dasha had been there. Dasha knew.

But suddenly the surfer was clear, coming out of the tube in a balancing crouch, arms spread like wings, streaking away down the turning slope of water before hitting the bottom and cutting up for another ride. Tucking the towel around her, Dasha squinted at the distant figure swooping up and down the wave, then reached for the binoculars that her husband kept by the window to search for whales. Adjusting the focus, she could make out a man. On a red board. Mungo McKay. That red board, this early in the morning, it just had to be Mungo, one of the best board-makers along the West Coast. Knowing Mungo, he'd probably spotted the swells before dawn and been catching rides ever since. Which meant that the other surfer out there was sure to be his girlfriend, Miche, now paddling fast on to the last swell of the set, catching the crest, rising to her feet and dropping away until the two of them were lost behind the headland.

All so long ago, Dasha mused, putting down the glasses and wondering how she'd make out now if she gave it a try. Wipe-out. Laundered. Just creamed. That was then, this is now.

Dasha glanced at her watch. A little before eight. She'd need to get a move on. She might not be paddling out for the Melville breaks any time soon, but her schedule today was likely to be just as tough and demanding. A two-hour drive up to Pearse-Caine's Wilderness project

9

for an on-site meet-and-greet with Mrs Courtney Sutton, who'd gone and bought their first unit off-plan after reading a magazine article about the project. She'd got it as a birthday surprise for her husband, and had called the previous afternoon to say she was bringing him in for his first weekend. 'He can be a little difficult sometimes,' Court had confided. 'You know men. Sometimes they need some stroking . . .'

Which had made Dasha giggle some when she put down the phone. Stroking? Is that what the woman had said? After spending two million dollars on the first of Pearse-Caine's Wilderness retreats without telling hubby? Was that all it took? Either Courtney was a toaster in the sack, or Win was some pushover. And from what Dasha knew of software billionaire Win Sutton of SuttonCorp Seattle, the latter seemed very unlikely. No wonder the wife wanted back-up.

'Hey, Momma. When's breakfast? Blister's hungry.'

Dasha turned from the window. Standing in the bedroom doorway, rubbing sleepy eyes, was her five-year-old daughter Alexa. Clasped in her arms was her teddy, Blister.

'Waffles,' Dasha replied, going down on her knees and gathering her daughter in her arms, smelling the sleepy warmth of her.

'With maple syrup?' came a second voice. It was Alexa's nine-year-old brother, Finn, coming up behind his little sister and deliberately pulling a tuft of hair from Blister's balding head.

'Finn Pearse,' cried Dasha. 'I don't believe I just saw you do that.'

'I didn't do a thing,' Finn lied, barefaced, eyes widening and innocent, as Alexa's mouth opened in a silent scream. It didn't stay silent for long.

'Just you wait till your father hears about this,' said Dasha, as the bedroom filled with a rising wail of indignation. 'Just you wait till I tell him.'

2

Hauling his board up on to the narrow skirt of beach, Mungo McKay turned in time to see Miche take a tumble at the end of her ride, her own board slicing at too steep an angle off the breaking lip of the wave, stripping away her ankle leash and dumping her unceremoniously into a creamy wash of boiling surf.

'Way to go, baby,' murmured Mungo, and plumped himself down. The air was still damp from the night, and a thin crust had started to form on the surface of the sand as the sun rose above the hills behind him and warmed it. It would be a fine day, with some fine surf, but Mungo knew it wouldn't last. Even now, far out beyond the waves, where sea met sky, a long thin line of black separated the two, running the horizon's length between the headlands that enclosed Melville Bay. Leaning back on his elbows, pushing through the sand crust, he watched Miche tumble towards him with the surf, her board sluicing up the beach ahead of her. 'One of these days, my lady, you're gonna give the word wipe-out a whole new meaning.'

Mungo was tall and tanned with a wet slick of greying blond hair that reached to his shoulders, cream-coloured eyebrows and eyes as brown as old kelp. He'd have been a very good-looking man if it hadn't been for a ragged line of scars slanting across his left cheek, from the point of his chin to the lobe of his ear. Back in his teens, as a careless carpenter's apprentice, he'd let a sander pad work loose from its mounting. Leaning into the wood, the spinning sand-paper disc had ripped free and gouged its way across his face. Nearly twenty years on these same scars had worn themselves into deep angled creases that gave his smile an odd lopsided tilt and turned handsome into rugged. He was smiling now as Miche, sputtering angrily, rolled to a stop not ten feet away from him, the wave that had carried her up the beach streaming back past her to the ocean.

'That was your fault,' she snarled, shooting him a menacing look, her black Makah Indian eyes blazing.

'Hey, me? I didn't do a thing,' said Mungo, chuckling. 'What did I do?'

'You . . . you didn't put enough wax on the board, that's what.'

'And if I'm not mistaken, that's your board, not mine,' countered Mungo. 'Which means it's your job to see it's waxed.'

'And it's your job to keep an eye on me, and look out for me, y'know?' Sitting in the streaming surf, she slid a finger beneath a slick of wet black hair and flipped it off her cheek. 'That's what the good guys do.'

'Who said I was a good guy?' Mungo replied, springing up to retrieve her board before the next wave got a hold of it, then hauled her up on to her feet.

'And I've got sand in my suit,' she said, squirming, plucking at the neoprene skin. 'And a bathload of ocean too. Real cold.'

'And I suppose that's my fault as well?'

'Sure is, white man. Who else's?' Miche snatched the board from him, and feinted away when he leaned down to plant a kiss on her cheek. 'Hey, you! Good guys only, remember?'

'Maybe it's time you got yourself a new board,' said Mungo, as they trudged up the beach towards a flight of steps set in the sea wall. They'd been out for nearly three hours and his thighs and shoulders had that pleasant, drilling ache that comes with good waves and better rides. Nothing put Mungo in a better mood.

'So you gonna make me one?' Miche teased, knowing that that was a little too much to expect, even after the three years she'd been sharing Mungo's bed. The shortest of her lover's surfboards, the 6-threes, took a minimum of two months to shape, cost a small fortune and were legendary up and down the coast – sleekly sculpted boards made from hand-picked sustainable paulownia, finned with plantation-grown cedar, and each signed with the entwined 'M's that could also be 'W's depending on which way you looked at them. Two thousand a pop, easy, and a six-month waiting list. For the last five seasons, all the big pro boys in Hawaii had ridden a Mungo McKay Wave-Walker – the 6-threes, the 6-tens, the 7-fives, and that beautiful nine-foot-eight-inch 'Pointer' for the real steep-and-deeps at Waimea and outer reef Pe'ahi.

Mungo waited until they reached the steps, hefting the board under his arm. 'Already done it,' he told her. 'Reckoned a 7-three would suit you.'

13

Two steps behind him, aiming to whack his butt with the end of her board, Miche stopped dead in her tracks. She ran the words through her head, to make sure she hadn't misunderstood. Then ran them through again. Her own board? Her very own Wave-Walker? She couldn't believe it. He had to be joking? After all their time together the man still managed to catch her when she least expected it. By the time she got her wits back Mungo was up over the top step and heading for home.

Back in his workshop, an old timber-frame rope shack fifty metres behind the sea wall that smelt sweetly of ocean salt, warm sawdust and gum turpentine, Mungo slid his board on to trestles, switched on the local radio station out of Astoria, then reached for the tag behind his shoulders to pull down the zip on his wetsuit.

'. . . and it's looking like some fine sets coming in off the ocean this a.m., all the way down from Desolation Point to Cape Tribulation. So if any of you surf boys listening in got a good excuse for a day off work, head on down to Titus Bay or Ringwood Beach or the Melville Bluffs for some of the best breaks you'll likely see all season. Swells are high now but expected to peak this p.m., with outer buoy readings suggesting there's more to come tomorrow and into Sunday . . .'

'Been there, done that,' grunted Mungo, watching Miche scurry around the workshop as he peeled down the black neoprene sleeves of his wetsuit.

'Forecast is good along the coast rest of the day, with high blues and the mercury tipping 24 celsius,' the weather man continued. 'But word is, it's all set to change by day's end, with a whiplash tail-ender coming in from the islands and a front heading down from our friends up in BC. No need to tell you folks that it's gonna get wet

14

before it gets dry, all the way from the highlands to the ocean . . .'

'So where is it then? Where're you hiding it?' asked Miche impatiently, checking under the clamp-table and behind the saw-bed, shaking her head as every possible hiding place drew a blank. 'You better not be kidding me, you hear?'

Stepping out of his wetsuit and carrying it to the tub-sink, Mungo turned and pointed over his shoulder, up at the rafters where ropes and fish-nets had once hung to dry. Lying across two beams was a red-bellied board. When Miche saw it her heart gave a lurch and her throat tightened.

'Needs a bit more beeswax to finish her off. But the way I hear it, you're good at . . .'

Mungo McKay didn't have a chance to finish. Miche was in his arms, legs wrapped around his waist and her mouth clamping down on to his.

3

'Momma's wearing scarara. Momma's wearing scarara,' chanted Alexa from the back seat of Dasha's silver Lexus Hybrid.

'Mascara, stupid. It's mascara,' said Finn, sitting beside her, thumbs flying over his DS keyboard.

'Don't say "stupid", Finn,' Dasha chided. 'It's not a nice word. Say "silly" instead.'

'Silly. Stupid. Still means she's a dumbass,' replied the boy, this last word spoken cautiously, under his breath.

'Finn Pearse, I heard that. Where did you learn a word like that?'

'Dad,' he replied, with an unmistakable 'so-there' edge to it. 'And Gramma too,' he added for good measure, to hammer the point home.

Dasha grimaced – typical, she thought. Some father. Some grandmother.

But now was not the time to let it bug her – she was more concerned that if Alexa had noticed the mascara, then maybe she'd applied her make-up too hurriedly or thickly. It wouldn't do to turn up for lunch with the Suttons with mascara globs in her eyelashes and dotting the tops of her cheeks like a high school prom queen. Pulling up on a red at the set of traffic lights at the bottom of South Bluff Drive, Dasha flipped down her visor and checked in the vanity mirror. She tipped her head from side to side, winked one eye and then the other in the mirror, then jumped in her seat when the driver behind her beeped his horn. The light had turned to green. Snapping back to the road, she promptly stalled the Lexus and a couple more angry blasts greeted this further delay. By the time she'd gotten started again and pulled away, the light had switched back to red and the line of cars behind her stayed right where they were.

And good riddance, thought Dasha, looping down on

to Promenade and along the harbour front. She was heading for The Quays, Pearse-Caine's wharfside development where she and Zan kept an office, and where Dasha's mother, Shelley, had an apartment. Just a block from the office, Gramma's was the perfect place to dump Alexa and Finn when the schedule got crowded.

In a perfect world, of course, Zan would have been around to help with the kids and do the driving, and she'd have had time to get herself into some kind of presentable order. Not that she was a slouch when it came to high-end meetings or corporate presentations and all the social bally-hoo that went hand in hand with maintaining a successful architectural practice. But three days earlier, her husband had gone off on his annual fishing trip, up to the high lakes on the Hanish Stream. And as Dasha Pearse knew only too well, nothing, not even Mr and Mrs Win Sutton, came between Zan Pearse and a cutthroat trout. Not that she begrudged him his break. He worked hard, he was a great dad, and he deserved the down time. Dasha hadn't even bothered to phone and tell him about the meet. Knowing her luck, she'd call his cell just as he hooked the big one. He'd never forgive her.

'Hey, Mom,' said Finn, breaking into her thoughts. 'Why's there a police car outside the office?'

The question brought Dasha back with a jolt. Up ahead, where Lower Main joined Promenade and swung round the north side of the port, she spotted the squad car in The Quays' parking lot. As she came off the harbour bridge, made the lights on Main and turned through the development's anchored entrance she also saw the reason the squad car was there. Daubed across

17

the opaque front window of their office were four spray-painted words, each letter two feet high, each dripping paint down the window in alternating red and green ribbons. And just a week before the offices were finally going to be fitted with security cameras, goddammit!

Rather than park in her reserved bay outside the office, and right next to the police car, Dasha drove past without stopping. In her rear-view mirror she could see Big Bill Mulholland, the town's police chief, leaning on the bonnet of his Durango four-wheel drive, boot heel resting on its fender, surveying the damage.

As she sailed by, Dasha hoped Mulholland didn't recognise her car. She was running late already and if she wanted to make it to the Suttons she didn't have time for police enquiries and questions and commiserations. Her office manager could handle all that. And get someone in to clean that damned paint – and message – off of their window. And fast.

But as Dasha pulled into a space at the far end of The Quays' parking lot, it wasn't just the damn timing thing with the security cameras that bothered her, or the paint that would have to be cleaned off, or the possibility that she might be delayed. What really concerned her about this new message was the fact that the usual two-word aerosol instruction – 'STOP NOW . . .' – had been added to.

Another two words completed the line, and it was this chilling addition that prickled the small hairs on the back of her neck:

'. . . OR ELSE!'.

4

Warming up her breakfast coffee with just a small slug of Jack's sour mash, Shelley Caine left the galley kitchen in her Quays' apartment and went through to the living room. Slipping her fingers between the blinds she watched her daughter's Lexus pull into a parking bay two floors below and the kids tumble out. She glanced at her watch. Running late as usual, rushing around like a fly on one wing, thought Shelley. Just like her dad. And her husband, come to that. All three of them. Take on anything, they would, but pretty much damn hopeless when it came to a schedule. Dropping the blinds, Shelley took a sip of the cooling coffee and felt a scalding glow. Whoa – maybe a splash too much sour mash. She'd need to keep a line on it if she was looking after the kids.

Shelley had always liked a drink. From way back. A vodka rocks on the stroke of six, wine with meals, social stuff. But after her husband, Mack, passed on, she'd taken to it with a real relish. Pretty soon the vodka had given way to bourbon – it was always a good thing to vary your diet, she liked to think – and come winter, bourbon had a warmer, richer taste than the icy Ivanoff Sixes she bought in two-litre kegs. Jack, Jim and Hiram were now among her best friends – a splash in the morning to oil the joints and get the old body moving, a dash in her morning coffee as a reward for unloading the dishwasher from the night before, a couple of tugs around lunch and maybe a little something to see her through the afternoon. But she could handle it. She knew when to hold off.

Melville-born and bred, Dasha's mother had been one of the first to move into The Quays, taking a two-bedroom unit with harbour view just a few months after her husband passed away. At first she had missed the old family home with its creaking wood stairs, heavy panelled doors and gingerbread verandahs. But she'd quickly discovered that the new condo was much better suited to her current needs. Not only was she close to the shops, a deli, a couple of bars, a Starbucks, and an Austrian bakery, but The Quays' recycling was a damned wonder.

Back in the old house, there had always been a problem getting rid of empty bottles. Most of her neighbours had just a few to recycle – mostly jars for sauces and preserves – but whenever the garbage crews came to empty her bins, it sounded like a Niagara of breaking glass out there on the sidewalk, and she'd turn up the radio to cover the din. One time, a friend had applauded her sense of civic pride – recycling bottles for the whole street. Shelley Caine had not disabused her of that assumption. But here at The Quays, set into the worktop beside her kitchen sink, there were three bin lids. One was for plastic waste, one for paper and board, and one for glass. She just lifted the lid and dropped the bottle in. At the bottom of the chute, two floors down in the basement, was a large sealed container that serviced the six apartments in her block. She might have been getting through more liquor than any of the other residents but there was no-one to point a finger or raise an eyebrow.

Out in the hall, the buzzer sounded and Shelley went to answer it.

'Hey kids, come on in, why don't you?' she said, stepping aside as Finn and Alexa bowled in through the door.

'I'm running late, Mom,' said Dasha. 'Can I just leave them with you and split?'

'You go on ahead,' her mother said, receiving a hug from her daughter and a kiss on each cheek, but remembering to keep her mouth firmly closed so that her breath wouldn't give her away. 'I got their favourite fish pie for lunch and if you don't make it back by teatime I'll have 'em fed and watered by whatever time you do. Only don't rush yourself, you hear?' said Shelley as Dasha headed down the corridor. 'And check out that mascara, honey. You got it on a little thick, you ask me.'

5

In a small town like Melville, even with weekenders coming in from Seattle, a chief of police soon got to recognise certain cars. And Big Bill Mulholland recognised Dasha

Pearse's silver Lexus the moment it slid by. A hundred yards ahead he saw the brake lights shine, and watched the car pull into a parking bay two rows over. Not that he was surprised she hadn't stopped by the office. The woman had the kids with her, looked like she was in a rush, and well, it wasn't the first time that this kind of thing had happened.

Three times in the last five months – since Pearse-Caine started construction on the Wilderness project up-country – Mulholland had been called out to see the spray-painted threats smeared across their office windows, or across the glass-bricked entrance to The Quays. On each occasion he'd been blunt and honest. 'Until we catch them with the spray-gun in their hands, Mrs Pearse, there's not a lot we can do beyond give you a crime number and tell you to call your insurers,' this advice levied with a take-it-or-leave-it shrug. 'And maybe fix yourself up with some of those CCTV cameras in the meantime.'

And every time he spoke the words, he wished he could do more. Descended from a long line of Melville whalers – back in the days when you rowed the whaling boat, threw your harpoons and hung on while the whales took you for a sleigh ride – Mulholland didn't take kindly to anyone messing with his town, nor the people who lived in it. And what he saw each time he answered the Pearses' call fair made his blood boil. Some damned hooligan troublemaker, some damned do-gooder eco-nut who couldn't think no further than the end of his busy-body green nose. Like, just how many chemicals were they gonna have to use in cleaning agents to scrub that shit off the windows? Did the asshole ever think about that before he pulled out his aerosol can and started spraying? No damn way, thought Mulholland, hitching up his gun belt. As if the Pearses were doing anything that deserved that kind of attention anyhow. Far as most of the townsfolk saw it, it was the Pearses that had helped put Melville back on the map, renovating those old captains' houses up on South Bluff, converting the flensing sheds, and bringing in those houseboats to liven up the deserted quays. Got them featured in all those magazines, didn't they? Stoked up the interest, good for the local economy. And everything eco-friendly as you please. Sustainable this, renewable that. What was there to complain about? Let alone go making threats. And this latest message was certainly that, far more chilling and direct than the ones that had come before it.

Course it wasn't locals doing it, Mulholland was certain of that. In a small town like Melville he'd have heard about it, known whose door to go knocking on. When he discovered the aerosol cans couldn't be bought nowhere but Seattle, he was even more certain the perps were out-of-towners.

'At it again, Chief?'

Mulholland turned. It was Lindie Cass, out walking her dog. Big and blonde and blowsy, turquoise rings and necklaces matching her eyeshadow, Lindie owned Mama Surf, Melville's oldest and best-loved tavern down on Promenade.

'Sure looks like it, don't it?' replied Mulholland, taking off his trucker's hat and pushing a wad of freckled fingers through a thatch of greying red hair. As he settled the cap back down, he spotted the Lexus heading back in his direction. Just Dasha this time. Eyes straight ahead. Kids dropped off with their gran. Looked like she was dressed for a meeting too, hair done up and all. He pretended not to see her, and turned back to Lindie as a green Toyota truck pulled out of a bay and followed after the Lexus. 'Course, it needn't never have happened,' he continued, noting the Toyota's out-of-town plates, 'if our Mr Pringle hadn't voted against it when the council were talking security cameras for downtown.'

'Tell me about it,' said Lindie, calling her mutt to heel. 'They should have left that fucker in sanitation. Where he belonged.'

Mulholland chuckled. Since David Pringle had taken up the job of Town Works and Resources Director, he had made more enemies than al-Qaeda, and become the town's favourite whipping boy. Anything went wrong, seemed you could always trace it back to Pringle.

'You know what he's planning this time?' asked Lindie, who had no good reason to like the man – her planning application for a pontoon bar across from her premises on Promenade had been turned down by Pringle just the week before.

'Now you gonna spoil my day, Lindie? This early on?' asked Mulholland.

Lindie drew close. 'The little dipshit wants to introduce a sport licence for the beach. You surf, you pay. Like parking a car. Waves by the hour. Says we need to regulate the numbers. Too many coming in. Too many coming in? Without the surfers, this town would have been done for when they stopped the whaling and the logging.'

Mulholland sucked in his breath. Now that was news. Right from out of left field. For a second or two he couldn't credit it. Had Pringle completely lost the plot? Because Lindie was right. If it hadn't been for surfing, and the crowd it brought in, and the work that the Pearses were doing, bringing life back into Melville, the town would have gone down. Two great industries lost and surfing saves the day. Who'd have believed it? Surfing.

For a while back then, after the last whale carcass was hauled up the harbour slipway, and the last lumber loaded along South Bluff Quay, it had looked like Melville was a busted flush, couldn't even turn itself round as a sailing marina like some of the other ports down the coast. To get in and out of harbour, you needed a steady nerve and a strong ship to make it through the surf that rolled into Melville Bay nine months of the year. It had been worth the risk for bales of fur and timber and whales, but weekend sailing was a different matter. Pretty soon the fine old houses the town's well-padded traders and skippers had built up on South Bluff were peeling with neglect, the raised sidewalks along Main Street sagged wearily, and its deserted cobbled quays had been left to the crabbers.

And then the surfers arrived, back at the start of the seventies, a Beach Boys soundtrack and a small band of pioneers who reckoned Melville's big-wave surf breaks better than anything further south. Mulholland remembered them. Tanned, young guys with easy smiles, and pretty girls waiting for them on the beach. Not a care in the world if the waves were high, and never any trouble for a rookie cop called Mulholland just starting out after a spell in 'Nam. Pretty soon he'd caught a few swells himself, and most evenings he'd find himself down at the beach, smoking dope and talking waves.

Hell and high-water, it was down on that darned beach, sitting round some driftwood fire, he'd met his wife.

For a couple of seasons, those first surf boys kept Melville to themselves, but word soon spread there were some awesome walls up in north-west Washington State. One minute it was a few camper vans parked up for the season, a few gunslingers riding the waves. The next the whole damn world's out there. Surfing, or watching. Most just watching.

And if those first surfers didn't really do any work, and had a kind of stoned hippy look to them, the ones who followed were a very different breed, software and telecom execs from Seattle who were wealthy enough to invest in some prime weekend real-estate but still young enough to surf. It was this market that the Pearses and a whole bunch of other locals had lucked into, with board shops, accessory stores, and surf-wear boutiques up and down Main, not to mention bars like Mama Surf along Promenade and Jap diners serving sushi and saké.

And men like David Pringle to keep everyone in line, thought Mulholland.

A ticket for the beach? A licence to surf? The bird-brain had to be joking? Then again . . .

'Whaddya bet he'll get it through?' asked Mulholland.

Lindie shook her head. 'It'll never happen, Chief. Not in Melville.'

Mulholland seemed to consider this, rubbing a hand through his walrus moustache. 'A ten says he does.'

'And your ten taken . . .' replied Lindie, and the two of them shook on it.

6

Elroy Baker had never bought a woman's product before. It was about as bad as buying that first Trojan when he was fourteen. No, he decided. It was worse. Even at this time in the morning and Delaney's Supermart open just an hour, it had taken three idling strolls down the cosmetics aisle before it was clear of customers – all of them women, all of them intent, it seemed to him, on reading every word on the back of every bottle or tube or packet they picked up. Didn't they know what they wanted? Didn't they have anything better to do?

On his fourth pass, a tinny muzak piping out along the aisles, Elroy hurried over to the relevant shelf. Or rather shelves. It wasn't just the one brand he had to deal with, but what looked like dozens. In seconds a kind of numbing panic swooped in. He hadn't figured on a choice.

Tampons, that's what Mort had said. Just tampons.

And fruit. And duct tape. And torch batteries. And a good sturdy padlock, and a whole load of other stuff – all of which he could handle, no trouble.

But tampons? What sort of tampons? Did he need

the Super or the Regular? Did he need the green packet? Or the blue one? Or the pink? And then . . . Wings? Night time? Jesus. What kind? What was he supposed to choose? Tampons? Sanitary towels?

To cover himself, Elroy took a packet of each, burying the items as best he could under the other supplies. It wasn't until he reached the check-out that he realised his mistake. He was going to have to empty out his basket on to that strip of conveyor belt, all laid out for anyone to see. And just how was he going to explain needing so many different brands? He was about to turn back to the shelves and unload everything, make do with just the one brand, when he realised he'd left it too late. Two of the women who'd held him up earlier on the cosmetics aisle were now settling in behind him, waiting their turn.

Lowering the bill of his baseball cap, Elroy started to unload his basket. First went the rolls of duct tape, then the padlock, the apples, the bananas, the avocados, rolling down the conveyor belt like flotsam on a patched black river. Finally, with what he hoped would pass as a bored indifference, he brought out 'Night-Time' in the blue packet. Then 'Wings Supreme' in the pink, followed by assorted packs of 'Beyond', 'Softeeze', and 'GentleGlide'. And as he did so, he leant forward an inch or two, angled out his elbows and broadened his shoulders in an attempt to cover the nature of his purchases from the women behind.

'You want help packing, son?' asked the check-out lady, as she swiped the last 'GentleGlide' across the scanner.

Son? Why did everyone over the age of forty call him *son*? He was twenty-five, chrissakes, six foot one in his socks, and been working the crab boats since for ever.

28

'No thanks, ma'am. I'm just fine,' Elroy replied. 'Do it myself, no problem,' he added, suddenly wondering if there was any hint of sarcasm in her offer to help with the packing. He glanced at her to make sure. She was slouched in her spin-round chair, chewing gum and testing each of her lacquered fingernails with a click-click against her thumbs. No sly smile, no odd looks. She could have been on a different planet. Probably was.

'Then that'll be fifty-eight bucks fifty, son.'

Gritting his teeth, Elroy slipped three twenties from his pocket, moved past the till, and started shovelling his purchases into a plastic bag.

'Hey dude, havin' a party?'

Elroy swung round to the voice. Standing right behind him, dressed in a white butcher's apron with a paper trilby perched on his big round head, was Tod Breamer. A lay-off back in high school and now clearly working shifts on Delaney's meat counter, Breamer's broad red face was split into a leering grin, piggy black eyes flicking between Elroy and the packet of Softeeze he held in his hand.

'Your change, son,' drawled the check-out lady, holding out a palmful of dimes and a curling till receipt.

Elroy took them with a nod of thanks, threw them into the bag with the Softeeze, then turned back to Breamer. His old high school chum might have been bigger and broader and older, but Elroy knew he was smarter. And out of school smarter really counted. It gave him a surge of confidence. He'd managed the check-out lady; he could handle this.

'How's it going Breamer? Good to see ya,' he said, tucking a pack of GentleGlide into the bag and reaching for Night-Time.

'I mean,' continued Breamer, not to be distracted. 'I mean, your mom and sis stockin' up for a rainy day or something?'

'Breamer, you wanna talk girl's talk, that's fine by me,' replied Elroy, surprised at how level and sure his voice was. 'But me, I just buy 'em and pack 'em.'

Breamer took this in, not sure whether to nod or frown.

'You wanna know,' Elroy continued, suddenly inspired as he packed away the last items. 'I get 'em for lagging.'

'Lagging?'

Elroy hefted the two bags from the counter and set off for the Exit doorway. 'Gotta leaking pump on the boat. Skipper wants to lag it till he's got the money for some proper parts and repairs, know what I'm sayin'?'

Breamer decided on a nod, not wishing to appear uninformed when it came to boats, about which he knew very little.

'See you round, Breamer,' called Elroy, as he ducked through the automatic doors.

'Yeah, you too, Elroy.'

Outside, Elroy headed for his truck, slung the bags on to the front seat and got in after them. There was sweat on his forehead and his heart was still thumping.

Lagging? Jesus! Where did that come from?

But he'd done it. Exactly what Mort had told him to do. And he'd handled big dumb Breamer into the bargain. Mission accomplished. Which was just as well. In the last few weeks Elroy Baker had learnt one very important lesson. Do what you're told, and don't never mess with Mort Johannesen.

'You sure you want to do this?' said Mungo, turning his flatbed Mitsubishi on to Main and heading up town.

Beside him Miche was checking through her backpack. Satisfied, she tossed it on to the back seat. 'Two days, two hundred a day says I want to do this.'

'You're gonna get wet.'

'I'm boarding. Of course I'm gonna get wet.'

Mungo grunted. 'You know what I'm saying. If there's rain coming in, it won't take long to fill those canyons.'

'Then I'll be back sooner than we thought. Deal is Gimball pays the two days even if I'm up there just the one.'

'That's what Gimball told you?'

'You were there.'

'It was Mama Surf on a Wednesday night. I didn't hear a thing. Just saw those fat wet lips moving.'

'Well, that's what he said. Why? You gonna miss me?'

Mungo pulled up at the lights on Delamere and glanced across at her. She was looking right at him. That look she had, always challenging, always testing. The answer-back princess. And that straight, black hair, the long fringe that reached to her arched black eyebrows, those soft almond eyes. Yup, truth was, he was going to miss her. But he wasn't altogether sure he could trust himself to say it, without reaching into the glove compartment and giving her the second present of the day, his mother's wedding ring, three small twinkling diamonds in a thin gold band. He'd been planning it for weeks, just hadn't quite found the right time to spring it on her. Three years together, it was time to get the whole thing up and on a proper footing. And he did love her, like really love her. He'd had his share down the years, hanging round the beach, surfing the breaks. But Miche was way different. There was just something about her – wilful, stubborn, sexy as hell. Like two hours back when she'd taken him upstairs after she found the board, just pushing him down on the bed and sliding out of that neoprene suit like it was silk. No-one should have been able to get out of a wetsuit like that. But she had. Even the sand felt good.

The lights saved him. Mungo shifted gears and pulled away. 'There's gonna be some waves,' he said. 'Wouldn't want you to miss them. Not with the new board and all.'

'Four hundred bucks says the breaks'll have to wait, lover.'

'Just take care. If the Susqua looks like it's gonna fill, you tell Gimball it's a no-no. He'll try and railroad you . . .'

'He'll try what? Railroad me? You are kidding, right?'

Mungo chuckled. A ridiculous idea. No one railroaded Miche Tomak. But four hundred dollars was some lever.

'You think he'll pay up?'

'Tell you what,' grinned Miche. 'If he doesn't, you can always go round and get it off of him.' She shot him a look. Mungo and Gimball did not hit it off. Knowing Mungo, he'd love a chance to steam in on Charlie Gimball.

'Well now, there's a prospect,' replied Mungo, pulling off Main and into Gimball's lot. 'Just don't forget to give me a call, let me know how it's going.'

'It's the Susqua, remember? No signal till after the canyons.'

'You could always light a fire. Send me some of those smoke signal things.'

Miche reached for her back-pack and threw open the passenger door. Leaning over, she gave him a long, whispering kiss on the side of his mouth. 'Only smoke signal you're gonna get is when I'm back Sunday and smokin' your ass on the breaks. Or in bed. Take your pick, surf-boy.'

And with that she was out of the truck, door slammed behind her, and striding across the lot.

8

Charlie Gimball looked at the clock on the wall of his office and wondered if Mungo's girl had remembered. If she hadn't been squaw, he wouldn't have worried. But she was, and he did. You never could tell with the natives.

33

The girl might look like a *Cosmo* cover but like the rest of them Makahs her brains were in a different place. Smoking too much dope and swinging one too many crystals, was Charlie's opinion. He'd offered her the job two days earlier at Mama Surf down on Promenade. Said he was short a board leader for today's college trip and maybe she could help out? Two days running the gorges from just above the Susqua Falls? She'd seemed keen enough at the time and was a good, experienced canyoneer, knew the water like the back of her hand. But you couldn't rely on that, not with squaws like Miche Tomak, even if he was paying top dollar.

Charlie shook his head miserably and was leaning forward to pick up the phone, put a call through to Mungo's place, when he saw the Wave-Walker van pull into the lot. The passenger door swung open and Miche jumped out, reaching back in for a rucksack. In the driver's seat Charlie could just make out Mungo, flicking a return wave to Miche and turning back out on to Main.

'So you made it,' he said, as she pushed open the door and dropped her kit by his desk, took a chair and stretched out.

'You think I wouldn't?' she asked with a sly smile. She knew Charlie Gimball a whole lot better than he knew her.

'Never can tell. Those margaritas down at Mama's don't do much for the memory,' he replied, letting his eyes graze over her. Shoot, but she was just gorgeous, thought Charlie, pretending to wipe an eye but taking it all in. Wearing jeans and a tight polo neck, she was long and lean with a chest on her that screamed 'look at us, look at us', straight black hair cut to the shoulder, high Indian cheekbones and eyes as black and shapely as the ace of spades.

'Wouldn't miss it,' she said, not fooled by the eye-wiping routine, feeling his gaze drift over her – just as she'd expected. 'So, what's the brief?'

'Like I told you the other night,' he couldn't resist saying, 'a canyoning club from Fairbanks College over Tacoma way. Six students, two teachers. They're bringing their own gear, including wetsuits. All we gotta do is provide the boards and chow, and meet up with them at the Lodge up in Shinnook. I already loaded everything, you'll be pleased to hear. You'll be paired up with one of the teachers, guy by the name of Pete Conway who made the booking. Me and his wife'll drive the vans, set up lunch drops and deal with the camps.'

'How's the river?' asked Miche, remembering the forecast back in Mungo's workshop. 'You been up recently?'

'Couple of weeks back. Good late summer flow but nothing too high or fast. Deep enough for jumping some of the higher chutes, but no standing water to speak of. If we can get up there by two, you should be able to squeeze a couple of hours in. Warm them up some. Maybe get as far as Susqua Falls. Tomorrow, if you start early enough, you could make it down through Lobo and Cougar canyons. I was thinking we could camp up the last night below Fiddler's Chute and paddle-raft the rest of the way down to Shinnook.'

As Charlie outlined the itinerary, Miche ran it through in her head. Headwaters to Susqua Falls a fairly straight-forward twelve miles to start, another twenty or so Saturday – fast and furious – and back in time to try out her new board. Two days out, less than fifty miles tops. And four hundred dollars cash in her pocket, say eight bucks a mile. It didn't get better than that. Just so long as the peaks out on Melville Bay stayed high till she got back Sunday afternoon.

'When do we leave?'

Charlie glanced at the clock on the wall. 'How about right now?'

9

Moving his feet carefully over the muddy bed of the lake so as not to cloud the drifting water, Zan Pearse waded along the high bank towards his camp, keeping an eye on the still surface. For the last couple of hours he'd been stalking the top end of Bear Tree Lake, chasing a speckled shadow that had come to nothing, and time was running out. He was due back home that evening and with camp to break and a three-hour trek to the trailhead where he'd left his Jeep, there wasn't much casting time left.

Of all the lakes on the upper levels of the Hanish Stream, ranging in size from a suburban front lawn to a college football pitch, Bear Tree was Zan's favourite.

It was the highest of all the lakes, on the top-most level, long and narrow but large enough to provide good water, with shadowing overhang banks and sluicing currents where the Hanish Stream entered and left it. The water was tea-coloured, chill from snow-melt and clear as glass, knee-high at the top end, sloping down to waist height around the edges of the lower pools.

Zan had come here first with Mack Caine, Dasha's father, nearly twenty years earlier, his fourth summer in Melville. The first two seasons they'd fished stretches of the Susqua in the neighbouring valley where the old man had watched how the boy handled himself. When Mack was satisfied, he'd taken Zan over the ridgeline and brought him to Bear Tree.

'They'll tell you the trout are finer and fiestier over in Idaho,' Mack had told him. 'Or down south on Steamboat, Umpqua and Deschutes, or up north in BC on the Babine and Morice. But don't you believe a word of it. The best darn fishing for trout is right here on the Hanish, and Bear Tree's the jewel in the crown.'

And twenty years later, Zan was in no doubt that his late father-in-law was right in all but scale. Bear Tree wasn't just a jewel. In his opinion it was the whole damn crown.

At the end of every summer Zan took a week's break from Pearse-Caine to fish for steelhead and cutthroat. It didn't matter what was in the diary – meetings, deadlines, presentations – he'd pack his four-by-four and head up-country. Parking at the trailhead and shouldering his kit, he'd hike uphill in a lazy zig-zag before levelling out on to the first of the three shelves that led to the upper Hanish lakes. Brushing a path through ferns that had never seen the light of day, and climbing up past moss-covered cedar and ghostly hemlock that looked as though they'd shrugged on green overcoats to keep off the chill and the wet, he'd smile at the echoing, insistent drill of a distant woodpecker, pause for the bugling of elk, and keep a wary eye out for cougar and bear. Up in these hills, miles from the nearest shack, it didn't do to take chances, his right hand never straying too far from the butt of his Colt .44 Magnum.

There were no map-printed names for the puddles and ponds and finger lakes that lay up here (Zan had checked), and, far as he could tell, it was Mack who'd given Bear Tree its name. And it was Mack who'd shown him why. Set around the water's edge were more than a dozen red cedars that bore the marks of bears' claws, bark ripped and shredded, moss and lichen piled high in dead grey pillows around their roots. Just the cedars – not the hemlock, not Douglas, not alder. Neither Mack nor Zan knew the reason for the choice, but they both agreed that if a bear could do that to a tree, what they could do to a man didn't stand thinking about. Yet in all the time Zan had been coming here, he'd only ever seen one bear – a large brown sow with her cubs – loping along the opposite bank as though she was in a hurry to make the shops before they closed. That night, he'd slept light in his tent with his gun beside his pillow.

It wasn't just fishermen the bears spooked. Up here, as Mack used to say, the trout were as difficult to lure as a nun on sabbatical. Which was half the fun. You could dry-drift a fly over the head of a cutthroat a dozen times and he'd just watch it float on by. You could drop a Big Hopper on the bubble line and a bull would turn his back on it. You could find a pod of rainbows, finning against the top-end current, drop a wet-fly between them, and they wouldn't stir more than a fin to get out of its way. And all the time you'd be looking over your shoulder, just in case some old grizzly decided to drop by, pay a call.

All of which made a strike a prize worth having.

The other great thing about Bear Tree was its inaccessibility. From trailhead to campsite, it was a tough uphill hike that usually took Zan most of the first afternoon – he rarely made his first cast before dusk shadowed the water. Also, the tree cover around Bear Tree might have been close and thick enough to cause problems with your back cast, but it kept away the floatplanes and the helicopters. In twenty seasons – apart from the early days with Mack – Zan had never had to share the water with another angler.

This was Zan's last day up-country and so far the catch had been good. A bull trout the first evening at a tad over five pounds, followed by two red-jawed cutthroats, one of which he'd spit-grilled for his supper. His second day had begun where the Hanish Stream fed into Bear Tree, which meant tracking through a squelching moss meadow cut in the middle with a narrow, fast-moving pelt of water where he knew the trout liked to line up in squadrons. Three good-sized rainbows hit his Royal Wulff in the space of an hour, all of them a respectable weight and all of them returned to the chill swirling stream to fight another day. By lunchtime, the sky was high and blue through the treetops and it was hot. He'd retrieved his net of import Grolsch lager from where it had been chilling in the coldest water he'd been able to find, snacked on a protein bar and snoozed on the bank until the evening fish started calling him.

And that was how he'd spent his time, trolling both sides of Bear Tree, working the moss meadows at either end of the lake and finding some new sweet spots along an eddying twist further up the Hanish. It was all he'd hoped for, all he could have asked for – hard fish, sly fish, runners and sinkers, all of them cool and cunning. But last night, too dark for more casts, stripping off his waders on a skirt of bankside pebbles close to camp, he'd seen the fish you dream of.

It started with a tell-tale plop not ten feet from the beach, close enough for a ripple to reach him. It was just a flash but it was enough – a long silver side, hunched shoulders and a flick of the tail that left a rolling swirl on the surface. A 'summer-run' steelhead. Maybe thirty inches. And twenty pounds easy, or close to it.

Zan had spent the night thinking about that fish. Where it might go, the pools and eddies it might favour, the flies that might attract it. He wished with all his heart that the old man was there. Mack would have known what to do; Mack would have known where to find it. But this time he was alone, no other fisherman on the water. The fish was his if he could find it, lure it, take it.

With just one final morning to play with, Zan had dressed in the dark and was out on the water before the surface mists had slid away. By ten o'clock he'd passed a dozen rainbows that he'd have cast for just a day before. But now he wasn't bothering. There was only one fish he was looking for, only one he'd cast for. He checked the time. Maybe another hour's fishing before he'd have to break camp and head off down to the trailhead. He looked across the lake and knew it wouldn't be enough. Clambering up on to the nearest stretch of bank, he hurried back to camp, dug out his phone from his rucksack and dialled Dasha.

10

A low insistent hum, four seconds long, followed by a second's silence and the hum again. Jenna Blake let it ring three more times, praying she'd switched on the answer phone before falling into bed. Literally falling, and still dressed from the evening before so far as she could make out.

By the fifth ring it was clear she'd hadn't remembered to switch on the answer phone, but she let it ring on, hoping the caller would give up. Squeezing her eyes shut, she burrowed down under the duvet. But she could still hear it. Whoever was calling really wanted to get through. Wearily, she reached for the bedside table and grappled the phone into bed with her.

'Is that Jenna Blake, the world's most celebrated TV news reporter?' were the first words she heard. She recognised the voice immediately. Her brother, Greg, in his last year at Washington State, working towards a doctorate in animal behaviour. Another three months and he'd be let loose on the world. God help it, thought Jenna with a burst of annoyance. Always her little brother calling at the wrong time. At least there was no-one in bed with her.

'Greg, for chrissakes. Do you know what the time . . . ?' Jenna's eyes focused on the green digital read-out on her bedside clock. 10:36. Shit, it wasn't even midday yet. Her day off and it was starting way earlier than she'd planned. Thanks to Greg.

'Don't tell me you're still in bed?'

'And sleeping, Greg. Happily sleeping.' Or rather, unconscious, thought Jenna. The previous night she'd covered Seattle's latest club opening downtown, realised too late it was pretty much gay, so she'd found herself a perch at the bar and gotten loaded. She wondered if Gerry Coons, CTACtv's news-desk producer, had known when he gave her the ticket. She just bet he did. 'So whaddya want? Speak now, or . . .'

'One word. Jellyfish.'

Jenna groaned. 'Please Greg, not another animal thing.' For the last two years her zoologist brother had been researching human–animal conflict, and the increasing incidence worldwide of animals turning on man. Two months earlier, he'd called to tell her about a fifty per cent rise in cougar attacks in British Columbia. Before that it had been bear maulings in Romania, wolf attacks in Uzbekistan, and death by dog in Beijing. It didn't matter how many times she tried to tell him, Greg seemed not to realise that his sister worked for CTACtv Seattle, not the National Geographic Channel or Discovery, and that her viewers, let alone her news-desk editor, weren't too concerned by how many kids in Uganda were getting bitten by the resident chimps, or why twenty-foot long salt-water crocodiles were terrorising bathers along Australia's Queensland coast.

Now it was jellyfish.

'Greg . . .'

'The bay's full of 'em, Jen. You could walk out to the Kerry Light on them.'

'Kerry Light? Where are you?'

'About twenty miles north of Titus Bay. Out on the coast. And they've never seen anything like it up here. I'm telling you, this is a scoop, baby. It's all here.'

'They sting, these jellyfish? They bite?'

'Sure they sting.'

'I mean fatal sting, Greg. Like you die screaming in agony. Or a set of teeth that'll snap your leg off.'

'They're jellyfish, sis. *Chrysaora fuscescens*. You get a sting, sure. But they won't kill you. It's just they don't often come this far north, and it's some colony out there. Awesome. Just swept in from nowhere.'

'Anything else get swept in? Something a bit more dramatic.'

'We had sharks,' Greg replied. 'Couple days back. I left you a message, but they moved on.'

Jenna's interest was piqued. Sharks were good. 'Moved on? You happen to know where?'

'Who knows? They weren't saying. North, south. Coulda headed back out to sea.'

'Is this usual? Large numbers of sharks getting together?'

'Sure, it's called schooling. Happens all the time. But you don't usually get it so close to shore.'

'If they come back, you just make sure and call me, y'hear?'

'What about the jellyfish?'

'When they grow teeth and fins, Greg. Teeth and fins,' she replied, and jammed the phone back on the stand.

43

11

Forty minutes after leaving Melville, driving along a two-lane black-top that never strayed far from the Susquahanish, Dasha saw the stone ramparts of Drivers' Cut rise above the treeline. It was here that the river narrowed and took its first real deviation, a slow left-right-left through the ridgeline separating the Melville and Shinnook valleys. Easing the Lexus into the first of the bends Dasha passed into cool shadow, the mid-morning sun lost behind two rising slabs of limestone that squeezed road and river together. As usual she felt a familiar shiver along the back of her arms.

Back in the old days, this dog-leg twist on the Susquahanish had been a real problem for the logging industry, the only spot between Shinnook's sawmills and Melville's lumber yards where timber was given to jamming up in a wall of raw red wood. It was here that the log-drivers, after whom the Cut had been named, came into play, finding the one log that, when released, would set the rest free. It was dangerous work, hopping from one piece of rolling trimmed timber to the next, and a memorial plaque on the wall of the

Cut commemorated those brave men who had been crushed to death when things didn't go according to plan. Every time Dasha passed that plaque, that's when she shivered.

Swinging the Lexus past the memorial Dasha rattled over a planked bridge, found the sun again and felt the land start to rise, the road straightening and the Cut walls dropping back. From here the valley narrowed and the Susquahanish took on a faster pace, its steepening banks not twenty feet from the side of the road. Ahead lay gentle slopes of alpine meadowland fenced to pasture, rising up into a staggered fringe of Sitka spruce, the road Dasha followed passing orchards and farms and isolated stands of garryana oak and red paper-barked madrone.

Five minutes later Dasha saw the left-hand turning for Shinnook and, glancing in her rear-view mirror, she flicked the indicator and slowed. A mile or two behind her an old green Toyota truck also indicated left and followed at a safe distance.

From here the Melville – Tacoma highway branched away to the right, bypassing Shinnook and heading on south-east. If you wanted up-country this was your last chance, two single-lane black-tops the other side of Shinnook winding up into the Silver Hills, roughly following the tributary courses of the Susqua and Hanish Streams. Take the left fork along the Hanish and the road carved a path through the spruce and fir for nearly twenty miles before petering out into a rarely used trail at the end of which Zan had parked his Jeep. The Susqua went further, rising higher and promising a pass through the mountains but delivering nothing more than a rutted track that led nowhere. It was up here that Dasha's land started, and where the first of Pearse-Caine's wilderness homes had been built, three miles along a cleared firebreak on the upper banks of the Susqua.

Normally Dasha would have driven straight through Shinnook, a quaint, tightly huddled community of stone and wood-shingle housing set around the logging pool and old saw mill, now trading as the Saw Mill Lodge, and the only accommodation in town. That's what she would have done, except a light on the dash and a soft beep let her know that she was low on gas. If she wanted to make it to the Wilderness site and back she'd need a refill. Checking the time, she pulled into Shinnook's only garage, filled the tank, bought herself some water in the shop, and was getting in behind the wheel when her cell phone rang. Hoping it wasn't her mother calling to complain about Alexa and Finn, Dasha was relieved to see Zan's name come up.

'I thought you were supposed to be fishing?'

'I am. Just thought I'd call, see how you are.'

'Liar. You never call when you're fishing. I call you. And only in the evening. Those are the rules. Your rules too.'

'Rules are there to be broken,' he replied.

Dasha smiled. She knew why he was calling. His voice was jerky and excited, a whisper really, just as he sounded when he showed her a new design, outlined a new project. 'I'll remember that when you next go fishing,' she said.

'So where are you? What are you up to?' he asked, holding back.

'I'm in Shinnook, on my way to greet the Suttons.'

'They're coming in? You didn't say.'

'Mrs Sutton called yesterday. They want us there for lunch. I told her you couldn't make it, so it's just me.'

'You should have let me know.'

'Really? And that would have made a difference?' she teased.

'Well, the Suttons . . .'

'Zan, I know you, right?'

'Okay, okay. Not a whole heap, no.'

'So what can I do for you? I suppose you're calling to say you want another day. It'll be tomorrow night, not tonight? There's a fish you've seen.'

'Only if you can spare me?'

'I think I can manage. Tell me about the fish.'

'Oh baby, you wouldn't believe . . .'

12

'Doughnuts. A dollar each. They gotta be kidding,' said Eddie Dougan, dropping behind the wheel of the green Toyota and slamming the door behind him. There was no inside panel on the door and the sound shook tinnily through the truck. 'Here,' he said, taking a doughnut for himself then passing the paper bag to his companion. 'She still on the phone?'

In the passenger seat Gene Dickens yawned, scratched the side of his head. He wore a vicious buzzcut and the marks of his passing fingernails showed on the scalp like three red tramlines. 'Still on the phone,' he replied lazily.

'You ask me, this is the best shot we've had,' said Eddie, chewing on his first mouthful, looking down to pick crumbs from between his check shirt and T-shirt. He was thin and wiry, with narrow eyes and a slim mouth. 'We oughta call Mort. Let him know.'

'Best to be sure,' said Gene, wrapping the bag around one half of his doughnut and biting off the other. Mort was right, he thought, chewing through the soft, sugary dough. Anxious Eddie. Just no holding the guy back. Like every other small-time local activist he and Mort had had to work with, just desperate for action. Couldn't wait.

'If she's going to the site,' Eddie continued, 'she'll turn right at the fork and up the Susqua. Then we'll know. Then we call it in.'

A hundred yards ahead, on the other side of the road, the two men could see Dasha's Lexus pulled up in a garage forecourt. This was the first time she'd left Melville since they'd started keeping tabs on her, and Gene had a feeling that Eddie was right. This just might be the moment. They were certainly ready. In the last few weeks they'd settled into base camp, gone over the routes and worked out a dozen different scenarios. None of them looked as good as this one. The kids dropped off with grandma, the husband out of town, and a dozen miles of up-country trail for the lady to negotiate – alone – if she was heading for the Wilderness site. If she took that right-hand turning, he'd call Mort like Eddie said and they'd likely do it.

'She's on the move,' said Eddie, straightening up behind the wheel. Up ahead, Dasha pulled out of the garage forecourt, heading up the slope towards the logging pool. If she wasn't stopping at the Lodge for a meeting or lunch there was only one other place she could be going – no point in coming all the way out to Shinnook just to fill up with gas and take a phone call.

'Give her till the Lodge then take off after her,' said Gene, balling the paper bag and tipping it into the back seat. Brushing his hands together he reached for his cell.

'You callin' it in?' said Eddie, starting up the Toyota.

'Let's just see what she does.'

Three minutes later, keeping their distance, they watched the Lexus pass the Lodge and carry on out of town.

'You gotta call it in now,' said Eddie. 'It's the only place she could be going, and a good hour to get there. Gives us all the time we need.'

'Just keep on the way you're going,' Gene said quietly. 'No need to follow. Now pull in here.' As the Toyota braked to a halt by North End Bridge, he watched the Lexus disappear into the trees then punched in a number on his cell.

'Let's see what Mort has to say about it,' he said.

13

An hour behind Dasha, making the journey from Melville to Shinnook in Wild Water's specially adapted SUV and trailer, Charlie Gimball and Miche Tomak arrived right on time for their rendezvous with the Fairbanks group at the Saw Mill Lodge.

Pulling a trailer stacked with float-boards, and with the back seats and boot of Charlie's van loaded with camping gear, they'd rattled along at a steady fifty, any conversation pretty much exhausted by the time they reached Cedar Creek gas station a few miles out of Melville. While Charlie filled up with gas Miche crossed the road and took a look at the river. It looked to be running a little faster than in Melville, a soft, whispering pelt of coppery water clear enough to see the weeds and pebbles on its sandy bed, cutting an open course through sloping pasture, shaded by stands of old hemlock. In spring, fed by snowmelt and steady rain, it was a different creature altogether – a rush of muscly water that reached within a foot or two of the bank – but right now it seemed settled enough.

Standing at its edge, Miche picked up a stick and

tossed it into the centre of the stream. As soon as it hit the surface, it was off, bobbing along with the current, but not too fast or wild to alarm her. She watched it for maybe twenty feet then heard Charlie toot his horn.

From Cedar Creek, curled up on the front seat, Miche watched the river run alongside them and took in the scenery. It didn't matter how many times she made the journey, the countryside never failed to impress, the pasture land either side of them starting to steepen the closer they came to Shinnook, the fir-clad valley sides closing in on them and the Silver Hills beginning to loom up ahead.

As well as admiring the scenery, she also took in her travelling companion, hunched over the wheel and picking at his teeth with a thumbnail. Miche didn't need to see a resume or read references to know the kind of man Charlie Gimball was. Tracking into his late forties, Charlie liked to blame his increasing failings on anyone but the real culprit. Charlie was always right. Charlie knew better than anyone else. Truth was he wasn't, and he didn't. For all the bluster, life was slowly getting the better of him.

According to Mungo, Gimball had arrived in Melville after learning the ropes with a wilderness outfit down in Oregon. He'd set up Wild Water Adventures on a wing and a prayer and for five or six seasons had built up a reputation for fair prices and always finding good water – not difficult with the Upper Susqua so close. But when the money started coming in, old Charlie had sat back and let standards slip, blaming the down-turn on sloppy staff, the kids he pulled in cheap to run his trips. No-one stayed long with Charlie Gimball.

Sooner or later he'd hit on the girls who worked for him, or square up to the boys. And Charlie Gimball was not a pretty sight when he'd sunk a few margaritas at Mama Surf and started rolling those shoulders of his.

From the word go, Wild Water's big earner had always been canyon-boarding, an activity that Miche had loved as a kid, but which Mungo regarded with a grunting disdain. Body-surfing, that's all it was, he told her. Lying on a board rather than standing on one. And Miche had found it hard to persuade him otherwise. Sure, it wasn't like surfing Melville's breaks, but the ride was longer, a lot of fun, and the canyons of the Upper Susqua were just magnificent. The previous season she'd taken a few groups down through those canyons when Gimball was short-staffed, but even without Mungo's advice on the matter she'd made it plain she was only prepared to stand in on a casual basis. Money and fun, it didn't get much better than that.

'You like country and western?' asked Charlie, switching on the radio. Miche shrugged. She knew that Charlie wasn't bothered whether she liked it or not, would play the station whatever she said.

'You hear the weather reports this morning?' asked Miche, as Gimball spun the dial for something suitable.

'I heard 'em,' replied Charlie, eyes flicking between tuner and road until he found some Johnny Cash and slumped back in his seat.

'And?'

Charlie shrugged. 'Some front coming down from across the border. Due to reach the Cascades some time this afternoon and the Silver Hills tonight or tomorrow morning. But it's just more of the usual – bigging it up for a splash down in Idaho and the Plains before heading on east. Shouldn't do more than brush past.'

'How much rain? They say?'

'Not enough to fill a butt. Maybe there'll be some heavy water getting up tomorrow evening, maybe not. But by then we'll all be down through the gorges and sitting round a campfire. All we got the last morning is a bit of fun on the Susqua shallows. Easy stuff. No trouble.'

Miche, who knew the canyons and gorges of the Susqua and knew what even a thin shower on the wrong side of the Silver Hills could do, hissed softly through her teeth.

'Hey, I'm telling you it's not a problem,' said Charlie, catching the sigh. The last thing he wanted was his guide causing problems or playing up. 'You been down them canyons in worse than this,' he continued, flicking his thumb to the skies above them. 'Not a cloud. Lookit. See for yourself.'

'Charlie, you know as well as me . . .' Or maybe he didn't, she thought.

'Listen, girl. It's Wild Water Adventures, remember? That's what they pay for, that's what they want, *capisc*? They get a good ride, they come back for more. Tell their friends.'

'Even so, we should keep an eye on it.'

'And we will. We *will*. Course we will. Be stupid not to.'

Miche nodded. Stupid, sure. And in big trouble if they didn't. Not that a cancellation worried her. Just so long as she got her money, Miche was prepared to go with the flow.

By the time they pulled into the Saw Mill Lodge

beside the old logging pool at Shinnook, the Fairbanks crew were already there. Their minibus – with 'Fairbanks College' on its flanks – was already parked in the Lodge car park, its occupants snacking on doughnuts and sipping beakers of coffee. Miche gave them the once-over: four guys and two girls, all around seventeen, eighteen, all dressed in identical college slickers with FCC embroidered on their backs. Two of the party stood away from the group, chatting beside the driver's door. They didn't look much older than the kids they were in charge of, but they had to be teachers, thought Miche. Despite the slickers, they had that look about them – older, in charge.

Beeping his horn, Charlie rattled in beside them.

'So you made it,' called Charlie, pushing open his door and swinging down from his seat. 'Looks like we're in for some fun,' he added, shaking hands with the teachers and looking up at the sky. 'Hope you brought your factor fifty.'

Twenty minutes after meeting up, introductions made, the two vans set off, with Pete Conway's wife, Alison, driving the students, and Conway travelling with Charlie and Miche. He was somewhere in his thirties, Miche guessed, with a crop of brown hair and an easy grin. It would have been a great smile, she thought, if he spent some money at the orthodontist. There just looked to be too many teeth in his mouth and it turned what could have been a good deep voice into something of a gargle.

'We got far to go?' he asked, leaning between the two front seats, arms up behind Charlie and Miche's head, peering ahead enthusiastically at the narrowing black-top and thickening woods either side of them.

''Bout an hour, Pete. Maybe more,' replied Charlie. 'Least there won't be any traffic hold-ups.'

'And we'll get some boarding done?'

'Warm-up stuff to start with. Just to see how your guys perform. Tomorrow we hit the fun slides. A few miles of rapids, maybe some standing water, and then the canyons. Fourteen miles of them, cut through the bedrock. No more than forty feet at the widest, and going right down to twenty. Water's up and you get a real wild ride, just like it says in the brochure. And a couple o' real good chutes. Takes some *cojones*, I'm tellin' ya.' Charlie slipped a hand from the wheel and slid it between his thighs, winked at the teacher in the rear-view mirror. 'Ain't that so, Miche?'

Miche managed a nod. Always the same lines with Charlie. Just words – brochure-talk. She knew better. And she'd be the one in the water. If the river was up just a couple of feet, what Charlie described as a 'wild ride' was an understatement, his 'chutes' nothing less than fast twenty-foot drops into pools that could keep you spinning for a week if you lost your board or your nerve. When the water was really up, most of the groups she'd led preferred to porter those jumps, rather than take them.

'I said, ain't that so, Miche?' Charlie repeated, a grin on his face, but menace in his eyes. 'Good and fast, right?'

'Sure is,' she replied, glancing round, stitching on a smile. 'Fast and furious.'

14

Mort Johannesen laid the blade to the stone and, applying pressure through his fingertips, he moved the damascened steel in a series of sawing circular movements that gave off a soft whisper of sound, the grey wood-grain pattern of the knife blade shimmering in the sunlight.

The Japanese had their swords, but Mort had his knife – eleven inches of Solingen steel beaten and folded, beaten and folded until the blade resembled an Ordnance Survey map of swirling seamed contours and could slice through a sheet of paper floating through the air. He'd seen the knife in the Quartermaster's store in Mosul. 'The personal property of Mr Saddam Hussein hisself,' the Quartermaster had assured him, and it was priced accordingly.

The moment he'd set eyes on it, felt the weight of it, tested the fine balance, Mort had known he just had to have it. Since he didn't have the money to buy it, he stole it instead. And killed the Quartermaster with it – first blood – when the bull-shouldered supply sergeant caught him exiting the stores at three in the morning. And from the moment he wiped the sergeant's blood off the blade, Mort had never gone anywhere without it.

That knife was a constant in Mort's life. Wife, mother, brother, sister, father, son, daughter – none of which Mort Johannesen possessed – all rolled into one. Not even the army had managed to get as close to Mort as that knife.

Like many before him, Mort had joined up to get away from something – in his case a big, fat Texas nothing. Lured by the prospect of foreign postings, he'd looked at the map and dreamed of the places he might be sent – Grenada, Puerto Rico, Hawaii, the Philippines, the Maldives, Guam. For a panhandle boy they were the rainbow's end. Except, of course, he got to visit not a single one of them. After a six-week boot camp induction up in the Adirondacks, and a holding transfer to Camp Wyeth at the end of Long Island Sound, Mort's president George W. Bush declared a second war on Saddam Hussein. Instead of Hawaiian beaches and Philippino bars, Mort found himself posted to the northern Iraqi town of Mosul, manning roadblocks on one or other of Mosul's five bridges across the Tigris. One month after the president touched down on the deck of the USS *Abraham Lincoln* and announced an end to hostilities, Mort was on one of these roadblock duties when an improvised explosive device concealed in a passing vegetable cart blew up. Four of his six-man squad were killed by the blast, while Mort and a corporal sustained just a few slicing shrapnel cuts that left their faces puffy and raw for a couple of days. It was just bad luck that one of these tiny pieces of shrapnel sliced across the cornea of Mort's left eye. Which was why Mort Johannesen wore an eye patch.

'Your war's over, soldier. You're going home,' the medic had told him at Mosul base, and forty-eight hours later he was resting up in a field hospital in Germany, Iraqi sand still prickling his scalp. Three months after losing the eye – 'easiest and best option', they'd assured him – he was judged unfit for further active service, offered discharge and given a flight ticket stateside.

And that was that. Mort was out of the army, back home, with a stack of final settlement and disability dollars in his pocket, a Purple Heart, and just the one eye. An eye that continued to need treatment.

'All that sand, son. There's something back there we need to get out,' was what the doctors told him. In the end, with no assistance from the military thanks to his discharge and no medical insurance he could afford, it took most of his settlement to cover further treatment.

By the time he was finished with the medical profession, Mort had started to build up some head of steam. War, he came to realise, was just one big beanfeast – so long as you got yourself on the inside track. Exxon. Abrams. ConSec. Halliburton. Every goddam independent contractor worth his desert boots – and some of them not even that. Snouts in the trough, the lot of them. But not him. Not Mort Johannesen. Four years serving Uncle Sam and all he had to show for it was empty pockets and an empty socket.

But you can still do a lot of reading with one eye. And the more Mort read, the madder he got. All those big-note backhanders, the contracts, the mark-ups, the skimming – eating up honest-toil tax dollars and getting them all into worse shape than they were at the start of it.

And it wasn't just I-raq, no sir. Stateside too, they were

hoovering up the greenbacks and, so far as Mort could see, mostly raping the land to do it, lining their nests with oil and coal contracts, GM crops and whatever else they could coax or rip from the earth. And no-one doing a damn thing about it, excepting a rag-tag corps of Greeny do-gooders who tried to shame the big boys into their way of thinking and mostly failed or compromised.

But shaming never worked. Not with the big boys. Mort knew that and told them so, soon as he joined their sandalled ranks. Look at Union Carbide and that Bhopal place in India, he'd say, and Exxon and the Valdez thing, just now coming round to settle up near twenty years after they spilled a million tons of crude on to the finest coastline on earth. They don't care. They got an army of lawyers to sit on it. Till you forget about it, or lose the will to live. The way things are going with these big corporations, he told them, you'll be dead and gone before anything happens. Direct action, that was what it was all about. And choosing the right target. Something that made a mark.

But not everyone agreed. It was six months before he managed to muster any kind of support, a half-dozen hard-core misfits who thought the way he did. Men like Gene, good ol' Gene. Tough as turtle shell, the one guy who'd stayed the course with Mort. He was busted out of the forces for going AWOL to visit a dying mother and got no leave from his hard-time sentence to attend her funeral, so when he came home to find the house bulldozed to make way for a gas station, old Gene-boy hadn't stopped to think. He'd blown that gas station and hit the road. In the last couple of years the two of them had been involved in a dozen separate actions

59

around the States, ranging from open-cast mine sabotage in the Virginia hills to the tar-fields action in north Wyoming earlier in the year.

When a proposed gas-drilling project in Montana had been wound up shortly after the Wyoming gig, without any need for Mort's kind of action, he'd been on the look-out for something new. He found it in a cover story in *Time* magazine about logging contracts up in the north-west. The feature – the usual tale of greed and graft in high places – also carried a small sidebar on a firm called Pearse-Caine who'd secured permission to develop some first-growth forest on the borders of a national park. According to the story, the firm had established itself with eco-friendly housing in converted warehouses along the whaling quays of a place called Melville, and a line of luxury harbour houseboats that made Sausalito look like a trailer park. And now they'd decided to develop up-country, in some of the most beautiful landscape in the States.

It hadn't taken Mort long to do the maths. A ten-million-dollar development in town, plus houseboats for $800,000 a mooring, and now the two-million-dollar Wilderness retreats – ten of them, apparently. To accompany the sidebar – mostly favourable in tone, which made Mort madder still – there was a picture of the firm's managing director, some guy called Zan Pearse (Zan, for fuck's sake – what kind of a fuckin' name was that?).

It wasn't just the name Mort took against. It was the look of the guy too – all preppy short blond hair and good teeth, down on the beach with a surfboard, chris-sakes, ballin' chicks and making fuckin' millions while he, Mort, was out there on the front line getting his ass kicked for Uncle Sam. The story, and its glowing endorsement, outraged Mort and he was outraged even more when he looked up Pearse-Caine on the internet. There they were – husband and wife – on-site in hard hats, conferring at an office draughtboard, making presentations to corporates. And then the domestic: the kids, the fancy house, the sailing, the fishing, the surfing.

It was all Mort needed to get himself real fired up. Making a buck out of Mother Nature and giving it the spin, trying to make it sound good, making out they were giving back, contributing, saving the planet. Bull. Shit. All they were doing was stuffing dollars in their pockets and smiling all the way. Taking, taking, taking. But sometimes, Mort knew, Mother Nature had a way of biting back. And this time round Mort was going to be there to lend the old lady a helping hand.

Within days of reading that story, he and Gene had come in from Montana to scope the place out. Melville, up there top of the west coast. And Pearse-Caine. The perfect target. Big enough to matter, but small enough for Mort to make a real mark. Not a dent, this time, but a major statement of intent. Down home and dirty.

Quietly, over the weeks, they'd started looking for local support, sounding out a few of the protest groups who'd campaigned against Pearse-Caine's development plans. Mort had done the same in all his campaigns, pulling in donations and supplies and accommodation of one sort or another, and usually ending up with a group of badasses to lend a hand.

He hadn't been so fortunate in Melville County. Sure, there were people who didn't like what Pearse-Caine were doing but it hadn't taken long to see that they weren't the guys Mort was looking for. Most of the people he talked to preferred the idea of sustained demonstration and pursuing legal routes to gain their ends, rather than embracing Mort's more realistic proposals. Few of them seemed prepared to accept the idea of direct action. The only ones who came close were Eddie Dougan from out-of-state, down there in Astoria, Oregon, and Elroy Baker whom he'd brought on board as a local back-up resource.

Melville born and bred, Elroy worked the crabbing trawlers and had never been out of the state, probably never been out of the county. Twenty-five, a college drop-out, he lived in a small three-room walk-up at the top of Melville just off the Shinnook road. From the moment Mort shook his hand, he knew he had the boy. Nothing the kid wouldn't do for him. Like some of those Iraqi kids. Their parents'd beat the shit out of them, but it didn't stop them coming round for gum and chocolate, learning how to high-five and cuss like a marine! Just the kind of man he needed.

Dougan – Anxious Eddie – was cut from the same cloth, tipping towards his mid-thirties, but all tossed up and looking for someone to throw him a line. After a five-year spell with the US Navy, he'd come home to stand on the belt in one of the last canneries on the Columbia River. He'd lasted six weeks before moving to telesales in Portland, then insurance door-to-door – just a trail of dead-end jobs that had given him an abiding sense that he deserved better. That he was owed. Instead he was on the road to nowhere, so better make the best of it. Have some fun. If he'd met a bank robber instead of some girl in the environment movement, Eddie would likely have turned bank robber. As it was he balled the girl and joined her club. It's how he'd met

Mort – everything he was looking for that he'd missed since leaving the navy.

Six weeks earlier, after picking up Eddie in Astoria, they'd moved into the old logger's cabin that Elroy had found for them up in the Hanish Forest, an hour's cross-country drive from the Pearse-Caine's Wilderness development on the Upper Susqua. When they'd discovered a few days earlier that Zan Pearse was fishing a lake not fifteen miles further upstream, Eddie had been concerned. It was too close, he said; they were just a mile or two from the trail. But Mort had been delighted. It was that closeness that added to his excitement. 'He'll go right past and never realise she's here. No one will,' he'd told them with a sly grin.

The cabin that Elroy had found for them was in poor order when they took possession but in the last few weeks, as they tracked Pearse-Caine employees and left their spray-painted messages on Pearse-Caine's office and developments, the four of them had turned it into a first-class base for operations. There was a serviceable bunkhouse under the eaves, a large kitchen, a sitting room with a stone-breasted fireplace, a basement fit for purpose, and a yard where the elks came browsing early morning.

It was here, sitting on the sleepers that stepped up to the porch, that Mort had taken to sharpening his knife, a daily ritual that seemed to sharpen his brooding resentment as much as his blade, a time to settle into silence and focus. He'd finished sharpening and was applying a coat of bergamot oil to the blade when he heard his Mitsubishi grunting and jolting down the narrow trail that led to the cabin. A moment later Elroy jounced through the last cover of trees and swung into the clearing, coming to a halt with a squeal of worn brakes. Mort watched the boy hop down from the cab and lean into the back for his purchases.

'You get everything?'

Elroy, lugging the bags to the cabin steps, nodded, his eyes straying to the glinting blade in Mort's hands. 'Sure did. Just like you said.'

'Put 'em down,' said Mort. 'Show me.'

Dropping the bags Elroy reached in and brought out the padlock. Using the tip of his knife, Mort opened up the moulded plastic wrap and tipped out the lock. It was just what he'd asked for, a two-inch 'Weatherbuilt' with a long shackle for a chain. He nodded. 'Tape?'

Elroy handed over a roll of silvered duct tape and watched Mort slice away the wrapping with the knife.

'You get everything else I wanted?' he asked without looking up.

'Sure, boss. Batteries – three-volt lithiums, spare bulbs, fruit and . . . the rest of it.'

Without saying anything Mort indicated with a wave of the blade that Elroy should show him.

One by one came bags of apples, bananas, avocados, a pack of steaks, bacon, bread – everything that Mort had said. He noticed the boy was trembling. Good. He liked that.

'So what's in the other bag?' asked Mort. 'What else you get?'

'Just what you asked for. Nothing more.'

Mort leaned forward and looked in the second bag. He frowned, the black eyepatch shifting on the wrinkles.

'How long you plan on us keeping her?' asked Mort slowly, fixing Elroy with his single blue eye. 'You got us enough there for a year easy.'

Elroy felt himself redden. 'Just didn't know what type, boss. Reckoned I'd best get us a choice . . .'

It was then that Mort's phone bleeped. Sheathing his knife, he wiped his fingers on his combat pants and pulled out his cell.

He listened for a moment, nodded, then came to a decision.

'We do it now.'

15

Four miles from the trail-end on the Susqua Stream, Dasha Pearse turned down a narrow track, a two-wheel-rut corridor where the undergrowth scraped even the belly of her high-axle Lexus. Through the thickly woven blanket of spruce and fir and pine and redwood that covered the Caine Reserve, loggers from a previous century had cut these pathways to access logging camps and timber yields, bringing out the logs by horse-drawn skidder carts when the stream was too high or too dry to send them downriver. It was these tracks that Pearse-Caine had opened up to reach their Wilderness sites.

Twenty minutes of lurching traverse later, Dasha pulled out of the trees that had flanked her the whole way and entered a slanting meadow of blue-sky brightness. A century earlier a logging camp had stood here – a dozen plankwood cabins half a mile from the Susqua Stream, the cabins and any sign of them now long gone. Instead nature had taken the land back. Dasha had seen the old black and whites of camps like this one in the family photo albums, her own grandfather and great-uncle working their whipsaw together, or standing in a clearing much like this one with a felled tree behind them, all open waistcoats and jaunty headgear, big moustaches and fat cigars, posing against a ten-foot sawn cross section of timber.

The thought of the destruction her family had caused to this extraordinary landscape all those years ago still sent a thrill of guilt through Dasha. It had made the Caines rich and she, personally, had benefited from that family wealth – private education, European holidays and access to various family trusts to buy the land on South Bluff Drive, to build their dream house, and to underwrite many of Pearse-Caine's developments. But Dasha still felt uncomfortable about it, where the money came from. At least she was trying to make amends, create something worthwhile, their new Wilderness retreats making no impact on the environment, eco-sustainable from the first driven hardwood dowel to the source of their power.

Pulling to a stop, Dasha got out of the Lexus and stretched her legs. The air up here was clean and fresh, a warm resinous scent that seared through her sinuses and made her blink. On all four sides of the meadow stood a line of spindly spruce and fir, what lay behind its branchy screen a shadowy darkness impossible to see more than a dozen feet into. Beyond the trees, maybe ten miles to the north and rising to a blue tree-cropped skyline, was the Hanish Ridge, on the other side of which her husband Zan was that very moment casting for trout.

Dasha was wondering about his big fish when she detected a distant, elusive whisper of sound breaking in from the east. She looked around, shaded her eyes and tried to place it. A moment later she saw a black speck heading in her direction. Two minutes later the sound had risen to a blast of rotors as a Bell 430 came in to settle on the meadow, the down-draught flattening and chasing the long grass in frantic swirling circles. The aircraft shone like a new toy, its bodywork not so much painted as lacquered a deep royal blue, almost black, with a gold line streaming between its main rotor and tail-fin and the legend SuttonCorp stencilled into its livery.

Courtney Sutton was first out of the helicopter, dipping below the slowing rotors and only waving when she was clear of them, a tall, elegant woman in immaculately pressed jeans tucked into cowboy boots and a blustering poncho that she gripped tightly in the rotors' wash. Behind her, Dasha caught a glimpse of the Bell's plush executive interior. No plastic quilting or metal frame seats here – rather two pairs of luxurious armchairs facing each other over a wood bench table, the carpet a rich pile that showed above the sill of the sliding door. Dasha could almost smell its perfumed interior – no jet fuel fumes for the likes of the Suttons, just a breeze of clean, fresh air-con. That back compartment was probably soundproofed too.

'How lovely to see you, my darling,' began Courtney, giving Dasha a hug, her grey eyes sparkling with excitement. 'And I'm just so thrilled you could make it,' she continued, looping an arm through Dasha's and drawing her close. 'And such terribly short notice. You are an angel to be here, you really are. But everything happened so quickly – some boring old convention down in San Diego cancelled at the last moment. Which means our first weekend together in I don't know how long. Win and I, just the two of us. Can you believe it? And I know he's going to just adore it. Even if he doesn't know it yet.'

Courtney gave Dasha a grim, apologetic look and the two women turned as a short, trim fifty-year-old with ice-blue eyes and the same kind of Eddie Bauer country gear as his wife, stepped down from the helicopter. He didn't bother to stoop beneath the sweeping blades and up close gave Dasha a swift look-over before dropping their bags and offering his hand. Dasha took it, his grip firm but fleeting.

'I've been told a great deal about you, Mrs Pearse,' he said in a clipped, whispery voice. 'And all of it in the last twenty minutes. I'd never heard your name before, but apparently you're my wife's new best friend. In the whole damn country.' He gave her another sharp little look, as though he was not yet convinced, and not overly amused by this impromptu excursion. Then he turned to the Bell's pilot and circled his finger in the air. With a roar from the rotors that put an end to any further conversation, the helicopter lifted from the meadow and turned back the way it had come, swooping low over the trees and setting their tips asway. 'So if you're such a damned good friend,' Win Sutton continued, once the scream of his helicopter's rotors made it possible, 'maybe you can tell me just how the hell Courtney here gets a convention cancelled, has me togged up like John Wayne and brought out on a picnic when, quite honestly, I have better things to do with my time?'

'You'll find out soon enough, my darling,' said Courtney, releasing Dasha's arm in favour of his, pretending not to have caught the shortening edge to his voice. 'Dasha? Shall we get going? I just can't wait a second longer.'

With their bags stowed and the Suttons loaded into the Lexus – Win in the front and Courtney sitting behind them, hanging on to the back of her husband's seat – Dasha swung away from the meadow and rocked over the uneven ground, lurching down on to the firebreak that led to Wilderness One.

'I'll be frank, Mrs Pearse, if this is one of Courtney's hare-brained schemes wanting me to invest in some land speculation of yours, I can tell you right now that you've got the wrong man.'

'Oh, Win, you're being just horrible to Dasha. Apologise right this minute or I'll be cross.'

'I'll apologise when I don't see a "For Sale" sign nailed to a tree.'

'Well you won't see one of those, my darling, because the sale's already gone through . . .'

Win Sutton turned and gave his wife a look. It wasn't hard to see that the man was about to be not very amused at all.

Dasha felt her stomach tighten. Dear Lord, let Courtney know what she's doing, she prayed, as Win turned back in his seat and looked grimly ahead, jaw muscles clenching.

Five minutes later, most of it spent in silence, Dasha saw the firebreak open up ahead as they closed on the stream.

'Dasha,' said Courtney from the back seat. 'You've got to stop right here. Just a moment. There's something I need to do before we get there.'

What she needed to do was tie a black, silken blindfold around her husband's head. He didn't give in graciously, but he finally allowed the prank to go ahead. 'No peeking,' warned Courtney as they started off again, coming to a halt just a few minutes later.

Courtney was out of the car first, opening the front passenger door and taking her husband's hand. 'It's just a few steps, my darling. There, that's perfect.' Coming up behind him she untied the blindfold and a big smile beamed out of her face. 'Well, what do you think?'

Win Sutton rubbed his eyes, patted down a patch of thin grey hair that had been pushed out of place by the blindfold and looked around. The first thing he saw was the Susqua Stream, a wash of chuckling water driving happily between mossy banks. The next thing he saw were trees, crowding down to the banks.

'Court, what have you done?' he asked, in a voice suddenly soft with menace.

'Why I bought us a country cottage, sweetie.'

Win paused to take this in. 'And this country cottage is where exactly?'

'Why right up there, honey-bun.'

Win Sutton turned to look where she was pointing and shaded his eyes.

Dasha looked with him. Three weeks earlier, the construction team had finished Wilderness One and moved on to the second site further upriver. In their planning application, Pearse-Caine had guaranteed no footprint – nothing that could point to the hand of man. And in three weeks, in addition to the stringent clearing and cleaning of the site, Dasha could now see that nature had also done its part. A thick carpet of fresh, green, mossy grass now covered the land where the saw-tables

70

had stood, and the Portakabin office and bunkhouse for the crew. After a ten-week building programme no sign of construction work could be seen – no sawdust puddles, no campsite fire, no off-cuts, no felting, not a thing – and Dasha felt a rise of delight and pride.

The forest was as they had found it.

With one exception.

And here was her first client, one of the richest men on the west coast according to Forbes' latest *Top Twenty* list. And he was looking right at his new home and he couldn't even see it. He just couldn't see it. For a moment Dasha wished she'd brought along a film crew. Courtney had set it up perfectly – even if she hadn't needed the blindfold – and Win was playing the part any director would die for.

He. Couldn't. See. It.

'Courtney, you're getting me riled . . . What damned cottage? There's nothing but . . .'

And then he saw something. Something in the nearest four trees overlooking the stream. Something that didn't quite fit.

'What the . . . ?'

Dasha spotted the angle of his gaze and knew at once what had caught his eye. The block steps, made of red-barked fibre-glass that looked for all the world like rotting tree stumps rising in an ascending line, what appeared to be the only man-made pattern in this natural setting. The stumps had been Zan's idea, based on the Buren columns in the main courtyard of the Palais Royal in Paris. The two of them had visited that city just six months earlier to celebrate their anniversary, a week of long lunches and slow lovemaking. In between these attractions they'd chanced upon the Palais Royal and the striped Buren columns. The moment Zan had seen them, he'd pulled out his notepad and started sketching. When he gave her the sheets all he'd said was, 'The way up.' When Dasha saw the sketches she knew exactly what he was talking about. And there they were. The way in to the Suttons' new home. Steps up to their front door.

Win Sutton crossed the clearing and made for the blocks. And then he looked up, shaded his eyes again and whistled again. 'Jesus H . . .'

Courtney squeezed her hands together and shot Dasha a conspiratorial grin. Dasha was no longer holding her breath, but her heart was still beating fit to bust.

What would he think? What would he say?

'A treehouse? A treehouse, Court? You bought us a treehouse? You gotta be kidding me?'

'Just climb up and take a look, my darling. And then come back down and tell Dasha she's the most brilliant architect you ever met in your whole darned useless life.'

16

As hangovers went, it didn't quite make the Richter scale, but Jenna Blake knew she wasn't going to get off lightly. At least she wasn't still dressed. After hanging up on Greg, she'd stripped off her clothes under the duvet, kicked them out on to the floor and snuggled down again, feeling somehow better for the effort, cleaner. Slowly, carefully now, she slid from beneath the duvet and stood up, made for the kitchen, found herself some Tylenol and washed the pills down with a vitamin drink. Only then did she open her eyes more than a squint.

An hour later, showered, teeth cleaned, mouth-washed, but still in her dressing gown, Jenna felt herself coming round. Another hour she'd be on the mend and last night would just be a bad memory, rather than a painful bad memory. She perked some coffee and managed to pour herself a mug and carry it to her desk without spilling a drop. She took a sip and flicked on her laptop.

Holding the coffee mug in both hands, she scanned her home page – LA Times, New York Times, Seattle Herald, ReportTV, HeadlineCom – taking in the two-line leaders, sometimes following up an item that caught her eye. It was the first thing Jenna did every morning, even on her day off. Take in what was happening out there, looking for the lead, looking for direction.

And right now she needed some direction. And luck. The last two months she'd brought in just two good pieces – a sixty-second slot on a visitor suicide in the tiger enclosure at Seattle Zoo, and a tanker-ramming on Puget Sound. If she didn't come in with something solid, and soon, Coons would start giving her that look of his. *Come on, baby, where's that story? I thought you were good. I thought you had talent. You're making me disappointed*. He didn't have to say a word of it. Just that look. That's all it took.

When Jenna found nothing to interest her, she checked

her horoscope – her sign was Aries – almost as important as headlines. According to Yahoo.com, it was all just waiting for her. Great things coming. Just be there and do it. Best damn news she'd had in ages, but exactly how long was she going to have to wait? This month? This year? And where was she going to have to be, so as not to miss the great things coming?

Sharks. The word seemed to drift in over her shoulder, whisper itself in her ear, lodging itself in her consciousness like some flash from a dream. She remembered what her brother had told her, punched into YouTube and did a search. First up was a CBS news report from Marina del Rey filmed just a few months earlier, a handful of leopard sharks close to shore, schooling, or spawning, or just hanging out, no-one seemed to know. But not much to see, beyond an aerial shot that made them look as threatening as koi carp in a pond. She tried another report. This time the shark was bigger, its fin slicing through the waves. Some nut on a surfboard with a fishing rod and a lump of meat. Shark takes the bait and gives him a tow-in. Unreal.

Half an hour later, after viewing a dozen or more clips, Jenna quit the laptop and reached for the phone.

'Greg, it's me. Tell me about the sharks.'

'Jellyfish, sis.'

'I said sharks, Greg. I want to hear about the sharks.'

'Well, there was a heap of them, okay. But like I said they're gone.'

'But gone where? If you had to guess?'

'Judging by the current and the swell coming in, I'd figure south. Causeway, Ringwood, Stover Park. Any of those beaches down south from here. Seems like the sharks might be going with the weather.'

'Weather?'

At the other end of the line, she heard her brother sigh. 'Jesus Jenna, for a news reporter you sure got your finger on the pulse.'

'It's my day off, okay? So tell me about the weather.' She glanced out of the window of her attic apartment, a wide blue sky above the flat roof of Lowe's Hardware across South Rainier Avenue.

'According to the forecasts we got some big storms heading our way. One coming in from the islands – tail-end of a tropical depression – and another moving down south from British Columbia. Then there's the currents to consider. There's been some anomalies, and tides are higher than they've been for years. You listen to the news, rather than reporting it, you might get ahead of the game.'

'Thanks for that, Greg. I'll bear it in mind.'

17

With its creaking suspension, the old Toyota made heavy weather of the Susqua Trail, rattling and shuddering over the uneven ground, Eddie clinging hard to the tipping wheel, Gene braced between the door and dashboard, a boot wedged against the transmission tunnel.

'So how long you two been hooked up, you and

Mort?' asked Eddie, as he swung the truck around a large tree stump in the middle of the track. Since joining up with them down in Astoria Eddie had been keen to find out more about their operation, get himself involved, maybe stay on with them after the Melville job was over. But Mort kept a tight lid on things, always around, creeping up on you when you least expected it. A tough son of a bitch, and no mistake. Didn't seem like there was much the man wouldn't do to get his own way. Which was fine by Eddie, just so long as he could trail along and make some money.

'A while,' said Gene, glancing across at Eddie.

'Where d'you meet?'

'Out east,' replied Gene, who could be just as tight as Mort when it came to straight talking.

'Marines wasn't it?' probed Eddie after a suitable silence.

Gene nodded. 'Doin' our patriotic duty, son. Only it don't pay. Not then, not now.'

'I never got out of Hawaii,' said Eddie, looking forlorn.

'Then you're one lucky fucker,' said Gene, with a chuckle. 'But don't go tellin' Mort, is my advice.'

They drove on a while until Eddie eased his foot off the gas. 'Looks like we're there,' he said, pointing up at the side of the track. A hundred yards on was the cross-country cut-off for the cabin. 'And looks like we beat him to it,' said Eddie.

'Just let's wait and see, huh?' replied Gene. 'Just pull up ahead. Right here. I think I see him.'

'You see him?' said Eddie, peering through the windscreen. 'You're bullshittin' me, right? There's nothing but track.' Pulling on the brake and letting the engine idle, Eddie climbed out of the Toyota and looked around, started forward. He was about twenty yards from the front fender when Gene saw a green shadow rise from the grass behind him and start to stalk him. Next minute Eddie was on the ground with Mort's knife at his throat. Watching from the passenger seat, Gene chuckled again. That'd teach him.

Pulling Eddie to his feet and sheathing his knife, Mort flung an arm round his shoulders and led him back to the truck, stopping to pick up his rucksack from the edge of the trees. By the time they got there, Gene had surrendered his front seat and left the door open for Mort.

'We set?' asked Mort, pulling himself up into the Toyota.

'Ready and waiting, Cap',' replied Gene, making himself comfortable in the back.

'So let's get going,' said Mort, pushing his rucksack down in the footwell and slinging an arm out of the window. 'Time to teach our lady friend the facts of life.'

18

Dasha and the Suttons had lunch on the main terrace, thirty feet above the ground, shaded from a slanting midday sun by a screen of shifting spruce branches that whispered above their heads, with the Susqua Stream gurgling past not fifty feet away, and the air sharply scented with a resinous tang. Albany, the Suttons' butler, had arrived in a Sutton company four-by-four while Win was exploring his new home, and had rustled up a delicious picnic lunch of home-made terrines and warm sourdough bread, smoked salmon and cold cuts of Wagyu beef, the meal washed down with the kinds of wine that Dasha had only read about.

'You've done a remarkable job, young lady,' Win told her as the table was cleared. 'Truly remarkable.'

Courtney clapped her hands and beamed. 'Didn't I tell you?'

'But let's be serious here just a moment,' continued Win, as though he hadn't heard his wife. He leaned back in his chair. 'Just exactly how much has this little nest cost me?'

'Win!' exclaimed Courtney. 'It's a gift. From me to you. And it's very rude to ask how much something cost.'

'I'm guessing here . . .' said Win. 'I'm guessing somewhere in the region of two million bucks? The materials, the finish, the power and services, the land . . .'

'And don't forget fishing rights to a half-mile of grade-A stream,' added Courtney.

'So, am I in the ball park?' He reached out a hand, placed it gently on Courtney's arm, to quieten her. But his cold blue eyes never left Dasha for a moment.

Dasha glanced at Courtney who gave a helpless shrug, as if to say there was no ducking the man, or his questions, and that Dasha might as well tell all.

'Right in the diamond,' said Dasha. 'On pitcher's base.'

Win nodded. 'I'd guess it's a fair price,' he said at last. 'We talking freehold or lease?'

'Twenty-year leasing. And Pearse-Caine has first refusal on sales within, or at the end of, that lease period.'

'Two grand a week. Not bad,' he nodded. 'Any leaning to rental or fractional ownership?'

'Not if we can help it,' replied Dasha, keeping her voice level. In the last twelve months, Pearse-Caine had been more tightly leveraged than they were used to, and in order to secure funding for the Wilderness project she and Zan had told their bank that they would offer renting and timeshare options in order to secure finance and guarantee loan repayments. 'What we'd like,' she continued, 'is single ownership. We want our clients to see Wilderness as a lifestyle choice, rather than as part of an investment portfolio, or a shared residence.'

Win shot her a thin, knowing smile. It made Dasha feel a little uncomfortable. Had the man seen through her? Had he guessed how tight things were, that it was only his wife coming in so early that had made things happen?

'So tell me, how many of these "retreats" are you planning?' he asked.

There was an edge to his tone that reminded Dasha of an initial meeting with accountants to discuss the project, and a meeting that followed with their bank in Seattle. All the same kinds of questions. And always that undercurrent of fiscal scepticism. Ask the same question enough times and sooner or later you got to the truth. She wished that Zan was there with her. He was so much better at this than she was. But she took a breath and soldiered on. 'This is the first,' she explained. 'Work's just begun on a second site a few miles upriver. There'll be ten, maybe twelve in all.'

'How d'you get planning?'

'They made it difficult for us, but we found a way round.'

Win nodded his approval. 'I like people who find a way round. And how have you covered your overheads? The land, materials . . . You got private backers? Shareholders? Bank loans?'

Once again, Courtney started to tell her husband off but he held up a hand and kept his eyes firmly on Dasha. 'Of course, you don't have to tell me if you don't want to,' he cautioned, with an understanding smile, knowing very well that she would.

Dasha smiled back. 'The land was left to me. It belonged to the family. The Caines were loggers. Made their money in timber. Sixty thousand acres, right here, between the Susqua and the Silver Hills National Park.'

'Nice bequest, but still it's gotta cost.'

Dasha nodded. 'To be perfectly honest, Mr Sutton . . .'

'Win, please.'

'To be honest, Win, it was your wife buying off-plan that gave us the means to go ahead.' There, she'd said it. And she felt better for it.

'So you're . . . leveraged?'

'There are interest payments we need to keep up on an initial loan.'

'You gonna sell 'em all? You got buyers?'

'I don't think we'll have too much problem . . .'

'. . . Once word gets out that you've sold the first one to the owner and chief executive and president of SuttonCorp,' said Win with a sly glint in his eye.

'Well, we like to think that ownership details will remain confidential,' Dasha countered. 'We believe that's how our clients would prefer it.'

'And I'm sure you're right. I'm sure they would. So, you got any other projects lined up?'

'A few things,' replied Dasha.

'Such as?'

'Well, we've put in some plans for the Melville bridges. There's three of them cross the Susquahanish along Main Street. Two road bridges, one footbridge. They're old and not particularly pretty. Zan and I thought we could start with the footbridge and see what happens.'

At that moment Albany appeared on the terrace with a tray of coffee. Win watched him pour it and helped pass round the cups.

'Blue Mountain,' said Win, as he took a sip and Albany retreated inside. 'From the mountains of the same name in Jamaica. It's my wife's favourite, though I think it's overrated. And horribly overpriced. But there you are.' Then he put down his cup and got to his feet, walked to the terrace rail and took in a deep breath as though savouring the pine-scented air. Then he turned back to the two women sitting at the table and levelled his gaze on Dasha. 'Young lady,' he began. 'I have a proposal that I would very much like you to consider.'

19

Miche headed for the shallows beside a stretch of over-hung bank and slipped off her board. She was wearing a helmet, rubber hood, wetsuit and fins and used the latter to bring her closer to the shore, into her depth and out of the current. There may have been no rain for a while but the river was still quite boisterous, tugging at her board and pummelling her wetsuit.

Twenty metres away the first of her group spun round the bend. It was Clyde, topping six foot, with a red bandanna tied round his neck. Seeing her wave to him, he paddled over to join her, a big grin squeezed tight by his hood.

'Hey, that was great,' he said, unbuckling his helmet and pulling off his hood to reveal a wild thatch of red-top.

'You did all right,' said Miche. 'Good work round those rocks back there.'

'They came up real fast,' he said, grinning with delight. 'First I thought it was just water and then . . . Whoa, hold on there. That's no water.'

For the last forty minutes Miche had been leading the group down the first stretch of river, assessing their expertise on boards. Charlie and Pete Conway, who'd persuaded his wife, Alison, to swap with him, had dropped them at the start then driven the two vans downriver to set up their first night's camp, now just a few miles further on. They'd be there in less than an hour, the only remaining hurdle for her group the Susqua Falls just two hundred metres ahead. It was no more than a twelve-foot drop into a deep safe pool, but it was the first real obstacle her group had faced. So far they'd handled their boards well, read the water wisely and whooped with delight whenever the current threatened to spill them. No-one had looked in any kind of trouble and when the water did speed up they knew how to handle themselves.

One by one the party gathered around her – the two girls, Naomi and Kelly, real cheerleader types; Pete's wife,

Alison, shivering as much from the excitement of the ride, Miche guessed, as the chill water; a geeky-looking guy called Bradley with a healthy mix of freckles and acne; and the two quarterback types who pulled their boards right in beside Kelly and Naomi. The taller and better-looking of the pair was called Taylor and the older, shorter one, BeeJay. If they weren't on the job already, Miche decided, it didn't look like it was going to be too long before they were.

So, seven in her group and all of them proficient enough to give Miche a confident feeling.

'Okay, listen up, guys,' she began. 'Right round the next bend we hit the Susqua Falls. It'll sound like Niagara as you come up to it, but it's just a twelve-foot drop into a deep, rock-free pool. Any of you not do a jump before?'

Alison held up a hand, as though she was answering a question in class.

'Okay, Alison, you come with me. I'll talk you through it. The rest of you, I want you to come off this bank in pairs, on my signal, one pair at a time, and head for the centre of the stream. Paddle fast into it, pull up the head of your board when you go over, and hold on tight. When you're clear of the drop, give a blast on your whistles so I can bring on the next pair? Any questions?'

There was a shake of heads, and Miche herded Alison back into the current. A hundred metres on, they finned towards the bank and wedged themselves into a line of rocks. Upriver they could see the group waiting for the sign, while from fifty metres downstream came the rushing bellow of the falls.

'Just watch how and where they make the jump,'

Miche shouted to Alison over the roar of water. 'When it's our turn, we'll go together.'

Ten minutes later, the last pair — Kelly and Taylor — rode out into the stream and took the falls side by side, whooping like Tarzan as they disappeared into a cloud of spray.

When she heard the whistle blast, Miche tapped Alison's shoulder. 'You ready?'

The teacher nodded, smiled bravely.

'So let's you and me go and show 'em how.'

20

Mort watched Gene and Eddie manoeuvre the Toyota into the side of the trail. The boys were wearing the Forestry Department overalls which Mort had brought with him from the cabin, and both looked the part in their hiking boots and Forestry billcaps. From where he sat in the shade of a trail-side spruce it looked for all the world like their truck had broken down. Eddie swung up the bonnet and Gene set a toolbox on the roof.

Mort ran a fingernail under the edge of his eyepatch, then glanced at his watch. A little after three. Sometime in the next hour, he estimated, a silver Lexus would come trundling over that hump a hundred yards back and see their truck. There was no way, seeing a breakdown way out here, that she wouldn't stop, see if she could help. Things like that just didn't happen. It was a shoo-in. And Mort had estimated exactly where she would pull in. Ahead of the truck. Not behind it. She was a woman, after all, and here were these two guys, way out in the boondocks. They might have been wearing Forestry Department kit, but if he'd learned one thing about Dasha Pearse it was that she was canny and careful. It would be pure instinct on her part to pull up ahead of the truck. Ten, maybe fifteen feet, he was guessing. Which was just about where he was sitting under his tree. And like Eddie, she would never see him. She'd get out of the car, come round to the trunk and call back to see if they needed any help. And that's when he'd get her. His right thumb pressing hard down on that magic spot an inch below the ear lobe to incapacitate her, followed by a quick jab with the hypodermic in his pocket. A shot of sodium thiopental would give them all the time they needed to get her secured and back to the cabin before she could cause any trouble.

Just so long as she pulled up ahead, and didn't stop beside the truck, buzz down her window. That could prove a problem. But not an insurmountable one.

He'd find out soon enough.

21

Dasha felt a great wash of excitement fizz through her as she pulled out of the firebreak and got back on to the main Susqua trail. Even now she still couldn't quite believe it, still couldn't quite get a grip on Win Sutton's proposal.

'You've got the land, the taste, the design and the technical know-how,' he'd begun. 'And I've got the money. Lots of it. So let me tell you what I'm thinking here . . .'

What Win Sutton was thinking was this. SuttonCorp was looking to attach itself to an eco-friendly sustainable energy platform to underpin a major advertising pitch even now in the planning for the following year. Pearse-Caine's Wilderness Project fitted the bill so exactly that Win Sutton wanted a part of the action. In short, he would underwrite construction costs for the remaining Wilderness units – at a building rate of three new units per year over the next three years – an investment, he explained, that would be interest-free and part sales-refundable. What he wanted in return was a twenty per cent stake in future Pearse-Caine projects. Having asked a ton of questions about the Wilderness project's waste retrieval and power sourcing – the bore holes and water system that Zan had come up with – Win Sutton also wanted to take a further twenty per cent stake in developing new technology. He might have made his billions in software, thought Dasha, but he clearly wasn't averse to new business ideas.

As far as Dasha was concerned, neither she nor Zan would have any problems accepting his proposal and terms. There was, however, one final condition that Win Sutton had stipulated which she wasn't so sure about. Win Sutton wanted the project to have a new name: Sutton Wilderness. While Dasha wasn't too bothered, she knew that her husband might baulk.

She was wondering just how she'd play this through to Zan when the Lexus crested a slope and dropped down through the trees. Up ahead she could see a truck pulled into the side of the trail, the bonnet up and two men working on it. The vehicle looked vaguely familiar but she couldn't place it. Then she saw the Forestry Department overalls and wondered what they were doing on her property. Even thirty minutes away from the Wilderness project she was still on the land her father had willed to her. They certainly couldn't have been passing through, and the only reason they might have been there was a fire – about as likely in this mossy, damp environment as a whirlpool in a goldfish bowl.

As she drew closer she saw a tool kit opened up on the roof of the truck. One of the men was leaning into the engine bay and the other was juggling with a couple of spanners. When they heard her car, they both turned and the juggler waved.

Pulling up beside them she buzzed down her window. 'You guys need any help?'

'You got any charger leads might help,' said the man with the spanners. 'Seems like the alternator's actin' up . . .'

'There's leads in the back. You're welcome to try.'

Dasha pulled forward and parked about ten feet ahead of the truck. She kept the engine running, pulled on her brake and got out of the car. The two men hadn't moved, staying by their truck, still absorbed in whatever it was that had brought them to a halt. She was lifting up the hatch when she sensed a shadow pass behind her and a whispering scent of pears in syrup, like a kind of bergamot. The next thing she knew there was a hand on her shoulder and something pressing against her neck.

But there was no time to react. Her legs simply buckled and a moment later, lying on the trail, she heard her cell buzzing and felt a sharp prick on the inside of her elbow.

And then everything went black.

22

Sometime after lunch Shelley Caine had dozed off. When she came to, she wasn't altogether sure what was happening. Her mouth must have dropped open because her lips and tongue were as stiff and dry as old planking. The last thing she could remember was the two kids watching TV. Now Alexa was sitting in Mack's old armchair with a towel wrapped round her shoulders while Finn snipped away at her long blonde hair with a pair of kitchen scissors. As her eyes focused, Shelley could see that a good amount of hair had already been taken off, caught on the nap of the towel, in the little girl's lap and over the arm of the chair.

'Gramma's awake, Gramma's awake,' trilled Alexa.

'FINN!' cried Shelley, lurching out of her chair and clawing for the scissors before he could cut off any more of his sister's hair. 'What in blue blazes do you think you're doing?'

'Alexa needed a haircut,' her grandson replied artfully. 'She asked if I'd give her a trim.'

'How does it look, Gramma?'

'Gee, honey, it looks . . .'

It didn't take more than her Gramma's wide-eyed, disbelieving look for Alexa to realise that something had gone wrong. Badly wrong. Her proud smile started to melt. She'd known something like this was going to happen. She'd just known it.

It took a while for Shelley to calm the little girl down, and then she had to set to with the scissors herself, trying to balance out Finn's initial work on just one side of his sister's head. By the time she had finished, Shelley decided she hadn't done that bad a job, all things considered. A little ragged, maybe, and Alexa certainly didn't suit a fringe. But it would do. 'There you go, honey. Good as new. Don't you just love that fringe?'

Alexa looked mournfully in the bathroom mirror. 'I don't know. What will Momma think?'

'Well, I think she's just gonna love it. Tell you what. Why don't we go call her and you can tell her all about it.'

Back in the sitting room, Shelley put Finn in front of the TV and settled Alexa on the sofa, punched out Dasha's cell number and handed the phone to the little girl. By now her daughter ought to be closing on Shinnook and getting within phone range.

'I'll be back in a moment,' she told the kids and went through into the kitchen. Now where had she put old Jack, she thought to herself. She needed a little lift after that rather shocking awakening. Not bothering to find a glass, she pulled the cork and tipped the flask. A mouthful was all it took. Ooh Jack, you're a bad, bad boy. She glanced at the clock on the kitchen wall. A couple more hours and Dasha would be back. A couple more hours making sure her grandchildren didn't do any further damage. With Jack's help she knew she'd manage it.

'Gramma?' came Alexa's voice from the next room. 'Momma's not answering.'

23

Laying down his electric sander, pulling off his eye protectors, Mungo McKay ran a calloused hand over a two-metre curve of dusted board. Enough for the day. He'd been working that length of paulownia since dropping off Miche at Charlie Gimball's place and he knew he was way past doing his best work. He rolled his stiffening shoulders and stretched into a yawn, hands on his hips, tipping back, feeling the dry itch of sawdust in his hair, in his ears, across his parched lips.

Downtime. Beach time, he thought. A beer, a quick shower, pull on the wetsuit and in ten minutes he'd be paddling out for some rides on Melville Bay.

That Friday evening, with a big orange sun balancing on a shelf of distant black cloud, the beach was busy. Walking along the sea wall with his board under his arm, Mungo remembered that morning's radio broadcast. Mention big swells on the air and every surfer within tuning distance was going to be hightailing it to Melville: an early weekend for the young silicon-chip brigade from Seattle and Tacoma who'd bought into the new Quays apartments and studios; the college guys who roamed the coastline looking for the best bombs; and the high-school kids just out of class. And that's exactly what had happened. Behind the sea wall, that morning's empty parking slots were now filled with two-door Beamers, Mercs, Porsches and a rusting, dented collection of camper vans.

But most of the new arrivals, Mungo noted as he climbed up on to the sea wall, seemed to be hanging out on the beach, watching the waves rather than riding them, the broken surf racing up high, before rinsing back like orange quicksilver. As Mungo trotted down the steps, it was easy to see why. There was a surprisingly warm breeze coming off the water and the waves were as high as he'd seen them in months, real combers racking up one behind the other, caroming off the Bluff reefs either side of the bay and powering down the centre line. Whatever was happening out there in the ocean – that tail-end storm they'd been warning about on the radio – it was just how Mungo liked it. Big rolling sets with twenty-foot faces, maybe higher, just gnarly enough to keep the traffic light, the reason he always hit the beach so early in the morning when all the other board-boys were sleeping off hangovers or serving up early morning seconds for the girls they'd met the night before at Mama Surf. Not that he had anything bad to say about Mama's; it was where he'd met Miche after all.

With maybe a couple of hours till sunset, there were just a handful of boards out there, the few guns brave enough to take on the breaks that were coming in, looking like they were getting bigger and higher with each set, their distant thunder carried to him on a breeze that was sharp with the storm-stench of salt. He could almost feel the beach tremble as he walked down to the sea and threw himself on to his board, paddling strongly through the wash of broken surf, feeling himself pulled out into the swelling ocean.

With the shoulder surf riffling along the rock-tumbled shoreline of South Bluff, Mungo steered a line some twenty metres out from the rocks but not so far out to be caught by the rising breaks. It was a narrow, choppy passage and as he headed out he could feel the pull from the ocean, a dangerous malevolent tugging that twitched the point of his board and set the adrenalin pumping. No wonder there were so few boards out here, he thought. Word had got back to the beach. For a lot of the Melville crowd, just a single ride would have been enough. In conditions like these, there wouldn't have been too many coming back for seconds.

Up ahead, Mungo saw a familiar figure – Jed Roberts, a deputy at the Sheriff's office. For the last couple of months he'd been dating Ginny Farrell, from the Harbour Master's office. According to Miche, who knew everything that was going on in Melville, Ginny had taken a real fall for the guy, but was determined not to let him know it. Lucky guy, thought Mungo. That Ginny was a piece of work.

Right now Jed was facing away from him, having taken the same line out, and was waiting for a suitable ride, like a jet lining up in a runway queue. The upturned soles of his feet were a pinky white – big, splayed surfer's feet wrinkled with the cold and the salt. Normally he wouldn't have waited to catch a ride – it was Mungo who had taught him to surf in the first place and he was a good strong boarder – but Mungo could see that the waves coming in were getting bigger than Jed could handle. And Jed knew it. Sooner or later, he'd buck up his nerve, find a wave and take a ride. Until then . . .

Knowing that his voice wouldn't carry over the sound of the incoming surf, Mungo paddled in Jed's direction, pausing to bang the flats of his hands on the front of his board. It was the steady beating rhythm that Jed finally noticed, turning to find Mungo coming up behind him.

'How's it goin', Jed?'

'Hey, Mungo. Looks like you and me are the last to go.' Jed glanced back nervously at the breaks where the three boarders ahead of him picked up the same wave and curved below it on their way to the beach. In seconds they were no longer visible, lost behind the wave's racing, tumbling, glass-green hump.

'Looks like some good rides coming in. You wanna do one together?' asked Mungo, as if Jed would be doing him a favour.

'Sure, why not?' the off-duty deputy replied. It wasn't difficult to read the relief in his face, hear it in his voice. If he was going to have to take the biggest wave he'd ever ridden, at least he was going to be doing it with Mungo McKay beside him.

'Come on then,' said Mungo, edging ahead of him and pushing up on his board to look out over the breaks. 'Third one back, just a little lower than the one behind it. Let's take it.'

Stroking to the right, away from the South Bluff shore-line, the two boarders set themselves up for a swift paddle as the second wave passed them and the third started to build just fifty metres off.

It was then that Mungo saw a slim shadow rise up through the wall of the water, two maybe three feet in length, travelling in the same direction as them, like another surfer moving in for the same break. Only this one was underwater.

'Hey,' shouted Jed. 'Dolphin. You see it?'

'Yeah, I see it,' Mungo replied, wondering how long it would take the younger man to realise it wasn't a dolphin. Or a porpoise.

It didn't take him long.

'Jesus, it's a shark,' Jed suddenly exclaimed.

'I think you're right,' said Mungo, wondering if it was too late to quit the wave or if they'd gone just that little bit too far. It was, and they had. If they chickened out now there was a good chance they'd be spilled and churned into the reef. They certainly wouldn't be able to ride it out into the following trough because the crest was forming up fast. Too late now to get over the top and down the other side.

Which was when Mungo noticed another shadow in

the wave. And another. And another. Dark grey tops and shimmering white bellies. Great whites, by the look of them. But not big ones, nothing fully grown. Just babies. Baby great whites. Like a nursery of them, following each other through the wave.

And then, as Mungo and Jed turned and lined up for the wave, there were sharks all around them – more baby whites, and what looked like equally young bulls and tigers and white tips. None of them more than a metre but all of them with a head full of teeth. In all his time surfing the Melville Breaks, Mungo had seen nothing like it. Shapes moving below them, dark torpedo shadows shifting through the incoming wave, and on all sides fins breaking surface.

'Jesus, Mungo. They're everywhere. There's hundreds of them!' cried Jed, his head flicking from left to right, taking his paddling arms out of the water and clamping them to his sides, repositioning himself on his board.

And there was the wave bearing down on them, fast, rising up not ten metres back, several million tons of water filled with an arching barrel-load of teeth and terror.

'Hey Jed, keep on your belly,' shouted Mungo as the rising swell caught them and they lifted up towards the crest. 'Just don't stand, okay? We just ride it on our bellies, you got that?' And with his fingers clamped to the rails, Mungo slithered his way up the board and pointed its tip south.

In an instant the wave was on them, and they were picking up speed, tilting across the face of the rising wall at maybe a forty-degree incline, hands gripping the edges of their boards and powering down the slope, looking for the fastest line but anxious not to crash into

95

each other, or any of those fins between them and the shore.

When, finally, they made it safely back to the beach, panting with the ride, dragging their boards through the shifting wave-cream, Mungo turned and looked back out to sea.

'Don't reckon I'll be going out there again any time soon,' said Jed, digging the tip of his board into the sand and leaning against its tail.

'You and me both,' replied Mungo. 'You and me both.'

24

There was nothing Dasha could do to stop it. Within seconds of regaining consciousness she felt her guts heave, her chest rise and a great uncontrollable rush of vomit spewed from the back of her throat. Instinctively she reached up with her hands to stem the flow, but something held them back, something cold and hard around her wrists, something that cut into her skin and made her gasp. The gasp brought a scalding acid sting to the inside of her throat. She gagged again but there was nothing left to bring up. Taking a series of shallow breaths, she opened her eyes. But it wasn't easy, her eyelids scraping against what felt like a rough band of material. There was nothing to see. Eyes open, eyes closed – it made no difference. Just a deep black darkness.

She'd been blindfolded.

Like Win Sutton.

The name came into her head from nowhere. But it set off a chain of images she couldn't stop, as memory flooded back.

The Suttons and the Wilderness treehouse.

The lunch served by Albany – most of which she had just deposited all over herself.

The drive back down the trail.

Her excitement at Win Sutton's offer.

And then . . .

A broken-down Forestry Department truck.

Except it wasn't Forestry. She could recall no markings. Just a green Toyota that had somehow seemed vaguely familiar.

It was the men by the truck that had made her think of the Forestry Department. Those brown overalls with the green stripe, the baseball caps with the light brown bills.

She remembered pulling up beside them, rolling down the window. An older man, and a younger one with his head under the bonnet. She hadn't recognised either of them.

They needed charge leads. She had some in the trunk.

So she'd pulled in ahead of them and gotten out of the car . . .

It was then that Dasha, lying there in the darkness, felt two completely separate sensations: a deep dull ache in the side of her neck, in that hollow where the shoulder

97

connects, and a numbed, stiff patch of muscle on the inside of her arm.

An injection.

She'd been drugged. Kidnapped.

And this was where she'd ended up, lying on her side, on what felt like a rough mattress, her head resting on a rubbery pillow that was hot and wet and already smelling bad, her hands clasped above her head, cuffed and, by the rattling sound of it, attached by a length of chain to a metal bed frame.

So, she'd been drugged by those Forestry guys. Or rather, by an accomplice. Because she recalled that neither of them had moved from their truck when she pulled up ahead of them and got out of the Lexus to get them the leads.

Someone had come up behind her, put her down, put her out.

And they'd brought her here, wherever the hell she was.

But what for? What did they want?

It didn't take her long to work it out. The spray-painted message she'd seen just that morning on the windows of the Pearse-Caine office. 'STOP NOW . . . OR ELSE!' Whoever it was who had left that warning hadn't waited long to implement their threat.

Lying there in the darkness, putting it all together, Dasha also remembered the sound of a phone ringing, seconds before she blacked out. Alexa. Finn. She was certain it must have been them. She'd been about to call them herself, close enough to Shinnook for her cell to work, to say she was on her way home and would be with them in a couple of hours.

And there they were, calling her.

Alexa. Finn. Her children! And then – thank God it wasn't them who'd been taken. Right now they'd be sitting down for Gramma's fish pie.

Or would they? What was the time, she suddenly wondered? How long had she been under?

Instinctively Dasha moved her left hand to check her watch. But she'd forgotten the handcuffs, and the bracelets rasped against her wrist bone, rattling the length of chain. But she could feel that her watch was missing. And her gold bracelet on the other wrist. And her wedding band and engagement ring! Someone had removed all her jewellery. Even her earrings. She pressed the side of her head against the pillow to make certain. No doubt about it. They were gone too.

And her shoes. She wasn't wearing shoes either. Whoever had brought her here had taken them as well. But her legs had not been shackled and moving them slowly, carefully, she swung them off the bed and managed to sit herself up, a grinding throb in her head. Reaching out a foot she felt for the ground, a rough uneven surface. Dirt. Hard-packed earth. And by reaching a little further she found where the floor met the wall, a cold stone wall.

Where the hell . . . ?

Who the hell . . . ?

What the hell . . . ?

Sitting on the edge of the bed she shivered, a flood of pinprick goosebumps racing across her skin from scalp to toes.

She suddenly realised she was cold.

And scared.

Very scared.

25

Chief Mulholland watched Jed Roberts cross the squad room heading for the locker room. Looked like he'd come straight off the beach. T-shirt, cut-off jeans, flip-flops. Probably had, judging by the tangle of sun and salt-streaked blond hair sticking off the top of his head. Kids, thought Mulholland. Lived in a different universe. Different set of rules.

'Hey, Jed,' he called out. 'How about wearing some trousers the next time you drop by?'

Jed looked up guiltily. 'Sure Chief. Sorry about that. I got kinda held up.'

'Out on the beach by the look of it. And just so's you know, you're the last one in. Again.' Before he could get any further, the phone on his desk started ringing. He looked at his watch. If he wasn't out of there in the next ten minutes, he'd get his hide whupped by the wife. Every Friday. Bridge at the Lessermans'. The date was written in stone and he didn't dare be late. For a moment he was tempted to leave the phone ringing but Mulholland wasn't the kind of cop to let a call go unanswered. He picked it up, waved Jed away and settled back in his chair.

'Melville Police Department. Chief Mulholland speaking.'
He recognised the voice at the other end of the line
immediately. 'Mrs Caine. How're you doin'?'

'Why I'm just doin' fine, thanks, Chief. But it's my
daughter I'm worried about.'

'And how's that, Mrs Caine?'

'Well I'm looking after the kids and I was expecting
Dasha home by now, to pick them up.'

'And she hasn't got there yet?'

'That's right, Chief, and I'm worried.'

'You called her?'

'Course I called her. Just to let her know the kids
were fine and I was feeding them their suppers. Fish pie;
they love it. I called the house, too. Up on South Bluff.
Just in case she went home first.'

'And there was no answer?'

'That's right.'

'When did you last speak to your daughter?'

'This morning, when she dropped off the kids. Then
again from Shinnook round lunchtime. She was headed
up to the Wilderness site and I told her not to worry
about rushing back if she was held up. I'd give them
supper. But she hasn't called in, and I can't get through
to her. Tried a dozen times.'

'What about Zan?'

'That's what she called about from Shinnook, to tell
me Zan was staying up another day, fishing the Hanish.
Which means, if he's anything like my Mack, he'll be
up to his butt in water and left his cell in camp. I was
going to wait an hour or so, try him when the fishing's
done. No point any sooner. But it's Dasha that's worrying
me, Chief. It's not hearing anything, you know? And
those damn-darnation signs painted up on Dasha's

windows again . . . I guess it's just gone and got me jittery.'

'I understand that, Mrs Caine, course I do. But I'm also sure there's a good reason . . . How're the kids by the way?'

'Why they're just fine, you know. Watching TV right now.'

'And you're okay with them staying there?'

'Sure I am. Sure . . .'

Mulholland detected a note of hesitation in her voice. As though she was getting tired of the babysitting. Wanted a break. A drink, too, knowing Shelley Caine.

'What's worrying me,' Shelley continued, 'is there's been some kind of accident. I called the hospital here and up Shinnook, but they couldn't help any.'

'Well there's been no traffic incidents called in, I can tell you that. Maybe she's broken down up on the trail, and her phone's out of power. Or she's still up round those canyons and can't get a signal.'

'Could be, Chief. Maybe you're right. It's just . . . I'm worried, is all.'

Mulholland thought for a moment. Normally he'd have given it a few more hours before doing anything. People getting home late, it happened all the time. But that morning's spray-painted threat on the Pearse-Caine offices gave him pause for thought. 'Tell you what, Mrs Caine. I've got a unit going up Shinnook way. I'll have them liaise with the boys there and get them to take a look out on the Susqua Trail. Then swing round to the Hanish, see if they can find anything. I'll get right on to it. Soon as I have something I'll call you back, how's that?'

'That's very kind, Chief. Thank you. I'll be waiting.'

'My pleasure, ma'am.'

Mulholland put down the phone and winced when

he saw how late it was getting. Pushing away from his desk, he grabbed his hat and keys and headed for the door. Across the squad room, Friday night-duty sergeant Jim Calley and a couple of the boys emerged from the locker room. 'I'm off out of here, Cal. Over to you. Quiet so far, but I need a squad car up to Shinnook and the Susqua Trail. Maybe the Hanish, too. There's a chance Dasha Pearse might have gone and broken down up there. Might be needing some help. Drives a silver Lexus. Send Jed along. Keep him entertained.'

'You got it, Chief,' replied Calley.

The two men exchanged a private smile. They both knew that Friday nights Jed Roberts liked to take the Promenade beat, keeping an eye on the bars and clubs along the main quay. And the other eye on the look-out for that Ginny Farrell.

26

'Ya wanna hear a funny story?' asked Eddie, throwing down the cards he'd been practising shuffles on.

Gene, with his feet on the table and his ankles crossed, lowered the magazine he was reading and settled his gaze on the man.

Sitting by himself on the stone hearth, Elroy looked up nervously. Ever since Mort and the boys had come back with Mrs Pearse, bundled her comatose form down into the basement and chained her to the bed, Elroy had been keeping a low profile. In the past he'd always been one of the first to promote direct action, but now he was involved in it, right at the sharp edge, he wasn't so sure.

'Guy I know up Hyannis works for the Environment Agency, right?' continued Eddie, keen to establish his eco credentials, his contacts. 'Wanted to test some sewage outlets and chart current changes, so he decides to put oranges in the outflow pipes, right? See where they head when they come out? Trouble is they don't. Him and his boss check the shore every day right around where the oranges are supposed to appear, but they find doodly. Then, one morning, they see this old lady with a put-up shack on the highway selling home-made marmalade, right? In Hyannis? In winter? So they stop and ask where she gets her oranges and, like, she tells them she's just been finding all these oranges along the shore, just swept in like, and it seemed such a pity to waste them so she's been making marmalade. And selling it to every car comes past. Done a roaring trade, she has. Course they don't have the heart to tell her . . .'

Gene had heard the same story a good few times already. From any number of different people.

So had Mort.

Without anyone hearing him, he had made his way down the stairs, not a single board creaking. He was dressed in combat pants tucked into black corp boots and wore a green Marines T-shirt. He had a webbing belt round his waist with a scabbard and knife attached.

He looked neat and creased and dangerous. 'I get to hear that story just one more time, Gene,' he said. 'And I swear I'm gonna have to ram it right up whoever's ass it's coming out of.'

Eddie blanched, but tried to laugh it off, muttering something about the old ones were the best, and reached for the comfort of the playing cards.

Over on the hearth, Elroy seemed to flinch. The flinch turned into a nervous shuffle along the hearth as Mort made straight for the fire, picked up a log and threw it on, sending a cascade of sparks barrelling up the chimney. Even this early in the season, it was chill in these parts, and they had still to burn off the dampness in the cabin.

'Anyone hear anything?' Mort asked, looking at one of them after another.

They all knew he was referring to their prisoner, Dasha Pearse, locked up in the basement beneath them. When Mort's eyes lingered on Elroy for a second longer than the others, Elroy felt a spin of fear. He was saved by Gene.

'Rattle a chains a while back, and what sounded like she was throwing up,' replied the old marine, rolling up his magazine and tossing it on to the table.

Mort turned back to Elroy. 'You got any coffee out there?' he asked, nodding towards the kitchen.

'Nothing hot, but I can brew some up.'

'Sounds good,' said Mort. 'Get to it.' Then he turned back to Gene and Eddie. 'So let's find out how our guest is enjoying the facilities. Bring her up,' he said. 'But keep the blindfold on. And no-one says a word 'cepting me. Understood?'

With a heave out of their chairs, Eddie and Gene went to the trapdoor, levered up the ring from its bed

105

and pulled it open. One after another they stepped down into the gloom.

Out in the kitchen Elroy busied himself with the coffee, making a fresh pot rather than heating up the dregs of the last. He'd learned early on that Mort was particular about his coffee. The first time Elroy had made coffee for Mort in his three-room walk-up, Mort had tipped the mug on to the floor – right on to the carpet, just like that. 'When I want diner coffee, I'll go to a diner, okay? When I ask for a coffee, I want real coffee, right? Not slop.' That's what he'd said, just like that, rubbing the spilt coffee into the carpet with the toe of his boot. Just to get the message across. And back then, Elroy had warmed to it – that strength, that determination, that fuck-you attitude that came off Mort in waves. There was nothing the man couldn't do and Elroy had loved it, being a part of it all. Right now, though, hovering over the Cona, he wasn't feeling quite so certain.

Through the kitchen door he watched Mort take Eddie's chair and poke a finger through the jewellery they'd taken off Dasha Pearse. The bracelet was chunky, two bands of interwoven pink gold and platinum. The stones in the ear-studs were diamonds, small but good, and the watch was an Ebel. Elroy watched Mort pick it up, examine it and then swing it round on his fingers. You didn't need to know the name, thought Elroy, you could just feel its value in the heft and workmanship. Ten thousand dollars and no change, he'd guessed when he took a look at it. Minimum. Some families, Elroy knew, lived a year on that kind of money. And less. For a moment, just a brief moment, he'd felt the old hostility rise up in him. But it didn't last long. Talking about doing something, he had discovered, was a great deal easier than actually doing it.

Whether he liked it or not, it was now clear to Elroy that he was in this up to his neck, in way deeper than he'd ever anticipated, just hauled along by the abstract but compelling prospect of it all. And Mort's dangerous presence. He was scared, too. Scared shitless. It hadn't seemed to register before, but it did now: kidnap was a federal offence. You got caught, you went down for a long time. If he'd had the choice right then, he'd have been out of that cabin quicker than spit. But it was too late for that.

Returning with the freshly brewed coffee, Elroy poured a cup for Mort and pushed it across the table towards him. Mort reached for it, took a sip, nodded his approval to Elroy and then his single eye switched to the trapdoor as Eddie and Gene reappeared with Mrs Pearse. When they'd brought her back to the cabin a couple of hours earlier, Elroy had noted the sweet smell of her perfume, but as they hauled her to the table and dropped her down in a chair, the reek of vomit hit him like a wave, a wide pink stain down the collar of her jacket and jumper.

Of course, being local, Elroy knew Mrs Pearse. He'd never spoken to her, but he'd seen her round town – shopping, parking the car, out with the kids, going in and out of her office at The Quays. The last time he'd seen her, she'd been on stage at a town hall debate where she'd explained what Pearse-Caine were doing. It all sounded like she was saving the planet single-handed, but Elroy hadn't been convinced. Still, she must be shitting herself now, he thought, watching Eddie and Gene settle her at the table. Her crop of blonde hair was a mess and her lipstick was smeared, but with her hands cuffed in front of her and the blindfold she looked, well, kind of sexy and vulnerable. He licked his lips, not quite sure how he felt about it. Attracted to her, sure, but sorry too.

He wondered what Mort was going to do, how he was going to play it. It didn't take long to find out.

'Well, good evening, Mrs Pearse,' began Mort, running the links of her watch against his cheek.

Elroy saw her head snap around towards his voice, her shoulders square up.

'So nice of you to join us,' Mort continued.

'Just who in the hell are you?' she said, taking Elroy by surprise. He hadn't expected her to be so . . . well, vocal. But she wasn't even halfway finished. 'And just what in the hell do you think you're doing?'

Mort looked across at Gene, shook his head and smiled. 'Oh, I think you know who we are, Mrs Pearse,' he said at last. 'And I think you know what we want.'

'Don't tell me,' she snapped. 'You're low-life scum who go round spray-painting people's cars and office windows with threatening messages. Yes, I know who you are. But boy, have you overstepped the mark this time.'

Putting the coffee pot down on the table, Elroy moved away from the action, taking up position beside the kitchen door, safely out of range and stunned by her nerve. Jesus, he'd never have dared speak to Mort like that. Yet here was this woman . . .

'Well now, ma'am, I think you might well be under-estimating the opposition a tad,' purred Mort, gently rubbing the skin around his eyepatch, the watch still held in his fingers. 'And in these particular circumstances, if you don't mind my saying, that would be a very . . .

intemperate thing to do.' Mort reached for his coffee, blew on it and took another sip. 'But yes, you're right, we are the ones who spray-painted your cars and your office. Just little messages you chose to ignore. Which is why you're sitting there in that chair. Because, see, we're not your usual run of polite little protestors who come to church halls and take a vote. We don't write letters to the local paper, and we don't spend our evenings making placards. We're just a little more . . . direct than that.'

'If people like you think they can change the world with a can of aerosol paint, then you're very badly mistaken, mister. What we are doing is important work. Researching new ways to power our homes, new ways to build those homes, new ways to conserve and protect, and leaving no—'

'Please, please, please,' interrupted Mort, dropping the watch on the table with a solid clunk, and leaning forward. 'Spare me the PR guff. Researching, protecting, conserving? Enough. You can defend what you've done till the birds fall out of the sky – which they will do soon enough if you'all carry on the way you are – but the fact remains that you have gone into the forest and . . . you have raped it, pillaged it, turned it into a profit-making machine. Not for mankind, not even for the suckers who buy into your ideal fuckin' world dream. But for yourselves. You know it, I know it. In fact, you're no different to the rest of your family, are you Mrs Pearse?'

Dasha stiffened.

Mort chuckled. Sometimes the army taught you something useful, he thought. Not just how to get information, but how to use it. 'That's right,' he continued, his voice soft, cajoling. 'You know what I'm talking about, don't you? The great Caines. The Timber Caines. For generations your family cut down every damn tree they bumped into – to build houses, ships, sure, but also to make money. A lot of it. To fill the family coffers. It's how you get to wear stuff like this – the watch and the jewels . . .' he picked up the bracelet and tossed it into Dasha's lap.

The surprise of it striking her made Dasha double up, as though the weight had been far heavier than it was, and it dropped to the floor between her legs.

'But you know what?' continued Mort. 'Sometimes, just sometimes, old Mother Nature gets to bite back. And this, believe me, is one of those times.'

There was silence for a moment, just the rustle of logs settling in the hearth and the creak of Mort's chair as he leant forward, sniffing theatrically. 'You know something, Mrs Pearse, seems to me you're starting to smell a little high.'

'It must be the company I keep,' she replied, quick as a whipcrack, head tipping back, chin jutting out defiantly.

'That's my guess, too,' replied Mort. 'All you property speculators and corporate bloodsuckers getting together sure must heat up a room something bad.'

Over by the kitchen door, Elroy smiled with the others, but he felt a chill when he saw Mort reach for the knife in its sheath and draw out the blade. Pointing the knife at Gene and Eddie, and then to Dasha, he indicated that they should hold her down.

Before Dasha had time to react, the two men had her pinned in her chair, Eddie at her feet, Gene coming up behind her and gripping her elbows. For a moment or two she was able to rock her chair back and forwards but that was all.

'Time to remove the offending articles,' said Mort, pulling up a chair and sitting down in front of her. Lifting the blade to his mouth, he breathed on the steel as though to warm it, then slipped it under the hem of Dasha's jumper. Instinctively she tried to reel away from the touch, but Gene and Eddie held her tight.

'Careful now, Mrs Pearse. Just would hate to prick you,' whispered Mort. As he raised the knife, the jumper tented then parted, sliding off the blade as the steel cut through it from hem to neckline. Leaning forward, Mort pushed the jumper back to her shoulders with the tip of the knife and started in on the blouse. Six pearly white buttons gathered in her lap and the blouse opened.

'Stand her up,' said Mort, and Dasha was pulled to her feet. With sawing butcher-like slices, Mort opened up the sleeves of her jacket and jumper and blouse and watched them drop to the floor. 'There, that's better. No smell now.'

Instinctively Dasha tried to hunch forward but Gene held her back. She also started to shiver, more from the sudden exposure than the cold. Her bra was white, a small section of the right-hand strap soiled from the vomit. Mort ran his knife along the mark, slid the blade beneath the strap and drew it out, as though testing to see how far it stretched. Elroy, frozen in the kitchen doorway, was certain he was going to slice through it at any moment, and cut the bra from her shoulders. But he didn't. Instead Mort returned to his seat and said to Elroy: 'Fetch the lady a T-shirt. The one on my bed.'

Two minutes later, Elroy was back with the T-shirt. It was black with a green tree on its front framed by a red heart. *Love the Forest* ran the message. While he was away, the handcuffs had been taken off and Mrs Pearse was back in the chair. Elroy handed her the T-shirt and her hands scrabbled for it, tried to find the right openings.

Mort chuckled as she finally pulled it on. With a nod to Gene, the handcuffs were snapped back around her wrists.

'There. How's that?' he asked, but Dasha said not a word. 'Cat got your tongue?' he continued. 'Well now, little pussy better just let it go, because right now we got some important business to attend to.'

'If you think for a single second . . .'

'Hey, Mrs Pearse,' Mort whispered. 'You really are pushing it here, you know? Really trying my patience. I mean, if you got a problem about helping us out here, well I got just the two words for you.' He waited a moment before he spoke again, smiling as he did so. 'Alexa. Finn.'

Back near the kitchen door, Elroy saw Dasha flinch, as though she'd been hit.

'You were easy enough to pick up,' continued Mort in a soft, reasonable voice. 'Can't see no reason why your kids shouldn't be no different. Can you?'

Hoisting himself out of his chair, Mort picked up his cell phone. 'So why don't we have ourselves a little word with hubby,' he said. 'See if we can sort all this out.'

He tapped in the number that he'd copied off her cell up on the trail, then moved behind her and held the phone to her ear.

'Nice and gentle now . . . Nice and gentle . . .'

27

The light had started to go. The sky, a lace-edged oval break in the canopy above Zan's head, was still a pale grey with shafts of pink and purple, but the close rise of the trees around the water made the evening seem darker than it was. If he was going to catch this monster Zan knew he was going to have to do it in the next few casts. Pretty soon it'd be too dark to see anything.

Apart from a break at lunchtime Zan had been following the fish all day, across the upper meadow end where the underwater reeds shimmied with the current, and all the way along the left-hand bank where the trees sloped right down to the water and made casting a nightmare. Right now he was on the edge of the lower pools, balancing on a shingle ledge, waist-deep in his waders, not forty feet from a six-foot overhang that threw an arc of black evening shadow over the lake's glittering evening-sky surface.

And suddenly, there it was. A silvery smudge passing along in a slow leisurely trawl just a few inches below the surface. A lazy flick of the tail, a spurt, and then a gentle turn back. It was mesmerising, as though the fish knew Zan was there and was just playing with him.

Try. Go on and try. See if you can do it.

A twenty-pounder, thirty inches, thought Zan. Maybe more. A record breaker. He felt a pulse of excitement shiver through his body, prickling at the tiny hairs on the back of his neck.

Gathering in his line for what felt like the hundredth time, Zan lay the rod back across his left shoulder, gave the cork handle some right-hand wrist to lend it a curve, and watched his Green Darner Headdress sail out over the water. It dropped in a circle of ripples exactly where he wanted it, ten yards back from the outflow stream which slowly tugged it in that direction, closing in seconds on the silvery shape below. But the fish didn't show the slightest interest in the fat lure passing above its head.

Reeling back his line, Zan kept his eyes on the water. What worried him was having the fish so close to the lake's outlet, a narrow chute of water that tumbled down to the pond below. If his fish got spooked by the heavy fly, or the pulling stir of current, it'd do one of two things. Either head back into the lake with a swift and powerful flick of its tail, or it'd go with the flow and drop down to the lower level. If the fish stayed where it was there was a chance that Zan could hook it. But if it went with the current and dropped down into that lower pool, there'd be no time to strike camp and follow. The record-breaker would be lost, and all the way back to his Jeep, Zan would hear Mack's chortling laugh. 'You struck out, boy. You missed a record-breaker. Now, if I'd been standing there . . .'

With ten feet of trailing leader and glistening line dancing between the tip of his rod and the surface of the water, Zan started a series of soft whipping movements, and cast again, the damp clot of feather and fur at the end of his line sailing over the water to drop no more than a yard beyond the fish.

Holding his breath, Zan drew the rod back and up and watched the fly tumble and dance across the surface of the water in the black shadow of the bank. And suddenly the shimmering silvery tube just inches below it seemed to hold and pause. Zan knew at once that the fish had seen the fly, and he knew too that it was starting to rise.

This time he had its attention, this time the fish would strike . . .

At first Zan thought he was having a heart attack, a dull wincing vibration in the left side of his chest that seemed to grow stronger. And then came a low buzz and he knew it was not a heart attack. It was his cell phone. Of all things, his bloody cell! He never fished with his cell, always left it at camp, buried in his rucksack. Only this time, after calling Dasha to say he'd be staying another day, he'd slid the phone into his shirt pocket, not back in his rucksack, and headed out to the water. And now, at the very moment it should have remained unheard, it rang and the feel of it and the sound of it made him start and the shingle beneath his feet shifted as the fish began to rise, mouth opening . . .

And in that unexpected moment the fish sank back, the fly untaken.

Zan tugged the phone from his pocket and flipped it open just to put an end to its bleating. How could Dasha be calling now, he thought angrily? She knew never to call until late, around the children's bedtime, when he was sitting by his campfire and they were in their pyjamas, smelling of the bath.

'Yup. This had better be a real . . .' he began.

'Zan. It's Dasha.' Her voice was tight and low, and he knew immediately there was something wrong. His first thought was the children.

And then there was another voice, just as low but darker, more venomous. A man's voice. Texas someplace, southern states for sure. 'Mr Pearse,' the voice began. 'That was your wife. And those are the last words you will ever hear her speak unless you do exactly what I say. Do I make myself clear?'

'Who is this?'

'I said, sir, do I make myself clear?'

Zan took a breath, tried to steady himself. 'Yes. Yes, of course.'

'So. Let us begin. Tomorrow morning, first thing, you will issue a press release to the media – local, state and national – confirming your company's decision to abandon its Wilderness Project and to pass the Caine Reserve into the stewardship of the National Parks Commission. You will not negotiate with them, or insist on any conditions, in any regard. No ifs . . . no buts . . . When full and clear title has been legally signed over, sir, your wife will be released. You have forty-eight hours to effect this transaction. As for the authorities . . . call them by all means. There is nothing that any of their agencies can do in the time available to them. They will never find us.'

'Now just a goddammed—' said Zan, the words just leaping into his mouth.

But the speaker paid no attention, and his message continued: 'You will not hear from me again. And nor, more to the point, will you hear from your wife if you don't do exactly as you are told. Do I make myself clear?'

Zan gritted his teeth. 'Yes, I understand.'

'Good. I thought you would.'

And the phone went dead at exactly the moment that the fish came back for another bite, streaking on to Zan's bobbing lure and snatching it from the surface of the pool.

Zan felt the tug on his line and the jerk on his rod and heard the sudden whining spin on his reel. For a second he watched the action, eyes wide and uncomprehending, the line cutting and jerking through the surface of the lake. Then he flung down the rod and, pushing through the water, turned for the bank.

28

Miche's heart dropped. After bashfully refusing to perform for most of the evening, geeky freckle-faced Bradley had finally been persuaded to go find his guitar and play them something. There was always one, thought Miche wearily. Another evening of tuneless strumming and endless, hopeless reaching for unreachable chords. Please God he doesn't sing as well, Miche prayed. And everything had been going so well.

Her team had arrived without mishap at the camp which Charlie and Pete Conway had set up for them. She knew the site well, a level stretch of soft mossy pasture in a half-circle of rustling spruce, close enough to the river to hear the water shifting and shuffling its way downstream. A row of tents had been set up either side of the two vehicles, hurricane lamps glowed like cream beacons through the canvas, and with the moon just a day off full, it was just a magical spot to be.

By the time they had hauled themselves out of the river, stowed their boards, hung up their wetsuits and got themselves changed for cocktail hour – beer and wine for the grown-ups, cans of soda and a surreptitious flask among the kids – the sky had darkened, steaks were sizzling on Charlie's charcoal brazier, and foil-wrapped potatoes were heating up on the edge of the firepit. Now, after their first campfire dinner, the ten of them were settled in their various picnic chairs and van backseats, sitting round the firepit chatting among themselves, Yuma bats flicking above them, a drying line of wetsuits throwing dancing fire shadows among the trees.

As usual Charlie had been monopolising the conversation, always in his element with a captive audience. And the man sure knew how to lay it on. The thrills and spills. High, fast chutes he'd jumped; sucking pools he dragged himself clear of; and standing water – 'high as a kicking horse, I'm tellin' ya' – that he'd somehow managed to breach. 'And there it is,' he'd say, jerking a thumb over his shoulder at the splash of the river. 'The best stretch of water you'll find this side of Niagara. Just ready an' waitin' for us.'

Miche had heard the same lines a dozen times and he never deviated.

It was then that Bradley went looking for his guitar.

'He's good,' said Alison, leaning across her husband towards Charlie and Miche as Bradley headed off.

118

Which is what they all said, Miche reflected, promising herself that the next time she came out on a Charlie Gimball water adventure she was going to pack earplugs. As Charlie's group leader there was no way she could possibly, or politely, slope off to her tent. She'd have to sit through whatever hell was coming her way without a whimper.

Five minutes later, Bradley was back at the fire, hoisting his guitar over his neighbours' heads and settling himself into his seat. There were a couple of accidental twangs from the strings as he made himself comfortable (which Miche hoped wouldn't be the high point of his playing), followed by a moment or two's tuning, tightening the keys till he was satisfied. Even in the flickering firelight, Miche could see the guitar was a well-travelled, well-worn instrument, its coat of varnish long since scraped away where fingernails had strummed wood as well as strings, its soundboard plastered with various labels. It looked like the kind of guitar you might see in a pawnbroker's window.

Where a moment before there had been a smattering of chat and laughter among the group, an expectant hush now settled around them, as though they knew what was about to happen, and were looking forward to it. Miche, sitting furthest away with Charlie, Pete and Alison, noticed this shift in everyone's attention and a moment later she understood.

After a whisper's pause, Bradley began to play, fret fingers sliding effortlessly through the chords, the fingertips of his right hand picking their way across those six elusive strings to conjure up a passage of delicately executed and deliciously clear chords that rang out between the trees, bringing them all to a rapt silence.

Miche recognised the tune immediately. 'Light My Fire'. José Feliciano. Perfect pitch, perfect timing, perfect delivery. And unlike most of the guitarists Miche had suffered before on nights like these, he didn't bother watching his fingers pluck the strings or work the frets. Not even the more difficult passages. Tilting back his head, eyes closed, he just . . . played.

'Told you he was good,' whispered Alison.

'And some,' Miche whispered back.

But geeky Bradley wasn't just good, he was astounding. After Feliciano, he broke through that first burst of applause with the openings riffs of 'Listen to the Music' by the Doobie Brothers, then segued into some Beatles, Nina Simone, Simon & Garfunkel followed by a dozen other pop, rock and country classics – some Rolling Stones, Chuck Berry, George Benson, Jack Johnson – each with its own spin and flourish.

Sometimes he just picked his own way from one melody to another; other times one of the group would call something out and he'd just play it like he was on automatic. After a couple of requests had been shouted out and accommodated, Miche summoned up the nerve and called out 'Fire and Rain'.

Not recognising the voice, he'd looked up, caught her eye and nodded. 'Sure thing,' he said and launched into it – just like that. It seemed to Miche that there wasn't anything he couldn't play with that damned instrument. And he could sing too.

It started with 'Fire and Rain'. Not the whole song, not every lyric. Just the odd line – '*I seen lonely times when I could not find a friend*', or '. . . *thought I'd see you, baby, one more time again now*' – his voice a pitch lower than might be expected from so lanky and geeky a frame, sure and steady as his playing, warm and smoky as the fire. It was as if he was talking just to her – enough to put goosebumps up and down her spine – and she closed her eyes and felt a squeeze of longing for Mungo to be there, the big-frame strength of him to nestle right into, those big arms wrapped around her.

That was how well Bradley played, the kind of playing you'd pay money to hear in an auditorium, Miche decided. But there was something about hearing it out here in the middle of nowhere, with the logs shifting in the firepit and showering up sparks into the night sky, with the soft susurrus of the river not fifty feet distant, and with a treetop breeze shifting through the higher branches – nature's own accompaniment – that made it somehow very special. She wasn't the only one who felt it. The other side of Charlie, Miche saw Pete reach for Alison's hand and draw her closer, across the firepit she caught Kelly resting her head back against Taylor's chest, and Naomi had started combing her fingers through BeeJay's curling black hair.

It was then, just as they were getting lulled along, that Bradley suddenly changed direction and started picking out a gentle, shifting prelude of classical phrases that floated through the clearing, lingered in the air above their heads, held everyone captive. Miche didn't know the composers, couldn't have put a name to any one of them, but she knew it sounded Spanish. Not flamenco – nothing so brutal – but deeply intense and soulful all the same, gently building and rising, then dwindling away, weaving around itself like the twisting branches of a vine. Right there in the wilds of Washington State, Miche could smell the dust and taste the oranges in every plucked string. And never, not once, a dud note.

As far as Miche could tell Bradley played for an hour,

maybe longer, shifting seamlessly between classical and pop, rock and reggae, blues and soul. Playing what he wanted, playing what anyone wanted. Happy to oblige.

And then suddenly it was over.

'Punky's Dilemma', by Simon & Garfunkel. Light and tripping, soft and youthful, ending on a long, gentle, final brush of all six strings. And then he was pulling the strap over his head and zipping up the guitar in its cover.

When they realised what had happened – that he was done – a low moan of dissent spread through his audience. But nothing would entice him to break it out again and play one last number. That was it. 'Punky's Dilemma'. Over.

But it wasn't just the last tune of the evening.

It was the last tune that Bradley would ever play.

29

Twenty miles north, over the Hanish–Susqua ridge-line, Zan's torch cut a wavering path of light through the forest, shadows dancing away from the moss-covered trees as the spill of brightness passed. Travelling light, he'd made good time, and with the slope in his favour he knew it was going to be quicker getting down to the trail-head than it had been climbing up to Bear Tree. There was no question he was getting close. But how much further? How much longer would it take?

He'd left Bear Tree nearly two hours earlier, stripping off his waders as soon as he reached camp, pulling on his hiking boots and taking only the bare essentials – his car keys, wallet, rain-slicker and torch – leaving the tent, his fishing gear, rucksack, fire-irons, anything that might hold him back. He'd taken his cell phone too. The damn battery had been too low to make any calls – to Chief Mulholland, to Shelley – but he knew he could easily recharge it when he reached the Jeep.

The whole way down, Zan had replayed that slow, fearsome, threatening conversation in his head. Those first words of hers: 'Zan, it's Dasha . . .', her voice stiff and frightened and brave, before the phone was taken from her and that other voice had come on the line. There'd been a real malevolent confidence in the kidnapper's voice. Real meat to the threat. The threat towards his wife. *If you do not do as you are told, sir, you will never see her again.* As plain and simple as that. His blood ran chill at the memory, a shiver through his body as he lumbered on through the woods, pushing aside ferns, brushing low branches from his path. Right now he had to get to the Jeep as fast as he could, charge up his cell and make the calls from there. Which was why he had quit camp so swiftly, which was why he was close to running through the forest, moving as fast as he could. There was a lot to get done in forty-eight hours and the sooner he set to it the better it would be. He didn't have a moment to lose.

There was no doubt in his mind what he was going

to do. Never a moment's doubt about what his response would be. He was going to do exactly what the kidnapper had demanded. An announcement from him on the local morning news that the Caine Reserve was to be handed over to the National Parks Commission, and their Wilderness Project abandoned. As breaking news, he had no doubt that it would be picked up by State and National broadcasters – both press and TV. The National Parks Commission would make sure of that. When Pearse-Caine had put forward their proposals for the Wilderness project, the National Parks had been vociferous in their objections, and had been deeply embarrassed when permission to develop had been granted. They'd be only too delighted to take everything over, and Zan had little doubt they'd hang on to it too, even when it came out that the transfer had been forced, on account of a ransom demand. With Dasha's property bordering the Silver Hills Mountain Reserve and the Olympic National Park, the NPC would control a stretch of land nearly double the size of Yosemite. They'd make damn sure it would take years to get it back from them.

As he stumbled through the woods, his breath rasping hard in his chest, a light sweat seeping through his eyebrows, Zan started to focus on the calls he would make. The first would be to Chief Mulholland. When he heard about the kidnapping, he could start up some kind of search, liaising with other agencies to get men in the field, and the air. To search for his wife. Despite her kidnapper's belief that he and his gang could never be located, and Dasha rescued, it had to be worth a try. And in the time it took Zan to drive back to Melville they'd already be on the case. He'd also call Shelley and bring her up to speed. Since it was likely she wouldn't have heard a word from her daughter, and was now unable to get through to him on his cell phone, the old lady would be getting anxious, not to mention Alexa and Finn wondering where their parents were. Then, of course, there'd be a late-night call to Tom Gold in Seattle, the company lawyer, to start in on the paperwork and liaise with the Parks Commission. The sooner the transfer went through the sooner he'd have his wife returned to him.

Or would he?

Because Zan knew there was a definite possibility that her kidnappers – there had to be a gang of them, surely? – might not keep their word about releasing Dasha when the property transfer was completed.

Had she seen their faces? Could she describe any of them?

If she had . . . if she could . . . they would surely never risk releasing her.

He'd heard it in the man's voice. Absolute determination. Absolute ruthlessness.

His stomach took a roll at the terrifying prospect that, whatever he did, he might never see his wife again, that she would die some horrible, lonely death, and that their children would have to suffer the agonising loss of a mother. Without thinking, Zan squeezed his eyes shut and in that momentary loss of concentration he failed to see a gnarled length of root rise up in the light from his torch, a twisted moss-shrouded limb that was higher than those around it, high enough to snatch at his leading boot and bring him crashing down. The last thing he registered was a molten flash of pain in his left knee and the torch wrenched from his hand, tumbling away into the undergrowth, the beam blinking off.

Darkness.

Utter darkness.

30

For the first time in a long time Dasha began to weep. As far as she could tell it was nearly three hours since her kidnapper had made that call to her husband. Three hours since she'd heard Zan's voice, heard the demands, before being brought back down to the basement. Three hours spent running everything through in her head, trying to get a grip on what had happened to her. And when she'd gone through everything for the hundredth time and there was nothing new to add to the sum of her knowledge, she'd let herself think of her children – and the threat that man had made – and the tears just spilled out of her. Silently at first, then accompanied with muffled, desperate whoops of grief that made her body rack.

Soon, though, she brought the sobbing under control. She couldn't afford to lose it now, she told herself. She had to stay focused. She had to stay strong. It was then, trying to blink away the tears, that she decided to remove the blindfold. Raising her cuffed hands, she slid her fingernails into the cloth and wrenched it down. This single, insignificant act of defiance made her feel instantly better, infinitely more determined, though she kept the cloth around her neck to pull back up again when the trapdoor opened. Not that its removal seemed to make any immediate difference. Apart from a few thin cracks of light in the floorboards directly above her, the darkness was still there.

After a short time, however, her eyes began to adjust and for the first time she was able to take some stock of her surroundings. Roughly square, she discovered, pacing out the room, fifteen steps by fifteen steps. With three walls built of stone and one, behind the flight of stairs, made of wood planking. The floor was dry-packed earth, smooth in places, rough in others, sloping with the land from the stairs at one end of the room down to the bed at the other. The first picture that came into her head – and stayed there – was of a logging cabin, built on a hillside, definitely up-country, somewhere close to where she'd been taken. A cabin that wasn't used that often, maybe rented out just a few months of the year to hunters or fly-fishermen, a cabin chill enough for her to wish that she still had her jumper or jacket.

Of all the things that had happened to her since waking up in this basement, it was that experience of her clothes being cut away that had shocked Dasha the most, more than she would have imagined. Her jacket, jumper, blouse, simply sheared off her. The humiliation of it. The powerlessness of it. And such a terrible sense of vulnerability, of being stripped in front of these men, and her absolute inability to do anything about it. She hadn't been able to see any of them, but she'd felt their eyes on her, on the pretty little bra she'd put on that morning, its pink lace edging and ribbon trimmings, the way her breasts filled it. And when she felt the knife slide beneath the strap and pull at it, she'd expected any moment that it would be sliced through and her breasts exposed.

But nothing had happened. The next thing she knew, her cuffs were being unlocked and she was struggling into the T-shirt they'd given her.

Back on her bed, Dasha listened to the various sounds drifting down to her from the floor above – a chair being pulled across the floor, the canned applause from a TV programme, the occasional murmur of voices, and the creaking tread of feet. So far she'd managed to identify three different kinds of footstep – a leathery scuff of boots, and two sets of rubber-soled trainers. But there was another presence in that room, she was certain, what sounded like the soft tread of thick socks, a fourth person. The one who'd been sent upstairs to fetch the T-shirt? A woman, maybe? Maybe that's why the bra strap had not been cut.

Whatever the split, male to female, Dasha was sure that there were no more than four people holding her captive. She was equally sure that the two men who had brought her up from the cellar and taken her back down had to be the Forestry guys she'd stopped for, and that the man who had spoken to her was the man who had come up behind her and put her out. That lingering scent of citrus when his knife slid across her skin. She could smell it, too, on the T-shirt she'd been given. *The one on my bed*, he'd said. Whoever he was, he was big. Extra-extra-large, if the T-shirt was anything to go by.

He also had a deeply unsettling voice, a dangerous, piss-polite southern drawl that, despite her defiance, had put a chill clean through her. Not even the knife was as frightening as that voice. Low and cajoling, smooth and teasing. She was certain that it belonged to a man who knew exactly what he was doing, and a man who would kill without a thought. What frightened her, too, was the clear sense of anger radiating out of him. Angry, angry, angry. And quiet too. Dangerously quiet.

But at least her children were safe, she thought to herself, tucked up in bed by now in her mother's apartment. How much worse it would have been if Alexa and Finn had been taken, as the man had suggested. Or Zan, whose single, exasperated 'Yup?' was all she'd heard when he answered the call. He'd been fishing, stalking that record-breaker of his, and madder than hell at the interruption. She was certain of it. What surprised her was that he should have had the phone on him. He never fished with a phone.

Dasha wondered what he would be doing now. If she was right about the time, he'd be hammering down the trail to Shinnook and the road to Melville, having called up Chief Mulholland to let him know what had happened, that his wife had been kidnapped. Then he'd have called Shelley, told her too, checked that the kids were okay and could they stay with her a little longer? He'd also call Tom, their lawyer; have him draw up the requisite paperwork for an announcement first thing tomorrow morning. Because whatever else Zan did – alerting the police, her mother, getting a search-and-rescue under way – he'd also do exactly what he'd been told to do. To secure her release, he'd hand over the Wilderness land without a second thought. A done deal, regardless of what the police might say, regardless of the consequences, whether they'd end up losing it to the National Parks, or not. It was company land after all, a company asset, and as chairman of the board Zan had the right to dispose of it with or without her approval. It would have been just the same if he had been the one kidnapped. She had a similar right to dispose of assets. Two partners. One signature. Although, of course, in the normal run of things . . .

. . . But this wasn't the normal run of things. This was about as far from normal as Dasha could imagine. Kidnapped. Handcuffed. Held captive in a log cabin miles from anywhere . . . And then, out of nowhere, a thought occurred to her. Had her kidnappers known about the single signature? Just how much homework had they done? For all her brave talk up there about scumbags, these were, she suspected, very clever scumbags. Scumbags who'd thought out every last detail.

Which made her feel a new shiver of fear.

Because what hope did she really have?

Even if Zan did surrender the land . . .

What was the point of pulling the blindfold back on when the trapdoor opened?

She had to admit that the chances that they would kill her were just as high as the chances that they would set her free.

Which meant, she realised, that she should make every effort to get away from this cabin, and away from these men, before it was too late. Because she certainly didn't intend to just sit there and wait for something to happen.

But where to start? Where to start?

31

It was a heavy weight pressing down on his right arm, rather than the throbbing red-hot pain in his left knee, that finally brought Zan back to consciousness. It was as if the arm was twisted, held down fast from shoulder to wrist, elbow joint at full extension. For a moment he wondered if he might have broken it in the fall, and for that reason he didn't try to move it.

It was this caution, this unwillingness to cause himself any more pain or damage by some ill-advised movement, that probably saved his life.

Lying there flat on his belly in the darkness, the right side of his face pressed into the soft dampness of the moss and leaf litter, Zan opened his eyes. At first there was nothing to see, but gradually he became aware of a dim light, the kind of light that a cloud-covered moon trying to break through dense foliage might manage. A dark grey misty light outlined by black twisting shapes that he realised were trees. He took a cautious breath and flexed the fingers of his right hand, just the gentlest movement to find out if he'd sustained a break, or maybe dislocated his shoulder.

It was that minute movement that caused the weight on his arm to shift, now bearing down on his straightened elbow so forcefully that he almost shrieked with the pain. It was fortunate that he did not. Something stopped him. Because he suddenly knew what was on his arm.

Or, more precisely, what was sitting on his arm.

Suddenly, he could smell it – a deep woody stench of fur. And hear it, too – a low throaty grunting that he could feel shifting down through the weight on his arm.

There was a bear sitting on his arm. A bear. Brown or grizzly, he couldn't tell. While he was lying unconscious this bear must have got his scent, and found him there, on the ground. And sat on him. Just . . . checking him out.

What he did know was that it was not a big bear – thank God – but a small one. A cub maybe. The weight was just about manageable. A full-grown adult bear pressing down on his arm would surely have snapped it.

And then he felt the strangest sensation in the fingertips of his upturned right hand. Something passing over them, touching them, one by one. And he knew immediately what it was. A claw. A single talon. The bear had seen his fingers moving and was investigating.

And now the bear was swatting the hand with his paw, back and forwards as though trying to see if he could make the fingers move again. Zan could feel the fur with one swipe and the rough-padded palm with the second swipe. The bear was playing with him.

Playtime – it was almost fun, comforting.

But what happened next made Zan's blood freeze and his guts twist and his mind race.

The crack of a branch close by – nothing to do with

the bear cub sitting on his arm, nothing to do with the bear cub playing with his hand in the darkness.

Something else.

Cub, cub, cub. The word circled around in his head until he could pin it down. And then he had it. There might have been a bear cub on his arm, but bear cubs had mothers.

Which was the crack he'd heard maybe twenty feet away to his left.

And no longer just a sound. But movement too. One of the trees was moving. Or rather, something was moving through them. Another crack, and a grunt, like a deep throaty cough, and the shape dropped down and lumbered in his direction.

Brown bear or grizzly didn't really matter much now, he thought with a numbing stomach-clenching chill. Both of them could kill him with a single blow from one of their mighty paws, and as the black shape came closer Zan squeezed his eyes shut. He couldn't believe this was happening. He was going to be killed by a bear, his insides were going to be ripped out of his belly. He was going to die an agonising death. He would never see his wife or children again, he would never . . .

His mind went blank as a rank stench of hot, feral breath swept across the side of his face. *Phwoah-phwoah-phwoah* it went, backwards and forwards, great, hot stinking gusts of it. And then a warm wet nose burrowed down under his chin and nudged his head upwards, as though the creature looming above him wanted to see what her cub had found.

Zan did not resist, but he kept his eyes clenched shut, his face squinched tight, like you do when you know you're about to be hit. But he wasn't hit. Instead a long

133

wet strip of warm sandpaper rasped across his cheek. Once, twice, three times, scoring a path between jaw and hairline.

It was then, with a final jolt of pain, that the bear cub lurched off his arm and the clamping pressure eased. Instead he felt two paws, three paws, four paws tread uncertainly over his back and shoulders as the cub came to take a look at what his mother had found.

Zan's eyes might have been squeezed shut but he could see in his mind what he'd be looking at if he did open them. In profile there'd be that long conical snout and those hunched shoulders; full face would be round and wide, a great mutton-chop disc of fur. He tried not to think of the mouth, the teeth. If one of the beasts decided to bite him, he'd never be able to staunch the scream or stop himself trying to struggle free.

Once again a hot wet tongue slapped over his face. And again, and again. As though the bear – he was sure it was the mother – was trying out the taste of him before setting in with an exploratory bite.

But it was the cub that went for the bite. Pushing up under its mother, the cub got between the licking tongue and Zan's face and fastened his smaller jaws around Zan's head. Zan knew that if he opened his eyes now, he'd be looking straight down a bear's throat.

The cub gave a small shake of the head and Zan felt the sharp little puppy teeth break the skin, felt a trickle of blood pool into his ear and stream down over his neck and into his collar. The pressure of the cub's jaws tightened and it was as though his head was caught in a clamp that was closing fast. Any moment now his skull would shatter. If there was any comfort to be found, it was the thought that if the jaws had belonged to the mother, the shattering would already have happened.

Pushed away from licking Zan's face, the mother now turned her attention to the rest of his body, running her snout across his back, snuffling as it went, drawing in the scent of him. While the cub continued to shake his head, Zan felt the mother's snout press down between his thighs, snuffling at his crotch. If she decided she liked the smell and decided to take a bite there, Zan knew there was no way he could control himself. He would certainly react. Instinctively push her off, try to roll away. And then both mother and cub would be on him.

And that would be it. He'd be finished.

Killed certainly, probably eaten too.

Whatever he did, he knew he had to play dead. Or that's exactly how he'd end up.

It was then, with his head in the cub's mouth and his rapidly shrinking genitals being nudged and mouthed by the mother, that Zan remembered his gun. The Colt .44 holstered to his belt. He could actually feel the wooden grip pressing against his right hip. It gave him a surge of hope. Just the explosive sound of a high-calibre shell blasting from the six-inch barrel might be enough to see them off.

If only he could just . . .

With the two bears now fully occupied on his left-hand side, Zan slowly, carefully tested his stiffened elbow, then started to bend it, bringing his right hand down to his belt. Like a spider's legs spinning a web, his fingers worked at the holster buckle, and finally released it. Easing the gun free, he prayed that the two bears wouldn't notice the movement.

He knew what he had to do.

Two shots for the cub. Up close, into the neck and head.

Then the remaining four bullets for the mother, before she knew what was happening. Into the chest, and the heart if he was lucky.

With his head still clamped in the cub's jaws, and the mother burrowing into his crotch, Zan knew that time was running out, and that this up-close-and-personal examination would soon give way to something a great deal more aggressive. Right now the Colt was his only hope. Just so long as the mother didn't decide to shift position and sit on him. Fifteen hundred pounds of bear meat pinning him down was not an attractive proposition.

But just as the tip of the barrel pulled clear of the holster rim and he got a proper grip on the butt, slid his finger through the trigger guard, the cub suddenly released his head, and his smaller but no less sandpapery tongue began licking at the spilled blood on Zan's face and neck, the accompanying blast of meaty bad breath almost overpowering.

The relief at being released from the cub's vice-like jaws made Zan's head spin, and for a moment he lost all sense of direction and space. And then the cub sneezed and a warm, wet spread of mucus spattered across Zan's face. The sneeze elicited a panting, anxious grunt from the mother and she raised her head from between his legs to see what was going on.

For a moment neither beast moved, as though they were trying to work out what had happened.

Now was the moment.

Now was his chance, thought Zan and, holding his breath, he drew the gun up to his waist, was about to roll over on to his back and start blasting, praying to the gods to make his aim good, when he felt the mother's paw suddenly reach under his hip and tip him over. Just like that. It was as if she had seen the gun and was trying to deflect its aim.

And his body did exactly what she wanted, spun like a log, burying the gun behind his back, and driving a steely wedge of pain into his knee.

Before he could do a thing, he felt the bear cub do the same as its mother, its tinier paw slipping under his shoulders and tipping him over a second time, like a hamburger on a griddle, followed by a second seismic flare of pain from his knee.

Three times, four times they did the same thing. One after another. Mother then cub. Tipping him over, rolling him down the slope, bounding after him to tip him again, the gun wrenched from his hand by snatching tree roots without a shot being fired.

It was as though the two of them were playing a game and enjoying it immensely. If they could have laughed, he was sure they would have done. But there was no such release for Zan.

Either he would start to scream, or he would pass out.

He prayed it would be the latter.

Were he to scream, he had no doubt that the bears would tear him limb from limb.

On and on they pushed him, tipping him harder and harder, further and further, till they had to chase after him down the slope, lumbering between the trees, the three of them crashing through the undergrowth, tree roots and broken branches and moss-covered rocks beating against him until he realised he was finished, his senses slipping away from him, his resources no longer able to cope.

And then, suddenly, he was in the open, tumbling fast down a steep bank of mossy turf. With gravel at the end of it. He felt the stones crunch beneath him as the ground flattened out and he came to a halt, breath gasping from his body, senses spinning after that roller-coaster ride.

But the bears were still there. In the milky light he could see them loping down the bank after him, and coming closer with every bound, the mother finally rising up against the moonlit cloud-cover to come crashing down on him.

Except the mighty roaring beast hit something else, something above Zan's head, her claws smashing down on to metal panelling and shrieking off it like chalk across a blackboard.

The next instant, flashes of light beat out into the night, and a wailing horn slashed through the silence. For a second or two, Zan couldn't think what was happening – the trees, the bears, everything around him lit up in staggered strobe-like, hooting motion.

And then he did. He was back on the trail-head, with the front fender of his Jeep above his head. The impact of the bear's massive paws crashing down on the bonnet had set off the car's alarm.

With a long, roaring bellow from the mother and a whimper from the cub, Zan watched the two of them turn and lumber back into the forest as though they'd been scalded, their pelts a silvery shimmer in the strobing flashes of the Jeep's headlights.

Grizzlies. They were grizzly bears.

That was what Zan thought in the seconds before he passed out.

32

Deputy Jed Roberts was about done in.

First off, Calley had given the Promenade beat to Bud and Tuck – which had put leery smiles on their faces – and lumbered him with Tabitha Wain, Tabs, the department's sole woman deputy. On a small, skinny man, Tabs's uniform would have looked like a clown's outfit, but every time she pulled it on she managed to iron out every crease. She had tight, cornribbed hair that showed stripes of pale scalp, and she tied the braided ends of it into a stiff little pig tail that shot out the back of her billcap. She rolled at the hips when she walked, she talked through her nose, and she liked to take things serious, by the book. Tell her a joke and Tabs'd nod her head, as though considering delivery rather than content. And if all that wasn't bad enough, she was eighteen months senior to Jed, and didn't much care for Ginny Farrell. Worse still, Calley had put the two of them in a squad car and sent them off to Shinnook and the trails.

It was Jed did the driving, of course, while Tabs handled the radio, calling in every ten minutes or so – time, location, *nothing to report, over*. Flicking channels to let every other police department within a twenty-mile radius know she was on the road. Halfway up to Shinnook, just past the Cut, she'd taken time out to lean past the steering wheel and tap his speedo. A fraction over fifty, maybe sixty – Jesus.

As far as Jed could see, there had been no good reason to bypass Shinnook in favour of a road traffic incident fifteen miles out along the Shinnook–Tacoma turnpike. Like he said when she told him to keep on driving rather than take the turning for Shinnook, the scene would be well covered. They'd probably have units in from Tacoma, he told her. Which they did, a good half dozen crews, lights flashing, cones out for passing traffic, set around a dead elk and three seriously damaged vehicles. The ambulances had been and gone, but there was still some clearing to be done. The only good thing about the stop was the chance for a cigarette.

After an hour or so chatting with the boys out on the turnpike, Tabs had gotten him back in the car and heading off to Shinnook. They'd cruised around for five or ten minutes, checking for a Lexus, called in briefly to the sheriff's department there – just a single deputy manning the desk – then headed out for the Susqua Trail. Two hours later, having followed the narrow black-top until it petered out into a rutted trail, and going on as far as the axles on their Buick would allow, Tabs had him turn them round and head back down, radioing to report no Lexus encountered, *over*. By the time they reached the turning for Shinnook, Jed's arms felt like jelly, and he had trouble reaching the indicator.

'Let's just take us a peek up the Hanish,' said Tabs, as Jed started to swing round for Shinnook.

'Hanish? I thought the Sarge said she was up on the Susqua? Why would she be on the Hanish?'

''Cause her husband is up there, that's why. Maybe Mrs Pearse just decided to drop by, say hi.'

'The guy's fishing, Tabs. Wives don't just drop in when their husbands are out fishing. You just don't do it.'

'Says who?' asked Tabs, with a wiry determination. 'So let's take the right here, and go have us a look. Just in case.'

Now, with a sharp, persistent rain drumming on the roof of the squad car and the wipers hard pressed to keep it swept off the windscreen, they were humping and jolting their way up the Hanish Trail, working the Buick over a second stretch of untended trail which Jed had made the most of maximising, trying to shake Tabs's resolve with every lurch of the springs. For the last four miles neither of them had spoken, Tabs occasionally directing the searchlight between the trees, Jed keeping his eyes on the trail but thinking of Ginny, and what they'd be doing if he wasn't out here with Miss Piggy on the road to nowhere.

Ginny. Ginny Farrell, two years older than him, and two years more tantalising. She'd been on his radar a year or more but it was only the last couple of months he'd lucked out. Every minute since then had been a slayfest. There wasn't another girl in Melville who made it quite as difficult as she did. Or quite so rewarding.

'How much further you reckon on going?' Jed asked at last, chewing on his toothpick and longing for a cigarette. If there was one thing Tabs loathed — after drunks and rapists — it was smokers. He hadn't had a smoke since the Tacoma wreck and was aching to light up. The further they went, the longer he'd have to wait.

Tabs glanced across at him then turned back to the

pitching trail. 'We'll go a few more miles, but if this rain gets any . . .'

'Hey, you see that?' called Jed. 'Up there, over the brow, looked like lights – a glow, you know?'

And sure enough, a few moments later, a pair of headlights swung over the rise and dropped down towards them, the twin beams smearing through the rain on their windscreen.

On and on they came, bucketing down the trail towards them.

'Ain't no Lexus,' said Tabs 'Looks like a Cherokee to me. But he sure ain't slowin' down any, that's for damn . . .'

'Holy Mo,' said Jed, tugging the wheel round. 'He's gonna hit us . . .'

33

It was the rain, falling on his face, that had woken Zan. A chill uncertain spattering that had softened the dried scabs of blood on his face and sent trickling streams of bloodied water between his lips and into his mouth. It was the sweet, metallic taste of that blood that brought it all back to him. The bears. Being rolled down the hillside like a child's hoop. Being played with. Not that the play would have lasted long. Sooner or later, Zan knew, either mother or cub would have dealt him the killing blow.

And then, vaguely, he remembered why he'd been in the forest, the beam of his torch slicing through the trees, stumbling down to the trail-head, not watching where he was going: the phone call, the threat, the instructions he should follow if he ever wanted to see his wife alive again.

As he lay there, flat on his back with his shoulder pressed against the wheel of his Jeep, he thanked the lord that the bears hadn't finished him off. If they had, he'd never have made it back to Melville, never have gotten his lawyer to draw up the transfer papers, never have made the news. And the kidnappers, waiting for it and not hearing it, would almost certainly have followed through on their threat and Dasha would be dead. Him too. Alexa and Finn orphans.

But somehow he had made it – this far. He'd twisted his knee, survived the tender ministrations of a pair of grizzlies and had ended up right next to his Jeep. Luck, he acknowledged, didn't come in bigger parcels.

For a few more moments Zan lay there, not moving, going over everything. Then he lifted his watch and looked at the time, squinting in the darkness, trying to focus. Normally the luminescent figures shone out brightly, but now they seemed to dance in a bright green blur, flicking to left and right and leaving a trail as they did so. It was impossible to see what time it was, impossible to tell how long since he'd set out from his camp on Bear Tree Lake. All he could say with any certainty was that it was still night-time. And still dark enough for dawn to be some way off.

It was also clear that he'd suffered some kind of concussion. His memory might have been in one piece, just, but his eyesight was certainly compromised. As though to confirm this he was suddenly aware of a steely beat of pain in the left side of his head where the bear cub's jaws had clamped down on his skull and squeezed.

No wonder he couldn't see what time it was. Whatever he did now, he'd have to do it slowly, carefully.

Feeling through his pockets he checked for the Jeep's keys. He found them in an inside pocket in his rain slicker. All that rolling about and somehow they hadn't fallen out. Even more luck.

Knowing that both head and knee would object violently to any ill-considered movement, Zan tried to work out what he should do next and found it as hard to make a decision as it had been to focus on his watch. Definitely a concussion. There could be no other explanation.

Carefully, pushing up on his hands, the gravel biting into his palms, he sat himself up. Slowly, bringing his good leg into play, he bent it, tipped his weight on to it and, groaning with the pain and the effort, he got himself upright, hopped round to the driver's side, bleeped the Cherokee's lock and pulled open the door. For a moment a swim of dizziness washed over him, but he held on to the door, swivelled round and rested himself against the side of the front seat. Supporting his weight with his elbows, he hooked the heel of his good leg on to the foot-plate and pushed himself up behind the wheel.

Head still spinning and thumping – a real hangover headache that made him squint his eyes – Zan pulled the door shut and paused for breath, panting from the effort, grateful to be out of the rain that was now rapping hard on the roof and smearing down the windscreen.

At least, he thought, if the bears came back he'd be safe in the Jeep.

Trying to focus on the wheel and dashboard, the first thing he recognised was the dashboard clock. Right there in front of him, between the spokes of the steering wheel. But though the digital figures on the dashboard clock were bigger and brighter than the numerals on his wristwatch, it was still little more than a red blur. Carefully he tipped his head back and forward in an attempt to refocus, trying it with the left eye and then the right in case one of them was working better than the other. Finally he made out a 23 and what looked like 15. Not as late as he'd imagined. But late enough.

What next, he thought? What did he need to do now?

For a moment his mind was a blank and then he remembered. His phone. He needed to phone Chief Mulholland, he needed to call Shelley, call Tom. He reached for the glove compartment and pulled out the charge wire, managed to plug it into the lighter socket, then went through his pockets for his phone. Trouser pockets, slicker pockets, shirt pockets. But the phone had gone. He didn't have it. Somewhere, being tossed down that hillside by the bears, the phone must have flipped out of his pocket. He'd lost it. It was gone. The only thing he could do now was get down to Shinnook as fast as he could and start phoning from there.

With trembling fingers, Zan leant forward, slid the ignition key into its slot and turned on the engine. It started first time and the sound of it gave him a surge of confidence, a belief that his torment would soon be over. He found the switch for the lights and turned them on, twin pools of light illuminating the trail-head turning circle, a heavy rain now lancing through them.

145

Engaging gear, Zan turned the Jeep in a single, level sweep, tyres crunching over the puddling gravel, wipers pushing away the rain on his windscreen. It was a comfort to note that the movement caused few problems in terms of pain, or even discomfort, from his left leg. It was only when he straightened up and the gravel turning circle gave way to the rutted trail itself that the problems started, the Jeep bouncing and rolling over the uneven ground and his knee spurting with pain at every jolt.

It was close to fourteen miles to the start of the black-top, and Zan had travelled the route enough times to know that he was looking at forty minutes easy before he hit a smooth surface, and another twenty on top of that to make Shinnook. And in the dark, with the rain coming down and the trail already muddying up, it might take even longer.

The first fifteen minutes, he managed well enough, gritting his teeth every time he hit a bump and jarred his left leg. The next fifteen were harder, and the going got tougher. Gripping the wheel, he peered ahead through the slanting rain, praying for the rutted track to turn into black-top, and for the lights of Shinnook to show. His headache seemed to be getting worse too, and his eyes were starting to play tricks. Coming round a bend in the track he could have sworn an elk stepped out right there in front of him. It was only as he spun the wheel to avoid it that he realised the elk hadn't been there at all. It was just his imagination.

Hallucinations. He was so done in, so tired, he was starting to hallucinate.

He reached forward and turned down the heating, sending a chill, refreshing blast out of the vents. That would help, he thought; that would keep him awake. Then he remembered the dashboard radio and switched it on. The CD player came on first, Annie Lennox's *Medusa*. The last time he'd heard her voice, he'd been coming up this same trail with a few days' fishing in front of him. Rather than hear it through again, or try to find another CD, he switched to the radio – news, sport results, a late-night story, some country and western, a pop station. He settled for the news – some report in from Iraq – but five minutes later he found himself blinking, eyes dry and tired. He'd been wrong about the radio keeping him awake. If he wasn't careful the newsreader's voice combined with the tapping rain and bucking ride and rhythmic thumping of the wipers would put him to sleep. So he switched off the radio and started singing to himself – half-remembered lines, choruses, even humming, to keep himself awake. He'd have given a fortune to pull over and take a nap, but he knew he couldn't. Just keep your eyes open and on the track, he thought.

Sooner or later he'd reach the black-top and the driving would be a great deal easier.

And smoother. And faster.

Just keep your eyes on the track, keep your eyes on the track. Just keep . . .

Five minutes later, as the Jeep hit a rise and dropped down, Zan's eyes just closed. He knew he was going to sleep but suddenly he just didn't care. So what? He was tired, just so plain, doggone exhausted . . . and if anyone deserved a break it was him. A sleep would do him good. Sleep was the way to go. Let it just sweep him up. He deserved it.

Sleep, sleep, sleep was more important than driving, driving . . .

Jesus he was driving! His eyes sprang open and coming

147

right at him were a set of headlights. It was like driving towards a mirror, a reflection of his own headlights.

Just another hallucination, he thought. Just like the elk.

But he wasn't going to be fooled this time. He wasn't going to swerve out of the way a second time.

Damn phoney mirror, he thought, a smile breaking across his lips. *You think you're gonna fool me again, you got another think . . .*

Suddenly a horn blasted out towards him, followed by the start-up wail of a siren and a flashing bar of red and blue lights.

Zan squinted in the glare of lights.

No elk this. No mirror. No hallucination.

A goddam police car by the look of it, and heading in his direction, even closer now, about to hit.

Shit . . . this was real.

34

Chief Mulholland and his wife, Julie, had just gotten home from the Lessermans' after an appalling run of luck at the bridge table. Six rubbers down and forty bucks short on the evening. It wasn't the run of the cards that upset him, or the shaky bids, or the four tens he'd had to peel off his billfold at the end of the evening, it was losing to the Lessermans. He and Julie were way better players.

'They'll be crowing all week,' she said bitterly. 'If I'd kept those diamonds in the last hand, at least we'd have salvaged one game,' she continued, pulling off her coat and hanging it on the rack.

'It wasn't the diamonds, it was me,' said Mulholland. 'I just played the bids wrong. Guess I wasn't concentrating.'

'You want a drink before we go up?' she asked, standing midway between stairs and kitchen.

'Hey, why not?'

Off in his den, Mulholland heard the phone start up.

Julie heard it, too, and gave him a tired look. 'Go on, I'll bring it through to you.'

'Just a small one,' he said, heading down the hallway. He knew what the call was about. Dasha Pearse. Had to be. The whole thing had been nagging him all evening; he just knew there was something up, something not right. Maybe that's why he'd played such lousy hands.

When he reached his desk, he swept up the phone. 'Yup, Mulholland here.'

'Chief, it's Deputy Wain. We found him, Zan Pearse. Leastways we think it's him. It's his car – the Cherokee Jeep. His licence. His wallet. But it sure doesn't look like Mr Pearse.'

'Is it or isn't it?'

'If it is, he's been beaten up pretty bad. Got cuts all over his head, blood everywhere.'

'He conscious?'

'In and out. Keeps talking about bears – coulda easily

149

been one of them done this to him. And kidnap too. His wife, Mrs Pearse? Keeps saying someone's kidnapped her, holding her for ransom.'

Mulholland cursed softly.

Julie came into the den and put his drink on the desk, pointed to the ceiling. She wasn't staying up.

Mulholland blew her a kiss, held up five fingers. He wouldn't be long.

She gave him a look. After thirty years together she knew the way a lie shaped up. 'Where are you?' asked Mulholland, reaching for his drink.

'About ten minutes off the black-top – Hanish Trail – and it's tipping down something bad. We were just about to turn back when over the hill he comes. Didn't even seem to notice us – headed right for us. Then suddenly he swerves like he's just seen us.'

'Is he fit to travel? Can you get him to Melville, or you need to have him checked out at Shinnook?'

'I reckon we can make it,' replied Tabs. 'Get him fixed up and comfortable in the back. You want me to do that, Chief?'

'I want you to do it, Tabs. Get him down here quick as you can. I'll have them ready and waiting at the medical centre. Meet you there.'

'You got it, Chief.'

Putting down the phone, Mulholland glanced at the clock on his desk.

Midnight.

Some way to start the weekend.

35

Day-off or not, a little hungover, Jenna had been doing her homework. It was midnight when she finally switched off her laptop, scooped up the last of the noodles she'd ordered in, and pushed back from her desk.

After trawling through the various internet sites that her brother had recommended, and following up some links of her own, it seemed to her that there were two possible storylines worth exploring. Number one – sharks. There was something visceral about that fin weaving through the water, those razor-sharp teeth, those dead black predatory eyes rolling up in their heads as they launched themselves on a victim. And a pack of them together – hundreds, Greg had told her – well, that just had to be the cherry on the cake. And they were a lot more camera-friendly than a bunch of drifting jellyfish, even if the jellyfish did sting. Those fins, those teeth, those eyes . . .

The only problem was she didn't know where they were. She'd checked Google Earth and listed all the beaches and settlements south of the Kerry Light where Greg had first spotted them. There were more than a dozen possible locations – Stover Beach, Ringwood, Causeway Point, Melville Bay – but since she didn't know how much territory these sharks could cover in a day, and didn't really understand the tide and current stats she'd called up, it was difficult to be certain. Like Greg said, they could just have hightailed it back into the ocean and split up. And Coons, her news-desk editor, would want more than a hunch if he was going to send her out with a camera jack and outside broadcast van.

The second story – Jenna knew she was on even weaker ground here – was the storm front that Greg had also told her about, moving down from British Columbia. According to weather movement records from previous years, this incoming system was a seasonal fixture, usually bypassing the state and dumping on the parched and welcoming plains of Idaho. This year, though, fore-casts from the National Weather Service in Maryland, and the Northwest Forecast Center in Seattle – no more than a couple of miles from where she was sitting – were suggesting that this year the storm was drifting further west than normal and might easily get trapped over the high westerly ridges of the Silver Hills National Park.

According to a forecaster she'd spoken to at the National Weather Service, Jenna had discovered that this unseasonal redirection was the result of a range of other-wise seasonal patterns being radically upset. It had all begun off the west coast of Africa in late April when Hurricane Jax started her westerly trek across the Atlantic. Monitored by observers at the National Weather Service, of whom Jenna's contact had been one, this storm front had headed towards the southern Caribbean, rampaged across Trinidad and Tobago before sweeping into the larger playground of the Gulf of Mexico, spinning about like a prima ballerina and building up a substantial head of steam. When Jax had hit Galveston just a few weeks earlier it had been a mighty blow. Jenna remembered the footage – waves crashing over the seawall, palm trees bent to the wind, traffic lights swinging over deserted rain-swept crossroads, and metal sheeting tumbling along the street. She even remembered the name of the local TV reporter – Sharon Walker – who'd managed to file some great storm sequences. Walker, Jenna had heard, was now with CBS on a two-year contract and a hundred thou a year.

Of course, Jax wasn't like Katrina and New Orleans, her contact at the Weather Service had admitted. It wasn't as big and it wasn't as destructive. But when Jax came ashore, she came in from the south-east, at least a few points outside its forecast path, causing an incoming south-westerly to veer north. In a kind of climatic domino effect, this unexpected switch in direction caused a bank of warm air above the Great Plains to shift north-west, running up the spine of the Rockies towards the Canadian border. It was this band of unseasonably warm air that was now slowing the weather front bearing down on them from British Columbia, and holding it up over the ridge line of the Silver Hills. Unable to retreat north or continue south-east into Idaho, Montana and Wyoming, penned in by another depression coming in off the Pacific, it looked like the coastal side of the Silver Hills Ridge was in for a drenching.

All Jenna needed were a few good rivers raging over their banks, people swept away, and houses destroyed.

And all she had to do was work out exactly where this might happen.

Or pray those sharks started biting.

36

Old Jimmy Looking Eyes pulled up his truck in Totem Hill car park, switched off the engine and killed the headlights. It was still night-time, but with a near full moon lowering to the north-west and silvering the banks of sea-fog drifting in from the ocean there was enough light to make out the wooden posts that marked the trail leading up to the North Bluff look-out point.

Pushing open the door of his truck and pulling himself from behind the wheel, Old Jimmy dropped down on to the ground and leant back in for his hat, gloves and a folded blanket. This time of the morning there was a chill in the air and, slamming the door behind him, he tugged on his hat and gloves and pulled up his collar. The climb would warm him up soon enough, but right now he could feel the chill in his old bones. Tucking the blanket under his arm, he crossed the car park, passed between the trail posts and started upwards.

Ten minutes later, his breath shortening and a dew of sweat prickling his scalp, Old Jimmy came through the last trees and stepped up to the belvedere, one of the best viewing stations along the entire west coast. There were two levels here: the first terrace held a half-dozen wood benches where the sightseers could rest their legs and catch their breath, and an orientation table so they could see where they were. Incised on to a greening sheet of brass the coastline of northern Washington State stretched from Cape Flattery in the north to the mouth of the Columbia River and Cape Disappointment down south. On the topmost edge of this table, compass arrows pointed across the ocean to Sydney, Honolulu, Manila, Tokyo and Beijing, and on its three landward edges to Anchorage, San Francisco, Houston, Chicago and New York, with the distances bracketed in miles.

But old Jimmy wasn't interested in the map or the view and he didn't tarry. He headed for the short flight of steps that led from the belvedere to the top level where an ancient Makah totem pole stood on the highest point. A low chain-link fence had been set around it and a small plaque informed visitors that the totem had once been a tree, an ancient red cedar cut down to a twelve-foot column by local Makah Indians. It had been old when the first settlers found it, and it stood there still, its splintered, greying trunk carved into the shape of an eagle astride a bear's shoulders, the eyes of both bird and beast fixed on the distant ocean.

Stepping over the chain-link fence, Jimmy spread his blanket on the stiff grass and levered himself down on to it, arranging his legs as close to a crossing as possible and setting his spine along the totem bear's belly. Without thinking, Old Jimmy started to hum and after a few bars the words came to his lips, the old harpooner's song to the whale he chased, a promise to sing and dance and make offerings at the very totem he now leaned against, if the whale allowed himself to be caught and killed.

Jimmy's family had been whalers for generations. It was in their blood. While other coastal tribes waited for a whale to beach, the Makah and Susqua and Hanish, and the Nootka further north, had gone out looking for them, carving their twelve-metre dugouts from the cedars that grew all along the coast. Old Jimmy remembered the first whale he'd killed, his father at his shoulder singing the same song as they waited for the beast to rise, his hands trembling on the harpoon's trigger. And he remembered his last whale too. A mighty humpback that had come to his dreams not two hours earlier and brought him to this old place.

In the forty or so years since Jimmy stepped ashore for the last time down on Melville's main quay, the spirit of that slaughtered humpback had visited him three times. The first time he woke in a sweat, drenched through as though he'd fallen overboard. That same morning, on his way to the port, he'd slipped on a cobblestone step, broken his hip and never went to sea again.

The second time the whale came to him, Jimmy woke from the dream and knew immediately that something bad was going to happen. When he reached the quays where he worked in the flensing sheds, he heard the news that his old boat, the *Melville Scout*, had gone down with all hands, caught in a storm seventeen miles off Clayaquot Sound.

And now Old Jimmy Looking Eyes had had the dream a third time. It had woken him in his bed and he had come straight here to Totem Hill.

As the song he sang softly to himself came to an end, he looked up at the sky, still enough moonlight left to see a cover of higher clouds race in from the ocean, while a soft, woolly cover of sea-fog swaddled the bay beneath him.

He grunted. Big winds up there, but nothing down here. Not a whisper.

It surprised him. And then it didn't.

After all, something bad was on its way.

The whale spirit had told him.

37

The first real rain came down over the north Hanish ridge at a little after two in the morning, fifteen miles from Bear Tree Lake and a thousand feet higher. Since sundown there had been a low mist climbing up through the trees and shifting over the upper slopes before the rain arrived, but within minutes of it starting, the mist had gone as though beaten away in the advancing downpour.

Dropping down the slope the rain fell in billowing curtains, streaming through a thick pelt of pine and spruce, slicing through the branches and turning their moss shrouds into pointed dripping beards. Down on the ground, seeping through a carpet of twisting roots, drooping fern and matted pine needles, the rain soaked into the top soil. At a depth of seventeen inches it reached the stone shoulders of the ridge and could sink no further. In less than an hour, a million little streams had started up down there, sliding between the stone mantle and its carpet of topsoil, trickling unseen along the upper slopes of the ridge.

At Bear Tree Lake, the rain came in a sudden rush, over the treetops, puckering and rippling its way across the water to beat a vicious tattoo on the taut drumskin roof of Zan's abandoned tent. Somewhere in the forest an elk bellowed, but the only other sound was the belting rain – gusting through the trees now, splashing into the lake.

At the northern end of Bear Tree where Zan had waded through a squelching meadow of moss and grass to cast for rainbows, the incoming stream had grown far stronger now. If Zan had been standing there the rush of water would have easily sluiced over the top of his boots. An hour after that, he'd have been standing waist deep in the torrent.

Inch by splashing inch, the surface of Bear Tree rose, backing up into the stream and spreading out over its low banks. Within an hour of the rain arriving, the water was lapping just two feet shy of the top of the bank where Zan had cast for his steelhead. But there was no need to wait for the water to breach it. With hundreds of tons of run-off pouring through the cut leading down to the next level of lakes and ponds, the mouth of this tiny channel started to widen. The more water that poured through it, the greater the damage and the banks either side of it started to crumble with the weight pressing against them. With a sudden wrenching sound of tearing roots and crumbling earth, the sides of this channel gave way and the contents of Bear Tree Lake cascaded down on to the next level.

And the rain followed it.

38

Chief Mulholland was waiting at Melville County Hospital when Deputy Wain turned Zan's Cherokee Jeep in under the neon panels of the Accident & Emergency portico. Mulholland had arrived at the hospital twenty minutes earlier, introduced himself to the doctor on duty and explained about the imminent arrival. By the time Tabs braked to a stop, two nurses were on hand to help Zan from the back seat of the Cherokee and on to a waiting gurney. As the gurney was wheeled past him, Mulholland could see that Pearse's eyes were open, flickering a little wildly as the neon lights flashed past overhead. Normally well tanned, he looked pretty pale to Mulholland, his crop of blond-grey hair still wet, slicked back from his forehead, his neck and cheek and hairline a mess of tiny cuts and abrasions. He looked like he'd been pulled from a car wreck. Mulholland also noticed that Zan was wearing a gun belt and holster. As far as he could see, there was no gun.

'He have a gun on him?' asked Mulholland, turning to Tabitha.

'No Chief, no gun that we've seen,' she replied, unzipping her jacket and slipping her thumbs into her belt. 'Not on him, and not in the car, save a box of shells in the glove compartment. Musta left it at camp.'

'Or dropped it someplace,' said Mulholland. 'He say much on the way down?'

'Like I say, he was in and out,' she replied, going on to repeat pretty much everything she'd already told him over the radio.

While she was talking, Jed Roberts pulled up in the squad car and parked behind the Cherokee. As he hauled himself out of the driver's seat, Mulholland couldn't help a smile. The kid looked just about done in. Not exhausted. Just 'Tabitha'd'. Pretty near six hours they'd spent together. Mulholland almost felt sorry for him.

'So, good job, well done,' he said when Roberts joined them, cutting Tabs short. 'The pair of you check in with Sergeant Calley back at the office, and then you might as well call it quits.'

'Thanks Chief,' replied a much relieved Roberts.

'Happy to stay around if you need me, Chief,' volunteered Tabitha.

'No, Tabs, that's just fine. I only want a few words with Mr Pearse and then I'm outta here too.'

Fifteen minutes later, the doctor came to find Mulholland in the waiting room.

'You'll be pleased to hear that your Mr Pearse is going to be just fine. A couple of days' rest and he'll be good as new.'

'He beaten up?' said Mulholland, getting to his feet, throwing down the copy of the *Fishing Times* he'd been leafing through.

'You could say. But not in the usual sense. The patient says bears, and no reason to disbelieve him. There are clear puncture wounds on the neck, jawline and cheek and deep into the hairline. You can follow the wounds in an arc. Looks like a bear got the man's head in its mouth and clamped down hard. X-rays show a very tiny hairline fracture at the edge of the skull below the left ear. There are also numerous lacerations to his face and arms and hands compatible with fending off an animal attack, though they could also have been caused by running blind through a forest, trying to escape from an attack – branches whipping back, that kind of thing. He's also twisted the patellar tendon in his knee. It's not the worst I've seen, but it'll still hurt. I've immobilised it for now and given him a cortisone jab.'

'So he is awake then? Conscious? I can have a word? It's important.'

'It can't wait till the morning? The more rest he gets . . .'

'Now would be better.'

'Then you've got till I put the needle in his arm and he gets the sleeper he deserves. Five minutes max, and no argument.'

Mulholland found Zan in a recovery room along the corridor from A&E. The metal sides were up on the bed, and a drip snaked down into his left arm. He'd been name-tagged round the right wrist and attached to a monitor that bleeped encouragingly. His clothes had been taken off him and a surgical gown put on in their place. His head was bandaged and a cage lifted the bedclothes over his legs. On his face and neck and arms were a multitude of nicks and cuts and livid bruises. With the harsh lights overhead, he looked even worse than when he'd been brought in.

Pulling up a chair, Mulholland sat down beside him. 'Mr Pearse? Zan? Can you hear me? It's Chief Mulholland.'

Zan's eyes fluttered open and a thin smile creased his lips. 'I hear you, Chief. Not dead yet.' And then the smile faded and a frown settled across his features, as though he was trying to remember something important.

Mulholland cleared his throat. He knew he didn't have much time. He was going to have to get as much information as he could. The doctor could be back at any moment. 'According to my officers, you said something about your wife being kidnapped?'

'That's what he said.'

Mulholland frowned. 'That's what who said?'

'Whoever's damn well got her. I had a call. Up fishing on the Hanish. Said if we didn't hand over the Wilderness lands to the National Parks in the next forty-eight hours I wouldn't see my wife again.'

'This was a man's voice?'

'That's right. That's right. Sounded like he was from the south. Kinda slow Texas drawl.' Zan tried to sit up, get himself more comfortable, but all it did was draw a groan from him.

'And the call came through from your wife's cell? You saw her name?' asked Mulholland.

'No, I didn't,' replied Zan. 'I just took the call . . . I assumed it was Dasha.'

'And what time was this, when you got the call?'

'Seven? Around then.'

'And why didn't you call the Police Department at that time? Right after you got the call.'

'The damn cell was out of power, Chief. I just couldn't believe it.'

'So, you left camp . . .'

'. . . And came charging down through the woods . . .'

'. . . Which was when you fell? When you hurt your knee?'

'I just went flying. Tripped over something and that was it.'

'And the bear?'

'Bears. Two of them. A mother and cub.'

Mulholland whistled lightly. In his thirty-two years as a law enforcement officer, Mulholland had seen what a bear could do – campers dragged from their tents, attacked on forest paths. Sometimes you found the bodies, sometimes just bits of them. Sometimes nothing. 'You're a lucky man, Mr Pearse. Up there, just a twisted knee can kill you. And two bears certainly can. So, you got any idea who might be behind this?'

'Some eco-nut. Has to be. Probably the same guys who've been spray-painting the office.'

Mulholland nodded, thinking of the new message that had been put up just that morning. Either it was one mighty coincidence, or Zan Pearse was right.

'So what's next?' asked Zan. 'What are you going to do? I can handle my side of it, but we need to get the police involved. A search . . .'

'And I'll get on to it right away, don't you worry

about that. But there's other agencies we'll need to bring in on something like this.'

'We gotta find her, Chief. And fast. Whatever it takes.'

'So you're going to do what they want?' asked Mulholland.

'It's land, Chief. Trees, earth, grass. And they've got my wife. No contest.'

'It's just forty-eight hours leaves things pretty tight for us. The longer we can string this along, the more chance we'll have of tracking 'em down is all I'm saying.'

'Soon as I can get through to my lawyer, that transfer is going ahead, Chief. I want it on the news first thing. So they know I'm doing what they want.'

It was then that the door pushed open and the doctor came in. 'That's it, Chief,' he said, filling a hypodermic from a sealed bottle. He pointed the syringe to the ceiling and squirted out a thin stream. 'You're out of here. And so is my patient.' Pushing up the sleeve of Zan's gown, the doctor wiped the skin with an antiseptic swab, slid in the needle and pressed the plunger.

And that was that. Interview over. There was nothing more the Chief could do.

Pulling on his hat Mulholland walked past A&E reception, bid the nurses a good night and strode out into the parking lot. Getting into his car, he reached for his cell and put a call through to Calley.

'Brew up some coffee, Sergeant. We got us some work to do.'

39

Elroy Baker hadn't slept. And he hadn't slept because he had a plan.

For more than an hour he'd lain in his bed, facing the wall and feigning sleep, listening to Gene's soft snores across the room and Eddie, in the bed beside him, reading a paperback, licking a finger each time he turned a page. Judging by the time between each lick and rustle of paper, Eddie was a pretty slow reader. Finally, he had put aside the paperback and switched off his lamp. With a grunt, and squeak of bedsprings, he'd settled himself down and in less than five minutes was breathing low and steady.

The bunkroom, as Gene had called their accommodation when he first saw it, was at the top of the stairs, a long room running down one complete side of the cabin. Since the cabin was only ever used by weekend hunters out of Shinnook or Melville, it was sparely equipped with four single beds, two bedside tables and two small table-lamps. There were two Indian-pattern rugs laid between the beds, a double wardrobe behind the door, a chest of drawers and flimsy cotton curtains sporting an elk-head pattern stretched along a wire cord. Across the corridor from their bunkhouse was the bathroom and, at the front of the cabin, Mort's bedroom.

In the last hour a light rain had started to tap at the bunkroom windows, and to its comforting accompaniment Elroy had made up his mind, knew what he was going to do. Knew what he had to do. As far as he could guess it, the solution he'd come up with was the only way he was ever going to get out of this mess without spending time behind bars.

It was the knife that did it. Mort's knife. The way he sliced off her clothes, played the tip around her bra strap. For a moment down there in the sitting room, he'd been convinced there was going to be rape to add to kidnap. There was a greedy look of longing in Mort's single eye, and Gene and Eddie had watched the whole performance as though mesmerised. God, he'd thought. When Mort finishes that call to her husband, he's gonna give her to them. Or take her himself. Right there, more than likely. Up on the table. Held down and screaming. And like as not he'd be expected to take his turn with the rest of them, and implicated whether he did or not. Rape, or accessory to rape. His choice. But neither option sounded like the kind of thing he wanted to be involved in. It was to his great relief, therefore, that Mort had sent him up for that T-shirt and the bra had stayed in place.

It was this feeling of implication, of things turning bad, that had kept Elroy awake and forced him to re-appraise his role in this increasingly criminal endeavour. There was no doubt in his mind that the more time he spent with these guys the deeper into the shit he'd be wading. And if he stayed any longer, there was every likelihood that it would get a whole lot worse. Which was why he'd decided it was time to ship out. Taking the woman with him. He'd wait till Eddie was well asleep, then he was going to creep down, get Mrs Pearse out of the basement and the two of them were going to make a run for it. He knew the woods hereabouts, knew how to get back to Shinnook without using the trail. He'd just head for the Hanish and follow it downstream. And the way he saw it, Mort and the boys would never find them, never catch up if the two of them got a good enough headstart. They'd have to go on foot, of course. Nothing else for it. No point taking her Lexus or his truck; starting them up was sure to wake someone – Mort, probably, in the front bedroom. And that would be that. They'd just have to trek it.

Elroy waited another half hour before he made his move, listening to the rain grow heavier and heavier, drumming on the boards above his head, scratching against the window panes. Finally, comforted by the snores from Eddie and Gene, he swung his legs out of bed, picked up his clothes, and in his shorts and T-shirt crept out of the bunkroom, latching the door quietly behind him.

With no windows the corridor was a lot darker than the bunkhouse and he waited a few moments for his eyes to adjust. Up ahead, there was no light under Mort's door and no light coming from downstairs. Carefully, on tiptoe, keeping as close to the wall as he could to lessen any chance of creaking floorboards, he made his way down the corridor, held his breath going past Mort's door, and made it down the stairs.

Creeping into the kitchen, he pulled on his clothes and reached for his big padded jacket, and Eddie's smaller jacket which would fit Mrs Pearse. It was when he reached down for his boots, outside the kitchen door, that he remembered Mrs Pearse's shoes – flat-soled Timberlands. The woman wouldn't get a mile in those.

Shit, thought Elroy. Shit, shit, shit . . .

And then he had a brainwave. If Eddie had a jacket that would just about fit her, then maybe he had the right size boot. Elroy rooted around until he found them, then put them up against Dasha's boat shoes. Pretty close, near as he could tell.

Coming out of the kitchen, he crossed to the table, picked up Gene's battered black Maglite and went over to the trapdoor. Pulling out the ring from its nest he lifted the trapdoor. Very carefully. It creaked like crazy and he knew that if he lost his grip and let it slam back down it would wake the whole cabin. But he held tight, stepped round it on to the flight of stairs and then lowered it down on top of him as he descended into the basement. At the bottom of the stairs he flicked on the Maglite and spun the beam round the room until it reached the bed and illuminated a sleeping figure.

Silently he crossed the room and stood beside the bed, angling the torch to one side so that it didn't shine right into her face. It was the first time since she'd arrived that he'd seen her without the blindfold. Reaching out a hand, he touched her shoulder and gently shook it.

40

Dasha felt a hand on her shoulder, a quick shake. She was awake in a second, shuffling up on the bed and blinking her eyes in the torchlight. All she could see were a pair of washed-out blue jeans and thickly socked feet.

'What . . . ?' was all she managed before a voice cut in, whispered to her.

'Please keep quiet, Mrs Pearse. I'm here to get you out of here.'

'You're what? Who are you?'

'My name's Elroy. What's happening here is not right. I want you to know that.'

'You're one of them?' she asked, pushing back against the wall and swinging her legs down in front of her. She was awake enough now to be immediately suspicious. If this was some trick . . . if he tried to do anything to her, she'd lash out with her feet where lashing feet weren't supposed to go. If he tried to lay a finger on her, she'd fight like he wouldn't believe.

On the edge of the torchlight, she caught a shadowy profile and saw the nod. 'I am. I mean I was. I don't want to be a part of this. It's not right, so I'm going to get you out of here.'

He had a soft, warm voice and the whisper gave it a sense of urgency. She could tell he was quite young. Late teens, early twenties she guessed.

'Please, Mrs Pearse, you really have to hurry.'

Picking up on his urgency, Dasha swung off the bed, heart pounding, and held out her handcuffs for him to unlock them.

'I'll need these off,' she said, then sensed a sudden uncertainty in him.

He made no move to do so, just stood there looking at them.

'You have got a key, haven't you?'

'Mort's got the key,' he said quietly. 'There's no way . . . I'll sort it later. Come on now, and please keep very quiet.'

Dasha did as she was told, following him up the steps and out through the trapdoor where he switched off the torch. Shivering in her T-shirt and bare feet, she looked around the room in what little light there was. She'd been right. As far as she could see it looked like a logger's cabin or something for hunters. Plain, bare and very masculine. No high-end rental this, more authentic hunting experience.

With a creak, Elroy lowered the trapdoor back down and gathered up the pile of clothes that he'd left there – the parkas and boots. 'We'll put these on outside,' he said, nodding to the front door. 'Safer, and quieter, out there.'

'I can hardly put on a coat if I'm cuffed,' she whispered. 'If you haven't got the keys, you'll have to find something to break the chain. Is there an axe outside, or something in the kitchen?'

She felt the same uncertainty she'd noted earlier, just radiating off him. For a moment he seemed to freeze, as though he didn't know what to do next. It was as if he was more frightened than she was.

'Stay here,' he told her. 'Don't move. I'll go look.'

'And my phone?'

She saw him shake his head. 'Back on the trail,' he replied. 'Mort would've chucked it in the woods, or the river. Precaution. Never can tell nowadays what they can do with cells.'

'You got a phone of your own?'

Once again she saw him shake his head, and she began to feel very uneasy. If he hadn't thought it out this far, how was he going to get her any further? For a moment, Dasha wondered whether she should trust him. But what was the alternative? At least she knew her way round the forest, for that was clearly where they were. She'd been coming up here with her father since she was child, with Zan too. Once she got her bearings she could just give him the slip and head on down to the closest settlement. Just keep to the river, she could hear her father saying. It'll bring you out somewhere. She also heard, up in the hills above them, a groan of low thunder playing itself along a ridge-line.

'Okay, okay, it doesn't matter,' she whispered, as though she was now the one in charge, and telling him what to do. 'Just go find something for these damned cuffs.'

Laying the torch on the table, Elroy crossed the room towards a doorway at the bottom of the stairs which Dasha presumed led to the kitchen. She was wondering what he'd come back with – a butcher's sharpening steel, maybe even bolt cutters? – when she saw his shadowy form reach the doorway and suddenly stop, stretch up on tiptoes, then hunch forward. There was a gurgling sound and a grunt, and as Elroy slumped forward she saw another shape in the doorway, standing right in front of him, as though blocking his way.

Suddenly the sitting room lights went on, a pair of antlered sconces on two of the walls, and Dasha could see him. A man with an eye-patch, in T-shirt and combat pants.

'Elroy, Elroy, Elroy. Naughty, naughty boy,' he was saying, sliding an arm round the kid's shoulder.

It was the same voice she'd heard earlier, when she'd been wearing the blindfold. Mort. It had to be Mort.

Dasha froze where she stood.

'And Mrs Pearse. Up and about so late. And in such bad company,' he continued, pushing Elroy away from him. Like a tree that had been felled, the body just crumpled backwards on to the floor, stretched out.

Both Elroy's hands were clasped to his belly, clutching at the sides of a massive vertical wound, a fast pulsing spill of dark arterial blood spreading around him like a crimson cloak, his socked heels drumming on the floor-boards, frantically at first but gradually slowing. And as the drumming ceased, the hands eased from the wound and a bubbling sigh escaped from Elroy's lips.

Dasha reached for a chair to steady herself.

Just a boy, she could see now in the spill of light. Blond curly hair, a wide, open face and a long lanky frame. Twenty? Twenty-two maybe? Not much more.

And standing above him, the man who'd killed him. A curious frown settling on his forehead, looking down to watch the young man's life drain out of him.

And there, in his right hand, the light from the kitchen glancing off it, Dasha could see the long silver blade he'd plunged into him.

41

At first Miche thought it was just Charlie snoring in the next tent that had woken her. She straightened her head on her pillow so that she could bring both ears into play and listened out. Six heartbeats later, she heard another soft chesty rumble turn into a fully fledged grunt. But there was something else. Something else beyond Charlie's snore. Another sound, a low distant crumpling sound coming from the north, somewhere beyond the Hanish ridge, almost muffled by the mountains.

Thunder. Like a whisper. Far away.

Miche pulled down the zip of her sleeping bag and rested herself on her elbows, every sense alert, listening out for the next roll. It didn't take long coming, a little more sustained this time, a little more defined, as though it were gathering itself, drawing closer. Squirming out of her bag, Miche pulled on her jeans and moccasins, and felt around for her torch. Two minutes later she was passing the firepit heading for the river. If there was thunder in the hills, then there was likely rain as well. It was just a question of where the rain fell. Which side of the divide. Most years it dumped on the Idaho side and those vast dry plains stretching down to the Dakotas just soaked it all up. Very occasionally it tipped down oceanside and up-country streams like the Susqua and the Hanish could fill up fast. Snowmelt time was the worst. Mix that up with some heavy spring rain and you really had problems. This time of year, however, it was usually just coastal fog sweeping in and condensing in the hills – a few inches a month – nothing serious. Unless that storm bound for Idaho had decided to change direction.

All around the campsite the tents were dark and silent. Carefully, playing the torch beam away from them so as not to disturb their occupants, Miche made her way to the river bank, feeling the ground slope away and the sound of the river grow in volume.

Was it louder than it had been the evening before, as they sat around the firepit listening to Bradley?

Would the water be running any faster? Would it be any higher?

Miche glanced up at the night sky, expecting to see stars. But there was nothing there, no glimmer, no moonlight, just a dark cover.

Up ahead, in the beam of the torch, the bank dropped away towards the stretch of pebble beach where they had come out of the water the previous evening, stripping off their hoods and fins and wetsuits, crowing and cheering at their adventure. Stepping out on to that strip of pebbles Miche played her torch over the water. It was still and glassy close to, but further into the stream it became a silvery, muscled pelt.

But was it higher? Was it faster?

As far as Miche could remember the beach was about the size it had been the previous evening, and across the river she could make out a dead branch caught in a fold of rocks. It was hung with streamers of vegetation brought down on earlier high waters. So far as she could tell the height of the water seemed the same as it had been the evening before, those weedy streamers still dry and stiff.

But there was something different, she was sure of it. Something not quite right.

She played the beam over the surface, up- and downstream, looking for the boulders that the afternoon before had shown dry and proud of the water. They were still there, the current sluicing around them. But were there as many? Had some of the smaller ones been covered? She peered along the beam of light at the closest one to her and it seemed to her that the stone seemed a darker shade of grey, wetter maybe, as though splashed by rising water and a more powerful current. Or perhaps it was simply a night dew which, with the first sign of sunshine, would dry out.

'Beautiful night,' came a man's voice from just behind her.

Miche's heart leapt and she spun round. She jerked up the light without thinking and a face shied away, bringing up a hand to protect his eyes. She saw the red bandanna round the neck. Clyde. Did he wear that damn thing while he was sleeping too?

'Whoa, there. I'm sorry. I didn't mean to startle you.'

'You didn't,' Miche managed to say. 'It's just . . . not a good idea to come up behind people like that. Not out here.' She dropped the torch beam between them, but noted a slim smile spreading across his lips.

'You mean, I coulda been a bear and you'd have stuck a knife in me?'

'A bear doesn't creep up on you,' said Miche. 'He doesn't have to. One minute you're all alone, the next he's loping out of the trees, fast, looking for something to eat. And you'll be that something.'

'So you get many bears round here?' he asked, going over to a length of greying tree trunk that had been swept down the river in some season past and setting himself down.

'Oh yeah, they're about,' she replied.

'Better keep an eye out then,' he said, as though the prospect didn't bother him too much.

Miche couldn't help a smile. Just exactly what Mungo would have said, maybe even word for word, and followed up with the same kind of look that Mungo had. That single raised eyebrow look. A look that Clyde hadn't quite been able to pull off. He might have reminded her of Mungo – that slow and easy charm, that gentle smile, the comforting presence – but there were still rough edges there. All raw and spiky still. Clyde had some living to do to match up with Mungo.

Digging around in the pocket of his jacket, the younger man pulled out a joint and a lighter and held them up to Miche. 'You want some?'

For a moment Miche was taken aback, not sure how to respond. For all the charm Clyde was still a school kid – seventeen, eighteen years of age – with his supervisors not twenty yards away. And Miche was supposed to be his group leader. But hey . . .

Miche looked around. It was still dark, no sign of anyone stirring. She switched off the torch and in the dim light made her way over to the log and sat down.

The lighter flared and the tip of the joint glowed. Clyde exhaled appreciatively and passed it to Miche.

'You couldn't sleep?' she asked, holding down the smoke and then letting it out in a silent whistle.

Clyde shook his head. 'I heard you passing. Thought I'd see what was happening. Seemed to me you were looking for something.'

Miche passed back the joint, he took it, inhaled deeply, then pushed off the tip with a thumbnail and dug it down with the toe of his boot. 'Wouldn't want to start a forest fire,' he said, tucking the remainder of the joint back in his pocket.

'Up here it'd take a lot more than a butt end to start a forest fire. But you're right to take precautions. You never can tell.'

'So you local? You lived round here long?'

'I'm Makah. Native Indian.'

'Then you know these parts?'

'I know these parts.'

'So what were you looking for, back then?'

'I thought I heard thunder.'

'You did. I heard it too. But like a real long way away.'

Miche smiled. 'Not as far as you'd think.'

'Could it be a problem? I mean, holding up the trip?'

'If the river rises, it could be.'

Clyde seemed to take this in. 'But this is nothing. Couple of summers ago, my old man took me to India. We went up to Ladakh and rafted down the Zanskar. It was a whole lot rougher and hairier than anything I seen so far on this trip.'

'Rafting and canyon-boarding are way different things. I don't know this Zanskar, but I'll bet it's wide and fast.'

'You said it.'

'And maybe it drops something like five hundred feet in twenty kilometres.'

'Something like that, I guess.'

'Well this little stretch of river drops about the same in half that distance, and some stretches further down it's no more than forty feet across. If the river rises just a few inches, the power of the water really bulks up. And funnelling down through the canyons it gets to pick up some serious speed. Way too fast and dangerous to make the trip on boards.'

'So what do you reckon? I mean, it's not raining or anything.'

'It doesn't have to be. We're just a river away from any storm, and rivers move fast.'

'So what are you gonna do? Cancel? I'd sure hate that.'

There was a glimmer in the way he said the words. Unmistakable. Was the guy coming on to her? She switched on the torch, gave him a look. 'I'll leave it till morning,' she said, pushing herself off the log and sweeping the beam up and down the river – taking one last, uncomfortable look at the water. 'But right now I'm going to get some shut-eye. And you should be doing the same, kiddo.'

'Sure thing, ma'am.' Clyde pulled out the joint from his pocket. 'But maybe just another toke,' he said.

'I'll leave you to it then. See you in the morning.'

Clyde nodded. He waited till she was out of earshot, a shadow crossing the campsite, torchbeam sweeping across the ground. 'See you in the morning, Pocahontas,' he whispered.

42

Mungo hadn't bothered to put on his wetsuit and nor had he brought his board to the beach. Something told him there was no point. He wasn't the only one who'd had the same feeling. Sitting on the sea wall, and huddled in groups on the beach, more than a dozen early-morning surfers looked out to sea, pointing, whispering. One or two had boards, most didn't. The ones who'd brought their rides had stuck them upright in the sand or leant them against the sea wall. They weren't going anywhere, and they knew it.

Mungo pulled his parka around him and pushed his hands into his pockets as he trotted down the steps to the beach. After the previous day's high blue skies and warming sun, there was now a wide bank of fog drifting in from the ocean, the sea was grey as granite and the headland bluffs at either end of the beach were lost behind a shawling mist. He could feel its moisture settling on his face, softening the salt from the previous day, and he could taste it – chill and sweet – in the back of his throat. Not rain exactly, but getting close, Mungo reckoned. Settling his neck into his collar, he trudged down the beach and stood a metre or so back from where the racing water reached its highest point, the sand glistening for a moment then drying out as the creamy surf fell back. It was, Mungo noted, a far higher tide than normal for this time of year.

The swells were bigger too, way bigger than usual, fast-moving muscly walls of water rolling in from the bay, rising over the outer reef ledge and building up into towering faces marbled with streaks of spume. When they broke and fell they did so with a detonating force, barrelling over themselves in a cauldron of explosive surf. It was as though something far out to sea was sending in the biggest waves it could find, squeezing them between the bluffs, making them rise in power and height, the sets coming in faster and higher than forecast, higher than anything Mungo had seen for years. Some of the combers looked to be cresting around thirty, thirty-five feet, higher maybe, curling up and forward, white horse manes feathering off their tips. They were the kind of sets that only big-wave surfers would have had the nerve for, a half dozen locals maybe, and about the same from out of town – the blow-ins from Seattle and Tacoma and a few of the surf gypsies who followed the breaks along this western shore, boards stacked on the roofs of their camper vans. If it hadn't been for the sharks, short grey torpedoes lifted by the swell, still patrolling the breaks not thirty metres from the shore, they'd have been out there already, towing most likely. These weren't the kind of waves a surfer could easily paddle into. Too high, too fast, too mean.

As well as the swells and faces, Mungo also noted the wavering line of rubbish that marked high tide, a tangled wrack of netting, splintered wood and plastic strung along a wedge of brown, spongy surf-scum that shivered in the breeze. Apart from the bloated, bladdered clumps of blackened kelp, it was as if the ocean was throwing back everything that had been thrown into it. Mungo had never seen the beach so littered or messy. Not even the fiercest winter storms tossed up this much rubbish.

'You ever seen anything like it? Those sharks?' came a voice beside him.

Mungo turned. The man was in his late twenties, maybe thirties, clean-shaven with a crop of tousled blond hair. He wore the surfer's uniform – red-mirrored O'Neills on a worn leather cord, knee-length Billabong boardies, beach flips and a StormSurf hoodie – and had his arms wrapped round him, keeping off the early morning chill. Mungo didn't recognise the face. An out-of-towner. Probably owned one of the Porsches parked behind the sea wall, with a model for a girlfriend.

Mungo shook his head. 'Not that I recall,' he replied with a take-in glance and a smile at the stranger. And then a memory stirred. 'Though come to think of it, I do remember my dad telling me that when they had the whaling here, way back before anyone surfed these breaks, they'd see lots of sharks out there. Small ones, like now. Feeding off the outflow from the wharves and flensing sheds. This time of year. Kinda like a little nursery.'

'That's what's bothering me,' said the man. 'I mean, if these are the babies, where's mom and dad? Damndest thing is, it's the best surf I seen down here since I started coming. Better than the islands. Real Mavericks. And there ain't a body anywhere here's gonna give it a go.'

Mungo smiled again. 'Not anyone with a brain in his head. You from around here?'

The man tipped his head back over his shoulder. 'Houseboat, in the old harbour. Come out from Seattle most weekends. You?'

'Local. Born and bred.'

'Lucky man. If I could, I would, you know what I'm sayin'?'

Mungo knew exactly what the man was saying. No way was he going to earn the kind of money in Melville that he earned in Seattle. The kind of money to buy one of Zan and Dasha's half dozen custom-built houseboats moored off the inner quay.

Not sure whether to continue the conversation, or let it drop, Mungo just started out the way he'd been going, following the high-water mark. The younger man fell in beside him.

'The name's Ty,' he said. 'Ty Guthrie. Work for SuttonCorp across in Seattle. And that's my girlfriend, Carrie, back there with the shawl.'

Mungo glanced back. If the girl wasn't a model she certainly should have been. Even sitting on the beach, arms wrapped around her knees, now raising a hand to wave at them, there was a languid, long-limbed grace about her. A tangled mane of blonde hair, a pure oval face, her legs and arms gently tanned.

Mungo nodded back a greeting, knowing now that he would have to introduce himself. Not that he minded; he liked the look of the kid.

'And I'm Mungo,' he said.

There was a moment's pause as Ty took this in. 'Not *the* Mungo? Mungo McKay? "Wave-Walker" McKay?'

'The same,' said Mungo. He was used to people – surfers usually – recognising the name.

'Jeez, you're Mungo McKay? I got a board on order

from you. We spoke on the phone a few months back. I'm on your wait list. I thought you looked familiar.'

'The mug shot on the website?'

'That's the one.'

The two men laughed.

'Well, it's always good to meet a customer,' said Mungo. 'What did you order, I can't recall . . . ?'

'A six-ten "Wave-Walker". Paulownia wood, three cedar fins. Double concave with extra nose and tail rocker.'

Mungo nodded at the specs. 'Good board, but not the best for round here.'

'Oh, it's not for here,' replied Ty, pushing back a fall of hair. 'Taking Carrie to Tahiti in the summer. Try my luck on Teahupo'o.'

The name brought Mungo up short and he turned to his companion, took another closer look at the guy. If he was thinking of trying his luck on Teahupo'o, he'd have to be a pretty serious surfer. South Shore Teahupo'o was about as wild as it got. The ultimate bomb. Huge barrels, near vertical faces, double lips to trip you up in the zone, most times a guaranteed air-drop on to a mesmerising left-hand reef break that could skin you alive if you tipped the rail wrong or cut too sharp. Compared with some of the outer breaks on north-shore Hawaii it didn't get so high, maybe twenty, twenty-five feet on a big day, but a south-wester could turn it into a real monster. One minute there's nothing showing, the next it's there, jacking up as it hits the reef and sucking in every drop of water till you can see the fire coral just inches below the surface. Beautiful but deadly.

'"The wave at the end of the road",' said Mungo, with a brief little nod.

'You know it? You been there?'

Mungo didn't answer. Best not to. There'd be too many questions. Opinions sought. Let the guy find out for himself. That's what Mungo had done. And Mungo knew there was nothing he could do or say to stop his new friend going there and trying it. That's what surfing was all about. Going to the limit and trying to cross over. Mungo had done that, had felt that hot, howling gale of malevolence blasting out of a Teahupo'o tube, exploding across his shoulders. Five waves he rode, in two days. Three paddle-outs on the small day, two tows on the second, and bigger, day. That's all it took. Five rides, with the whole ocean chasing him, piling up behind him, trying to fall on him, wipe him out. Forever. Now he knew all he needed to know. Those looming Tahitian breaks had taught him a real valuable lesson – like, I've stepped over a line here, and now I'm trespassing. Sooner or later, I'm gonna get got. For good.

Instead he said: 'Did I say I'd have it finished by the the summer?'

'That's what you said.'

'Then I better get back to work, make sure I get it done in time.' They stopped on the strand and started back. For a moment Mungo wondered if he'd been too abrupt. To cover himself he said, 'You want to see the workshop, stop by some time. It's the old drying shed back from the wall.'

'Hey, I know it. Get all my kit from your store up front. Asked your assistant one time if I could take a look, meet you. Told her I had a board on order and all, but she wouldn't let me through. Tough girl. Cute too. She Indian?'

'Makah. Pure blood. They're dangerous animals.'

184

'Tell me about it. Carrie's got some Cherokee,' said Ty, as his girlfriend got to her feet, rubbed sand off her hands and, tossing her hair in the wind, started out towards them.

'Cherokee? She's a blonde.'

Ty laughed. 'What you're looking at there is a thousand-dollar dye job. Carrie's a model. They want her blonde, she goes blonde. Purple, it's purple. Goes with the territory.' Then he paused, gave Mungo an enquiring look, hopeful but uncertain. 'Say, why don't we all meet up later? How about dinner? My place. You free?' Before Mungo could reply, Carrie was there, and Ty was introducing them, and telling her who he was, and how he'd just invited him round for dinner that evening.

'Hey, why not,' said Carrie, holding her hair back with one hand and reaching out with the other to shake Mungo's hand. 'Sounds fun.'

For a moment Mungo held back, then thought better of it. Miche was away for another night. And the man was a customer after all. A customer who was thinking of riding Teahupo'o.

'Sure. Why not. Tell me where.'

'Last houseboat on the inner quay,' said Ty, reaching out a hand, a big, paddling hand, to shake on it. 'Below the light. It's called Fluke.'

'You called your houseboat after a whale's tail?' Mungo asked.

Ty shook his head. 'Nope. After the fluke that got me a job with SuttonCorp. I'll tell you about it . . .'

But that was as far as he got.

Twenty feet to their right, the water puckered and sprayed up into the air as a shoal of bait fish broke through a rinsing surf like a silvery cloud. Seconds later three fins followed not ten feet behind them, coming in from three sides, tails thrashing at the shallowing water. So great was the sharks' speed, so rapid their approach, that all three got an easy mouthful. But they were young, didn't know any better – or didn't care. They'd badly misjudged their trajectory, ending up high and dry on the sand, bodies arching, trying to get themselves back into the water. Their grey skin glittered and the jaws snapped and their eyes rolled. It was an extraordinary sight, the first time Mungo had ever seen anything like it. Carrie reached out for Ty, and further along the beach, other people had seen it too, gotten to their feet, were jogging over for a closer look.

'Whoa man, did you see that?' said Ty, as the last of the sharks rolled down into an incoming wash of frothing surf and thrashed back and away. 'I mean, those mothers must be hungry.'

43

Jenna arrived at the CTACtv studio forty minutes before the day's scheduling meeting. Normally it was a last-minute run down the corridor to make it into the conference room before Coons got there, but this time she was way ahead of anyone else. She took a seat at the end of the briefing table and leafed through the stack of incoming news bulletins she'd torn off from the print terminals. Five sheets, a dozen abbreviated news paras per page – car crashes, fires, muggings, burglaries, condensed PR items about new shops, designers, shows, court stuff, council politics and assorted corporate guff. From this was local news made, for the crews that reported it.

One by one colleagues drifted in with coffees and bagels and doughnuts – the edit boys, the camera jacks and the three other news reporters who'd never really be friends because each of them was out to bring in the best story and have Coons give them the bigger time slots. Like Jenna, they'd come prepared – notepads, laptops, reading though the same reports from the terminals that Jenna had just about finished. Up on the far wall, the seven o'clock news started with the day's breaking stories. While Jenna waited to see if there was anything about sharks, a young man in jeans and a blue plaid shirt open over a white T-shirt knocked at the door and leant in.

'Is this the briefing room?' he asked.

Everyone at the table looked up; no-one ever knocked when the door was open. One of the editors nodded and pointed to a chair. 'Come on in, bro, and join the circus. You the new camera jack?'

'That's right. Ramirez, Pico Ramirez,' he replied, nodding at the faces around the table, leaning forward to shake a hand. His voice, Jenna noted, returning his smile, had a soft hesitancy. Warm, polite, young. Late twenties, maybe a year or two younger than her. She turned back to the last page of reports, then found herself glancing up at Ramirez once more. Tall, rangy, with a tan as gentle as his smile and a ragged crop of wavy black hair. Hispanic for sure, but not full-blood. And probably the better-looking for it. Not so cocky, not so sharp, not so knowing – Jenna liked that in a man. Greyish eyes, not brown or black. And long strong hands, good nails. Without thinking, she checked for a wedding ring – nothing, no ring; in fact, no jewellery at all. She liked that too. She also noticed she wasn't the only one checking him out. Paula, Rosie and Nita – the other reporters – were also carrying out their own covert appraisals. Jenna looked back to her reports but listened in as Ramirez fielded the usual round of questions – up from Portland, worked for an indie outfit supplying news to local stations, before getting hired on contract by CTACtv. The usual way – indie to local, national if you had what it took. Or the stories that made you. Like Sharon Walker down there in Galveston. Bitch.

It was then that Jenna's eyes fastened on the word 'sharks', third para up from the bottom of the last page. Just three lines: sharks reported Melville Bay; schooling in the surf; none of them bigger than a couple or so feet, but big enough to keep the surfies on the beach. The information was credited P-LC/9:50 p.m. The letters stood for Phone – Local Call, and had been timed the previous evening. Someone on the overnight despatch desk would have taken the call, tapped it out on to the planning schedule, and filed it for this morning's briefing. Simple as that. Only whoever had taken the call, hadn't properly filed it. There was no contact name, no contact number. Which made the story – the facts – a whole lot harder to confirm, or get more info on. Which usually made a broadcast reporter like Jenna a whole lot more wary.

Up on the TV, the news team linked to weather and signed out. Jenna pricked up an ear. According to the forecaster – some wide-eyed clown who sometimes dressed up in costume for his shot – the storm fronts coming in from BC and the ocean seemed to be doing what Greg and her weather man had told her they would. It might be sunny right now, but the blue skies weren't going to last.

'Okay people, let's get to it.' It was Gerry Coons, barrelling into the room and kicking the door shut behind him. Jenna snapped to. 'So what we got? Who's starting?' he continued, dropping himself into the leather executive chair at the top of the table, and spinning round the faces.

For the next ten minutes Paula, Nita and Rosie punted ideas, argued their corners. It was a weekend, which meant Paula and Rosie would be going for city stories so they could get home for boyfriends, children, or parties. As far as Jenna was concerned, Nita was the only threat for the shark story. No way would she have missed it. It was a question of how you pitched it and when. When she saw Nita turn to the last page, to recheck the story, Jenna jumped in. It was the first time she'd spoken.

'You want me to do something on that Melville thing?' she piped up. 'Could be something there.' Out of the corner of her eye, she saw Nita grit her teeth. She'd been right. They'd both been after the sharks.

Gerry checked through the print-outs, found the last page paragraph and then gave her a skewed look. 'Melville? Hardly local. And it's a long way to go for a "could-be",' he added.

Jenna knew what he was saying. Earlier in the summer she'd travelled two hundred miles to cover a bank siege in Aberdeen that was over before she got there.

'You don't go, you never know,' she shot back. 'Hey, it's sharks. Sharks are good.'

Gerry gave it some thought, never shifting his eyes off Jenna. 'Twenty seconds lunchtime news,' he said at last. 'If it looks promising – someone gets a leg chewed off – or it gets picked up after broadcast, you stay and chase. Otherwise, since you're so fond of wildlife, you're back here for the ocelot cub birthday party at Woodland Park Zoo.' He gave her a sly smile. 'Why don't you take Ramirez. Show him the ropes.'

An hour later, she and Pico Ramirez were in the van and heading out of the station lot, Jenna wondering whether Gerry's sly grin had to do with giving her a zoo story, or sending her out with Pico. The guy was candy, and Gerry knew all about Jenna and candy.

Meanwhile, she had the sharks.

44

Charlie had the brazier lit and was cutting open a pack of bacon for breakfast when Miche came over to him. Most of the group from Fairbanks were down at the river, washing, shaving, cleaning teeth. There were shouts and whoops and a loud splash as one of them was pushed in. Miche recognised the high spirits for what they were. They all knew that today was the big one, that all the boarding they'd done the day before was just a lead-up to the main event. In a couple of hours they'd be taking on the Susqua canyons, Lobo and Cougar, along a twenty-mile stretch of winding river forced through sheer-faced gorges and dropping a good few hundred feet before they stopped for lunch. Even in the dry summer months it was a roller-coaster ride few would ever forget.

'You hear the thunder?' Miche asked, breaking off a crust of bread and popping it into her mouth.

Charlie pulled out a handful of rashers and started separating them. 'About a million miles away.'

'It'll be raining too.'

'Always does. On the Idaho side.'

'Maybe not this time, Charlie. I've got a feeling.'

Charlie couldn't hold himself back. He'd known when he peered out of his tent at daybreak and seen the grey overcast and a gentle drizzle thickening an early morning mist that Miche would be giving him a hard time, trying to persuade him to cancel the trip. Some chance.

'Listen, sweetie. It's cloudy. There's been thunder, like you say. And it's probably raining somewhere up beyond the Hanish. I'm not disputing that. What I *am* disputing is the fall coming this side of them hills over there and hitting us way down here on the Susqua. It just doesn't happen this time of the year. And even if it did, we're far enough ahead to outrun whatever might come down.'

'Outrun . . . ?' Miche was shocked. He had to be kidding, right? They'd both seen a river in spate. Outrun? It just wasn't an option.

'While you were sleepin' tight as a tick in a rug,' continued Charlie, 'I was down on the river and I took me a little look. You done that yet? Well, when you do you'll see what I saw. Not an inch rise in the level. No appreciable speed-of-flow increase. You ask me – and that's what I've told those kids over there – it ain't never been better. Just perfect. High enough for some good water, but not so high we're gonna have to bring in choppers to haul 'em out of there. Believe me, they're gonna have themselves the ride of a lifetime. Something they'll never forget.'

'That's what I'm worried about, Charlie. That's why . . .'

'And if you're gonna act up and get difficult,' he interrupted, laying the bacon slices down on the griddle with a hiss and a spit, 'then *you* can drive the van down to the next campsite, and *I'll* take them out in the stream myself. *That's* how sure I am. And oh, by the way. Drive the van and we're talking a lot less than the four hundred I promised you, *capisc*?' He turned and gave her a sly look. 'But I'm sure you'll appreciate that.'

Before Miche could reply, Alison and Pete came over to the griddle. Their hair was wet and slick from their wash and brush-up in the river, faces wide and bright and excited.

'Hey, how's it goin'? You need any help with breakfast?' asked Alison.

'Well now ma'am. If you're offerin' . . . ?' Charlie tipped her a wink and turned to Miche with a big happy grin. 'So what's it to be, Miche? The river or the van?'

'There any problem?' asked Pete.

Charlie kept his eyes on Miche, waiting to see if she was going to say anything. When she didn't, he turned back to the two teachers. 'The only problem I got, Pete, is how to feed that hungry mob of yours before they set out on the ride of a lifetime. Did you see how they ate last night? Near went through all my supplies, they did.

Reckon we'll have to catch ourselves some fish down at the next site just to keep them properly fuelled. Ain't that about right, Miche?'

'You're the fisherman, Charlie. I'll leave that one to you,' and with a short smile to share between them, Miche turned and walked away, over to the line of wetsuits still strung on the line. She found hers, took it off the hanger.

If anything happened out on that river, Miche knew the group would be safer with her than with Charlie.

45

It took just a few hours for each of the upper Hanish lakes to fill, and then break through or brim over their banks. One by one they spilled down from one level to the next, thousands of tons of water cascading on to the topmost Hanish slopes, flooding through the forest where, just the night before, Zan had played pattacake with a grizzly bear and her cub.

Most Septembers the stream immediately below the lowest of the Hanish lakes was deep enough to play a trout in a pool, and in spring it was strong enough to pummel your boots. But no more than that. Quietly fed by those high lakes and the Silver Hills ridge-line run-off, the Hanish

Stream was young and playful hereabouts, chuckling and gurgling between the rocks, flushing through narrow channels, its banks grazed by elk and darting with birds. It was as idyllic a spot as you could find anywhere in the Rockies – the sharp-spiny firs standing straight and high under a late summer sun, the land falling away from the blue-green hills to follow the twisting course the passing water had carved out for itself over the millennia. In spring there were butterflies here, flickering along the river bank; in high summer a plague of midges, and come fall the clear coffee-coloured water swirled and glittered with returning steelhead. And always, everywhere, that strong, resinous scent of pine.

A week before, a party of ridge-hikers from Shinnook had stepped across this part of the stream from rock to rock, but this September morning things were different along the Hanish Stream. The water was higher, brisker and altogether livelier. There were no still patches where you could see through the water to its pebbly bed, and there was more white than copper on its churning surface. It was in a rush and a hurry, spurred on by a sheeting, lashing rain that seemed to get heavier with each passing hour, as though the monsoon storm clouds from British Columbia had plenty more to deliver before they were done.

A mile below the trail-head where Zan had parked his Jeep, the Hanish was becoming more and more boisterous, impatient with the twisting course it followed. With some muscle behind it, it began to breach the banks as though looking for a faster way down and, like the Susqua at this height, the valley sides flattened a little, allowing the river to spread itself through the trees, sluicing past their trunks, racing over exposed roots and between moss-draped stones.

Close to the bank, the river had started up what sounded like a promising growl. Away from the river, however, it was the sound of rain that took over, slashing through branches and spattering on to the ground, followed by the rumble of approaching thunder.

And then another sound could be heard. A strange hissing, like the hiss of gritty snow falling, steadily growing in volume.

And it came not from the river, nor from the sky.

It came from the forest, from the trees.

46

Win Sutton sheltered from the rain beneath the dripping cover of the trees on the Susqua bank and watched the water tumble past. Was it higher than the day before? It certainly seemed to be going faster, and there appeared to be higher crests of white than there had been.

An early riser, Win had woken at a little after six that first morning at Wilderness One, his regular time in the city, and left Courtney fast asleep in their treehouse bedroom. He'd showered in water that if not luxuriously, bracingly hot was at least bearably warm, and he reflected that even in their hilltop mansion overlooking Puget

Sound, the view from his shower stall just didn't come close to this one, a seven-by-four-foot glass cubicle that made him feel he could reach out a hand and touch the red squirrel hunched over a cone on a branch not three feet away from him. And beneath the glass floor panel of his shower stall, there, between his ankles, he'd glimpsed an elk amble past, the tips of its furred knobbled horns passing not eight feet below him. It had made him start with fright, then mellow into a comforting sense of closeness with nature. He felt . . . he felt a part of it, and decided that Dasha Pearse, and her husband too, had created something quite extraordinary.

Nor was it just that incredible proximity to nature that entranced him. After his shower, in order to reach the towel rail, he had to step past a thick tree fork branching through the bathroom. As far as he could see, not a single scrap of lichen seemed to have been lost or disturbed in the room's construction. Remarkable. Quite remarkable. Such attention to detail. And once again he congratulated himself on the previous day's brainwave. SuttonCorp's proposed investment in the Pearses' Wilderness project. He wondered whether they'd go for it. They would be fools not to, but there were always plenty of those around. And Dasha really was a most handsome woman. It would be a pleasure doing business with her. As for the husband Zan, well, lucky man him.

Leaving the treehouse booted and parka'd and munching on a cold chicken leg left over from the previous day's lunch, Win had set off up the river bank for an early morning stroll. In Seattle he walked with his dog, before the chauffeur arrived for the trip into town. Out here in the wilderness Win had no choice but to walk alone (no pets allowed on the reserve), following what appeared to be a path beaten down by wild animals rather than humans – elk or beaver or marmot, maybe bears as well, who could say? Wondering whether he shouldn't find out a little bit more about bears before he went walkabout in the wild outdoors – and elks too, come to that – he followed the course of the river for another hundred metres then turned off between the trees. He hadn't gone far when the mossy, shadowing darkness – and the unsettling prospect of meeting up with a grizzly – made him turn and head back to the river.

It was here that he now stood, under the sheltering trees, watching the rain pelt down. When he'd set out it had been chill and grey, but it hadn't started raining. Now it was hammering down, the tall grass leading to the river bank drooping and flattening under its onslaught.

To his left, up in the distant highlands, beyond the grey mantle of rain and fog that seeped through the forest, a great drum roll of thunder rode along the ridgeline and swept down the hillsides. Like the squirrel, it seemed close enough to touch.

Win felt a shivering in his chest. It wasn't the cold – he was well enough insulated in his parka and padded trousers. It was another kind of shiver – the shiver he got when he went into a meeting and didn't know how things were going to pan out. It was, he realised, uncertainty. And in his experience, where there was uncertainty there was also fear lurking close by. Because that's what it was. He was out of his comfort zone up here, and he really did feel just a little intimidated. He shook himself. All part of the Wilderness experience, he persuaded himself. The Pearses weren't going to build their million-dollar homes in the middle of a zoo, for God's sake. What was he thinking about?

Shaking himself out of it, he looked instead at the river, trying to decide if it was higher than the day before, higher even than when he'd trudged up along it not twenty minutes earlier. All of a sudden there seemed to be something more muscular, more malicious about it. Hardly surprising, he thought, considering the amount of rain that was now battering down around him. Hey, Washington State. What did you expect, he wondered to himself? Then he set off back downstream, wading through the tall grass between track and trees, as much for the shelter as a desire not to stray too close to the river.

And, yes, he was certain now, it did seem to be growing. And the sound of it sure seemed to have risen a few decibels – a great churning, roaring surge of water only narrowly contained within the banks either side of it. If someone had shouted out his name from the other side of the stream, no more than twenty metres away, he was certain he'd never hear it. Hell, the other side of the river? He wouldn't have heard Courtney if she was standing right next to him. He could hardly hear himself think.

It was then, as he increased his pace and glanced nervously at the river powering down not twenty feet away, that his earlier sense of discomfort – no, fear – returned. How far, the hell, was that damn treehouse? he thought to himself. Better keep his damned eyes open or he'd go straight past it. It had taken him long enough the day before to spot it, and the last thing he wanted to do was go get himself lost.

But, then, there it was – those Buren steps grouped around a single trunk – and he hurried forward, his boots now slipping and sliding underfoot where before the ground had just been soft and giving.

The slips and the slides upset him still further, and he

threw out his arms to balance himself. Something was happening here. And he was pretty certain that whatever it was it shouldn't be happening. Closing on the tree-house, the long sodden grass that had soaked his trouser legs thankfully flattened out into a mossy bed that now actually squelched underfoot. By the time he reached the first of the Buren steps below his treehouse the water was sluicing past, lapping round his booted ankles.

No, he thought, this was certainly not meant to happen.

47

It was Eddie who found Elroy's body the following morning. He saw it first from halfway down the stairs and stopped dead. The curling blond hair and open mouth. The shocked expression on the white, bloodless face. That's what first registered. And then Mort. As if it was the most obvious conclusion to come to, that if Elroy was dead, lying there at the bottom of the stairs in a pool of blood, it was Mort who had probably put him there. Sometime between Eddie putting down his book and switching off his bedside lamp the night before, and coming down now to brew up some coffee.

At the bottom of the stairs Eddie stepped carefully

over the body, making sure he didn't tread in the blood that cloaked the corpse. In the kitchen, he turned on the gas and set about preparing the coffee, wondering just what Elroy had done for Mort to stick him like that. Shit, that Mort. It probably wouldn't have taken much, thought Eddie. You had to watch yourself round a guy like that. Tread careful.

Gene was down next. 'What'd he do?' he asked, stepping across the body with hardly a glance and coming into the kitchen.

Eddie, leaning against the sink and sipping his brew, shook his head. 'Pissed off Mort, I'd guess. Something like that.'

Taking up the coffee and pouring himself a mug, Gene strolled back out of the kitchen, coming round the side of the body rather than step over it again. Eddie followed him and they settled themselves at the table.

'What's your guess?' asked Eddie. 'Tried to ball her, and Mort didn't like it?'

Gene's eyes strayed to the pile of coats and boots on the floor by the front door. 'If I had to put money on it, I'd say our local boy got cold feet. Wanted out. And decided to take the woman with him. Rescue mission. Earn himself some gold stars.'

'And Mort surprised them.'

Gene nodded. 'Sounds about right to me.'

'Got himself good and gutted whatever he did, and no mistake,' said Eddie.

'Standard operating procedure,' came a voice from the top of the stairs. 'Put 'em down, and put 'em down good. So they don't go gettin' up again.'

Like Gene and Eddie before him, Mort stepped over the body when he reached the bottom of the stairs, and paid it no more attention than he would a sleeping dog. In the kitchen he pulled a carton of orange juice from the fridge and took a swig, then poured himself a coffee. Coming back out he rocked the body with the toe of his boot.

'Eddie, Gene, when you're done with your coffee, do me a favour and get this pile of shit outta here.'

'You wanna bury him or what?' asked Gene.

Mort thought about it for a moment, then shook his head. 'Just dump him in the trees. Ten, twenty yards in should be enough.'

Crossing the room, he went to the TV and switched it on. Settling down in one of the armchairs, he rested the mug of coffee on his belly, stretched out his legs and waited for the eight o'clock news.

48

While Win Sutton was taking his early-morning shower, the incoming rain had swept in across the Hanish Valley, climbed its southern slopes, and started drifting in over the Susqua watershed. Unlike the Hanish, there were no lakes on the upper levels of the Susqua, just a hundred different streams that fed into it.

In the time it had taken Win to pull on his boots and set out for his walk, those tiny headwater runnels a dozen miles further up the Susqua had started to swell, the small pebbles and splintered shale that formed their courses shuffling and chattering as the water shifted through them.

With far gentler upper slopes than the Hanish, the speed of this water flow on the Susqua was greatly reduced and it wasn't until it reached Wilderness One that it began to pick up some momentum. In a matter of minutes the river slipped over its low retaining banks a few hundred yards above the Sutton's tree-house and started to stream through the grass, spreading outwards into the forest, pushing ahead of it a rustling wave of pine cones and pine needles and knots of moss and other vegetation picked up on its sweep over the land.

Such swift but shallow flooding would continue in this manner for another three miles. It was at this point that the slopes of the Susqua Valley started to rise and steepen, forcing the spreading water to return to its original course. Within the space of just two miles, fed by these small but converging streams, the river started to swell and grow, cutting into tree-lined banks with enough power to snap away branches that hung too low over its course, and covering rocks that the day before had shown above the surface. Now contained by steepening banks, the Susqua started to perform, building walls of standing water around any submerged obstruction, high breaking waves that stayed where they were, fed by the oncoming flow, or spinning into foam-filled eddies in all those hollows and pools where normally the trout and the salmon basked.

It was here, too, just a few miles above the Susqua Falls, that the river's incline increased, from a gentle nine degrees to a more formidable fifteen.

And as the incline increased so too did the speed, and the power, of the water.

49

Treading carefully over the Susqua's stony bed, Miche waded into the river and looked upstream. The earlier drizzle had given way to a sporadic fall of rain, but the river seemed no different. As Charlie had pointed out, the current appeared to be no faster and the river level no higher than the previous day.

But years spent up in these canyons and creeks, on the Susqua and along the steeper, faster Hanish, had taught Miche that appearances were not to be trusted – a rule of thumb she had happily and successfully applied to her choice of men. She knew well enough that the river could change in seconds – like a lot of men she'd known – and what it could do. As she stood there, waist deep in the stream, she weighed up the pros and cons. Should she wait and see what happened in the next hour or so, or go now?

Right then, with the water stroking softly between

her legs, it had nothing to do with money, nothing to do with Charlie taking over, and everything to do with the safety of the group in her charge. Had the big storm moved on, as it usually did, or was it staying put their side of the ridge? Would this undecided spot of rain turn nasty or ease up? Would the river behave, or would it put on a show? Impossible to tell.

Go or wait? Go or wait?

It was like trying to read a wave she couldn't see.

With a deep breath, and heavy heart, she decided not to hang around. Let's get them on their boards and into that water. The sooner she had them through the narrow defiles of Lobo and Cougar canyons the better she'd like it. Turning back to her group, as Charlie and Pete loaded up the last of the tents and broke camp, Miche started in on her brief.

'So how're we all feeling today?' she asked, looking from one eager face to the next – Clyde, retying his red bandanna over the collar of his wetsuit; Naomi and Kelly isolated by the broad shoulders of the two quarterbacks, Taylor and BeeJay; Bradley looking nothing like the songster from the night before; and their teacher, Alison, just a little agitated, checking the leash between board and wrist a dozen times.

'Ready to roll,' said Clyde, giving her a smile.

'It's not going to get too fast or rough, is it?' asked Naomi with a sudden, panicked look.

'Don't fret, girl, I'll be right there behind you,' BeeJay reassured her.

Behind her, beside her, in front of her – Miche knew that there wasn't a whole lot the guy could do to help if the water in the canyons turned savage. They all thought they knew what was coming. They had no idea. What was waiting for them was a twenty-mile sleigh-ride of strong twisting currents and wild water that didn't take kindly to trespassers. It was like a bronco waiting for that weight in the saddle. In one section the river dropped near a hundred feet in less than a mile. And then there was the way out, at Fiddler's Chute, the other side of Cougar, a twenty-foot drop into a pool as clear as glass, with a *Last of the Mohicans* water curtain to paddle behind. Even in high summer when the river was at its lowest, maybe a couple of months earlier, the roar of the water coming over the lip, filling that cave of stone, was so loud that you had to read lips – not even a scream would cut through it.

Miche marvelled at how blissfully unaware they all were – just excited, up for it, another spin on the roller-coaster. All of them, with maybe the exception of Alison. She looked uncomfortable in her husband's wetsuit and Miche knew she'd have to keep an eye on her. Up at the campsite, Pete tooted his horn and he and Charlie turned out of the meadow and disappeared into the trees, heading for the trail.

'Okay, so here's the route,' began Miche. 'First forty minutes or so will be fast and straight, with lots of places to pull in along the bank if any of you want a breather. I don't want the party splitting up, so just let me know if you want to stop, okay?'

There were nods all round.

'About an hour from here, the Lobo and Cougar canyons start – maybe a couple of miles' breather between them. Lobo's a good introduction to what comes after. Think of it as a first date . . .'

'Been there, done that,' snorted Taylor, earning himself a slap on the arm from Kelly.

Miche paid no attention, carried on: 'After Lobo, it's Cougar. And the game changes. You'll see the sides rising up through the trees from about a mile off, and you'll hear it too. Like a soft roar. Before we get to it, we'll need to regroup and I'll brief you in more detail. There's a small rock shelf on the left-hand side of the river maybe a hundred metres after the end of Lobo – you can't miss it. I'll get there first and wave you in. Just keep a look out for me. I don't want anyone going down Cougar without me, okay?'

'You got it, coach,' said Clyde, rolling his shoulders.

'It's also likely that the river will rise a little and maybe speed up a tad. There's probably been rain up in the hills and sooner or later, it'll show down here. Just ride it and enjoy,' she said, hoping they'd be through Cougar before the swell really started.

'Okay, if everyone's set. Let's go get wet.'

Taking one last look at her group, Miche turned, threw herself on her board and started paddling. In less than ten feet she felt the river take her, swing the board downstream, and she couldn't help a silent whoop of exhilaration.

Something told her they'd be fine.

No problems.

50

Dasha Pearse lay curled up on her bed and thought about Elroy. Just a kid. Someone's son. Trying to help her. And now he was dead. She had never seen anyone die before – she'd been living with Zan in Seattle when her father passed away; a stroke, so quick, and he was gone. And she had certainly never seen someone killed. Actually murdered. Disposed of. So casually, so coldly. She could have sworn there was a smile on Mort's face when Elroy slumped on to the floor, socked heels drumming on the floorboards. Oh, what a horrible sound. She couldn't get it out of her head – that soft, frantic thumping. And then, with a bubbling whisper of breath, that final silence.

In her cold, dark basement, Dasha hugged herself. If she had known what she knew now, would she have been quite so brave, so outspoken, in that first encounter with her kidnapper, the killer? So challenging? If she had known what kind of man she was dealing with – that sly, knowing smile, that eyepatch, that knife – would she have been quite so provocative? She knew now that she would not have been. When Mort, standing in the kitchen doorway, told her to get back down in the basement, that's what she had done. She had obeyed. Without argument. Trembling with horror, she had gone to the trapdoor, lifted it and stepped down into the darkness. And he had followed, closing it after her and snapping a bolt into place. And as she'd crossed to her bed, feeling her way in the darkness, she had heard his footsteps above and what sounded like a whistled tune.

In the hours since then, she had lain shivering on the bed, falling into a troubled surface sleep, but always waking with a start – over and over again.

And now she knew it was morning, and there'd be no more sleeping. She had smelled the coffee, listened to the murmur of voices and an hour or so earlier had heard what could only be Elroy's body being dragged across the floor, a door kicked open and then kicked shut, the sound of boots going down a flight of wood steps and a disconcerting bump-bump-bump as though whoever it was couldn't be bothered to carry the body and had simply lugged it down.

Would they bury him or just leave him somewhere in the woods, Dasha wondered? If they were close to a river, which she suspected they were – she'd seen fishing rods in a corner of the room – maybe they'd just weight him down, toss him in and be done with it.

But what had happened to Elroy was fast becoming a minor consideration. What increasingly occupied Dasha's thoughts was what was going to happen to her? With her blindfold removed, she had seen Mort kill Elroy. She was witness to a murder. What chance was there now of her ever being released? She was doomed. He would never let her go. Better to kill her, get rid of the witness, and then disappear. In an hour, a day, whenever they got what they wanted, when the land was handed over to the National Parks, they would dispose of her, move on. Job done.

And there was no good reason, it struck her with a chill, why they shouldn't do it sooner.

The more she thought about it, the more sense it made. Unless she could think of some way of escaping, she was going to die. He was going to kill her – shoot her, stab her, cut her throat. Or get one of the others to do it. And then they'd dump her body wherever they'd dumped Elroy.

Would they ever find her body, she thought? Would Zan and her children ever discover what had happened to her? Oh God, she so wanted to see them again, to be with them, away from this hellish place. To see little Alexa's pixie, freckled face and hear Finn say 'dumbass'. To hold Zan in her arms, and to be held by him. She could see his curling grey-blond hair and gently stubbled cheeks, those marvellous blue eyes of his glinting with mischief. Let's take this wave, he'd say, relishing the challenge. Always the impossible one, the one Dasha wanted to paddle around. And he'd have that look in his eye – as if it was all a game. Surfing, designing, building – it was all the same to Zan. A game you had to win despite, sometimes even because of, the odds. It was what made him the man he was, the man she loved. Tough, resolute, fearless. A real man with a real heart. The kind of guy who never ever said 'love-you-too'. Every single time he beat her to it. And if she ever did get there first, he'd say something like 'not as much as I love you, my little surf chick.'

And now all that was at risk. Her husband. Her children. The future. But Dasha knew she musn't think like that. She *would* see them all again. She *would* hold them in her arms. That man upstairs might have killed Elroy, but he sure as hell wasn't going to kill her. Not if she could help it. When she saw an opportunity she was going to grab it. No fear. No hesitation.

Swinging her legs off the bed, Dasha made to stand up. But her feet slid away from her. She reached out her cuffed hands to hold herself steady, feeling for something to cling to. But there was nothing. The very next second she was sitting in a pool of mud. The hard-packed earth floor she had crossed just a few hours earlier, as Mort closed the trapdoor on her, had turned into a thick, soupy mud.

51

It wasn't the first time that Mulholland had woken in a police cell, and it probably wouldn't be the last. But as he pushed through the door of RubyRay's Diner, four blocks up from the Sheriff's office, Mulholland was still trying to roll the ache out of his shoulders, and swearing to himself he'd never do it again. He felt stiff and old and out of sorts and not even a hot locker-room shower had made him feel any livelier. Fifty-eight years old – he needed a good night's sleep to face the day. And a good night's sleep was something you didn't get in a sheriff's lock-up. He was relying on the Breakfast Special at RubyRay's to set him right.

'Chief's in,' called Ruby, as Mulholland hauled himself up on to a stool at the bar, hitching the crease in his jeans and settling the heel of his boot over the stool stretcher.

Through the service hatch Ruby's husband, Ray, laid some rashers on the hot plate along with four tomato halves and a slab of his curly kale hash browns. 'How you doin' Chief?' he called out with a wave of his spatula.

'Not so so bad. Yourself?'

'Better 'n most, Chief . . .'

'That's what he thinks . . .' added Ruby with a wink, pouring out a mug of coffee and giving Mulholland the once-over. 'Long night?' she asked, wiping away a spill.

'I look that bad?'

'Well, you sure as hell ain't no Brad Pitt, I'm tellin' you,' whipcracked Ruby, reaching behind her for the fridge. 'Juice?'

Mulholland shook his head.

'You want a paper, peace or company?'

Mulholland gave Ruby a look. He'd been coming to the diner long enough for her to read the signs.

'Peace is just fine with me,' she said, and sweeping up the Cona pot she bustled back down the duckboard. 'You'll get your breakfast soon as the old man's fixed it. You want more coffee, just holler.'

'I got it,' said Mulholland, and settling his elbows on the counter, wrapping his hands round his mug, he looked

211

around. There were four other men at the counter, and a couple of sales girls from Baxter's Mall sharing a slice of Ruby's apple pie in one of the window booths. Three of the guys Mulholland knew or recognised – RubyRay regulars, all of them in overalls – the fourth, in a suit, he didn't. Up above the counter a jokey TV weatherman in a yellow rain slicker and crumpled sou'wester was predicting some heavy weather in the Silver Hills above Shinnook, and some rough water coming in from the ocean. To make the point, someone off camera emptied a watering can over the forecaster's head.

Four times a week, usually breakfast, Mulholland dropped in at RubyRay's. Warm, familiar and welcoming as a soul could wish for, it was as close to home as any diner got. And when law enforcement was your beat, that counted. Ruby's coffee was always good and strong and freshly perked, and Ray's hash browns just a perfect fit for those empty places that needed filling. And this particular morning Mulholland reckoned he'd earned both.

It was past four in the morning when he'd arrived at the Sheriff's office after speaking to Zan at the hospital. The first thing he had done was brief Sergeant Calley, get out an all-points on Dasha's Lexus, and put a call through to Shelley Caine. There'd been no answer and he'd hung up after just a few rings. Next, just like it said in the book, he'd called in the kidnap to the State Investigations Unit down in Olympia. No way he wanted someone coming back at him down the road saying he hadn't followed the rules. At that time in the morning, there hadn't been more than the SIU switchboard to take a message and fill in the headings: Name of Hostage. Date of Birth. Description. Last Known Whereabouts.

Name of Investigating Officer. Contact number. After that, he'd put in a request for information on known or suspect hard-line environmentalists matching Zan's description – white, southern, male – with bureaus in Texas, Alabama and Louisiana. If he got nothing back from those, he'd spread the net a little wider. By the time he'd finished it was after five and Mulholland, who hadn't seen a bed for close on twenty-four hours, took himself down to the lock-ups. Just a couple hours later, Sergeant Calley had put his head round the door and told him SIU down in Olympia were on the line, a state investigator name of Davies who sounded like the narrator out of *Dragnet*.

Mulholland took the call in his office and filled Davies in on the background, running him through Dasha's movements, the possible time line, her car model and registration (which he'd already put out on the wire, he told Davies), the repeated and increasingly threatening spray-painted messages at the offices of Pearse-Caine, the environmental angle and Zan's sketchy description of the kidnapper. He took a certain pleasure in telling Special Investigations Officer Davies that he, Chief Mulholland, had already put in for a check with the relevant agencies down south. But if Davies wanted to follow it up . . .

It was when Mr *Dragnet* said he needed to talk to Zan in person and asked for a contact number, that something kicked in and Mulholland had bridled. He recognised a swerve when he saw it, knew he was being sidelined, and he didn't like it. Zan was in hospital, he told Mr Olympia Special Investigations Officer Davies. He'd been mauled by bears and was out for the count. Lucky to be alive. 'But anything else you need, just you

213

give me a call,' Mulholland had told him and promptly hung up. It might have sounded a tad short, but Mulholland persuaded himself that it would come out professional. We can handle it. Leave it to us. Not that he had any illusions that he'd be anything other than hired help and coffee-fetcher when Davies and the SIU team finally hit town and set up a command post in his office. But for now the case was his, even if there wasn't a whole heap he could do beyond call in on Dasha's mother down at The Quays and bring her up to speed.

Nodding an absent 'thanks' to Ruby, Mulholland set to on the Breakfast Special that she had slipped in front of him. As he cut into the hash browns and doused a piled forkful with egg yolk, he considered the one small piece of information he had failed to share with Davies. That Zan Pearse had received the ransom demand while he was fishing up in the Hanish Valley. On his cell phone. It was just another indication, if one more were needed, that the perp couldn't possibly be local – anyone who lived in Melville County would have known that you could only receive a cell call in the Hanish Valley if you were being called by someone in the Hanish Valley. Or on a straight line through Shinnook and down to Melville. And given they were likely to make that all-important ransom call from their base, somewhere safe and secure, it was Mulholland's opinion that whoever they were, they were holed up somewhere in that great swathe of forest between the Silver Hills ridge-line and Shinnook, or even, possibly, down here in Melville.

52

There'd been nothing about the Pearse-Caine/National Parks handover on the eight o'clock news, and nothing on any of the main nine o'clock broadcasts either. Which had done nothing to improve Mort's mood. Sitting out on the covered porch, he watched the rain tip down, soaking Eddie and Gene as they stepped out of the trees. Somewhere behind them, somewhere deep in the forest, was the body of Elroy Baker.

But Mort wasn't thinking about Elroy. What concerned him was the absence of any news coverage. Just how goddamned long did it take to issue a press release? He'd spoken to Zan Pearse and told him what he wanted more than twelve hours ago. What was the man up to, wondered Mort? Why the delay? All he had to do was call up his lawyer and public relations people and they could get the whole thing rolling. He had a cell, could have done it all from his camp, easy.

There was something not quite right about it, he decided as Eddie and Gene came in across the yard. Maybe he'd take the knife to the wife and send little old hubby some encouragement in the form of a tissue-wrapped body part – a finger? An ear? Just to make the point.

Of course, the National Parks deal was only a part of Mort's agenda. He might not have let his comrades in on the secret, but he had no intention of releasing Mrs Pearse when the news finally came through. Mort was no fool. He'd seen the house on South Bluff Drive, he'd seen the offices of Pearse-Caine in Melville and Seattle, and he'd seen the brand new Lexus and the brand new Cherokee Jeep; he'd even taken advantage of a show day to be taken around the next phase of Pearse-Caine's Quays' development in Melville. The show flat, still smelling of raw new wood and wet plaster, was a two-bedroom fully serviced condo overlooking both the inner harbour and beach. The half dozen planned apartments, occupying the last wing of the old flensing warehouses, were due to be completed by spring 2011 with an off-plan price of $847,000. Mort loved that 'forty-seven'. You're talking in hundreds of thousands and you can round it out to a seven? Jesus, who did they think they were kidding? Fact was these people were rich. They deserved to be taken. And taken for a whole lot more than a few pissy acres of forest. That was just the start of it.

Because there was no way that Mrs Pearse was going to be handed over in exchange for the land deal. That would be just plain stupid. He might have told the woman's husband that he'd never hear from him again. But that wasn't altogether true. Because Mort had every intention of calling Mr Zan Pearse and upping the ante soon as the Parks deal went through. Thanks for the land, but there's something else I want. Another million for the wife. It was time he took his own slice of the pie, and he'd already worked out how he was going to do it.

All Mort needed was the 'go', a news broadcast confirming that Zan was doing what he'd been told to do. After that Mort would quickly shift things up a gear or two. And Mr Pearse would have no choice but to go along with it.

53

Of the four units that made up their treehouse, each unit on a separate tree and connected by rope-and-plank walkways, Win and Courtney had settled themselves in the main salon, watching the rain splatter down on the terrace where just the day before they'd lunched with Dasha. Already the river was washing over the second Buren step, and sluicing past the four tree trunks that comprised the foundations of their wilderness retreat. Such was the power of the flow that it was possible to feel a very light trembling in the floor. At a rough esti-mate, Win reckoned the water to be a little over four feet deep, just a few feet short of the planked and sloping walkway that led up to their front door.

'Why don't we call Dasha?' Courtney suggested, as though Dasha would know what to do, would be able to correct the problem, just as she'd done during construction, accommodating all Courtney's extra whims and fancies easily and efficiently.

'I tried, but there's no signal,' he replied. He'd also tried to get through to Pearse-Caine's office in Melville and Seattle and to SuttonCorp headquarters, with the same result. Not that it worried him that much. For a man whose life relied on instant communication, he was surprised to find that the idea of being out of touch, isolated in the wilds of the Silver Hills, didn't really bother him. Right now, after that initial shiver of fear at the end of his walk – nature at work, the sudden unfamiliarity of it all – Win was starting to feel more comfortable, actually enjoying the prospect of riding out the elements in this extraordinary home his wife had found for them. He stretched back on the sofa, clasped his hands behind his head and looked up at the spread of branches supporting the salon's roof. He must have been smiling.

'I'm so pleased you like it here,' said Courtney, still swaddled in a Wilderness dressing gown, reaching out to pat his leg.

'Like it? I love it,' said Win. 'I really do. It's wild. It's remote . . . hell, just about a million miles from everything.' He took in a breath, looked around, then let it out in a long luxurious sigh. 'I guess . . . I guess I've been waiting for somewhere like this . . . Somewhere to just unwind, you know?'

'And be with me, of course. That too.'

'That too,' he replied.

'And judging by last night's little performance, Mr Win Sutton, the wilderness sure brings out the beast in you.'

'Why Mrs Sutton, that was you. Not me.'

'Well, how can you ever say such a thing? And not

218

even a blush of liar's shame. If I remember correctly it was most definitely you who made the first move.'

'Well, whoever it was, and however it started . . . it was fun.'

'You can say that again,' she replied, leaning towards him and planting a chaste kiss on his cheek. 'In fact,' she continued, moving her lips to his ear, 'how about you give me time to shower, and then just come look for me?' she whispered. 'Be a shame to waste all this wild weather, wouldn't you say?'

Ten minutes later, showered and scented and back in her robe, Courtney stood in front of the bedroom mirror and applied some lipstick. She hadn't felt this good in years, and she congratulated herself on her endeavour. She had been involved in this 'cottage in the country' almost from the moment the first wood dowels were knocked into place, had visited more times than she could count during its construction, and had spent sleepless nights wondering how Win would react. But everything had gone better than she could ever have imagined, ever have hoped for. Sometimes her husband got so involved in his work that she often felt invisible. She knew he loved her, of course, but invisible wasn't a nice place to be. A few days here, out in the wilds, looked like it was going to change all that. If she could make this first weekend special, she had no doubt that she would be able to entice him back here on a regular basis. And here was Mother Nature laying on just the most spectacular show. She couldn't see how it could get any wilder.

Courtney had put aside her lipstick and was mussing her hair, trying to get it to look unbothered but sexy, when her eye was drawn to a tiny crack in the bottom left hand corner of the bevelled bedroom mirror. For a moment she wondered if it had always been there and she just hadn't noticed it. But then it moved, lengthened, branching out across the glass like some deadly root system.

The next second, the bedroom floor shook and tilted, glass shards exploded from the mirror and Courtney was sent staggering back to the bed. Outside she heard a loud tearing wrench, and looking through the glass-panelled bedroom door she saw the wood walkway joining their bedroom with the salon stretch and twist and finally fall away into the floodwaters below.

For a second or two it didn't register. And then, with a lance of horror, she realised that she was alone, thirty feet from her husband whom she could see, even now, standing wide-eyed at the salon door.

But it wasn't over yet. With a slow, steady splintering, the main support branch above their bed began to break and the bedroom tilted far enough over for Courtney to see the river's spill racing hungrily below her.

54

The three of them were out on the porch. Mort and Gene with a chair apiece, and Eddie sitting on one of the steps, two up from where the rain spilled off the slope of the porch roof.

'It's getting heavier, you ask me,' said Gene, looking out into the yard where the downpour had wrapped misty silver haloes around Dasha's Lexus and the two trucks.

'Sometimes lasts for days like this,' said Eddie, with a local's smugness.

'Couldn't take it,' said Gene, tipping back on his chair. 'A few hours fine, but days?' He shook his head in disgust. 'Been here coming on a month and all I seen is a couple of days' blue sky. And now this. Worst so far.'

Ten feet away, the other side of the front door, Mort glanced at his watch. Time for the news. He was getting to his feet when Eddie, down on the steps, suddenly looked up, out past the trucks towards the trees.

'You hear something?' he asked, leaning forward and turning his ear to the forest.

Mort paused, bent down to take a look up the slope of the yard.

'Sounds like a snake,' said Eddie. 'Kinda like . . . hissing.'

All three men looked out at the belt of firs that began about fifty yards from the porch. There was certainly something in there – neither the distant rumble of the river, nor the rain hammering on to the roof of the cabin, splashing from the downpipes and battering down on to the yard quite loud enough to cover it.

And it was gaining in volume, this strange hissing. It was coming closer.

Gene put down his coffee mug on the arm of the chair and was getting to his feet when a figure suddenly burst through the trees and headed in their direction. A very familiar figure. It was Elroy Baker, arms waving, legs cartwheeling, bloodied clothes billowing around him as he surfed between the Lexus and Mort's Mitsubishi, rolling across the yard at the front of a knee-high wall of water.

Eddie, sitting on the steps, was the first to react, scrabbling back from his seat as Elroy's body smashed into the bottom step and rose up towards him, pushed and pummelled by the force of the water behind it.

'Jesus Christ, where the hell did all this come from?' shouted Gene, as Elroy's body rolled up the steps, bumping up each riser, blond hair slicking across a grey sightless face, arms reaching out for Eddie who still hadn't quite made it to his feet. A second later the surge spilled over the top step, swept across the porch and streamed through the open front door of the cabin, tipping Elroy's body on to Eddie's lap as it did so.

Still trying to stand, Eddie screamed out with horror and disgust – '*Fuck-fuck-fuck*' – and tried desperately to kick and push the body away, water gushing up, now surging over his chest, a swirling brown carpet of pine needles and cones breaking around him.

'Catch a hold, chrissakes!' cried Eddie, reaching out a hand to Gene as he struggled to free himself from Elroy's deathly embrace and the current's powerful grip. But Gene wasn't listening. His eyes were focused on the far side of the yard, up by the trees.

'The fuckin' cars are movin'. The sumbitch's movin' the fuckin' cars,' he shouted, as Eddie and Elroy, now hopelessly entangled, slid past him. The next moment they seemed to press together in the open doorway, before being sucked through it, hurled across the sitting room and jammed up against the back wall of the kitchen.

Out on the porch, clinging to the rail and up to his knees in a stream of rushing water, Mort looked at the cars in the yard. Gene was right. They were on the move.

The Lexus and Elroy's Toyota had been parked broadside to the trees and were only now starting to rock and pitch over, but Mort's Mitsubishi, facing down the slope, had already been picked up by the wheel arches and was surfing towards them, its bonnet bouncing along on the surge.

'Fuck, it's comin' right at us,' shouted Gene, trying to haul himself along the porch rail towards Mort, desperate to get out of the way but having to battle against the stream of water now splashing hungrily around his waist. The other side of the door Mort had reached for an open window and clamped an elbow over the sill, turning his back to the surge and trying to hook a leg over the window frame.

Five seconds before the Mitsubishi hit the porch, the stream caught the truck's rear end and swung it around. Instead of burying its nose in the steps, the truck, now broadside on, rolled over once then seemed to rise out of the flood as the water powered up behind and beneath it. It heaved up over the steps as though catching a wave and crashed through the porch rail and roof supports, snatching up Gene and slamming him against the cabin wall, just the other side of the front door from Mort.

Gene didn't stand a chance. Pinned between the log wall of the cabin and the roof of the upturned Mitsubishi, his mouth opened in a silent pink circle, a stream of bubbling blood shooting from between his lips. The weight of the water and the truck's rusting panelling ground the life out of his flattened, boneless body. As Mort watched, the Mitsubishi began to move sideways, rocking along the wall, rolling Gene's body with it. It was then, as if one truck was not enough, that the Toyota hit the porch, smashing up against the Mitsubishi's belly, with Dasha's Lexus, further to the right, spinning past and clipping the corner of the cabin.

The force of this glancing blow, and the grinding weight of the Toyota and Mitsubishi, provided enough impetus to rip open the corner of the cabin, tearing it apart like a badly stitched seam and stripping away the remaining section of porch roof. In an instant the mass of water hitting the building seemed to change direction, swerving away from Mort and powering the tangle of cars down the remaining length of now roofless porch. With a terrible screeching of wood and metal both the Toyota and Mitsubishi – and a crumpled Gene – reached the collapsing corner and were heaved away by the stream.

Chest-deep in the raging swirl of brown water, Mort clung desperately to his window sill, stunned by the flood's strength and malevolence. What had started just minutes before as a knee-high, hissing stream coming in fast across the yard was now a raging torrent, the roar of it filling his ears, the pummelling, pressing power of it pulling and tugging at his legs, trying to prise him loose and drag him away too. Unless he could get a firmer grip on his window sill and heave himself up on to it – or the water miraculously receded – he knew that he was lost.

But the racing water didn't look like it was going to let up any time soon, in no mood to release his legs, pinning him against the wall from the waist down. Reaching a hand to his belt Mort pulled his knife from its sheath and stabbed it into the cabin wall as far away from the pull of the water as he could reach. The point of the blade sank into the wood and without bothering to test it, he levered himself up. Trusting his weight on one elbow and the handle of his knife, he managed to shuffle himself a couple of inches along the sill. Working the knife free, he stabbed out again, a little higher this time, slowly hauling himself away from the current. Two stabs later, he managed to bring his chest up and over the sill, and was now able to use the force of the water to lift him even further. Pulling the knife from the wood, he stabbed out again, this time twisting inside the cabin, through the open window, and sinking the blade into the interior panelling. Again it held and he felt a quiver of satisfaction as his hips crunched against the sill, the water now spraying over his back. Half in and half out of the window, he felt the window frame shudder and saw the mortar gaps in the log walls start to crack and open up as the water smashed against them.

It was as if the cabin had been built with spit and glue. Everywhere Mort looked it was coming apart, the logs in the front wall shifting under the weight of the water and pulling free. With an almighty wrench that shuddered and groaned through the cabin, Mort saw the whole right-hand side wall of the cabin buckle and break away, swinging out into the surging current like a wayward windbreak to be snatched up and spirited away.

With one entire side wall ripped away it didn't take long for the rest of the structure, now critically un-supported, to fall apart. With a swooping horror Mort realised that, having gotten this far, having hauled himself out of the current, the river was going to take him whether he liked it or not. There was just no conceivable way he was going to get out of this, and he watched in disbelief as the sitting room's ceiling beams gave way one after another in a kind of splintering slow motion, the ceiling they supported crashing down, tilting over the staircase.

Bunkhouse beds, bath and other furnishings from the first floor came tumbling down into the main room to be swept away on the current, streaming through the now opened side wall. As if one wall wasn't enough to feed the fury of the flood, the kitchen at the back of the house where Eddie and Elroy had been trapped was promptly torn away from the main cabin, leaving a ragged hole looking down the slope. With a swerving surge, the flood now changed direction from the side of the house and poured instead through the open space where the kitchen had been, table, chairs, cupboards, fridge and cooker borne off after Eddie and Elroy in the roaring cascade. It was then that the roof timbers came crashing down, splitting open the stone firebreast. In an instant a cloud of thick soot settled on to the roiling surface of the water only to be whipped away like an oily black cloak, while a heap of blackened stones tumbled around the old sofa that had wedged itself up against the hearth.

It was this sofa, now pushed out into the room by the falling hearth stones, that the water promptly caught hold of and swung out into the main stream, hauling it towards the staircase and kitchen. In that single, mesmerising moment Mort saw his chance. As the sofa sailed past him, he heaved himself through the window, using his knife as a lever, scrambled over the sill and flung himself on to it, praying that he wouldn't tip it over.

His prayers were answered and seconds later the sofa, with Mort Johannesen aboard, spun through the hole where the kitchen had been and plunged down the slope.

55

Win Sutton was idly leafing through the Pearse-Caine Wilderness brochure, wondering just how much time he should give his wife, when he heard a mighty wrenching sound. Bounding up from the sofa he reached the terrace door in time to see the planked walkway connecting the salon with their bedroom buckle and twist, and thirty feet away he saw Courtney stagger across the room as her tree tipped dramatically to the left. By the time he pulled open the door and stepped out on to the terrace, the walkway had snapped free from the salon unit and now dangled like a casually tied scarf from the floor of their bedroom, its planked length tugged and twisting in the racing stream.

For a moment Win stood there, frozen with disbelief, unable to properly take in what had just happened. It was as if he was watching something on television, a certain numbing distance between what the eye saw and the mind registered.

'Courtney? *COURT?*' he called out, hoping she could hear him over the rain, hoping indeed that she was physically able to hear him. Had she hurt herself in that fall? Was she unconscious?

Calling out again, already aware that there was precious little he could do to get anywhere near her if she had been hurt, he felt a deep flush of relief as she reappeared in the tilting bedroom doorway.

'Win? Are you okay?' she called. 'What happened?'

'I'm fine, I'm fine,' he shouted across to her. 'It's the tree. It looks like the river's tilted it over. Must have stretched the walkway until it snapped. But are you okay?'

'Okay enough to be thinking what I'm going to say to Dasha next time I see her,' Courtney shouted back.

Win shook his head, with amusement as much as relief. His wife might have looked dazed and frightened but it was clear she was getting a hold on the situation. Just like Courtney – never lost for a snappy reply.

'Well, since there's no-one going to be able to get to us any time soon,' he called out to her, 'and since we're too old to go in for any kind of rescue mission, I guess we'll just have to wait it out until the river drops. Just so long as you're okay?'

Win had meant it seriously, since he could see no manageable way of getting to her. Or of her reaching him. As long as the tree didn't tip any further she should be okay. But he'd reckoned without Courtney.

'Speak for yourself, Grandpa. Too old, indeed. I'm not even fifty. And I'm damn well coming over there right now, you hear?'

'And how exactly . . .' he began.

But she was way ahead of him.

'There's the rope ladder the other side of the kitchen, back along the terrace there,' she said, pointing. 'Just unclip it from the brackets and you can sling it over here. I'm pretty sure it'll reach.'

'And what?' said Win. 'Please don't tell me you're gonna climb across it?'

'You betcha scrawny old ass I'm gonna crawl across it. If you think you're going to have the weekend to yourself, Win Sutton, after me spending all this time and money getting this little hideaway organised, well you've just got another think coming. So what are you waiting for, mister? Go get that goddam ladder.'

The ladder that Win reluctantly went to find had been installed as a secondary means of access down to the ground (to comply with planning requirements for a separate exit) which the evening before Courtney had discovered made the most marvellous swing.

Five minutes later Win was back on the terrace, dragging the rope ladder behind him.

'Now what you gotta do,' shouted Courtney, 'is secure one end your side, and chuck the other end over to me.'

Win shook his head. 'It weighs a ton, honey. There's no way I'll be able to . . .'

'Then swing it from the terrace, like a trapeze. And I'll grab a hold of it.'

'Jesus Christ, Court . . .'

'Just do it, Win. There's rain pouring in, I'm fucking soaked, and wet 'n' wild's never been a big thing with me, you hear what I'm saying?'

Despite himself, despite their situation, Win couldn't help but chuckle as he set about securing one end of the ladder to the terrace. No wonder he'd snapped her up. Shoulda met her years ago before those other buzzards he'd married had taken far more than their fair share. This was a woman – a wife – worth having.

Maybe it was because Courtney had suggested it, that Win wasn't surprised the trapeze idea worked. There was enough heft to the ladder to get it swinging pretty quickly and pretty effectively, and it wasn't long before Courtney grabbed a hold of it from her side. Twenty minutes later she had it secured.

She was just about to start out across the rope ladder (it looked frail as all hell, but Win had no doubt that somehow his wife would manage it) when he saw her pause.

'Just hold on a minute,' she yelled out. 'I need to get some dry clothes.'

'Jesus, Courtney, just get across here.'

'Hey, it's not you soaked to the skin, mister,' she shouted across at him, and then she ducked back inside.

Maybe it was that sudden shifting of weight from terrace back to bedroom, or the water pummelling away at the bottom of the tree, or the support branch in the bedroom finally breaking clean off, but as Win watched his wife make her way across the tilting platform, there came a single mighty crack, like a gunshot. In an instant the rope ladder was wrenched from its mooring like the walkway before it, the tree tilted over another twenty degrees and the entire bedroom unit seemed to fold in and collapse on itself.

With Courtney trapped inside.

Eyes wide with disbelief, Win watched in horror as their bedroom crashed down between the trees and smashed into the racing flood.

At first the pile of logs and wood panelling and roofing and decking just sat there in an ugly, broken mess, the river spraying over it. But as Win stared down, the water began to work away at this obstacle in its path – loosening a plank of wood there, snatching away another there, and then another, and another, followed by a whole section of roof dragged off in the stream, the whole place disintegrating, until finally Win spotted a flash of white, the towelling robe Courtney had been wearing, now snatched from the splintered rubble of their bedroom and swept away.

Somewhere beneath him, passing below the terrace on which he stood.

Spinning round, Win ran to the other end of the terrace and looked down, praying that he would see her, praying that, somehow, she might have survived the fall, the crush of timber, and might still be alive. Praying that she would see him, that she would raise a hand and shout out something down and dirty – that it was his goddam fault, that she was going to get him, just you wait . . .

But there was nothing to see, nothing to hear – the trees too dense, the hissing rain too thick and that sluicing pelt of water too fast and deadly to spare anyone or anything.

Courtney was gone.

Just . . . gone.

56

It hadn't taken long for the inch or two of mud that had snatched Dasha's feet from under her to become significantly deeper, a thick gloopy syrup that slowly but surely rose up the legs of her bed, forcing her to seek refuge on the staircase. She wondered where the water that fed it was coming from, gradually turning the basement's earth floor into a mud bath. Was it welling up from the ground, or leaking in through the walls somewhere? At no time had it smelt particularly damp down here, just a little mouldy, but now the shadowy darkness had a swampy stench to it. She remembered it had been raining when Elroy came to get her, and raining when Mort told her to get back down below. Perhaps it was raining still and leaching in beneath the walls?

Playing the architect Dasha had already decided that she was being held somewhere in the Hanish Valley, across the ridge-line from the Caine Reserve and their Wilderness project. Along the Susqua, cabins like this were usually built on wood pilings to allow for any rainfall run-off. But with its own quarry, Hanish Valley cabins boasted sturdier foundations. Dug into the slope, they were usually set on a levelling stone skirt, which provided the space for earth-floored basements like the one in which she now found herself.

As for the accommodation above her, that too had a Hanish feel to it. Despite the darkness and the short time she'd spent up there with Elroy, she had noted the exposed staircase and the interior log walls planked up to window-sill height, the loggers' hearth – long and high and wide enough so each man got his fair share of the fire – and the sashed windows either side of the cross-beamed cabin door. She had little doubt that the door led out to what was most likely a wide stoop or stepped porch, and that the staircase led to a bunkhouse with space for maybe a dozen men sleeping under the pitched roof. She was also prepared to bet that the kitchen at the bottom of the stairs was an add-on, set on stone pilings, the kitchen where Mort had hidden, stepping out in front of Elroy and slitting him open like a laddered hog.

Pushing away that chilling image, Dasha took advantage of the thin light coming through the few gaps in the ceiling to properly take in her surroundings. As far as she could see the room was long and narrow, running the width of the property, its furthest corners lost in shadow. Three of the walls comprised the cabin's stone skirting, almost certainly outside walls, but the fourth, set behind the trapdoor staircase on which she now sat, was made of panelled planking. Since the space down here was more limited than upstairs, and the cabin built on a slope, it stood to reason that the higher reaches of the basement were too low or cramped to be useful for anything, and had been sealed off.

Dasha wondered what was on the other side of this wood panelling and decided it might be worth investigating. If she could find any loose timbers she might be able to break through and burrow her way out, and she wondered why she hadn't thought of it earlier. She was pushing herself off the staircase to go and investigate when she heard a crashing sound from above as though someone had fallen off a chair, or kicked open a door. For a wild, wonderful moment she imagined rescue. But the sound didn't stop, didn't diminish. If anything it increased in volume until Dasha realised what the sound was – water, gushing overhead and now spraying through the gaps between the floorboards and the sides of the trapdoor, pouring down the staircase in a kind of stepped waterfall, and streaming across the basement's earth floor into the muddy pool around her bed.

Flood. They'd been hit by a flood, and a big one

judging by the dull thumping tumble of furniture in the room above her.

But it wasn't just the sound of water she heard. Moments later, the floorboards above her head shook as something large crashed against the cabin. It felt like a mighty blow. Something huge and monstrous.

Had a tree fallen? Had a tree toppled over and come crashing down on to the cabin? What was happening up there?

Then came another crash, not so loud this time, but still strong enough to shake the floorboards once again, followed by a wrenching, tearing sound as though the walls of the cabin were being torn apart.

Suddenly the planked wall she'd been about to investigate split open with a splintering crack and water blasted out of it, a chilling, deafening cascade that brought with it a slanting ray of half-light. Eyes wide with shock, Dasha watched it gush into the basement with an angry roar, slamming up against the bottom wall, tipping over her bed and churning the mud into a foaming tide that began to rise up the slope of floor towards her.

The panic was immediate. If it rose any faster, and with the trapdoor bolted from the other side, the prospect of drowning in this bubbling, swirling pool of mud suddenly became a real possibility. Pushing herself backwards, Dasha mounted the steps one by one until her back was hunched against the trapdoor, water pouring down over her shoulders and through her clothes as though she were standing under a shower.

Above her she could still hear the mighty wash of water rushing through the cabin, tearing at the insides of the house. From the direction of the kitchen came another fearsome wrenching sound and, seconds later, an explosive crash as something hit the floorboards a few feet above her. In the half-light now showing through the broken wood wall behind her, and coming in along the top of the side wall where a length of floorboarding had sprung loose, Dasha could now clearly see the water banking up against the stone wall where her bed had stood. It seemed only minutes since the flood had spilled into the basement, but it was rising fast now, backing up towards her, climbing the staircase a step at a time, suddenly lapping against her bare feet. If it went on at this rate she'd be under water in just a few more moments. If she didn't die of the smell first. Somewhere along the flood course a cistern or cesspit had clearly been breached.

Although there seemed little point in crying out for help, she did so anyway, a couple of feeble screaming *help*s, *help me*s lost in the sluicing rage of the water, beating her fists against the trapdoor. But she knew it was useless. As if anyone up there was likely to spare her a thought. In all likelihood they had planned to kill her anyway, so why should they bother coming to rescue her, given they had themselves to look after?

Or maybe there was no-one up there? If it was bad down here in the basement, it must be monstrous up there, she thought. Maybe they'd already been swept away, or were injured, or trapped like her?

And as the water crept up around her ankles, and streamed down on to her head, the tears started.

She didn't want to die, she didn't want to die. She wanted to see Zan again and hold her children. She didn't want to die like this. Alone, in the darkness.

Please God, she whispered, *Please God, don't let me die. Not here. Not now.*

57

As a means of transport, the sofa that Mort clung to may not have been ideal in the middle of a raging torrent but it was clearly better than nothing. So far he was still alive; his friends had not been so lucky. Digging fingers and toes into its sagging upholstery, he pressed his cheek against the sofa's stinking sodden weave and spat out the water as it gushed around his face. As far as he could judge the torrent that had hit them was probably no more than waist deep, but travelling at such a startling speed that it had been impossible to fight against it. Not a single one of them out there on the stoop had stood a chance, and had he not chosen to sit a few feet to the left of the porch steps, there was no doubt in his mind that either the surging water, or one of the trucks, would have taken him out as easily as Gene and Eddie. Yet so far all he had to show for the encounter was a pumping heart and, somewhere along the way, the loss of his eyepatch.

Looking out from the seat of the sofa Mort caught sight of the two trucks, now just a tumble of overturned wreckage pulled up short in the lower treeline, the water spraying up around them. It was then that he spotted Elroy and Eddie. Thirty feet from the trucks, the current had pressed the pair of them against a wide cedar trunk, and its pummelling strength – many tons per square inch – held them there in a gruesome embrace, Eddie's head resting on Elroy's shoulder, his wide, surprised eyes gazing back sightlessly at the cabin. He also looked as though he'd been half-crucified, thought Mort as his sofa whipped past, an arm slung over a branch as if he'd been trying to drag himself up out of the water and get free of Elroy when his ribcage splintered and the life was crushed out of him.

But there was no time for further reflection. Once in the trees, Mort's progress became much more precarious, a spin down the water slide exchanged for a session on the bumper cars. Hanging on tightly to his sofa surfboard, Mort rode the current through the trees, scraped by the lowest branches, bucking over high roots and spun round viciously after contact with tree trunks. Sometimes he was facing uphill and sometimes downhill. On one occasion the sofa turned lengthwise on to the flood and actually flipped over a couple of times, ducking Mort and filling his nose with a bubbling froth that made him spit and splutter when he surfaced, with no time to draw breath before he was ducked again.

But at no time did Mort lose his sense of direction. He knew exactly where the water – and his sofa – were headed. There'd clearly been heavy rain higher up the valley and the resulting floodwater had been strong enough to break over the Hanish's bank further upstream where the river looped around the cabin and take a shortcut through the woods. Any second now, the flood would bring him and his sofa back to the river as it came around again below the trees.

It was not a prospect that Mort anticipated with anything other than dread. In the last few weeks, since they'd moved into the cabin, he'd walked along the Hanish Stream enough times to know that the banks were steep along this section, and would probably still be steep even in the middle of a flood like this. The sofa, he knew, would take off when it came out of the trees.

And that's exactly what it did.

With a jarring half-tumble that had his feet lose contact with the arm of the sofa, Mort and his transport sailed over the bank in a cascade of water and crashed down into the river ten feet below, deep enough now to save him and the sofa from explosive contact with the stony river bed.

Mort and his sofa stayed together for the next two miles, crashing over rapids, spilling through walls of standing water and spinning across raging eddies before he heard the roar of Quarry Falls up ahead.

Before he went over he saw where Gene had ended up, his old friend skewered on a branch rising out of the stream, hanging from its tip, crushed and bloodied, the river splashing around his waist, tugging him further and further along the spear-like branch that jutted from his chest.

Gene's broken body was the last thing Mort registered before he and his sofa were suddenly dragged into the centre of the stream and catapulted over the falls, flying out smoothly into a swirling mist-shrouded cloud, now tumbling down with the roaring cascade into a pool nearly thirty feet below.

58

Spitting out a mouthful of water, Miche spun herself out of a whirlpooling clash of currents below Lobo Canyon's final sliding chute, spotted the rock shelf, and paddled over to it. When she reached it, she slid from the board and felt her feet touch the bottom. Fifty feet away, Clyde and Kelly whooped as they surfed down into the churning pool, followed by Bradley and Alison, with BeeJay, Taylor and Naomi close behind. They'd been on the Susqua a little over an hour, which was longer than Miche had planned for this stretch of the route, and they were now running about twenty minutes behind schedule. Ahead, clearly visible a mile downstream, the sides of Cougar Canyon rose above a spiky crown of treetops, its limestone walls fading away into shawls of mist and drizzle.

Waving to her group, Miche pointed out the shelf, then hauled herself up on to it, waiting for them to reach her.

'Not too mean for a bunch of freshers,' she said, as they gathered round, picking up on their delight and being pleased by it. These kids would be talking about this for days, weeks. Years maybe. A real adventure. Their faces, pinched into their surf hoods, looked red-cheeked and wide with smiles – even Alison's – though Bradley's spots showed more vividly against the chilled skin.

'Unreal,' said BeeJay, pulling off his hood and shaking out his hair.

'Awesome. Just freaking awesome,' said Taylor, putting his fingers between his lips and letting rip with a whistle that echoed across the river and rose up into the hills.

'And there's more to come, people,' said Miche, quietening them down. 'But first, just a few rules. The dos and don'ts. Some of you will know this already, but bear with me. Repetition's the best teacher and there's others here need to know,' she continued, thinking of Alison but not wanting to single her out. 'Think of it as a flight safety drill before take-off. Because that's what we're gonna be doing.'

There were more whoops from the quarterbacks, the smacking exchange of high fives, and another ear-shattering whistle from Taylor. Every time Miche gave this little speech, every time she said that line about 'take-off', they all did the same thing – whoop or whistle or hoot, often all three. Well, not all of them on this occasion. Clyde just looked cool, probably stoned, and Bradley seemed a little nervous. Like Alison, she'd need to keep an eye on him. An accomplished guitarist maybe, but he was not such an accomplished white-water boarder.

'So. Listen up,' said Miche. 'Number one – we all still got our whistles?'

Everyone checked the collars of their buoyancy vests. Nods all round.

'BVs pumped?'

More checking. More nods.

'Fins secure, and board leashes tight?'

Arms reached down under the surface to last-minute-check fins, and leashes were tugged.

'Okay, so here's what you need to know about Cougar. Just the three things. It's fast, it's deep and it's narrow. In the next twelve miles we'll drop a couple hundred feet, maybe more, and for most of the way there's not a whole heap of opportunity to pull in and rest up. Given the flow rate this morning, I'd guess it'll take somewhere around forty minutes to make it through. And riding a belly board, that's gonna seem pretty fast, believe me, maybe faster than some of you have done before. Just remember to go with the flow. Use it, don't try to fight it. You won't win, believe me.'

She looked at each of them in turn, to hammer the point home. Pumped up after Lobo, they just couldn't wait. Even Alison had a sparkle in her eye.

'One more thing,' said Miche, holding them back. 'Unlike Lobo, I want us to go in order. Alison, Clyde and Naomi, you go first. Then Bradley and Kelly.' Turning to the quarterbacks, she said, 'BeeJay and Taylor, you two stay with me as much as you can – not because you're not good, but because you're the ones who'll be helping me if someone starts whistling and help's needed. Okay, then. We all set?' She looked around the line of faces. 'So let's go find us some wild water!'

Teaming up as directed, with some more whoops and whistles and high fives, Miche's group turned and paddled back into the current – Clyde first, followed by Alison and Naomi, then Kelly and Bradley. Miche waited till Clyde started to line up for the bend, then slid off the shelf she'd been perched on and finned away from the bank with BeeJay and Taylor either side of her.

As soon as they hit the stream, twenty feet out from the bank, Miche knew something was different. The way the current shifted beneath her, the way her board started to duck and weave as she paddled after her group. It couldn't have been more than fifteen minutes since she'd come off Lobo, but in just that short space of time the river had changed, the way the stream sucked at her fins and splashed around her elbows and snatched at her leash. She felt . . . uncomfortable. It wasn't raining any harder than it had been at breakfast, but the water was different somehow. She was certain of it.

Glancing over her shoulder, as though she was on a lonely street and checking to see if someone was following her, Miche looked upstream and felt a chill twist of anxiety. She tried to shift it, shake it away, but it lingered, a cold finger coiling round her guts as the bend in the river straightened and the canyon rose up through the mist, two sheer faces of golden grey stone facing each other across forty feet of surging water.

Maybe, she thought to herself, maybe it was just the proximity of Cougar – knowing what was waiting for them up ahead. It didn't matter how many times she rode Cougar, it still had the power to scare hell out of her. Scare hell out of anyone. But it was too late now for second thoughts. The best thing she could do was get her party through as quickly as she could, and worry afterwards.

Pushing up on her board, she watched Alison, Clyde and Naomi slide fast and safe through the pillared entrance to the canyon. Then Kelly and Bradley. There were whoops from Clyde and Naomi, but these were quickly lost over the roar of the water pounding down through the canyon.

Just seconds later, it seemed, it was Miche's turn, she and her two companions pulled into mid-stream as the water bunched up into a smooth, fast, muscly pelt to funnel through the gap, the three of them picking up speed, slicing one after another between the bookend stone buttresses of the canyon, bucking and tossing their way down the first of the sheer-walled straights.

Another forty minutes, thought Miche. That's all it was.

Fifty minutes max.

And they'd be out of there.

59

Somewhere in Dasha's basement prison the rising flood had found a way out, fast enough to keep the water lapping at her chest and reaching no higher. Shivering in the cold, she sat on the top step, hunched beneath the trapdoor, and wondered what she should do, listening to the water suck and gurgle hungrily around her.

Since the flood had hit she'd heard nothing from her captors. Were they still up there, hanging on like her? Or had they been swept away by the blast of water? As far as she could tell it had been a massive hit, certainly enough to snatch anyone off their feet and haul them away. It seemed reasonable, then, to assume that she was now alone, and that if she did somehow manage to break out there'd be no-one up there to stop her.

But how to break out? There was no way she could force her way past the cascade pouring through the gap in the wood wall behind her, and the trapdoor, when she pushed against it, felt as if something had landed on it. There was now far less give in it than there had been before and she was certain it no longer represented a way out.

It was then that a floor joist running across the centre of the basement ceiling began to creak, as though it was supporting a weight it had never been designed to bear. Peering up she tried to make out where the stress to the wood was greatest – a bulge, a movement. And there it was – a prolonged and protesting creak and angry snapping loud enough to be heard over the water. In an instant what looked like a pile of stones from the chimney breast, one piece still in an unbroken block, tumbled down and splashed into the basement, a heavy enough fall to send back a small wave in her direction.

And after the stones the water, as though someone had pulled out a bathplug and she was no more than that blessed spider trapped in the downpipe, a gushing column that filled the basement with an ear-splitting roar. In an instant she could feel the water creeping over her chest and lapping at her shoulders.

But before she had time to register any sense of fear at the rising level, the extra weight of water suddenly brought down a section of the stone wall at the far end of the basement. In an instant the water spun towards it, so violently that she felt the sudden pull of receding water, and she had to hang on tight to the step as the water drained away from her, dropping past her shoulders, her stomach, her trembling thighs and then, step by step, down the staircase.

And there, as the level of the water dropped, the breach in the stone wall revealed itself: a ragged square of daylight, the outside world – a line of trees, and hammering rain silvering the distance between them.

A great and overwhelming sense of relief swept over her, shivering up through her limbs, filling her with a great flush of hope and confidence and possibility. So close, everything in the real world was suddenly so close. Right there, just twenty feet away.

But escape through that breach in the wall was not an option. She'd have been sucked off her feet before she was halfway there, pummelled by the great weight of water still gushing down through the floorboards. She'd be dead by the time she reached those trees that she could see shimmering through the rain.

There was nothing for it but just sit there on the staircase and wait.

Wait for the rain to stop and the flood to ease.

Then she could get herself out of there, get herself home.

60

Taking advantage of every crest, every rise in the stream, Miche sought out the group ahead, counting them off, a pack of black seals ploughing through the wash and crash of the water. So far everyone seemed to be handling the ride well, everyone taking it seriously, and everyone, Miche had no doubt, feeling that explosive rush of adrenalin that always came with Cougar.

As they passed the halfway mark, a tall bushy cleft on the right-hand wall, Miche felt her spirits begin to rise. She was in control. They'd done the first fast slide where the water bulged with muscle, successfully negotiated the board-bouncing rapids without mishap, and comfortably roller-coasted the switch-back curves and corners that followed. And right now they were far enough down the canyon for Miche to feel the end was in sight – even if it wasn't.

As she and BeeJay and Taylor swung out into faster water on one of the bends to pick up speed and make some ground on the others up ahead the rain suddenly came down in a rush, far heavier than before. It also seemed to be coming from two different directions, a shawl of misty rain drifting upstream, right into their faces, and a harder rain slanting down from behind them. With the canyon walls towering up either side, it seemed to concentrate the downpour, small spraying cascades starting high up, showering down and already staining the canyon's walls.

Seconds later came a burst of thunder. The last time Miche had heard it, just before breakfast, it had sounded low and distant. Now it was much closer, somewhere behind them, a crackling whiplash rippling through the heavens followed by a long, low grumbling bellow that seemed to take an age to trail off. Like the rain, the canyon seemed to amplify the sound, and the thunder's dying groans bounced back and forth from one wall to the other.

Taking her eye off the water ahead, Miche glanced at her watch. Close to thirty minutes into the ride, by her reckoning. And with the speed they were doing, and no real hold-ups, there was probably no more than another quarter-hour to go before they were through. But fifteen minutes suddenly felt like fifteen minutes too long, and Miche tensed, some sixth sense coming into play. Some ancient pulse of Makah intuition.

The rain was too hard, too insistent.

The thunder was too loud, too close.

And Miche knew they were speaking to her, telling her something, warning her.

Hell and high water, thought Miche, taking the lead in her threesome. If the rain was coming down this hard up in the hills behind them, it surely wouldn't be long before they felt the effect down here, with a dramatic rise in river level and speed. And already the water seemed to be getting rougher, wilder, suddenly splashing up on to the sheer sides of the canyon which only minutes before it had just seemed to slide past.

For another five or six minutes the current stayed steady, even seemed to settle, and a thin sliver of confidence crept back into Miche. They were going to do it, she realised. They were going to get through. In another hour they would be sitting round a lunchtime fire, drinking beers and telling their tales in excited voices.

But her confidence didn't last long. Up ahead, as her party of boarders bounced through another set of swirling rapids, Miche saw two of them take serious tumbles off their boards. She couldn't tell who it was at first but then she saw a blue board leap out of the white water and, still leashed to Clyde's wrist, slam back down. Thankfully, she watched him haul it in, grab hold and scramble back on to it before diving out of sight into another trough. But Kelly, some thirty feet behind him, was not so fortunate. Somehow her board had broken free from its leash and was flying through the air, caught like a kite in the surface draught. Flung past a standing wall of water that was breaking like a bow-wave mid-stream, Kelly was spun down a small side chute, swallowed up in a grinding eddy and then spat out to end up in an almost still pool behind a large boulder. For a moment she simply floated there, hardly moving, spluttering and coughing.

Not good, not good, thought Miche, as Kelly's companion, Bradley, tried to get alongside her, reaching out a hand to grab her. But the river had other ideas. With their fingertips just inches apart, he swirled past her and was caught by the main stream again, no way for him to get back to her.

Paddling as fast as she could, finning with all her

might, Miche crossed in front of Taylor and lined herself up for the bow-wave of standing water mid-stream, taking the same route as Kelly.

It was then, as she swung past the standing water and dropped down the side chute, that Miche heard a low, rising groan from behind her, still distant but closing on them, a sound that chilled her blood. It wasn't thunder, and it wasn't the roar of the water that swung her now towards Kelly. It was something far more terrifying. And she knew what it was. Somewhere in the hills behind them, up on the higher reaches of the Susqua, the flood wave she'd warned Gimball about had built up and was coming after them. By the sound of it, the deadly rush of water had already reached the entrance to the canyon, rapidly gaining height and velocity as it funnelled between the sides of the canyon, carrying with it a crashing, churning mess of debris – snapped branches, wrenched-up vegetation. God alone knew what else it carried on its surging, swelling crest, like a giant broom sweeping all before it.

Turning to BeeJay and Taylor who had followed her to see if they could help with Kelly, Miche waved them on. 'Go on, go on. As fast as you can!' she shouted. 'Get the others to speed up and once you're over the falls paddle back into the overhang. You understand? Paddle back into the overhang. You'll see the way in on the left-hand side.'

With a nod and swift change of direction the two boys finned away while Miche came in to circle Kelly, paddling against the edge of the current until she was close enough to reach out a hand and grab hold of the girl. With no chance of retrieving Kelly's board the two of them would have to double up and share Miche's for the rest of the ride. If no-one else took a spill Miche reckoned they stood a fair chance of staying ahead of the swell, still a few miles behind them but gaining on them with every second.

Turning her board broadside so there'd be room for the two of them, Miche hauled Kelly up beside her and together they clamped their fingers over its leading edge, sending up a spray that snapped back into their faces, making them squeeze their eyes tight.

'I'm so sorry,' cried Kelly. 'I just . . . I don't know . . . the leash . . .'

'It's okay, it's okay,' Miche shouted back, her voice just making it over the splash of the rapids and the rising thunder of the oncoming swell. 'We'll be out of here in no time.'

Beside her, Kelly frowned, jerked her head round. 'What's that noise?' she asked, looking back upriver.

'Flood water coming down from the hills. It's nothing. Don't worry,' said Miche, finning hard to get into the stream, feeling it start to pull them forward. If they could just stay ahead for the next mile or so they would make it. Once past the falls, they'd fin back into the overhang, the storm surge would shoot over them and they'd miss the worst of it.

But Miche had underestimated the speed and fury of the bore. Judging by the rising sound, it was catching up fast, and with her board turned broadside to the stream and carrying an extra person, it was heavier, harder to steer – and slowing them down.

'You take the board!' screamed Miche.

'But you . . . you . . .'

'Just go. Just go now. Get over the fall and then paddle back into the overhang. You'll be safe there.' And with that, Miche twisted the board until it was resting under Kelly, snapped her leash on to the girl's wrist and then flung herself to one side.

Without a board, Miche's speed dropped and in just a few seconds she had fallen well behind Kelly. Inflating her buoyancy vest, lifting herself higher in the water, she finned into the centre of the stream and started reaching forward with her arms, pushing the water past her. If she could stay ahead of the current, go a little faster than the river itself, then she stood a chance. She would make it. She would be safe.

Sliding and swerving, rising and falling, Miche raced along with the stream, a wild rage of white water breaking over her, the canyon walls racing past and falling behind her. Up ahead she caught a glimpse of Kelly riding fast and straight, her board hurtling along.

Good girl. Good girl. They were going to make it, they were going to make it. That was what Miche believed – truly believed – until she saw a length of stubby broken branch overtake her, on her left, midway between her and the wall of the canyon, and heard above the roar of the water the grinding, snapping, crashing of the deadly cargo the flood bore carried.

More branches followed, on both sides of her now, a mess of moss and fern and twisted boughs borne along beside her on the flow. She felt the water start to rise, just as it did on the swells in Melville Bay, and an image of Mungo sprang into her mind. It made her feel safe, calmed her, made her smile.

Mungo. Mungo.

That was the moment, as she mouthed his name, that the current suddenly sucked her under, thundered in her ears, pummelled against her body, tore off her fins, her helmet, her watch. Tossed her, spun her, rolled and tumbled her, just like a wipe-out on a Melville Bay break.

But on Cougar Canyon there was no safe beach to be flung onto . . .

No-one waiting for her . . .

No-one to tease her . . .

Instead, there came a mighty, crushing, concussive blow . . .

And . . . darkness.

Silence.

61

With Naomi just a few feet in front of her, Clyde back alongside her, and just a mile or so left to go, Alison was beginning to regret that their ride through Cougar Canyon was coming to an end. With no-one in the group ahead of them on the river, it was as if the three of them had been pathfinders, the first to navigate the Cougar's wild, twisting course, the first to take on its adrenalin-pumping glory and live to tell the tale. And not knowing what lay around the next bend had given that ride an added piquancy.

So, too, did the scenery. Although it was misty, although it was raining, there was a giant, towering majesty about the canyon – raw, wild and untouched – that had made Alison's heart beat faster. The way its walls rose out of the swirling water, straight and true and smooth, with only the tiniest ledges and cracks on their surface to accommodate only the stubbiest and hardiest of growths. The way those same walls closed in on them, fell back, drew in again, forever sculpting and directing the mighty flow of the river. The river they rode. Boisterous, determined, pulsing with life, bulging with energy.

Right from the start, after setting off from that last stop, the current had been far stronger than Alison had anticipated, far more powerful than Lobo. She hadn't expected it to tug at her legs quite so hungrily, she hadn't expected it to spit in her face and snatch at her elbows the way it did, or rock and buck her board so enthusiastically. If it hadn't been for Naomi and Clyde staying so close, she'd never have made it down in one piece. Apart from Clyde's tumble, which she was relieved to see he'd recovered from, the two young-sters had never strayed far from her and it was their company and their contagious enjoyment of the canyon's thrills and spills that had given her what she needed, her confidence growing with every passing mile. Sometimes, when they dropped down into a trough, or swerved round a bend or rose up over a crest of standing water, she'd even felt like whooping just as they did.

Now, suddenly, she understood why her husband loved it so much – riding water like this – and she understood why he'd been so keen that she take the board and not him. He wanted her to see what it was all about, taste the excitement, feel her guts twist on this celebrated roller-coaster ride. She loved that man so much – letting her do it when he would have given anything to ride it himself. That was the kind of man he was. That's why she loved him the way she did. Ten years married and he still made it feel like the first week.

Up ahead, beyond the cheek-lashing spray and breaking crests, from somewhere around the next bend, Alison suddenly sensed something new in the rhythm of her progress, a certain thudding pressure reaching up to her, a drumming pulse she could feel in her chest, now beating off the walls of the canyon and battering her ears. Bouncing along ten feet to her right, Clyde glanced across and gave her a snatched thumbs-up. He'd sensed it, too, and she nodded bravely, not quite daring enough to take a hand off her board to give him the same signal back.

With her attention so firmly focused on the river ahead, deciding she'd follow the tighter, slower line through the inside of the bend, it came as some surprise to Alison to hear a sudden whistling, frantic and repeated, coming from behind her. At first she imagined the whistles were a kind of enthusiastic acknowledgement from the rest of the group that the climax of the ride was upon them, an excited accompaniment to the whooping that was sure to follow.

But there was no whooping. Just the whistles – sharp and shrieking and strangely unsettling.

Not wanting to risk looking back as the final turn approached, Alison slowed her finning until Bradley, BeeJay and Taylor caught up with her, shouting across at her that she should increase her speed, and something about paddling back when she got over the falls.

Paddle back? Had she heard right? But it was too late to ask. The three boys had moved on, passing along the same instructions to Clyde and Naomi by the look of it.

Just a few yards further on Kelly came up alongside her and also screamed something to her. Again, it was difficult to make out what she was saying over the roar of the river and the approaching falls, but Alison assumed she was asking for instructions.

'Once you're over the falls, you gotta paddle back,' Alison shouted back at her, repeating what she'd been told by the boys, and wondering what had happened to Miche. Surely their guide should be up there with them, shepherding them through this last section?

But Kelly either didn't hear or didn't understand. Instead, she swung across the stream towards BeeJay and Taylor who, with Clyde, Bradley and Naomi, were taking the outside line on the upcoming bend where the water was faster. It seemed a strange approach to Alison. She'd have thought they'd want to stretch out every moment of the ride, make it last, just like her. Instead they were powering forward, arms wheeling, fins beating wildly at the water, as though they wanted to reach the falls as quickly as they could, and as fast as they could. They looked for all the world as though something was chasing them, and they were anxious to get out of its way.

It was then that Alison heard something behind her that hadn't been there before, growing even more insistent than the rising thunder of the falls up ahead, something that made her turn her head and glance behind on the sharp left-hander. What she saw chilled her blood, numbed her senses. A hundred feet back a wall of water rose up the sides of the canyon, hurtling into the bend as if no bend was there, straight and fast, curling and cresting over a mass of churning debris that thrashed like the rotating blades on a combine harvester.

It was on them in a moment.

Despite their speed, the youngsters were hit first, just a matter of seconds before they cleared that last bend and turned on to the final straight. Spinning her board to the right, looking out across the stream, Alison watched as, one by one, they were lifted up against the far canyon wall then plucked away by the grinding swell. Clyde and Bradley swallowed up, then BeeJay, Taylor and the girls engulfed in a splay of outstretched limbs and soundless screams.

As swift, and as final, as that.

And then, when the grinding mass reached its highest point on the canyon wall, Alison watched it drop back and come racing towards her.

Now it was her turn.

Gripping the sides of her board, lifting it up like a shield, she squeezed her eyes shut and felt the swell lift her upwards, sweep her backwards, toss her up into the air before grinding down on top of her.

Alison was the last in the group to die.

62

The rain was pelting down when Charlie Gimball and Pete Conway turned off the Susqua trail and drove through the trees to a patch of open ground a mile past the bottom end of Cougar Canyon.

Rigging up a sheet of tarpaulin between the two vehicles to keep off the rain, they set about preparing lunch, opting for salads and fruit and sandwiches rather than getting the gas griddle up and running. The guys could make do with a cold lunch and wait till evening for something hot – if the rain allowed.

Before leaving the previous night's camp ground, Charlie and Miche had agreed to rendezvous at this lunch spot around midday. By the time the tarpaulin had been secured it was past midday and there was still no sign of them.

Pulling his parka over his head, Pete Conway went down to the river bank thirty feet away and looked anxiously upstream. Watching from the cover of the tarpaulin, Charlie wondered how anxious he'd have been if his wife hadn't been one of the party. It was an uncharitable thought, but Charlie reckoned he knew human nature better than most. Pete might be the teacher in charge of six kids, answerable to six sets of parents and the Fairbanks school board, but if push came to shove he'd want his wife to make it through before anyone else.

'You think this rain could be causing them any problems?' Pete asked when he ducked under the tarpaulin and pulled up a chair.

'It's a long way down from the head of the stream, Pete,' replied Charlie, cracking open a beer from the cold chest and reaching across for one of his ham subs. 'You see anything bad about the river down there? She's just as she always is this time of year, you can take my word on that. And if you've got to go through Cougar, well there's no-one better than Miche Tomak to keep an eye out for you.'

'She seems pretty young for the job,' said Pete, catching the can of beer that Charlie tossed to him.

'Twenty-five going on forty,' replied Charlie. 'Injun blood right the way through. Susqua, Makah – one of those. So she knows these waters better'n most. If there'd been any problem, if she'd had the slightest concern, you can take my word on it that she'd have said so. Woulda told me to cancel. And with her in charge, I'd have done it. Even if you didn't get to make the canyons.'

Pete flipped open the ringpull and sipped up the beer froth. 'She just seemed . . . I don't know, she seemed a little . . .' And then he stopped, his attention caught by something over Charlie's shoulder. 'Is that a rat, or . . . ?'

Charlie turned, looked where Pete was looking. 'Marmot,' he replied. 'Male by the size of him. Should be bedding down for winter pretty soon. They whistle, you know. Kinda cute.'

Which is exactly what the marmot did, a short trilling whistle laced with alarm. Seconds later another marmot appeared from the tree cover, scurrying over to the first. Then a third marmot appeared, and a fourth.

Charlie frowned. He couldn't remember the last time he'd seen a marmot. Heard 'em call, of course, but they mostly kept to themselves. Shy little critters. Now here were four of them, halfway between the vehicles and the river, rising on hind legs to sniff the air.

In the wood from which they'd appeared there now came the sound of breaking branches and out from the shadows leapt an elk, then a second, accelerating across the open ground, scattering the marmots.

'Well I'll be—' began Charlie, but a loud roar from the river drowned out his words as a rising wave of white tops and twisted debris hurtled round the bend. Before either Pete or Charlie could move from their chairs, the wave swept in over the bank where they'd pitched their camp, hit the side of the Fairbanks school bus and slammed it against Charlie's SUV.

Sitting between the two vehicles, drinking their beers, the two men stood no chance.

They were dead before they got wet.

Part Two

'*Located just a few miles west of the confluence of the Hanish and Susqua streams, Shinnook is a busy centre for the local logging industry, though travellers to these parts should be aware that the town's rough collection of timber-frame homes and commercial enterprises offer little in the way of commodious accommodations . . .*'

Shaws' Travelling Companion to the
Northern Pacific States, 1923

63

When Jenna Blake and Pico Ramirez arrived in Melville, they followed the signs down Main Street and headed for the beach, turning at last into the parking lot behind the sea wall. Despite the shawling drizzle there was already quite a crowd gathered there, and as soon as she saw the line of people looking out to sea Jenna knew that it hadn't been a wasted journey.

While Pico looked for a space to park, Jenna jumped out of the van and headed for the sea wall. If there was a story here – which she prayed to the god of network syndication there would be – they didn't have long to set it up for the main lunchtime news. The drive out of Seattle had been a bitch, a vicious, slanting rain that slowed traffic to a stop-start queue on the freeway slip road. By the time they were out of the city limits and heading for the coast, the rain was still bucketing down and she was starting to fret. She didn't look good wet, and she hadn't brought an umbrella.

Fortunately the rain in Melville was softer, less bullying, more a dull grey sea mist sweeping in over the town, frosting beards and jackets and windscreens, bringing with it the salty tang of the ocean. Flat light, Jenna thought as she climbed the steps and came out on the sea wall. Not good. She hoped Pico wouldn't make a fuss. In her experience, moody cameramen made lousy lovers. But that was for later. Right now it was work.

At first all Jenna could really take in were the crowds. There seemed to be hundreds of people lining the wall and gathered in groups on a narrow skirt of sloping beach. All of them were looking out to sea. So that's where she looked.

Even to a non-surfer, the waves pounding in between the headlands looked awesome, a line of rising swells that towered up into the sky before crashing down in a furious, looping curl from left to right. If the sharks didn't come to anything, she could always do a piece on the waves, get some good-looking guy to show them how it was done. It was then that Jenna noticed there were no surfers out there. Not that she was too surprised; the waves looked just too damn high and dangerous for anyone with brain cells to take on.

That's when she realised that it wasn't just the waves that were putting off the surfers, but what was in them.

Every time a swell rose, in the seconds before it broke, at a certain angle, she could see the sharks trolling gently through the wave, lifted up by it. And in the troughs between the swells were fins, dozens of them, slicing through the surface. Wherever she looked, from one end of the beach to the other, all she could see were sharks and fins, passing up and down like pedestrians on a busy sidewalk. She'd never seen so many. They might not look all that big, but there were just so many of them.

'Jeez,' came a voice beside her. It was Pico, open-mouthed, staring out to sea.

'Let's get moving,' said Jenna, 'before they head off someplace else.'

'Doesn't look to me like they plan leaving any time soon,' replied Pico, and shouldering his camera he began a long sweep of the beach.

Jenna smiled to herself.

Not a word from Pico about the flat light.

64

So they'd made the news at last.

Propped up in his hospital bed Zan Pearse reached for the remote and switched off the TV, thanking his lucky stars for a lawyer who did what he was told without asking tiresome questions, or complicating matters with tedious legalese. In just three hours – since Zan had told him about Dasha's abduction, the ransom demand, and his decision to play ball – Tom Gold had made it happen. A short sign-off piece on the midday local news confirming that Pearse-Caine had decided to donate sixty thousand acres bordering the Silver Hills National Park to the National Parks Commission. The fifty-second slot included aerial footage of the upper Susqua valley where Pearse-Caine were building their 'controversial' Wilderness homes, a computer-generated impression of the treehouses that they had used for their planning application, followed by an on-screen confirmation from Tom outside Pearse-Caine's Seattle office that the transfer would be finalised by day's end. No reason had been given for Pearse-Caine's change of heart and no mention had been made of Dasha's abduction, or any ransom demand. The story concluded with a spokesman from the NPC expressing delight that their persistence in trying to halt this scandalous development had finally paid off, and that Pearse-Caine were setting an admirable example which the National Parks hoped other wilderness developers would pay heed to.

You could almost taste their complacency, thought Zan; as though they had been the ones to secure the land, and not a bunch of eco-terrorist kidnappers who were holding his wife prisoner. But if the National Parks had anything to do with it, he was certain the story would make national news in the hours ahead. And somewhere along the line, whoever had taken Dasha would see that their demands had been met.

From the moment he'd received the kidnappers' phone call, Zan had had no problem conceding to those demands. If it meant getting Dasha back, it was a done deal, whether or not the NPC could be persuaded to return the land when they learned that the transfer had been part of a ransom demand. Knowing the NPC, Zan suspected it would be no easy call, but right now all that mattered was getting Dasha back, in one piece. If her kidnappers kept their word, she ought to be released some time after the transfer was confirmed. Later that day. Maybe sooner.

Just so long as they kept their end of the bargain.

Thinking back, it astonished Zan that it had ever happened at all — getting that story on the news. By all accounts, he should have been bear turd up on the Hanish by now, or still crawling down to the trail-head. The various cuts and scrapes and bites he'd received from the bears had been treated and taped, but he could still feel the cub's jaws closing round his head and pressing down. According to the doctor, who'd visited earlier that morning, there'd been enough pressure to inflict a tiny hairline fracture along the lower edge of his skull.

Which was why, Zan supposed, he had the headache, barely mitigated by the drugs they'd administered, and the reason why his head spun if he moved too quickly. No wonder he'd been unable to focus on the drive down the Hanish Trail. Concussion was just the half of it.

Zan eased back in the bed and looked out on to the small well-tended garden courtyard outside his room. It had started to rain, tap-tapping at the window, the kind of rain that never looked up to much, but somehow always managed to find a way in and soak you to the skin. For a moment, lying there in his hospital bed, Zan remembered what it felt like to lie on a board down there in the bay and see the same patter of rain gently pucker the swells.

But thinking about the weather and old surf days wasn't going to get them anywhere and, snapping to, Zan decided on a plan of action. Reaching for the lift control on his bed he buzzed himself into a sitting position and carefully turned his head from left to right, noting gratefully that the pain behind his eyes seemed to be fading. His knee, too, was not as fiery or tender as it had been the night before, so long as he didn't try to bend it – pretty near impossible given the heavy bandaging. Swinging his legs round until he was sitting on the edge of the bed he reached for the monitor trolley and eased himself up on to his right leg. Taking a deep breath he then brought some weight to bear on his left leg. A wince of pain flared lightly. But it was a wince only. It was bearable. He could handle it. He'd have to handle it.

65

Sitting together in the back of the CTACtv van, Jenna and Pico watched the forty-second loop they'd filmed and sent to the studio. It began with Pico's long sweep of the Melville shoreline, then cut to Jenna standing on the sea wall with her back to the raging ocean. She watched herself push a whipping strand of hair behind her ear and start in.

'Here in Melville, one of the west coast's most celebrated surf beaches, surfers have left their boards at home today. It isn't that the waves are too high' – as if on cue, just behind her left shoulder, a massive wall of water toppled over into a churning roll of spitting fury – 'it's what's in them that's keeping everyone's feet dry.' She turned to the sea and Pico zoomed in on the sharks.

'According to locals,' Jenna continued in voice-over, 'the first sharks arrived late afternoon yesterday, and close on twenty hours later they're still here. Patrolling the shore from one end to the other, and back again.'

The tape cut to a grizzled old fisherman in a roll-neck sweater. With his weather-beaten cheeks and squinting blue eyes he'd have been a shoo-in as an extra for a Ralph Lauren knitwear ad were it not for the holes in his sweater and the lack of teeth. 'Used to have 'em like this back in whaling days. But that's been thirty years or more,' he told Jenna.

Next up was a surfer Jenna had found who certainly would have made the grade for that Ralph Lauren shoot. He was a typical surf boy, early twenties, long straggly blond hair that looked like it was stiff with salt, and a dazzling white grin that stretched a mile into creased suntanned cheeks.

'You go out surfin' in that,' he said, hooking a thumb over his shoulder, 'and it's not the waves gonna get you.'

With a final shot of shark fins breaking the surface and her sign-off, the screen cut back to the studio news-room. 'That was Jenna Blake, folks, out there on Melville Beach,' said the lunchtime anchor, shuffling papers behind his desk before turning to a second camera. 'And now, in other news this hour,' he began, 'as reported earlier, and in an extraordinary turn of events, Seattle-based architectural practice Pearse-Caine has today gifted sixty thousand acres of virgin forest to the National Parks in what insiders are saying is one of the biggest land hand-overs . . .'

'We back to town now?' asked Pico, turning away from the screen.

Jenna sat back in her chair, and gave her cameraman a contemplative look. 'Why don't we just hang round a while? See what happens,' she replied. 'Maybe get something bigger for the six o'clock?'

'Now how did I know you were going to say that,' grinned Pico.

66

If ever Shelley Caine had needed a drink, it was after Chief Mulholland came calling. Not a phone call, a personal visit. First thing. Breakfast time. Told her he'd called the night before as soon as he'd heard that they'd found Zan, but there'd been no reply. Shelley knew why she hadn't heard the phone. With the kids asleep, and the worry and all, she'd finished off the bottom end of a Jack Daniels bottle and started in on a fresh Jim Beam. She'd fallen asleep in her lounger which is where Finn and Alexa had found her just minutes before Chief Mulholland rang on her doorbell. In the time it took him to get up to her apartment, she'd run a comb through her hair, straightened her dress, and poured cereal for the kids. When she opened the door she reckoned herself presentable. While the kids made a mess of her kitchen table and argued over the TV remote, Chief Mulholland had sat her down and run her through what had been happening. Dasha kidnapped, ransom demands made, and Zan laid up in hospital pretty near eaten up by a grizzly by all accounts. For the sake of the kids, Mulholland told her, Zan had decided not to visit; he'd likely phone later, but didn't want to scare Alexa and Finn with his face all cut up and taped.

For Shelley, it was chilling confirmation of everything she'd felt the night before. Something just hadn't been right. Her daughter should have called. Zan should have called. The fact that they hadn't, and that she hadn't been able to get through to either of them, had filled her with an uncomfortable, anxious coil of dread. It had only been with Jack and Jim's help that she'd gotten any sleep at all. And next thing she knew, there was Big Bill Mulholland, sitting opposite her, telling her that they were doing all they could to find her missing daughter, that Zan had already acceded to the kidnappers' demands, and that they expected Dasha to be released as soon as news of the land transfer had been aired on radio and TV.

'Once they know they've got what they want, she'll be dropped off someplace,' Mulholland had assured her. 'She'll find herself a phone and call in, and we'll be there to fetch her. You see if I'm not right,' he'd told her, getting to his feet and reaching for that old bill-cap of his.

As soon as Mulholland had gone, Shelley had phoned the hospital, asked for Zan and been told to call back later. Her son-in-law was fine, they'd told her when she said who it was speaking, but he was still sleeping. Putting down the phone she wondered what to tell the kids. A surreptitious slug of Jim Beam in her coffee provided the answer.

'Your mama has been held up in Seattle,' she told them.

'I thought she was going to Wilderness,' squeaked Alexa.

'And so she did, my darling. But then, last night, she had to go into town. Seeing some clients, she is.'

'What about Dad?' Finn had asked. 'He was supposed to be back last night.'

'He's staying up in the hills an extra day, won't be back till later,' she lied smoothly. It seemed to work.

For the rest of the morning, Shelley had operated in a kind of daze, keeping up a perky front for the kids, yet worried sick for Dasha. Where could her daughter be? Who was holding her? Was she okay? It was those damn graffiti artists, she was certain, carrying through on their threats. And Zan, attacked by bears. It was all too much to take in – and her with the kids to look after. What on earth could she do to keep them entertained?

And then she had one of her bourbon brainwaves. 'I tell you what,' she said, warming up the remains of yesterday's fish pie for lunch, 'why don't we go see a movie? Special treat. There's always something for kids at the Delmont. Or the Drive-In. We could stop off for a pizza at Leoni's on the way back . . .'

The kids got very excited – what movies were showing? What kind of topping to the pizza? It was only then that Shelley realised there was a downside to this proposal. She'd have to make sure she didn't drink too much, or she'd never be able to drive.

And the one thing she really wanted right then, as the kids wolfed down the last of their fish pie, was another fortifying slug.

67

It had taken Zan just a few minutes to hobble from his hospital bed to the closet. When he got there, all he had found were his rain slicker and boots. The rest of his clothes were missing. It took him a moment to work it out – that his clothes had been soaked through and filthy, and that more than likely they'd been bagged up and stored someplace. In fact, he seemed to remember that his trousers had been scissored off him. But whatever had happened to them, he wasn't going to get anywhere in a hospital gown that came to his thighs and tied up the back. Knowing he wasn't going to get out of there without some help – and some heated objections from the medical team – he'd pulled the monitor clamp from his finger and waited. It hadn't taken long. Twenty seconds later a nurse pushed through the door.

'I need my clothes,' he told her. 'And I need them now.'

Just as he'd expected, there was every kind of objection. But he'd prevailed. His clothes had been brought to him and he'd clambered into them – cold and wet, the left trouser leg flapping open to the top of the thigh. Absolving the doctor of any blame, he'd called for a cab to take him home and, under a sea of disapproving looks from the nursing staff, he'd limped down to the entrance to wait for it.

By the time he got home, his knee was pulsing. But the pain was manageable. Bearable, just. He swallowed another of the painkillers he'd been given at the hospital dispensary and settled himself down by the phone.

There were more than a dozen messages waiting and he played them through one after the other in case there was something from Dasha or the kidnapper. There was nothing. Apart from a few domestic calls – their housekeeper calling to say she'd be delayed, some friends inviting them for Sunday lunch – every message was about the National Parks announcement.

The first call he made was to Shelley, running her through everything that had happened, assuring her that he was fine, that everything was being done to find Dasha and that he needed his mother-in-law to look after the kids just a little while longer. She could either stay where she was at The Quays, or bring them up to the house. Shelley told him she'd promised the kids a movie at the Drive-In and that it would be easier if they stayed where they were. Zan agreed and then asked to speak to them.

'When are you coming home, Papa?' asked Alexa.

Briefed by Shelley, he told his daughter that he was

274

up in the hills fishing and would be back either later that evening or the following day.

As Zan broke the connection, a thought suddenly occurred to him.

If he'd spoken to Dasha on his cell phone up at Bear Tree . . .

Heart thumping, he dialled another number.

'Chief, it's Zan Pearse. Any idea where my Jeep is?'

68

Jenna and Pico were celebrating their lunchtime news story with prettily decorated china flasks of warm sake and bamboo platters of nigiri sushi at Mama Surf's long bar when Jenna's cell bleeped.

'You still in Melville?' It was Gerry Coons at the studio.

'Just getting more on the shark story,' lied Jenna, cupping the phone to her cheek, hoping Gerry wouldn't pick up on the hubbub around her.

'Well, drop the sharks for now. There's been flood warnings coming in all morning for a half dozen counties out your way. The weather boys here are saying there's a shitload of rain coming down. Some weather front from BC that should have slid into Idaho got waylaid in the Silver Hills and is dumping fit to bust. There's also reports there are some high school kids rafting or boarding or something up around Shinnook. And you can't be more than an hour's drive away. If you can get any action, I'll give you a sixty-second lead for the six o'clock.'

'Why don't you send Nita and Sly? They're a lot closer than us,' tried Jenna, helpfully, hopefully, still wanting to follow up the sharks. Nita was Jenna's main competition for the outside news slots. A rain story would suit her well.

'Because we can't get to it from this side. Nita just called in. One of the bridges out of town is down and there's a tail-back on 101 right to the city.'

'But these sharks . . .' Jenna persisted.

'Sharks done. Flood waiting,' Gerry snapped and broke the connection. He must have known she hadn't packed an umbrella.

Jenna flipped her cell phone shut and turned to Pico who was pouring himself another slug of sake. 'Toss it back, bro,' she said. 'We're on the road.'

The rain had thickened since they'd dropped in at Mama Surf, the low drizzling shawls more insistent now. Unprepared for the downpour, they were soaked by the time they reached their van, and with every mile they drove out of Melville the rain worsened. Traffic was light but those cars that passed them all had their headlights switched on, as though they'd come through some nasty weather up ahead, and tyre spray billowed out from their wheel arches. By the time Pico took the van through Drivers' Cut the wipers were finding it hard to keep the windscreen clear.

It took them just over an hour to reach Shinnook where they came up against a police barrier on the far side of the town – a half dozen traffic cones set across the road leading to the Susqua and Hanish trails. The barrier was manned by two local cops, huddled in rain slickers by their squad car.

One of them came over to the van and Jenna wound down the window. 'CTACtv. What's the story?'

The cop ignored her question. 'Can't let you any further, miss.'

'Yeah, that's fine. Not a problem,' said Jenna in her most obliging voice. 'So what's happening? You got the look of a guy who knows what's goin' on.' Jenna flashed him her famous smile – confiding, intimate, flattering – and licked a fall of hair behind an ear.

The cop took her in – the smile, the friendly face – then looked back at his colleague. Rain coursed down from the plastic cover on his hat, dripped from the peak.

'Like I say, can't let you go no further. You'd just be two more people we gotta go in lookin' for.'

'There's people missing?' asked Jenna innocently, looking beyond the cop at the forested hills that rose above them. The trees seemed to be steaming, spiky layers of them drifting in and out of a low plug of cloud. Somewhere in the mist a loud, rolling crackle of thunder punctuated the spattering of rain, echoing down through the hills.

The cop looked back at his colleague again. There was seniority involved here, and Jenna knew he'd have to be careful what he said. But the famous Blake smile had clearly done its job.

'Far as we know it's a bunch of school kids,' he began.

'Some wild-water trip up in the gorges. The people who own the Lodge back in town said they saw them leaving yesterday, round midday. But no-one's seen nor heard of 'em since. We're getting some volunteers together to go look, but right now, we gotta keep this road closed.'

'How many in the party?' asked Jenna lightly. This was sounding better and better.

The cop shrugged. 'Half a dozen kids, plus teachers and guides. They took off in a couple of those mini-coaches.'

'So how far are these gorges?' As soon as she said it, Jenna knew she'd gone just one step too far.

The cop gave her a suspicious look. 'Like I said, miss, I can't go letting anyone through.'

'No, no. I understand that. And it's not a problem. In fact, we could do a piece right here. If that's okay? Just need some background.'

Hearing this, Pico switched off the engine, pulled himself out of the driver's seat and slid into the back of the van to start getting his gear together.

The cop watched every move, eyes flicking over Jenna's shoulder.

Jenna milked it. 'It's okay if we do that? I mean, right here? With you and the other guy by the barrier? That's all I'd need.'

Pico pulled open the side door and stepped out, leaning back in to wrap the camera and check batteries.

'Don't see it could do much harm, miss. But I'll have to clear it with my sergeant.'

With a nod and nervous smile at Jenna – she had cracked him – the policeman walked over to the barrier and conferred with his sergeant. Turning back to Jenna he lifted a hand and signalled it was okay to film.

Forty minutes later, Jenna and Pico checked into the Saw Mill Lodge in Shinnook and asked for a room with a balcony overlooking the hills and logging pool. The higher the better, she told the receptionist. Oh, and did they happen to have an umbrella? Ten minutes later, hair dried, some make-up applied, she had Pico film another face-to-camera piece.

'Make sure you keep the balcony rails out of shot and the roof too,' she told him, as he shouldered his camera. Stepping out on to the balcony, she opened her umbrella. 'It'll look like we're still out there. Getting soaked. Gerry'll like that.'

69

It never just rained, it poured, thought Chief Mulholland. For a Saturday morning, after just a few hours' sleep, he'd have preferred a quieter time of it. Slow and easy. Melville-style. But that wasn't going to happen. As soon as he'd arrived back at the office after his visit with Shelley Caine and the pit-stop breakfast at RubyRay's, he'd found a stream of flood alerts building up on his desk. Bear attack, kidnap, some kids lost up on the Susqua, and now a stack of weather warnings to deal with.

With his bear attack victim resting up in hospital, the Shinnook boys dealing with lost kids and all formal procedures pertaining to Mrs Pearse's kidnap already in place – so far there'd been no sighting of her Lexus, and no response to his request for eco-terrorist information from down south – there wasn't much he could do until Special Investigator Davies made an appearance. Which no longer looked like it was going to happen any time soon. While Mulholland had been working on Ray's Breakfast Special, Mr *Dragnet* had left a message saying he'd been held up on a flooded section of the 101. Served him well, thought Mulholland, watching the rain slap against his office window. Trouble was, if he planned doing something about the storm alerts – and soon as he'd seen them, he'd known something needed to be done – he was going to have to deal with Mr David Pringle, who ran Melville's Works and Resources division from a plush suite of offices in the Town Hall. Problem was, on a Saturday afternoon Dave Pringle was tucked up at home and couldn't be convinced of any real threat down here in Melville.

'Far as it ever gets is Drivers' Cut,' Pringle told him testily when Mulholland called him up. 'Just spreads out after that and drains off. You know that well as me, Chief.'

Mulholland also knew that in Pringle's scheme of things, civic responsibility took second place to a TV ball game when it came to weekends.

'Best be prepared than not,' pushed Mulholland.

'I already spoke to Olympia,' Pringle replied, probably from the comfort of his Lazee-Boy recliner, remote in hand, volume down. 'They confirmed there might be risks further up, but assured me it was unlikely there'd be any problems down this end.'

'That's not what it says in these flood reports I'm getting from Seattle,' said Mulholland.

There was a patient sigh down the line. 'It's how you read 'em, Chief. It's how you read 'em. Flood reports and imminent flood warnings . . . well, see, they need to be considered in the context they're sent out. In this particular case, it sounds to me like someone up the ladder's looking to cover his ass.'

And that was all he could get from Pringle. With a curt 'Good day to you, Chief,' the man had rung off.

Putting down the phone Mulholland wondered who else he should talk to. If this came down to covering asses, he better make damned sure his own was suitably protected. If there was no-one prepared to put any faith in these weather reports, well he'd head upriver and take a look himself. Make his own judgement. He was pushing away from his desk when the phone rang.

He picked it up, listened a moment and then said:

'You're supposed to be in hospital.

'So you just worked that out, have you?

'And you reckon you can drive, do you?

'Where you callin' from?'

Mulholland nodded, thought for a moment, then said: 'Well, I tell you what. Why don't you get yourself down to that front gate of yours, and I'll drop by and pick you up. Not much you can do by yourself, now is there?'

'Give me an hour,' Mulholland said, and put down the phone.

70

Mungo was working on a Wave-Walker cedar fin when Miche's elder brother, Paulie, knocked on the door of his workshop and put his head round.

'Hey, Board Boy, how's it going?'

'Hey there, Makah Man.' Mungo lay down his planer and waved Paulie in. Paulie was a couple of years younger than Mungo and a couple of inches taller. He was married, had three kids and lived out the far end of North Bluff Road, up towards Totem Hill. He wore his hair long, loosely tied between his shoulder blades, and his face was round, brown and heavily pockmarked. The two men clashed knuckles, hugged.

'I was looking for Miche,' said Paulie, casting around the workshop. 'She's not out front.'

'She's on a trip with Charlie Gimball. Up on the Susqua. Left yesterday, back tomorrow. Didn't she say?'

Paulie shook his head and suddenly looked anxious.

'Anything the matter?' asked Mungo, noting the look.

For a moment Paulie said nothing, as though he was embarrassed. Then he realised it was Mungo he was talking to. 'Maybe nothing, I don't know. But Gramps has got it in his head we all – the family – we gotta look out. Keep close, you know? Put the word out we should check on each other.'

'Reckon Old Jimmy's a guy worth listening to,' said Mungo, who'd only got to know the old fella after starting up with Miche. Back in the whaling days, Jimmy had been a famous Spotter – hence the 'Looking-Eyes' – and the way Miche told it, her grand-daddy had the same 'looking eyes' when it came to dealing with the spirits of his Makah ancestors – about as close to a Makah shaman as it got. 'He worried about anything in particular?' asked Mungo, thinking of the sharks and the swells out in the bay. He'd been feeling odd about that, himself. More than twenty years surfing those breaks and he'd only ever seen a couple of sharks. Now there were hundreds of them out there.

'You know Gramps. He says something, we all listen. Sometimes we go along with it, sometimes we don't.'

'And this time?'

'This time we do. Because he's sure worried about something. Maybe a couple more days and it'll be past. Back to normal. But for now . . .' Paulie shrugged. 'I just wish she wasn't up there,' he continued. 'Weather boys are saying there's some big rain coming.'

'Miche knows the score. She'll be fine.' Mungo checked his watch. 'Couple of hours they'll be paddling in for cocktails and tall stories.'

Five minutes after Paulie left, with a promise to keep in touch, Mungo blew a layer of sawdust off his cell phone and punched in Miche's number. Just in case.

283

He got her voicemail: 'Hi, I'm not here right now. Leave a message and I'll get back to you.'

Mungo smiled. That voice of hers – all breathless and backwoods husky – just did it for him.

71

Deputy Craven of the Shinnook Sheriff's department was getting just a tad weary. And wet. For the last half hour, since his sergeant had taken the squad car and headed back into town, he'd been sheltering under a stand of spruce near the up-country road-block, thinking about that lady reporter from Seattle, and when exactly his sergeant intended sending someone back to relieve him. Not that the barrier needed much in the way of policing. So far the only vehicles that had gone through were the two vans with search volunteers aboard, maybe a dozen locals crammed inside, windows creamed with condensation, rain slanting through the beams of their headlights and hammering in a halo of mist off their roofs.

All in all Craven was surprised they'd managed to round up so many volunteers. It had to be raining pretty damn hard up here in Shinnook before anyone took too much notice. Last time the town was hit by a flood, he'd been a kid and the run-off hadn't gotten high enough to get him sent home from nursery, let alone needing search parties for a bunch of high-school kids who'd likely called it quits the end of the first day and headed off home without telling anyone.

All a lot of fuss about nothing, 'cepting him having to stand out in the damn rain and listen to the marmots whistle.

Suddenly there was a burst of static from his radio. 'Craven? You there?'

'Yeah, Sarge. It's me.'

'How's it going? The search crews back yet?'

'They only just went up not twenty minutes back, Sarge.'

'Well, wait till they're back down, you hear? Then grab a lift with them. Shouldn't be long now.'

Shit, thought Craven, holstering the radio on his belt. Shit, he could be here hours yet. He looked at his watch. And less than an hour till his shift ended, goddammit.

It was then that something caught his eye, moving out of the trees on the other side of the road and sliding on to the road like a long brown snake. Thinking he'd go take a look, just to pass the time as much as anything, Craven pulled up his collar and jogged across the road. Soon as he got there he could see it was a stream of chip-bark sliding along the path that led to a picnic area beside the river no more than a hundred feet off through the trees. Had to be run-off surely, thought Craven. The river couldn't have risen that much. Last time he'd seen it, coming up from Shinnook with the Sarge, the current had sure looked weighty but it wasn't any way near what you'd call high.

A ripple of thunder rolled down from the hills and crackled overhead as he headed on through the trees to go check it out. Five minutes later he stepped out into the picnic area and gaped. A couple of miles downriver from where the Susqua and Hanish streams came together, the newly formed Susquahanish was higher than Craven had ever seen it, pretty much contained by the slope of the land on the far side but splashing up over the bank closest to him, streaming past a line of picnic-tables and picking up some bulk as he watched it.

He was reaching for his radio, thinking he'd better call this one in, when a roaring sound filled his ears. It came from upriver, and he turned in that direction. For three, maybe four seconds, there was nothing to see, just the sheeting rain, a coppery pelt of river and shadowy treelined banks curving round to the left. And then one of the rescue volunteer vans came tumbling round the bend, rolling side over side like a silvery yule log ahead of a tidal wave of debris that was now turning and heading straight for him.

Craven wasn't stupid. He was young and he was fit and if he moved fast he knew he could make it back into the trees and maybe find something to climb or cling on to before the wave reached him. He'd certainly be safer in the forest than just standing there on the bank gawping, waiting to be wiped out. So he spun round and started back down the path, splashing through the trees, looking for a likely refuge, then remembered that the other side of the road-block the land started to rise. Higher ground. If he could make it there, he stood an even better chance.

Seconds later he came out on to the road, the half dozen traffic cones he'd put up as a road-block carried off by the flooding and already a hundred yards down the slope. The water hit him when he was halfway across the road. The tree cover may have slowed down the deadly roll of debris but it hadn't stopped the flood, which came shooting through the trees like a high-pressure jet, a wall of hissing horizontal surf that snatched away Craven's hat, smacked against his shoulders and wiped his feet from under him. In a second he was spun like a pinball through the stand of trees on the far side of the road.

There was nothing he could do to protect himself.

He made the higher ground, but he didn't do it alive.

72

Jenna flicked through the Saw Mill Lodge brochure she'd found on the bedside table.

Back in the summer of 1896, she read, *it took thirty-two white settlers and a hundred and fifty Chinese labourers three months to dig Shinnook's tear-shaped logging pool. Five miles below the confluence of the Susqua and Hanish streams, the pool is the only stretch of level ground in Shinnook. At its widest point the pool is three hundred metres bank to bank, more than twenty metres at its deepest point and nearly six hundred metres from the inflow channel to the barrage, the stone and log barrier that regulates the flow of the Susquahanish and keeps the pool full.*

Jenna went over the information a second time. And

then a third. It was always the numbers that did for her. 1896 the year. 32 settlers. 150 Chinese labourers. 3 months. 5 miles. 300 metres. 20 metres. 600 metres. And on, and on . . .

Jeez! They never ever made it easy, that was for damn certain.

Closing the brochure she tried to decide what she could use and what she should dump. She and Pico may have got the sign-off out on the balcony but she was still short a good intro, a little bit of local colour to place the piece, give it some resonance. It was always a delicate balance – colour and news – and she had to get it right. Too much travelogue and Gerry Coons would carve rather than cut. *It's news, baby. News.* That's what he was always telling her, and if she wanted that slot on the Six then that's what she was going to have to give him.

So far she and Pico had filmed at the road-block, got some footage at the Sheriff's Office where the search for the high school kids was being coordinated, and interviewed the Lodge manager who'd seen the party of high school boarders head off the day before – 'Met up with their guides in the parking lot, they did. Nice kids all of them. Well-behaved, good manners, you know?' All Jenna needed now was a good strong intro, to carry a flood story with no flood footage – the police barrier out of town had seen to that.

Lying beside her, Pico gave a soft snore and burrowed his head into her hip. She looked down at him, pushed aside a fall of his hair and smiled. Oh, to be a camera jack, she thought to herself. All you had to do was point the damn machine and pull the trigger.

Right from the start, driving out of Seattle, Jenna had known that this was how they were going to end up.

And he'd probably known it too. Easy on the eye, and easy company too, fun and sharp and bright. The way he looked at her, the way he smiled when she caught his eye. Rattling through the rain on Route 101, they'd traded resumes, talked music and books, TV and politics, and by the time they hit Melville she'd made up her mind. It was like they'd known each other for ever – and this was the day. And he was just a gorgeous-looking guy – straight, intelligent and no emotional baggage that she'd been able to dig up. Eight months out of a relationship, two months longer than her. As far as Jenna was concerned, it was simply a question of when and where, and sooner rather than later. If Gerry Coons hadn't called about the flooding, she'd have checked them into the motel she'd spotted at the top of Main Street. The enforced delay had only served to sharpen everything, and the Saw Mill Lodge was a far classier hang-out than the Melville Court. By the time they'd finished filming on the balcony, both of them were ready for it and Pico had made his play. He'd laid down the camera and just kissed her right there, under the umbrella, out on that balcony. And boy, could Pico Ramirez kiss.

But for now the kissing was done. There was work to do. She had to get her intro right. Closing her eyes, Jenna concentrated on the numbers and tried to get the balance right.

'Back in 1896, when timber was king and the saw mills were humming, it took some pretty tough men and a whole heap of dynamite to carve out the logging pool you can see just behind me, here in the old logging settlement of Shinnook. Today the pool's still here, but the loggers are long gone . . .'

No, no, no . . . thought Jenna. Gerry'd kill it dead.

'Back in 1896,' she began again, 'it took tough men and a ton of dynamite to carve out Shinnook's logging pool. Right now, though, the town is the base of operations for an ongoing search for six missing high-school kids on a wild-water . . .'

Beside her, Pico jerked his head up, wide awake. 'What was that?'

'What was what?'

'Can't you hear it?' he asked. Pushing aside the quilt, he crossed to the window and Jenna watched him slide open the balcony door.

Now she could hear something.

'Jesus,' he whispered. 'It's a goddam tidal wave.' Then he spun round. 'Where's my fucking camera?'

While Pico lunged for his equipment, Jenna leapt from their bed and ran to the terrace.

'What wave? Where . . . ?'

73

Three miles downstream from the police barrier and just a five-minute walk upstream from the Saw Mill Lodge, Selma Beggins turned left off Saw Mill Road and started out across Shinnook's North End Bridge. Sixty-feet long and wide enough for a single-lane black-top with a narrow sidewalk either side, the bridge spanned the newly formed Susquahanish and connected those houses on the north side of the logging pool and river with the centre of town. In fine weather, the bridge was a favourite photo-stop for visitors. Downstream lay the clustered shingle rooftops of Shinnook set around the logging pool and, beyond the pool's barrier, a curving valley of spruce-lined slopes dropped away to Drivers' Cut. Upstream, the distant ridges of the Silver Hills etched a sharp wooded profile against blue skies, with the Susquahanish rolling down from the treeline, cutting a coppery trail through an almost alpine meadowland of lush emerald green. But with rain pelting down and a lid of low black cloud screwed down tight over Shinnook and the surrounding hills, there wasn't much of a view to take in that Saturday afternoon.

Selma had just finished her shift at the town's Donut Parlour and was wishing she hadn't stopped at the Shinnook Mart to pick up groceries. The bags were heavy, her fingers were already beginning to burn with the weight and she was still a half-mile from home. Glancing ahead through the rain she spotted a familiar figure heading in the same direction. It was her neighbour's son, Gene Donnelly, hunched against the rain and halfway across the bridge, hood up and hands thrust into his pockets. If the rain hadn't been hammering down she'd have called out his name; instead she put on a spurt, planning to catch up with him and off-load some of the bags. At that moment sixty-year-old Walter Merivale drove his pale blue Chevrolet Sahara up over the ramp on the far side of the bridge, its tyres whumph-whumph-whumphing over the bitumen-covered sleepers. As they closed on each other, none of them noticed the river beneath.

Just minutes after sweeping up Deputy Craven, the Susquahanish broke through the treeline above Shinnook and powered down to the North End Bridge. A slip wave came first, like a fast silent ripple, a two-foot surge that stayed level, didn't crest, and didn't break. When this initial surge hit the four redwood pilings that supported the bridge it finally broke, four bow-waves of water detonating into the sky and washing up over the bridge's trellised handrail.

This sudden explosion of water drenched Selma Beggins and caused Gene Donnelly to leap away from it, stumbling off the narrow sidewalk into the path of the oncoming Chevrolet. If he'd lived, Walter Merivale would have recalled a shadow to his left suddenly looming towards him through a blurring sheet of water, followed by a hefty bump as Gene made contact with the Chevrolet's nearside fender and headlight. But Walter Merivale didn't live. Nor did Selma Beggins. None of them lived longer than the few seconds it took the following wave to reach them.

This main surge was substantially higher and stronger than its forerunner, a good fifteen feet above the river's usual level, which meant a good three feet above the bridge's handrail. While Jenna Blake was flicking through her brochure, with Pico sleeping beside her, the flood water broke over that handrail in a tarnished silver wall that swept Selma Beggins, Gene Donnelly and Walter Merivale's Chevrolet clean off the bridge.

For maybe another forty seconds North End Bridge held firm against the crushing power of the water and the wall of debris that jammed beneath its span. But then, with a shattering snap and wrench, it broke apart, torn through the middle, the two halves of the bridge swinging open like a pair of doors. In seconds, pieces of the bridge were snatched away by the raging torrent, sleepers and planking and flapping sheets of blanket-like black-top. In less than a minute only the bridge's stone mountings remained, built into the banks but already several feet beneath a rushing maelstrom of water.

74

At first Jenna Blake couldn't see anything. While Pico prepped his camera, not bothering to pull on any clothes, she peered through the rain, trying to locate the source of the rumbling. It sounded like low thunder, rolling down from the hills, sustained, growing in volume. And then, through the slanting, silvery rain, she saw it. A wave of water, far higher than anything she'd seen earlier that day down on Melville Beach, pushing ahead of it what looked like a churning knuckle-duster of grinding timber. She caught it in time to see it hurtle into the logging pool and smash through the boathouses that lined the bank, snatching up the wood-plank pontoons and fleets of canoes and sailboats that were moored there as though they were made of matchsticks, great sheets of planking whirling off the surf and sent spinning backwards into the cauldron that followed.

Still naked, Pico pushed past Jenna, hoisting the camera on to his shoulder and taking a bead on the action.

'Jesus Christ, it's coming right at us. It's gonna hit us . . .' said Jenna in a kind of disbelieving whisper as the massive tide swept across the parking lot and burst through the Lodge's front door four floors below, blasting into the foyer and sweeping all before it, a raft of creosote sleepers off the North End Bridge plunging through the swell and battering down a section of planked walls.

As the balcony she was standing on shuddered from the impact below, Jenna suddenly snapped to. 'Get me into frame,' she shouted at Pico. 'Get me into frame.'

'What're you talking about?' he screamed back, not taking his eye from the camera. 'You got no fucking clothes on . . .'

'Head. Just the head. Stand on that chair if you need the angle. You got sound?'

While Pico clambered on to the chair and tried to get her decently in frame, Jenna took five deep breaths and, glancing behind her, turned back to camera. Hair sweeping across her cheek, she launched into her report. No time for intros or local colour. No time to prep, no time to rehearse. This was real news, right on the line, and she had to get it right.

'Seconds ago, just four floors below us, a mighty wall of water from the flooding Susquahanish River swept into the old logging town of Shinnook, out here in Melville County . . .'

Cutting between Jenna and the flooding below, Pico had filmed approximately fourteen seconds of film when the two balconies between them and the corner of the Lodge pulled away from their supports and tilted over, tables and chairs spilling over the railing. Pico swung away from Jenna and focused on the action now no more than twenty feet away from them.

'As you can see, the force of the water is so great that it's literally tearing this old wood-built lodge apart,' Jenna continued in voice-over. 'Right now we have no real idea how many people have been caught in the flood, swept away or been trapped like us in their homes, wondering just how high and strong this water is going to get. And just how much danger we're in.'

There was a tremor in her voice, and she might have looked scared for the camera, but Jenna Blake was surprised to discover that she felt no real fear. Despite the disaster unfolding around her she felt somehow removed from it, and the realisation gave her a jolt of confidence. This was what the job was about – if you were lucky enough to be in the right place at the right time. And this was how you played it.

Forget sharks. This was the story. Here. Now. And she was doing it. Doing it better that she'd ever done it before.

Up on his chair Pico turned the camera back on her but after a few moments he started pulling his finger across his throat. Cut . . . Cut . . . Cut . . .

What the fuck? thought Jenna. What the fuck did he want to cut for?

'I don't know how much longer we can stay here, or continue to film . . .' she began, but the next thing she knew Pico was hefting the camera off his shoulder and shaking his head.

'. . . Because your cameraman's out of power,' he told her, clambering down from the chair.

Standing naked on the balcony, feeling a chill rain trickle down her back, Jenna tried to take this in.

'But . . . but you've got spares, right? You have got spares, haven't you? Please tell me you've got 'em right here and not left 'em in the fucking van . . .'

Pico looked away, then back at her. He put down the camera and spread his hands. 'The van,' he said quietly.

'Well, then you're just gonna have to go down there and find the fuckin' things . . .'

So much for sloppy cameramen who weren't bothered about flat light, she thought, pushing past him into the bedroom, spitting with irritation. When she needed Frederick fucking Fellini, what did she end up with? A great lay, maybe, but a cameraman who ran out of batteries.

Now that she'd slept with him she could say that.

75

Judd Nichols was one of the last loggers left in Shinnook. Twenty years earlier, after a slab of timber crushed his foot, he'd taken early retirement and, with his wife, Nona, had stayed on after the logging stopped, turning the family home on the North End bank into guest accommodation. To supplement this income, he'd also negotiated a part-time job as the log-pool barrier supervisor, responsible for the sluices that controlled the log-pool's water level. Too tight and the water could rise dangerously high, too loose and the surface dropped, revealing an evil-smelling sludge below the grassed and pontooned banks. What with the kind of rainfall they got in these parts, you needed to keep an eye on that water, know what was happening back up in the hills, and there wasn't anyone who knew those hills or the Shinnook log pool better than Judd Nichols.

Most times all he had to do was step out on his porch after breakfast, light his pipe and just take a squint at the pool. Sometimes he could go days at a time without needing to adjust the outflow, and in the last week he'd made the twenty-minute journey round the pool path to the control hut just the once. But like everyone else in Melville County Judd Nichols had seen the weather reports, knew what was headed their way. Not that he was too concerned. This time of year, those fronts came down from BC regular as clockwork. Year in, year out, come late September they settled a little juice on the hilltops but stored the rest of it for the dry plains of Idaho. It was the way these things worked. Idaho got it from up north, Shinnook got it from the ocean. And never the two of them met. The way it was.

That morning, however, stepping out on to the porch, he'd hardly been able to see the pool through the rain, and as for the old saw mill over the other side, why it was just a murky shadow shifting through the downpour. An hour later he was round at the sluice control hut and, just as he'd reckoned, the levels were well up. Unlocking the control grid, he'd opened three of the five sluice gates, raising the left and right gates by three inches and the centre gate by another two.

But the rain had kept coming, heavier and heavier through the morning, and stepping out after lunch Judd just knew he'd set the openings too low. If he left it another twenty-four hours the water would be lapping through the slats on the jetty at the end of his garden, and flooding Nona's vegetable patch. There'd be hell to pay.

With no road round the pool it was a fine walk for most, with great views on a clear day – up into the hills and down towards the Cut. When your left foot was mashed, and the weather was chill, it wasn't such fun. But he got there in the end, whistling in his labrador, Dixie, and unlocking the control hut door. Out of the rain, the dog shook itself dry and settled under the control desk while Judd checked the dials. Even with the sluices opened up earlier that morning, the water level was still steady. All he'd done was balance it out. But judging by the clouds crowding down from the hills, he'd need a little extra to keep it that way.

Flipping all five switches, giving each sluice a further three inches, he listened to the lifting gear power up and seconds later a steady whine told him the gates were starting to open below him. Going to the valley window, he looked down at the river bed sixty feet below him, a gush of water streaming from the opened gates, pushing out a swell of white tops across its surface and sending up a fine spray into the beating rain.

Behind him, under the desk, Dixie started to bark.

'Quiet girl. Won't be long now,' Judd called out, limping back to the control desk and settling himself down with his pipe. Give it thirty minutes and he'd half-close two of the gates and leave the other three where they were. That should sort it.

He was tamping down a wad of soft tobacco in the bowl of his pipe when Dixie sprang out from under the desk and jumped up at the window, pawing the glass and barking.

Judd was just about to kick out with his good foot and give the dog something else to think about, when he spotted a movement across the pool, through the rain. Putting down his pipe and tobacco pouch, he pushed up from his chair and went to the window. Not sure whether it was the mist outside, or condensation inside, he rubbed the glass with his sleeve. It was condensation, and through the semi-circular wipe, he saw what looked like a mess of timber cascade over the inflow channels below North End Bridge.

It was just like the old days – summer timber launched on to a winter stream from the logging camps up in the hills, and coming down to the saw mill. But this wasn't the old days, and no timber had come down that river in twenty years.

It wasn't just timber either. Behind it came a wall of water sweeping all before it. Standing there at the window, unable to fully comprehend what he was looking at, Judd saw the wave race through the boat sheds and pontoons on the saw mill side, and tear through the line of jetties along the North End bank.

And down the middle of the pool, with nothing to slow it, the water powered towards the barrier and control hut, a curving face studded with all manner of tumbling debris.

'Lord A'mighty . . .' was all Judd managed, before the rising wave slammed into the control hut and broke over the barrier.

76

Fucking camera jacks. Fucking, fucking camera jacks.

That was all Jenna could think of as she struggled into her jeans, lost her balance and fell back on the bed. Here she was about to scoop the biggest news story of her career – a real live fucking disaster story, for christ's sake – and her fucking cameraman was out of batteries. Or rather, he had batteries but they just happened to be down in the fucking van, which he'd parked outside the fucking Lodge, which had just been hit by a fucking tidal wave.

Please God, please God, let the van be down there somewhere, she prayed, pulling on her jacket as she followed Pico out into the corridor. And if the van was down there, please God, please God, let them find the batteries. It looked pretty damn certain that they'd never be able to transmit live, but if they found the battery packs at least they could tape some major eye-witness footage and get it out of there as soon as the roads were clear. Christ, with the kind of film they'd be getting, Gerry'd send them a fucking helicopter. Because one fucking thing was certain. She was not going to fail. This story was big, and it was hers, and she was damn well going to get it on film if it was the last thing she ever did.

Outside their room, the fourth-floor corridor was empty. And tilting. Just a degree or two off the level, but the Indian-pattern runner down the middle of the passageway was rucked and clearly sloped on its way to the lifts. Not that either Jenna or Pico were planning on taking a lift. Instead they went to the main staircase and peered down the stairwell. Four floors below what had earlier been a nest of elkhorn chairs around a magazine table, was now a raging mass of water, a spray of it arching out from the banisters it sluiced through, and giving a very clear idea of the water's power. You didn't want to get caught in that, thought Jenna.

Shouldering his camera, even though the power was out, Pico led the way down the stairs, keeping to the wall, the two of them occasionally going to the banisters and leaning over, but always returning to the wall.

At no time on their way down did they see another soul – three corridors of rooms apparently empty. Somehow Jenna wasn't surprised. At this time, on a Saturday afternoon, she reasoned, all the guests would have been downstairs – in the Sawyers' Bar, or out on the covered Log Pool terrace, or in the large sitting room with the crossed whipsaws above the fireplace, or in town shopping for postcards and souvenirs. As far as she could see, peering over the banisters, everything on the ground floor was well under water, and anyone who'd been down

301

there when the flood hit had either been crushed to death or swept away.

Slowly, cautiously, the two of them made their way down the stairs, the sound of the water in the foyer below increasing dramatically with every step, until a blast of stale, foetid air suddenly reached up at them.

'Jesus, that stinks,' shouted Jenna.

'You what?'

'I said it stinks. The water.'

Coming down off the first floor, they stopped on the half-landing above the last flight of stairs. Twenty feet below all they could see was a surging race of murky, muddy water, sluicing up around the banisters. Pico parked his camera against the landing wall and set off down the last few stairs, clinging to the rail when he reached the water, leaning down to get a better view of the reception area and some sense of the extent of the flooding.

He turned back to Jenna on the landing. There was a smile on his face. 'You know we left the van in the parking lot out front?' he shouted up.

'You. Not "we". You left it in the parking lot. And? So? Can you get to it?'

'Don't have to,' said Pico. 'It's about thirty feet away, wedged between reception and the bar.'

'You're kidding me!' shouted Jenna, thinking *thank you God, thank you God*.

'So you want me to go get the batteries?'

'No, just book us in for a spa, maybe dinner,' Jenna retorted. 'Of course I want the fucking batteries. And I want them just as damn quick as you can manage it.'

Coming down the stairs behind Pico, Jenna leant down and looked for herself. And there was the van, just as

Pico had described it, jacked up on its front end in the middle of the foyer, its front wheels well below surface level, its rear offside tyre a couple of feet above it, and floodwater streaming over its bonnet and in through the broken windscreen. As far as she could see, their van was not going any place, anytime soon. All they had to do was get to it and find those batteries.

Back on the landing Pico told Jenna what he planned. On the landing above was a fire hose. If they took it off the reel and tied it to the banister, the flow of the water would stream it towards the van and provide him with the lifeline he'd need to cross thirty feet of fast moving water, four feet deep, and get back again.

'You think you can do it?' asked Jenna.

'You want the batteries, there's no choice.'

'Okay, *muchacho*, let's go get that hose,' she replied.

77

The flood crest from the combined Susqua and Hanish streams hit Shinnook just seconds after Zan Pearse and Chief Mulholland crossed Drivers' Bridge and swung out from the Cut into Shinnook Valley. Ahead, through the Durango's rain-blurred windscreen, the land began to rise and steepen, road and river cutting shiny black paths through emerald pasture, the slopes either side of them darkly forested and the distant hills shrouded in drifting mist and shawls of rain.

Somewhere up there was his wife, Zan thought. He was certain of it. Not down in Melville, not in Shinnook, but up in those hills. Just being this close – and getting closer with every minute – made him feel better, stronger.

They'd been on the road an hour now, and for most of that time Zan had been working the muscles in his left thigh and calf, switching to his toes when the pain in his knee kicked in, curling them backwards and forwards as though trying to relieve a cramp. And the effort – and the painkillers he'd swallowed before leaving the house – seemed to be paying off. Wrapped tightly in the bandages, his knee may have been all but immobilised but the stretching of muscles seemed to have restored some strength and flexibility.

As promised, Mulholland hadn't bothered to come up to the house on South Bluff Drive. He'd done what he said he'd do on the phone, just waited there in the turning circle in his mud-brown Durango with its gold Sheriff's shield on the doors, watching Zan hobble down the drive.

'Reckoned if you couldn't make it to the gate by yourself, then you weren't going to be much use to me,' he'd said, as Zan levered himself into the passenger seat.

'Well, thanks for that Sheriff,' Zan had replied, trying to make himself comfortable and wincing with the effort.

Glancing across at his passenger Mulholland had caught the wince as it creased through Zan's cheeks, thinning his eyes and lips. As well as being worried sick, it was clear the man was hurting. He may have managed to hobble down to the front gates, but his face was pale and his left cheek tattooed with a curving line of iodined puncture wounds from his encounter with the grizzlies. He looked, thought Mulholland, like a man who could sleep for a week. But somehow Zan Pearse was managing to hold himself together.

'You sure you want to do this?' asked Mulholland, as he put the Durango into gear, hauled her round in the turning circle and headed back to town.

'Let's just get to Shinnook, Chief. Fast as you like. See what we can arrange from there. I know she's up in those hills somewhere and I know that we can find her.'

'It's a pretty big bit of jungle, Rambo. Gonna take some time if this rain keeps coming.'

'It's not going to last,' said Zan. 'That's what the weather boys say . . . just some isolated flooding, they said, and easing up by nightfall.'

Mulholland tried to remember what Pringle had said to him. '*It's how you read 'em, Chief. It's how you read 'em. Flood reports and flood warnings . . . well, see, they need to be considered in the context they're sent out.*' Mulholland liked that bit – *considered in the context they're sent out.* Yup, that had a ring to it.

'Soon as the rain stops,' continued Zan, 'we can get some teams up the Hanish, maybe even find someone at Forestry to lend us a chopper.'

Mulholland grunted. 'Never much liked choppers,' he said. 'Just don't see how they stay up there without wings. Me? I like wings.'

It didn't take long for Melville to drop behind them and for the first few miles out of town, the two men hadn't spoken much, lulled by the drone of the wind-screen wipers, and the swish of the Durango's tyres over the two-lane black-top as it followed the Susquahanish rolling smoothly past on its way to the sea. As far as Mulholland could see the river looked full but not especially high, muscling its way between meadowland banks but in no way bullying or cantankerous. Maybe Pringle was right, Mulholland thought to himself. Maybe it was how you read those alerts.

'You eaten today?' he asked, as they swung past Cedar Creek gas station.

Carefully, Zan shook his head.

'No breakfast at the hospital? Lunch?'

'This and that.'

Mulholland took this in. After a moment, he said: 'Got some of the wife's Whale-Watchers in the glove there, you fancy one. Don't want you passin' out on me on account your blood sugar's too low.'

'The blood sugars are fine, Chief. But a cookie sounds good.' He leant forward, flipped down the glove panel.

'In the tin there,' said Mulholland. And then: 'You got it.'

Levering off the lid, Zan dug one out, then offered the tin to Mulholland.

'Well, seems a shame to miss the opportunity,' he said, and felt around, pulled one out. 'I just love 'em,' he said, settling the cookie into his cheek. Then he chuckled. 'In moderation, of course.'

Whale-Watchers were an old Melville favourite. A little larger than a dollar piece, as thick and dirt brown as a dog biscuit, they were just the right size to pop whole in your mouth and suck on. Like real dog biscuits, they didn't melt or soften or make crumbs, so you could always keep some handy in a pocket. They were made with a healthy dose of caffeine in the mix, and a high cacao count, and locals joked that a Melville Whale-Watcher could wake a dead man. They were sharp and bitter – an acquired taste, most folks said – but they were warming, too. For tourists and out-of-towners a commercial brand – Withnell's Whale-Watchers – could be bought at Delaney's Mart, or the souvenir shops where they cost a dollar more. But anyone who'd lived in Melville longer than a generation knew that home-made ones, using some old family recipe, were the real deal. Out on some late-night road-traffic incident, a couple of his wife's Whale-Watchers and all of a sudden Mulholland's focus just snapped back in. Wide-awake. Any more cacao or caffeine in the mix, he reckoned they'd have to classify them amphetamines.

After finishing their Whale-Watchers, the conversation started up again, the two men still chewing their cheeks long after the cookies were gone.

'It's like you're looking for more chocolate, ain't it?' said Mulholland. 'Gotta be there someplace.' He laughed.

Zan laughed too, then gave a little grunt. 'Bit like Dasha. Out there someplace.'

'You never know,' said Mulholland, pulling a toothpick from his lapel. 'We get to Shinnook and your wife's maybe already been dropped off, reporting in. After that newscast, whoever's holding her got no reason to keep her. It's not like there's cash to get hold of, and a drop-off arranged. It's done. Ransom paid.'

It sounded good, but Mulholland knew in his heart it was a long shot.

Zan also knew that it was an optimistic take on the

situation, a thin splinter of hope, but he clung to it – that Dasha would be there, dropped off by her kidnappers, reporting in just like Mulholland had said. Or that they'd find her, beside the road somewhere, heading into town. Another twenty minutes and they'd be there, he thought, and as they passed the memorial plaque on Drivers' Cut, and rumbled over the bridge, he started in on his leg-work again.

They were just straightening out after coming through the Cut when a buzz of static flared on the radio, a police despatcher calling Chief Mulholland.

Still sucking at his teeth and cheeks for the last shreds of Whale-Watcher, Mulholland reached for the mike, freed the loops from the gear stick and pressed transmit.

'Mulholland here . . .'

There was a short pause, then another voice took over from the despatcher.

'Bill? It's Slater.'

Zan stiffened. Jim Slater was the Sheriff up in Shinnook. Had something happened? Something to do with Dasha?

'Hey, Jim, how're things?' replied Mulholland. 'We're about fifteen minutes away, just out of the Cut and . . .'

A blast of static suddenly screamed from the speaker. Even with the volume down, it sounded fearsome. Mulholland jiggered the transmit button a couple of times, like that was the way to clear static.

'Jim? You there?'

When they heard Slater's voice again, he sounded distant, distracted, like he was talking to someone else, calling out to someone in another part of the office.

And then: 'Jesus H! What the f—?'

With a strange little click, the line went dead. No static. Nothing.

'Did I just hear what I think I heard?' asked Zan.

Mulholland tried the transmit a couple more times, but finally replaced the mike in its holder, a frown creasing his brow. 'Sure not the kind of thing I'd expect from Slater,' he replied. 'Sounded like he just got a shotgun put up his ass.'

Up ahead on the left the clustered shingle rooftops of Shinnook came into view round the side of the valley, and the meadowland they'd been passing through on the Melville side of the Cut gave way to a steeper prospect, the trees dropping down towards them, the river and road closing on each other, just a metal barrier between the black-top and a steep stony slope down to the river.

Mulholland peered ahead, hunched over the wheel. 'You see that?'

Zan followed his gaze, but didn't know exactly where to look, or what to look for. Then something caught his eye, like smoke billowing up from between the rooftops of Shinnook, as if something was on fire in the old logging town. He half expected to see flames flicker through the smoke. But they didn't. Just smoke, drifting across the rooftops.

'Looks like smoke,' said Zan. 'A fire maybe?'

'Bad luck in weather like this,' replied Mulholland, still frowning, still peering ahead. 'You ask me . . .'

The two men realised what it was at exactly the same moment. Not smoke, but a vast torrent of water bursting over the log pool barrage and streaming out of town, a mess of timber and debris charging along at its head and racing down the black-top all the way to the Tacoma turning.

Jamming on his brakes, Mulholland pulled in at the side of the road. Pushing open his door, he clambered out on to the running board for a better look. 'Holy Mother . . .'

In seconds the wall of water had reached the Shinnook–Tacoma fork, blasted across the black-top, and climbed up the slope on the far side, a great curving wall of water as high as the treeline and now bearing down on the only other cars on the road, a pair of them a half-mile back from the fork, their distant desperate brake lights glaring angrily through the rain.

But stamping on their brakes was all the drivers in those cars could do as the water surged towards them. No chance to turn, or reverse, or race away. No possible chance of saving themselves – and whoever else was in the cars with them. In an instant they were gone, lifted up by the wave, rolled a couple of times then simply swallowed up.

Through Mulholland's open door, over the rattling of the rain on the Durango's roof, Zan could hear it too. A low swishing drone like lorry tyres over a wet surface, still some distance off but headed in their direction and growing in volume.

Any minute now and it was going to reach them.

'Chief!' he called out. 'Chief, I think we better get ourselves . . .'

But Mulholland didn't need to be told. Nor did he need to be told there was no chance now of them outrunning the flood, turning and heading back the way they had come. It was already too late for that.

Dropping back in the driver's seat, he rammed the Durango into gear and gunned its big V-6 engine. Spinning the steering wheel to the right he left the black-top and started up the slope, heading for the tree-line, away from the road. Slipping and sliding in the rain-sodden turf, tyres spinning and churning for grip, he was making for higher ground.

As fast as he could.

78

It didn't take long for Jenna and Pico to secure the fire hose to the banister rail and play it out into the water surging through the foyer. As Pico had guessed the length of canvas snaked out towards the van. All he had to do was hang on tight and get pulled along by the current. It would be harder coming back, of course, fighting against the flow, but still possible, even with the power packs.

Pulling off his shoes and his jeans, Pico went down into the water stair by stair, with Jenna watching. Suddenly she wanted to reach out, touch him. Suddenly, she was frightened for him. The feeling surprised her.

'Shit, but it's cold!' he shouted back at her, as the water piled around his legs, then climbed to his hips, one hand gripping the banister, the other getting a hold of the hose. 'Here goes nothing,' he shouted, and letting go of the banister he sank into the stream and let the current take him.

Coming down the stairs so she wouldn't lose sight of him, Jenna kicked off her shoes and took just the one step down into the flood. Immediately she felt the water start tugging and pulsing around her ankles as it raced across the stairs and through the rails, and she reached for the banister to steady herself against the flow. He was right. It was cold. Damn cold.

Riding the stream, clinging to the hose, floodwater spraying up over his head and shoulders, it took Pico no time at all to reach the van. In less than thirty seconds she saw him scramble up on to the bonnet and reach round for the driver's door, higher above the water than the passenger side and closer to the wall. Jenna let out a squeal of delight which he must have heard over the roar of the water because he turned and raised a triumphant clenched fist, before clambering inside the truck and looping the hose through the steering wheel. Then he slid between the two front seats and climbed up out of sight into the back of the van.

Three minutes later – though it seemed a lot longer to Jenna, now up to her knees in the freezing, swelling water – Pico was back, manoeuvring himself between the driver's door and the lodge wall, two belts of power packs over his shoulder. Pulling the hose loose from the steering wheel and swinging the belts round his neck so they hung down his back, he slid across the bonnet and dropped into the water.

Jenna watched him drag himself towards her. Hand over hand, he hauled himself forward, his head turned against the current now pummelling his chest and spraying up around his shoulders. He was trying so hard, being so brave, and without warning Jenna felt a warm and unexpected spread of affection for him. She wasn't sure that she'd have been able to do it herself – it was not so much the strength, but the nerve. Even if it had meant not getting her hands on the power packs, and not getting her footage. She sensed, too, that he was doing it for her, not for any filming, not for the studio, and not just because he'd been the one who'd left the power packs in the van. He was doing it for her, she was sure of it. Doing it because he didn't want to let her down.

'Come on, *muchacho*,' she shouted. 'Not far now.'

He turned his head to look at her, and through the spraying water she could see there was a smile on his face – that he'd actually managed to get this far, that he'd so nearly done what he'd set out to do – and the smile widened the closer he came.

He was no more than six feet away from her, one hand holding the hose, the other now pulling the belts over his head, when he suddenly seemed to lose his grip, the strip of canvas slipping through his fist. As if sensing a weakness, the floodwater pounced on him, swirled up over his head and hauled him down, just his arm and the power packs waving above the surface. Seconds later, his head broke through the streaming wash and Jenna saw him tip back his face to keep his mouth clear of the surging water, and gulp in air, one hand still clinging stubbornly to the hose and the other holding the battery packs out of the water. He wasn't smiling now, and for the first time since he'd set out for the van he looked frightened.

'Just hold on,' Jenna shouted, coming down a couple

more steps, the water twisting and coiling around her waist. She reached for the hose, got both hands round it and tried to pull it in.

'No, no, no,' Pico spluttered. 'You'll never do it. Here,' he shouted, and, swinging both belts round his head, he flung them past her on to the stairs.

'Just reach out then!' Jenna screamed, letting go of the hose and stretching out as far as she dared. 'And come closer. Closer.'

But the throw had tipped him off balance. Pico made a wild grab for the hose with his free hand, but missed it, and plunged back under the water. Only this time he didn't resurface. There was no sign of him. All she could see was the hose dipping and digging into the flood, like a giant fishing line with a giant fish on the end of it. Pressing herself against the banister, her body held there by the force of the water, she reached again for the hose and tried to draw it back, tried to reel him in. But the hose was too heavy, too unwieldy, and the current too strong for her.

Then, suddenly, he was up again, spluttering and spitting, black hair plastered across his face, both hands gripping the hose now, desperately trying to pull himself towards her. But he was weakening, unable to get any real purchase, just hanging on to the line now. And the freezing torrent, Jenna could see, was getting the better of him, the hose slipping in jerks through his fingers.

'Get back to the van,' she shouted. 'Just get yourself back to the van.'

But there was no time for that. With a splintering crack, the wood column they'd tied the hose to snapped clean in half and the knotted hose sprang free.

As Jenna watched, Pico's head was pulled beneath the surface and he was gone.

'Pico!' she screamed out. 'Pico . . .'

79

While Chief Mulholland fought the mud and the slope and wrenched at the steering wheel, the Durango sliding and jolting over the hazardous terrain, Zan kept his eyes on the crest of water surging down the valley towards them. As far as he could tell it was no more than twelve feet high, the kind of wave he'd have left for less experienced surfers in the days when he paddled out for the breaks in Melville Bay. What worried him about this particular break, hurtling down the Shinnook road and riding up their side of the valley, was its speed and its weight. And its evident savagery. Though not as high as the telegraph poles that marched along the side of the road, it snapped them off, one after the other, to join a tangled mess of other debris breaking through the surf.

'Getting closer, Chief,' warned Zan, not wanting to upset his driver but keen that he should know what was happening, that the torrent was gaining on them.

'Ain't gonna get us. Ain't gonna get us,' Mulholland replied through gritted teeth, shoulders hunched, fists clenched to the wheel, willing his vehicle onwards and upwards. Never once did he take his eyes off the route ahead, all the time wrestling with the muddy swings and slides of the pasture, watching out for those innocent-looking depressions that he knew would halt them in their tracks. 'We get to the trees, we'll make it. Wedge ourselves in,' he muttered, almost to himself, as though he was making up the plan as he went along.

Dragging his eyes away from the oncoming wave, Zan looked up the slope. The trees still seemed a very long way off, and the slope definitely steepened before it got there. There was also a solid-looking wood fence to negotiate. They'd have to get up a good head of steam to break through it without being brought up short and slipping back. If that happened, they'd be finished. The flood would have them.

Having already planned for this obstacle, Mulholland turned to the right, gunned the engine and came at the fence from an angle, midway between two posts, catching the rails with his nearside wing. For a second Zan saw the wood flex outwards, as though to accommodate the impact, as though it refused to do what they wanted, intending instead to catapult them back down the slope.

For an engine-grinding, tyre-spinning moment, the steering wheel juddering in Mulholland's hands, those wood rails slid by them, bending like rubber bands. And closing on them was a hefty post. Without saying anything, both men knew that if they hit that post it was all over.

Then, with a mighty crack, the rails finally snapped and the Durango leapt forward through the gap, like a straining dog released from it leash. Bucking and jolting the Durango roared upwards as though given a new lease of life, and a half dozen ponies that had been watching the charge at the fence now scattered, a pair of them bolting off towards the wave, their companions heading in the other direction.

But they still had to contend with the slope. Traction was rapidly becoming a problem and their speed was beginning to drop. And it wasn't just the increasing incline that was slowing them down. Creeping out of the tree-line were dozens of small, trickling run-off streams, no more than a few inches deep or wide but spreading through the grass towards them.

'Go right,' shouted Zan, pointing to a shallow depression where the land and the treeline dropped away a few feet.

But Mulholland had seen it too, knew they could use it. Stamping down on the gas, he swung the Durango over the bank, found some unexpected grip and powered across the bowl of land towards the treeline.

With just thirty feet to go they felt the first bouncing rattle of tree roots beneath their wheels, water from the streams trickling out of the treeline now spraying up from their wheel arches. But the roots provided grip and the Durango surged forward. As it made the first trees, Zan looked back in time to see the two horses that had bolted towards the wave be swept up by it and swallowed.

80

Jenna Blake had never felt more alone. And empty. And cold. And, yes, frightened. Like a little girl who'd lost her mummy and daddy and didn't know what to do next. It was as though all her thought processes had closed down. She sat on the half-landing and hugged her knees, wide eyes fixed on the surging water that had snatched Pico away. Suddenly the news story she'd so wanted to report didn't matter any more, the disaster unfolding around her just a white noise that had no meaning.

She had known Pico Ramirez for just a few short hours, but in that space of time he'd registered. He'd gotten to her. That soft, gentle voice, and those cool grey eyes. That flickering, uncertain smile, and that quiet, new-boy vulnerability. Right from the start, up there in the CTACtv briefing room, she'd felt strangely drawn to him, a feeling of rightness, a sense of comfort, that had grown on the drive out to Melville. Jenna had taken more than a few of her cameramen to bed – in her line of work they were often the only men she got to spend any time with – but she'd known right away that there was something different about this one. Not the usual kind of man she hooked up with, not the usual kind of camera jack. Someone special. Someone who could have been special if he hadn't been swept away by the flood, now dead, drowned, lost.

For the first time in a very long time Jenna felt her lips bunch and her throat catch and tears prickle at her eyes. It wasn't fair, it wasn't right . . .

And then, from behind her, she heard a voice.

'Jenna? You okay, Jenna?'

Jenna spun round. Pico was standing above her on the next landing. Sopping wet but alive. She struggled to her feet, raced up the stairs and flung herself into his arms.

'Hey, hey, hey,' he comforted her, feeling the sobs break through her.

'I thought you were dead,' she cried, tears spilling from her eyes. 'Drowned. I thought . . .'

'Me too,' he laughed. 'That water is way mean.' Gently he pushed her from him and looked down into her face. 'It's okay. It's okay. I'm here. I'm back.'

'How, I mean . . . ?'

Quickly, Pico ran her through what had happened. Instead of being sucked into the restaurant and out through the smashed terrace windows into the logging pool, he'd been hurled into the kitchen. Grabbing hold of some shelving, he'd worked his way to a back door, kicked it open and found a staff staircase leading to the floors above. 'Must be used for room service,' he told her. 'I just climbed up to the first floor and, hey presto!'

'You're hurt,' said Jenna, suddenly noticing a smear of blood across the side of his T-shirt.

319

'It's nothing,' said Pico, but he lifted the shirt and peered at the wound as if seeing it for the first time. The bleeding hadn't quite stopped. 'Just smashed up against something in the kitchen. Being wet makes it look worse.'

'You sure?'

Pico smiled. 'Hey, no problem. Really,' he said, reaching for his jeans and trainers. 'Just let me power up and I'm ready to roll. With the van like it is, we won't be going live any time soon. But we've got two belts, ten power packs, say twenty minutes' footage a pack. That should give us plenty enough to get one hell of a story.'

With the camera powered up, they started filming. First they showed the water pouring through reception and past their jammed van, making sure to catch its side-panel station logo. After that they worked their way up the floors, filming the flood from whatever vantage point they could find, their confidence and excitement growing with every phase they filmed.

From their first few feet of film it was clear they were stranded in the lodge. As far as they could see there was no way out, the floodwaters raging on three sides of the building: out over the logging pool, upstream towards the hills where the flood had come from, and down along Main Street. It was only when they reached the roof that they could see the full extent of the disaster, and wherever Pico pointed his camera the shots were there. Dashing through the rain from one side of the roof to the other they filmed the main floodwater cascading into the logging pool, now filled with a churning mess of debris from the boathouses and pontoons that the first wave had torn through; Shinnook's sloping main street, transformed into a fast-flowing river that reached as high as first floor windows; and upstream, beyond the parking lot, where the river seemed to rise up in a surging backward crest. From this distance it had a certain stillness to it, a wall of standing water that seemed to go nowhere, the wave straining upstream but somehow held back.

And to accompany the footage was a soundtrack of rattling, squalling rain smacking into them like liquid tracer fire and misting the flat tarpaper roof they stood on; crackling bursts of thunder that sounded as if the storm had settled directly over their heads; a blustering wind that couldn't seem to decide which direction to blow in, snatching Jenna's words away when she spoke to camera; and the great rolling roar of the water rising up to them from the streets below, accompanied by the snapping and splintering of wood-frame buildings being torn apart.

Wherever they looked, from whichever side of the lodge roof, there was racing water, dirty brown and churning with a deadly debris, sluicing through the streets, carrying all before it, a fast, mighty tide roaring past, a flood that seemed to have no end, that seemed to grow in strength and vigour as they filmed.

And bodies, of course. Lots of them. Spinning and tumbling through the torrent, tossed among the waves, sucked down and belched out by the evil swirling current. Old and young, naked and clothed. Pathetically alone, or in streaming groups as though a bus queue or a crocodile of schoolchildren had been snatched up.

From their rooftop observation post, Jenna and Pico could also see survivors. For an hour or so inside the hotel, it was as if they had been the only people alive in Shinnook. But from the roof, it was clear they were not. Down the length of Main Street and beyond, groups huddled on flat roofs watching the water race past, or leaned from upper windows praying the flood wouldn't reach them, or looking for somewhere higher, somewhere safer. Men, women and children, soaked by the rain, whipped by the wind.

Fifty yards down the street, Pico zoomed in on a man, two women and two children who had climbed out of a roof window and were crawling on all fours along a stretch of guttering. Unable to negotiate the building's steeply pitched roof their only option was to reach a metal fire escape on the front of a neighbouring property maybe thirty feet away, a fire escape that climbed up two more floors to a flat roof, and safety.

As they inched their way towards it, Pico filmed them and Jenna supplied the voice-over. Whether they were family – even related – Jenna credited them with that status in her breathless commentary. 'Just across the street from where we are filming – unable to reach them, unable to help them – this family of five are crawling towards that fire-ladder. Ten minutes ago the flooding Susquahanish reached as high as the first floor where they had taken shelter, but now, as you can see, it's only a few feet below them and still rising.'

Through the lens, Pico closed in on the lead figure – a man, in his late thirties, a T-shirt stuck to his back by the rain, his jeans sodden. Finally he made the fire escape and pulled himself off the guttering, turning back to reach out for the rest of his 'family'. The two children were first, a boy and a girl, maybe seven and ten, almost too scared to move. Jenna could see the man shouting out encouragement, but she couldn't hear his

322

voice. Finally, he had them, one after another, swinging them up to safety above the snatching torrent. Then it was the older woman's turn, as fragile and scared as the children, uncertain whether she could trust herself to let go her grip on the gutter and reach out for that saving hand. But she did it, and desperate seconds later she, too, was with the children, huddled on a fire escape landing. The younger woman – the children's mother, said Jenna – came next. More agile, more certain of the man reaching out for her, she caught his hand and swung herself up.

'And now she's climbing up on that fire escape and they've made it. They've made it to safety,' screamed Jenna as a clattering burst of thunder broke overhead. 'Now they can climb up the fire escape, two floors up to that flat roof. Out of the river's reach. Out of danger.'

The words were hardly out of her mouth when she saw the man and two women suddenly reach for the rail and look upwards. Jenna looked too and a cold, disbelieving dread gripped her.

'There, there. You see it? Up at the top of the fire escape,' she screamed at Pico, pointing out the metal brackets that held the fire escape to the top of the wall. They were shaking violently and stone was crumbling away, dropping down on the family below.

'From where I'm watching, further up the street, it seems . . . I can't believe what I'm seeing . . . but it looks like the fire escape is being wrenched off the building. From the top there. It's just peeling away. Surely, it's not . . . Oh God . . . No . . . Oh no.'

In the slowest seven seconds of her life Jenna watched as the fire escape the family were huddled on peeled away from the wall. The older woman, sitting on the metal grating, gathered the children to her and the man and woman grabbed each other. For a moment, the unsupported fire escape seemed to waver, sway, and the family clung on to each other. Jenna knew that the metal would be shrieking with the tension, bolts snapping and rails twisting, but she couldn't hear anything over the raging storm of thunder and rain and river.

And then the flood seemed to surge forward, as though it had suddenly spotted the family, sweeping up in a spray around the metalwork, catching a proper hold on that staggered, swaying zig-zag frame of metal. And just hauled it away, pulled it clear, free of the building.

On that fragile, sinking landing the family must have known they were lost. What tears, what words of comfort and farewell were being spoken now between them, Jenna wondered aloud? Or were they silent, just the screaming of the two terrified children, and the desperate prayers of the old lady who clasped them to her as the fire escape tipped and swayed and their parents staggered above them? As they saw what was about to happen, saw that they were doomed. Knew that the river would have them. Despite all their efforts.

In an instant the flood reared up at them, dragged the fire escape down into its tumbling waters, and one by one all five were snatched out of their metal nest and swept away.

'Oh, Jesus . . . Oh, Jesus, no . . .' whispered Jenna.

81

Having made the treeline, Mulholland wasn't taking any chances. Stamping on the gas, swinging the wheel to left and right he managed to push the Durango a good thirty feet into the forest before jamming it between two spruce trees, stripping off lengths of bark and snapping off his wing mirrors as he forced it in.

Both men looked to the left, Mulholland panting with the effort of getting them up that slope, Zan only now feeling the pain in his knee. Since they'd seen the flood dropping down towards them, he'd been so intent on getting out of its way that any pain he'd suffered in the jolting climb to the treeline had been forgotten. Now it surged back.

And with the pain came the tide, sweeping through the trees in a rushing, deafening stream, spraying up around the tree trunks, drawing closer and closer through the shadowy forest.

'Hold tight,' shouted Mulholland, buzzing his window closed, and the next instant the wave hit them broadside on, slamming into the door panels and cascading over them. Even wedged between the two trees the

Durango shook and rocked, the radio mike jumping from its holder, the glove compartment springing open and the tin of Whale-Watchers spilling over them.

On and on came the flood, as high as their window sills, pounding against the door panels, surging round the windscreen. But then, having reached its highest point on the valley side, the main flow of water swerved away from them, steered back by the slope of land to a lower level. Instead of beating against the side of the Durango, it now started to stream over the front fender, sluicing up over the bonnet and on to the windscreen.

'It's slowing down,' said Mulholland softly. 'I do believe it's slowing down.'

'Sure seems that way,' replied Zan, twisting round in his seat and looking through the trees behind them. 'It's dropping, okay. But it still looks mighty fierce.'

Buzzing down his window, Mulholland peered out at the ground. Then he pushed open his door and stepped down into a thin cover of water. Zan did the same, favouring his good leg. Without Mulholland noticing, he pulled a couple of painkillers from his pocket and swallowed them dry.

Across the bonnet Mulholland blew out a chestful of breath, pulled off his bill-cap and wiped a sleeve across his brow. 'That damn fence,' he began. 'Never thought we were going to make it through.'

'You and me both,' said Zan. 'So what do we do now?'

Mulholland leant back into the cab and reached for the mike. 'Call it in, first of all. Let them know down in Melville what's heading their way.'

While Mulholland briefed his boys in Melville, Zan limped back to the treeline, rain still tipping down from a low scud of cloud drifting across the valley and cloaking the hills from view. Two fields below him, a dirty brown Susquahanish roared and tumbled along, several feet wider than he'd ever seen it, several feet higher and much, much faster. The paddock fencing that they had only just managed to break through had been ripped from the ground like a line of forecourt bunting, and the picture-perfect pastures below him were now coated in a slick of filthy grey mud littered with debris left high and dry by that first giant wave – rolled cars, sections of building, logs, branches, telegraph poles.

Looking through the sheeting rain towards Shinnook, he could see the floodwater still pouring through the broken barrier walls of the log pool, still streaming down the approach road and banking up on their side of the valley, hundreds of millions of tons of water spilling down from those cloud-shrouded hills. If Dasha was up there, which he was sure she was, he prayed she was safe, prayed she was on high ground, prayed that the flood had spared her.

Turning to the left, Zan followed the roaring course of the Susquahanish back down to Drivers' Cut. Even from this distance – no more than a mile up the valley – he could see how the river was backing up, a mass of debris choking the narrow dog-leg bend. If he and Mulholland had hit that pass just a few minutes later, there'd have been no room for manoeuvre. They'd have swung round that last bend and come face to face with . . .

Zan shook his head, and his heart picked up a beat. It simply didn't bear thinking about.

'So what do you want to do now?' asked Mulholland, coming up beside him, whistling softly when he saw the strew of havoc.

Zan didn't reply.

'You ask me,' Mulholland continued, knowing what

was going on in his companion's head, 'it looks like Shinnook's gonna have to manage without us.'

For a moment Zan felt a flare of guilt. The road up to Shinnook may have been impassable, but it had taken him only seconds to make up his mind.

His wife, somewhere up in those hills?

Or his children, down in Melville?

For just the briefest moment, he wondered what Mulholland – what anyone – would have done in his place.

'You were good with the fence, let's see how you do with the bridge,' said Zan at last, nodding back towards the Cut.

Mulholland gave him a look, and rubbed a hand across his drooping walrus moustache. The two men were close enough for Zan to hear Mulholland's palm rasp over his bristles.

'Then let's hope we can fire up that old engine of ours,' the old man said softly.

82

When Pico pulled the camera from his shoulder, he was shaking. Head, arms, legs. And his eyes were as wide as saucers, filled with a stunned disbelief.

'I don't know if I can do this any more,' he said, resting the camera against the roof ledge and straightening up, running his hands through rain-soaked hair, pushing it back from his face. He shivered at the admission. He'd wanted to be a cameraman since his first Super 8, filming family and friends, weddings, anniversaries, bar mitzvahs, before starting with local TV news stations. In the last three years – in Portland and Olympia – he'd covered the waterfront: car spills, fires, street brawls and demonstrations. It wasn't reporting from the front line in some foreign war zone, but sometimes he reckoned it came close. And in that time he'd seen his fair share of dead bodies. But Shinnook was different. He had just seen five people die. Actually die. And filmed them. Filmed them dying. One minute they were there – alive, clinging to each other. The next they were gone – swept away, drowned. Children too. When they hit that water, they were dead. All of them. No-one could have survived that speeding, sucking, ruthless tide, its merciless pile-driver force. They wouldn't have stood a chance.

If it hadn't been raining, Jenna was certain she'd have seen tears on Pico's cheeks. There were certainly tears on hers, and a tight, acid lump in her throat. She wasn't sure if Pico had been speaking to her, or to himself, but she understood. She knew what he meant and for a brief moment she wasn't certain that she'd be able to continue herself. Those last few minutes, watching that family struggle along the guttering, reach safety, one after another, only to be swept away . . .

But as she stood there on the lodge rooftop, stunned by what she had witnessed, something kicked in.

'We gotta do this,' said Jenna, for herself as much as for Pico. 'It's why we're here. It's what we do.'

Pico was shaking his head, gripping it with his hands. 'I don't think so . . . I don't think so. Not like this.'

She went to him, pulled his arms down and held them tight to his sides. 'Listen up. Listen to me.' She gave him a gentle shake, caught his eyes and held them. 'Either we go back to our comfy little love-nest and wait it out. Or we do something. Which means we film, or we help. Who knows, maybe we do both? But we don't give up, you hear me? We don't give up.' She gripped his arms tighter, gave them another shake. 'So get that camera up on your shoulder, *muchacho*, and let's do it. Let's do it.'

83

The Durango was made of stern stuff. After being crashed through the fence, jammed between two trees and hit by a bonnet-high wall of water, the engine turned on the second hit. But it still took Zan and Mulholland more than twenty minutes to work it clear of the two trees clamped tight either side of it. While Zan sat in the driver's seat, pumping the accelerator, Mulholland raged like a bull at the front fender, trying to push and bounce the car free. Finally with a screech of metal, the Durango lurched backwards and Zan reversed out. Apart from a rattling manifold somewhere beneath him and a tug to the right on the steering, everything seemed to be in order.

Handing the driver's seat back to Mulholland, who used more brake pedal than gas, they slid down the slope like a toboggan on a gentle run, the front and back ends fishtailing through the slick of mud all the way to the road. Once on the black-top the grip improved, but so much debris had been left strewn across the road that on two occasions they had to leave the car and clear a path, slipping in the mud as they hauled stuff out of the way, the hungry waters of the roaring Susquahanish licking up at them just a few feet away.

Both men knew that their only chance of getting back down to Melville relied on Drivers' Cut Bridge still standing, but as they negotiated their way round a score of obstacles, keeping as much distance as possible between the Durango and the edge of the road, neither man mentioned it. If the flood had carried the bridge away, they'd be stranded, cut off, unable to go anywhere.

Finally they reached far enough down the road to see that the bridge was still in place, albeit with a stack of timber and wreckage piled up around its supports, the wild river spraying up over this obstacle of its own making. Back in the old days, log-drivers would have clambered out to loosen this kind of a log-jam. Because they had to. It was what they were paid to do. All Mulholland and Zan had to do was get themselves over the bridge and pray it didn't collapse while they were halfway across.

Coming round the last bend, Mulholland pulled up and leaned forward over the steering wheel, assessing the route ahead.

'Looks clear,' he said. 'But will it hold?'

'It'll hold,' Zan replied.

'You want to take it fast, or slow?'

Zan frowned, tried to think, tried to apply load-bearing laws to the problem. Fast or slow? Crawl or race? Which would be best? Which would be safer? Which would the bridge prefer? From somewhere he remembered something he'd heard about marching soldiers going out of step when they crossed a bridge. Breaking the rhythm? That steady beat? But how did that help him?

'Fast,' said Zan at last. 'Spread the weight. Take it by surprise.'

'Someone should walk it,' said Mulholland, without saying whether he agreed with Zan's suggestion or not. 'A body's lighter than a car. At least one of us gets across.'

'You volunteering?'

'I was thinking your knee might need some exercise. I'll stay here. Make sure Billy-Goat-Gruff don't get you.'

As Zan got out of the car, Mulholland rummaged around in the door pocket and brought out a two-way radio, handed it over. 'Just in case,' he said with a grin. 'Switches on there,' he said. 'And it's set to the right frequency for Melville, so don't go playing with the dial.'

'You'll get it back the other side,' said Zan.

'You bet,' said Mulholland, and tipping his fingers to the bill of his cap he caught hold of the door and slammed it shut.

Leaving Mulholland, Zan walked towards the bridge, the rain battering down on his head. Out of the car, the roar of the river was gigantic, a great wash of rushing water that generated its own chill breeze, slapping round Zan's cheeks as he drew closer. Normally the banks dropped down at least a dozen stony feet to the water, but now it was boiling and spilling over the log-jam pressed against the bridge supports, less than a foot below the level of the road. Given the pummelling weight of the water, Zan was astonished that the bridge was still in place.

But it didn't look or sound as though this state of affairs was likely to continue for very much longer. The stone buttresses on either bank looked strong enough to withstand the flood but the metal superstructure, and the sixty-foot stretch of black-top that it supported, creaked dangerously. Spurred on by the thought of his children forty miles downstream, Zan took a deep breath and set out across the bridge, keeping to the middle of the road rather than use the walkways either side. Drenched by the flying spray spewing up from the jam of logs, feeling the surface flex beneath his shoes, he kept his head down and moved as quickly as his knee would allow.

He was halfway across when he heard Mulholland sound the horn. He turned in time to see the old Sheriff start up the Durango and head towards him, flashing his headlights and waving upstream frantically.

It was clear that Mulholland had seen something, maybe something coming their way that would tear away the bridge and leave them stranded. But with the pile of debris banked up against the bridge Zan could see nothing.

'Jump in,' yelled Mulholland, slowing down beside Zan but not stopping.

Zan did as he was told, wrenching open the passenger door and pulling himself in.

'There's a coach coming down. A goddam tourist—'

But Mulholland got no further. There was a mighty crash up ahead and the bridge shook like a giant seismograph needle.

'Brake. Brake,' shouted Zan, spotting a movement in the wall of timber just a few feet in front of them.

Mulholland saw it, too, and hit the pedal. As the Durango slewed to a halt a splintered length of telegraph pole, loosened by the impact, slid from the log-jam and launched itself like a wooden torpedo over the bonnet of the Durango. Just a second's delay from Mulholland in stamping on that brake, and the pole would have smashed through the passenger-side window and skewered them both.

'And go, go, go!' screamed Zan, as the blackened underside of the coach suddenly reared up over the top of the log-jam, jacking itself up foot by foot, streaming with water and closing on the vertical. Any moment it would hit the perpendicular and start to topple.

Hitting the gas, Mulholland powered forward, leaning over the wheel and glancing up as the coach teetered for a moment, end on end, and then started to swing down towards them like a pitcher's bat. Instinctively both men ducked, but only the coach's dark shadow hit them, its roof smashing down just inches behind their back-fender.

Maybe it was the weight of the coach, or the angle it came down, but the sheer force of the blow, and the remorseless pressure of the flood, was enough, finally, to break the back of the bridge. Just twenty feet from the far bank, more than midway across, the Durango's back end suddenly dropped and the road ahead of them tipped upwards, high enough for a tangle of branches and fencing and other wreckage littering the black-top to start sliding down towards them. Flinging the wheel from side to side to avoid the larger items, Mulholland swung the Durango through the mess and powered up the rise.

But they were too late. With a screech of steel and stone, the end of the metal bridge tore loose from its anchoring buttress and swung away from the bank, out into the flood. The Durango was now stranded on a tipping, bucking forty-foot section of bridge span that rested – for the moment at least – on a grinding mass of freed timber.

Neither man spoke; they just looked out of their windows in stunned disbelief as they slowly settled in the floodwaters and started off downstream.

84

After filming the family on the fire escape, Jenna decided they had to leave the lodge roof and find some other vantage point. And some new footage. She also knew they needed to get away from there, knew that she had to find something else to bring Pico back on line. She loved him for his compassion, she loved him for his tears – and his hard little body and long eyelashes, too – but what she needed right now was a cameraman, a cameraman with his mind on the job. And there was nothing left for them up here.

Choking back her own dismay and horror, Jenna picked up a battery belt and hurried across the roof with it. There was nothing he could do but follow her. She was banking on it. But when she reached the door-well, he was still standing where she'd left him, looking at his feet and shaking his head.

'Come on, *muchacho*. What're you waiting for?'

With the rain drumming on the roof, she wasn't sure he could hear her.

But he had. He looked up, then reached down for the camera, and started towards her.

While they'd been up on the roof, things had changed at ground level. Once the log-pool barrier had given way and a hundred million tons of water had cascaded down towards the Melville road, the pool had emptied and the flood had been split into two lethal flows. A killer torrent was still roaring down Shinnook's main street, and an equally ferocious torrent poured through the log pool's open boom, but the emptying of the pool meant the lodge's elevated position now raised it above the flood. The water that had raced through its lobby two hours earlier had been re-routed, sucked away by the pull of water pouring through the breached barrier walls. Where Pico had been swept away, there was now just a small stream of water cutting a path through a tangle of debris and a bed of stinking mud. The only thing missing was their van, just a ragged hole in the ceiling where it had rested before the change in the flow dislodged it.

'Looks like we'll be walking home,' said Pico when they finally reached the foyer, the two of them standing ankle-deep in mud. 'So where do you want to start?' he asked, shouldering his camera, looking around as if trying to decide what to film first.

Jenna smiled to herself. Pico was back on track.

85

'You got any bright ideas?' asked Mulholland, gripping the steering wheel for no good reason, and peering through the windscreen as they caromed over the flood-water broadside on.

'Not a one,' replied Zan, as waves higher than the Durango rolled and swerved around them, a murderous, fast-moving pelt of churning dirty surf that would have sucked the Durango under in a single gulp if it hadn't been for the length of bridge span on which the car was marooned.

As he sat there, wondering how much longer they'd stay afloat, it dawned on Zan that if Mulholland hadn't driven across the bridge to get him, he'd have been flung off when the bus hit and pulled under by the flood.

Right now he'd be dead.

He wouldn't have stood a chance.

With a bolt of gratitude, he realised that Mulholland had risked his own life to save his. Another man might have seen that coach bearing down on the bridge and just tooted the horn, flashed his lights, shouted at him to run. And stayed where he was. But not Mulholland.

Mulholland wasn't that man. Mulholland had come for him. Whether he'd saved his life, or simply delayed the inevitable, still remained to be seen.

'I feel like a kid on a roller-coaster, just wishing like hell the ride would stop and I could get off,' said Mulholland, turning in his seat, scanning the murderous river around them as though looking for a way out.

But there was no way out.

There was nothing they could do.

Zan nodded. 'You and me both, Chief. But I don't see how.'

'Me neither,' replied Mulholland. 'Guess we just gotta sit tight and see where we pitch up.'

They didn't have long to wait. Something out of sight, something below the surface of the boiling river, suddenly caught at the pile of logs and debris jammed beneath the bridge span and sent them spinning round a full ninety degrees. Bucking and rocking in the middle of the stream they were now pointed upriver, watching a set of malevolent waves chase after them.

'I think we might just be coming to the end of the ride,' said Mulholland, glancing in his rear-view mirror. 'I'd hang on to something if I were you.'

Zan looked over his shoulder. Coming up fast was a massive wall of stone, the last bend in the Cut before the river opened up into Melville Valley. A surging wave broke hard and strong against it, leaping up at its sheer, blank face as though searching for a hand-hold.

But no longer broadside on, their Durango had picked up speed. The bridge span they were parked on now had its own more streamlined momentum, going as fast as the stream, fast enough to find its own direction, fast enough not to follow every whim of the torrent. With just five breathless seconds between their speeding raft and that last deadly slab of stone, they slid past with inches to spare and shot out into Melville Valley like a bolt from a crossbow.

But if speed had saved them once, it didn't look as though it was about to repeat the favour. Now clear of the Cut, they were heading straight for a rocky plug of stone standing high and proud above the river, the swollen current sluicing around it.

They never reached it. When the flood broke through the Cut, the river had reared up over its banks and spread across the surrounding meadows. Indeed, if Zan or Mulholland had thought about it, they'd have recalled that the stand of stone had always been a paddock's distance from the river.

They would also have remembered that the paddock rose away from the bank in a long gentle slope of land. It was this gradual incline that now began to snatch at the keel of their bridge span, the tangle of wreckage still trapped beneath them and what remained of the bridge's metal supports all ploughing into the topsoil and slowing them down. When they finally came to a stop, they did so with a gentle bump, like a Shinnook canoe knocking against a pontoon, and an accommodating lip of mud and turf slipped over the end of the bridge to form a makeshift ramp on to the meadow.

For a full minute the two men looked over their shoulders at that lip of mud without saying a word, the river roaring past not twenty feet from their front fender.

Mulholland broke the silence: 'If I'm not mistaken, there's the road up there,' he said, nodding to the top of the rise.

'I think you might be right, Chief.'

86

Jenna and Pico started in the foyer, with Pico filming a long sweep of the devastated ground floor.

'Just two hours ago,' said Jenna, in a hushed voice-over, 'here in the foyer of Shinnook's Saw Mill Lodge, guests were finishing lunch, browsing through the postcard racks, or maybe setting out for an afternoon's shopping in this picture perfect old logging settlement in Melville County. Just two hours ago the Saw Mill Lodge was full – thirty rooms, let's say sixty guests. And staff to take care of them – over there at reception, in the Sawyers' Bar and Cocktail Lounge, or behind me on the Log Pool Terrace. Now, just two hours later, after a raging Susquahanish River tore through town, the Saw Mill Lodge is empty. Since the flood hit we haven't seen a single guest or member of staff. Here in the foyer, or on the four floors above us. It's as if we're the only people here. Everyone else has just . . . vanished.'

After the foyer, Jenna and Pico squelched their way over to the terrace, hanging on to each other for balance in the slippery mud. Leaning over a stone balustrade, Pico swept the camera across what had once been the log pool, now a muddy bowl sloping down to the shattered remains of the barrier.

'Just two hours ago,' repeated Jenna, 'there were twenty tables set out here on this terrace. Now there are none. Back then, Shinnook's logging pool lapped at the pontoon behind me. Now that it's broken through its barrier and blasted down into the valley, all that remains is the swollen, angry river that feeds it, that raging torrent of water just below me.'

Jenna watched Pico tip the camera down and follow the river's course.

'That was good,' she said, when Pico finished filming.

Pico nodded. 'I went in real tight on the break in the barrier. It looked awesome. Just . . .' He took a breath, couldn't find the words.

'So, now we need to find survivors,' said Jenna, turning back into the hotel. 'Tape an interview.'

'You sure there are any?' asked Pico, casting about.

Jenna shot him a look.

Pico nodded, then chuckled. 'Don't tell me . . . Let me get it right. "We don't look, we don't find,"' he mimicked.

'You're learning fast, hotshot,' she replied, and, with a smile he didn't see, Jenna headed towards the foyer, the mud sucking at her boots.

87

It was growing dark and chill up in the hills. The rain was still lashing down but Dasha sensed that the flood-water pouring through her basement wasn't as full or as energetic as it had been. And the gushing, rushing noise it made had dropped too, she was sure of it. Sitting at the top of the basement steps she looked at the water blasting through the broken panelling behind her, at the column of water plunging through the hole in the floor, and the break in the lower basement wall where the water still tumbled away into the backyard.

Now that it had her attention, Dasha began to watch the water level with a more disciplined eye, switching her attention from the wall behind her, to the hole in the tilting ceiling and the far wall. Gauging the height and the force and the flow of the water. If nothing else, she supposed, it was a way to pass the time, but after nearly thirty minutes of close observation and comparison she knew for certain she was right. The flood was definitely growing weaker – but very slowly.

She crouched there at the top of the basement stairs

for another half-hour before she dared go down the steps and wade into the water, her limbs aching with inactivity, her muscles cramped and cold. For a moment, she just stood there, waist deep in the stream, stretching, bending, trying to loosen the knots of tension that gripped her body. As soon as she felt able to continue, she kept to the wall and steered round the central pillar of water cascading down from the floor above, feeling her toes sink into the mud, under no illusions that there was still enough weight to the stream to send her sprawling if she lost her footing.

At last she reached the break in the far wall where her bed had stood and, cursing her cuffed wrists and the water snatching at her feet, she edged around it, holding on tightly, testing for loose stonework before committing herself to any movement.

This sense of risk, and the fact that she was finally able to do something after hours of inactivity and dark isolation, made her feel better, stronger, braver. She had something else to think about. Something to take her mind off the kids and Zan, now that the primary threat had been removed. She hadn't heard any kind of human sound or movement from above her and she was certain her captors must have been swept away or seriously put out of action.

What she saw when she got out of the basement confirmed this. The whole back end of the cabin, the kitchen area where Elroy had been killed, lay hanging down from the few ground-floor joists remaining. It looked like a wood rug thrown from a window to air. Since she hadn't planned anything further than getting out of the basement, this sloping tumble of broken planking now provided her with the next step. All she had to do was climb up it and she'd reach the ground floor which, since there was no cascade coming over the lip, she could only assume was now clear of water, above the flood.

Praying the tangle of wood would bear her weight she started the climb, hauling herself up two-handed, astonished at the damage the flood had caused. She'd heard about floods like these, but in all her time in these hills she'd never seen anything like it – the kitchen snatched clean off the back of the cabin, the water still tumbling down the slope, a number of trees wrenched out of the ground completely or toppled against neighbouring timber. Briefly, it made her think of her kids again. And Zan. If it was like this here, what would it be like down on the coast? If it had gotten that far yet. She remembered Shinnook and the logging pool, and the way they worked those sluices. There'd been a few close calls around Shinnook, standing as it did at the joining of the Susqua and Hanish streams, but they hadn't had a flood alert, let alone a flood, down at Melville for . . . well, since before she was born, she guessed. She prayed that this would be no exception, that Zan would be back home and that they'd all be safe up at South Bluff. She was thinking of them when, a few moments later, she finally pulled herself up on to the cabin floor.

Quickly she looked round, making sure there was no company to surprise her. If there had been, there wouldn't have been too many places to hide. The whole far corner of the ground floor, two complete walls, had been wrenched away. Unsupported, the floor above had crashed down and now rested at a forty-five degree angle. Most of the roof had gone too, and the only thing still in its proper place was the floor she stood on and the lower half of the cabin's stone hearth.

It was here among the rubble that Dasha found the first shoe – a left-foot trainer – and, more important, a black Maglite torch. She switched it on and a beam of yellowish light played over the floor and tilted ceiling. The batteries were clearly low or wet, but having a torch was a godsend. Pretty soon the skies would darken and she'd be lucky to see a thing. Conserving its power, Dasha did a quick circuit of what was left of the cabin. Within just a few minutes, she'd found a second trainer, also left-foot, and a waxed fishing jacket wedged under a ceiling beam. Thanks to its waterproof outers, the felt lining was remarkably dry and she pulled it over her shoulders, hugging it round her.

She also found a knife, stuck on the inside of a window frame. It may have been dark when Mort murdered Elroy but Dasha was certain that this was the knife he had used, the knife that had taken the young man's life, the knife that had sliced off her clothes. There was just something about it – its horn grip, its curling brass guard and the ugly grey swirl of its damascened blade. For a moment she just looked at it, with a kind of horrified repulsion. But she knew what she had to do. It was a weapon, she was in the wilds, it would be foolhardy to leave it. Gritting her teeth she caught hold of it and tried to pull it out of the wood. She was surprised how solidly and deeply it was embedded, as though whoever had plunged it in there had done so with extraordinary force. Finally, though, easing the blade backwards and forwards like the handle on a pump, she managed to free it.

But that was all she found: just a pair of odd-sized left-foot trainers, a knife, a jacket, and her dying torch.

That was all she had.

That, and her freedom.

88

It didn't take long for Jenna and Pico to find their first survivor.

The woman was wide-eyed, in her thirties, Pico guessed, her blonde hair hanging to her shoulders in soiled, darkened rat-tails. She was trembling and moaning, barefoot and soaked to her skin, dressed in a cotton shift and cardigan that hung wet and heavy from hunched shoulders. Jenna had seen her first, standing with a man either side of her, the two of them clearly trying to comfort her. The three of them were sheltering in a shop doorway just a block down from the lodge on Saw Mill Road, the flooding water raging past not ten feet away from them, the raised sidewalk shaking with its power. Each man was holding an arm, the woman trying feebly to break loose. If she'd managed it, she'd have simply crumpled where she stood, or staggered forward into the flood.

When Jenna saw them, she tapped Pico's elbow, nodded towards them.

'Give me time to get there,' Jenna had told him, 'then kinda sidle up, filming. Okay?'

Pico knew exactly what she wanted. This might have been their first outing together, but working with Jenna had been a masterclass in how to get a story. Not just any story, but a good story. And Pico had worked with enough reporters to know the good from the bad, the work-shy from the talented. But Jenna was something else. A real pro, hungry for it, a born reporter. Sometimes, when she was speaking to camera, he was mesmerised by her. Those dark, serious eyes, that dash of blonde hair. The way she started her sentences, the pitch and roll of her voice, the concern she showed, the involvement that came across. You watched this girl on your TV news and you were right there. Wherever she happened to be, whatever story she was covering.

Sharks, floods. She made you feel them.

And she'd kept him together, when he lost it. He wondered if she realised how close he'd come to just jacking it in. His first day with CTACtv, the biggest news story of his career, a disaster unfolding right in front of him. And he'd frozen, thought himself unable to continue. But Jenna Blake had brought him round, kept the show on the road. She was one tough cookie and no mistake. And just the most gorgeous . . .

But there was no time for that. Not now. Maybe later.

Taking the camera from his shoulder, Pico watched her step and slide, step and slide her way along the mud-covered sidewalk towards the shop doorway. Leaning in she put out a hand to the woman, and with the other she motioned behind her back for Pico to come forward.

348

Re-mounting the camera he made his way towards the group, praying he could rely on available daylight rather than use the camera's bright halogen beam. So often that white flare of light just killed the moment, stalled the action, distracted whoever it was being filmed. He tried a test shot a few feet from the doorway, pulling in from the flood, but knew immediately there was no choice. Ten minutes earlier he might have managed with what light there was, but suddenly it was dark and gloomy.

He held his breath as he came up behind Jenna, raising the camera slowly. But the glare seemed to make no impression on the woman, just one of the men glancing in his direction as the pool of light fell on them, rain slanting through it, tapping off the camera's plastic cover. All the woman did was take another gasping breath and shudder.

'So tell me. What exactly happened?' asked Jenna softly, moving an inch or two out of Pico's way. As he took up the space, focusing on the woman, trying to keep Jenna's head and shoulder just in frame, he heard the mournful tale she told: how she was just coming out of the store, pushing the buggy. And this elderly gentleman, out on the sidewalk, leaning in to keep the door open for her. Then the water – from nowhere – suddenly sluicing around his ankles, rising to his knees, and a strange fearful look on his face when he turned and saw what was coming towards him. In the seconds before it hit, the first low wave swept him off his feet, there on the sidewalk. 'Right there, right where you're standing now,' the woman moaned, reliving that terrible moment. 'Like seconds. It was just seconds . . .

'And . . . he . . . reached up,' she told them, the words hiccuping out of her. 'And he just . . . he just caught hold of the side of the buggy . . . Just like that. Because there was nothing else, you see. Nothing else to grab. And I wasn't ready . . . I wasn't holding the buggy properly . . . just the one hand, the other on the door . . . And my baby was in it . . . I tried . . . I just couldn't hold on . . . I should have . . .'

That lone, lost, devastated mother wasn't the only survivor they found. There were many more in the hours that followed. With many stories to tell. And Pico and Jenna listened to those stories, and recorded them.

Sad terrible tales told to a soundtrack of raging flood-water, in a darkening gloom.

But tales of hope, too, and courage, and unbelievable chance and circumstance.

And, against all odds, survival.

Part Three

'Settled by French trappers in the previous century, Melville has profited much from the trade in fur, timber and, nowadays, whaling, these principal industries providing this bustling port with a prosperity best illustrated by the quaint confection of gingerbread and filigreed homes of its merchants and mariners that terrace the slopes of South Bluff . . .'

Shaws' Travelling Companion to the
Northern Pacific States, 1923

89

Tall, cadaverous, with beetling black eyebrows and a scrape of thin black hair, Dave Pringle was in his den, watching the six o'clock news broadcast and waiting for the weather forecast. If they had that same guy on from lunchtime, with his rain slicker and sou'wester, Pringle knew for sure there'd be no need for alarm. If he was wearing a suit, it would be a different matter altogether. The studio news anchor was just rehashing the lead stories, including details of the Pearse-Caine property transfer, when the Pringles' phone bleated in the hallway.

'I don't know whether he's in,' he could hear his wife telling whatever son-of-a-bitch was calling him at home on a Saturday evening. 'Just you hold a while, and I'll go see.'

Pringle swung round his Lazee-Boy just far enough to keep one eye on the TV screen and find out from his wife who was calling.

'It's Sergeant Calley at the Sheriff's Office,' she whispered, standing in the den doorway. Since her hand was clamped over the mouthpiece, and the phone buried in her bony chest, his wife's over-dramatic whispering enraged Pringle even more than the call. With a frown of irritation he waved her into the den and took the phone from her.

'Pringle here.'

He listened for less than two minutes, then handed the phone back to his wife and swung back to the TV.

The news anchor had just finished an interview with someone from the National Parks and, assuming a suitably concerned expression, he turned to the weather man on the edge of the set. 'I hear it's not that good out there, Harry . . .'

The camera switched to the weather man. He was wearing a suit and looked uncomfortably serious.

'It sure isn't, Jim. Just a load of rain coming down pretty much all over the state this Saturday p.m., between twelve and fourteen inches recorded in some places in just a couple of hours, with high tides and strong winds racing in from the ocean and more on the way . . .'

'Shit,' said Pringle, and launched himself out of the Lazee-Boy.

90

Mort Johannesen opened his eye and was instantly awake. It was the same when he slept; close that eye and he was gone. And it wasn't anything to do with having just the one eye. It had been the same from way back. As though he always needed to be alert, even when he slept. It had served him well in Iraq, and it served him well now, wedged into a crease of stone that just about kept the rain off him.

The sofa and Mort had parted company at the bottom of Quarry Falls. As far as he could remember he'd stayed with it until they struck the surface of the water, but in the bubbling, churning dive that followed they became separated. Instead he'd rolled up on to the surface alone, gasped for air and, having established that the sofa was gone, he'd looked around for something else to grab a hold of, something he could use to keep himself afloat. If he didn't find something real quick, he knew he'd drown. Just be swept clean away. And the way this water was running there didn't look like much of a chance of making it to the bank, and safety. Some kind of physics seemed to dictate that you rode in the middle of the stream where the power of the water was fiercest, and the banks furthest away. And there, it seemed, you stayed.

As though bidden to appear at that precise moment, a length of tree trunk stripped of bark and branches had come tumbling over the falls and plunged into the water not ten feet away from him. As the log surfaced and spun past him, Mort reached out and grabbed hold of it.

For all his boot camp training and front-line action, Mort didn't know much about rivers, or surviving in this kind of surging power. But keeping his legs up and close to his body looked to be a sound idea. God alone knew what they might encounter if he let them down – rocks to smash against, submerged tree forks to snare a foot and tear it off. He remembered his drill sergeant at Camp Wyeth: *You're a target: be a small one. You're a target: be a small one.*

Spitting out water by the mouthful, his ears filled with the sound of the raging river around him, Mort had finally managed to bring a leg up and over the tossing log he'd hitched a lift from. He was now riding it like a very narrow surfboard, praying it wouldn't roll over and duck him under.

It was then, looking ahead, that he saw what looked like a small promontory pointing out from the bank. But as he drew closer, tumbling through the water towards it, he saw it was an island, a great bank of splintered tree trunks, roots, branches and shrubbery caught up and trapped by a slab of rock jutting out of the water. Before he could do anything about it, the end of the log he was lying on caught against a piece of the trapped timber and swept him round into the current until he was looking back upstream, a great surf wave surging up over his face. If he hadn't hooked a leg over the trunk, he'd have been whipped away like a stone from a catapult. As it was he was just about in one piece.

Inch by inch, praying he wouldn't lose his hold, or the log break free from the mess of branches which held it, Mort had crawled along the trunk until he'd gotten close enough to the stone to catch a hold and haul himself out of the water, clambering up on to a ten-foot-square floor of tilting rock about twenty feet from the nearest bank. It wasn't much, but it was a good six feet above the boiling waters raging past. Which made him six feet better off than he'd been just minutes before.

And that's where he'd stayed, these last few hours, curled up like a dog beneath a small overhang, just about sheltered from the stinging rain and the blast of chill air that came off the wild river surging around him.

Without moving Mort tipped his wrist and glanced at his watch. Close on eight hours since he'd been swept out of the cabin, just over three since he'd gone to sleep.

And in those last few hours things had changed. He wasn't shaking any more, he wasn't as wet as he had been and, so far as he could see, his island wasn't an island any more.

91

Ginny Farrell heard her phone and smiled. She checked the time. Four calls in the last thirty minutes. Two on the land line, two on her cell, a message each time. Deputy Jed Roberts calling. She'd been soaking in the bath when the first one came through, but now she was sitting on the bed, waxing her legs.

And here he was again, more than likely.

The answerphone clicked in on the fourth ring. She was right. It was him.

'Great news. I'm outta here, baby,' she heard him say, and she felt a hot little bolt of pleasure. After being stood up the night before – midnight, he'd told her he'd finish – Ginny had been just certain that something else would crop up to spoil their fun. She'd been looking forward to the date – it was her birthday after all – and she'd have been pretty mad if he'd gone and cancelled again. Not that she was going to let Jed Roberts know that any time soon. Treat 'em mean, keep 'em keen was her motto, and it hadn't let her down yet. Even if he was just about the tastiest cop she'd ever set eyes on, and even if treating him mean just seemed to go against all her natural womanly instincts. Every time she saw those big hands of his, she just wanted to . . .

'Like I said earlier,' Jed continued, 'the Sarge is keeping me on reserve what with the bad weather coming in and all, but otherwise we're clear for tonight. We still on? Where are you? Call me.'

But hey, she thought, let's not make it too difficult for the guy. Leaving the wax strip to dry some, Ginny leaned over and picked up the phone before he rang off.

'So how can I be of assistance, Deputy Roberts?' she started in.

'Hey, you're there. I been calling.'

'Just finished work and back home.'

'So we on?'

'On what?' she asked, smiling as she said it. Oh boy, was she gonna make him cover some ground after standing her up the night before. Was she going to make him work his passage.

'I mean, going out. You said maybe we could meet up? Saturday night. Mama Surf.'

'I did? Mama Surf? When did I say that?'

There was a pause down the line. He was getting the message. He knew he was on the hook. 'Hey, honey. I know. I'm sorry. I shoulda called you last night but it was mayhem, I'm telling you. Didn't get home till dawn.'

'Is that so? Well, maybe you need some beauty sleep, lover. Make up for what you lost. Don't want my man falling asleep on me.'

It was the 'lover' and 'my man' that swung it, just as she'd known it would.

'Aw, Ginny, you know I'd never do anything like that. And I am sorry, I mean real sorry.'

She waited a pulse. And then, 'Mama Surf? Is that what you said?'

At the end of the line there was a pause, a hopeful pause, which Ginny noted.

'Well, hey, we don't need to go there,' replied Jed. 'I mean, if you don't want to. I could always swing past your place, you know, if you'd prefer?'

Ginny didn't waste a moment. 'Well, now listen up, dream boots. If you think I'm gonna stay in on a Saturday night and toss you up a salad, grill you a steak, well, you got a big surprise in store. I got just a few more hours till I'm one year older, and I intend to see out twenty-seven with a bang. And I'm not talking dirty there. Unless, of course, you've gotten me a real nice birthday present.'

She heard the swift intake of breath. He'd forgotten her birthday, she knew it. Or been too busy. She smiled again. More ground for him to cover. This was going to be fun.

'You won't believe what I got for you, honey,' she heard him say, and she just knew he was lying through his teeth, knew he'd forgotten what time it was, or was desperately trying to think what shops would still be open. There wouldn't be many.

'That's what they all say, big boy. But if I told you Mama Surf, then Mama Surf is where I'll be. And you better be there or this little lady's gonna start looking out for more appreciative and congenial company.'

Breaking the connection, Ginny sucked in her breath, caught hold of a corner of the wax strip and pulled upwards.

Sheeee-yit. God-dammit.

Why was it always the last one hurt the most?

92

Even though it was dark, even though the battery in the torch didn't look like it was going to last much longer, Dasha didn't want to stay at the cabin. It was dry – drier than the basement at any rate – and despite the flood damage it still felt reasonably stable on its skirt of stone. And if the rain picked up again, which it easily could, she could shelter under the tilting first floor.

But now that she was free Dasha wanted to be as far

away from the cabin as she could possibly manage. There was something doomed and shadowy about the place and the thought of spending one more night there was simply too much to bear.

She was well aware of the dangers, of course. If the cabin really was in the Hanish Valley it was unlikely there'd be any close neighbours she might stumble upon – given that her kidnappers would have wanted somewhere isolated to use as a base of operations – and she doubted there'd be much in the way of shelter out in the forest.

And if she really was out in the wilds, as she suspected, somewhere deep in the forest, she'd need to look out for bears. There were black and brown bears aplenty in these hills, though she knew that these were likely to see her before she saw them, and be more wary of her than she was of them. But there were grizzlies as well, and by all accounts they lived up to their name. She'd never seen one, but a friend of her father's had once gone missing, never found, and Zan had told her about the time a mother and cub had loped past his camp while he was fishing on Bear Tree.

Ever since then Zan had always packed a gun, and Dasha rather wished she had one now. A gun would have given her the security of distance; a knife meant combat at closer quarters. She knew what you were supposed to do if attacked by a bear. Play dead, apparently. But she wasn't certain she'd have the nerve; she'd want to run. Or climb a tree. And then the bear would have her.

But despite all these dangers, the prospect of moving, of getting away from that cabin, was too much to resist and, stooping under the tilting roof, she made her way to where the front door had been and shone the torch up the slope.

It was then that she remembered the Lexus.

Cars, there had to be cars here.

93

Saturday nights Tod Breamer had a date. Every Saturday. Without fail. Sometimes he managed to persuade a girl along too. Tonight it was Rita, the receptionist from the Melville Court Motel. She was new in town, lived out on the Shinnook road and had a way of looking at you that just squeezed the juices clean down to those important places. Tod had seen that look earlier in the week, delivering the strip sirloins and New Yorkers to the Melville Court kitchens himself so he could make his move. Ten minutes later, getting back in the van, he still had the hard-on.

Stacking away the last of the prime-cut 12-ouncers in Delaney's cold-store, Tod pulled off his white paper trilby, dumped his blood-smeared white counter coat in the staff laundry chute and signed off. For much of the day he'd kept an eye on the weather, but the rain just kept coming, getting worse by the hour, slapping and gusting against Delaney's windows as though it was looking for a way in.

Normally, rain this heavy was a deterrent but tonight he was going to make an exception. Thirty minutes after signing off, he'd showered, changed and right now he was heading for the lock-ups behind the Town Hall to warm up the real love of his life. It might be raining close to bust but if there was a sure and certain way of getting himself into Rita's panties, it was sitting her in the front seat of his old Dodge Charger. A 1969 Road and Track two-door hardtop out of Hamtramck, Michigan, with bucket seats in brown leather and the original Rallye instrument cluster, its seven-litre Hemi engine block kicked out a hefty 375bhp and made a standing quarter mile in a respectable seventeen seconds.

Turn that key and hear that growl.

It never failed.

Five minutes later, rolling down the door of the lock-up behind him and switching on the light, Tod was greeted with that familiar workbench smell of gas and oil and metal. For a moment, waiting for the neon strips to settle, he just stood there, breathing it in, then reached forward and pulled off the soft cotton sheeting that covered her.

And there she was. Deep scarlet bodywork spray-lacquered ten coats deep, with a thin black matte trim round the wheel arches, bonnet vent, and Corvette-styled light assemblies. Wing mirrors, fenders, and split-front grille had been re-chromed, as well as the original bolted petrol cap and newly fitted twin exhaust. He might not know much about boats, like Elroy, but Tod Breamer knew his cars. And for this little beauty, sitting right there in front of him pretty as you please, you didn't have to go buy women's things to keep her pipes lagged.

A gust of rain rattled across the metal door of the lock-up and Tod sighed. Fresh waxed just four days earlier, wheel arches sprayed a week before that. Shit, shit and double-shit again.

But then he thought of Rita.

Twenty minutes later, the door was up and that big Magnum V-8 was chortling gently, the rain already settling in glistening beads over its humped scarlet bonnet.

94

Once Mort was awake, it didn't take long for the anger to come bubbling back. Swept along in the flood, all he'd been able to think of was surviving. And stranded on his rock, waiting for the river to drop, he'd kept a lid on it because otherwise just the thinking about what had happened would have driven him insane with annoyance and irritation. Not to mention the sense of powerlessness he felt just sitting there. But now, as he struggled up the bank and looked back at the river that had nearly cost him his life, Mort let the anger sweep back in and take him.

Everything gone. The cabin, the trucks, Gene. Months of preparation. And everything going so well. They'd been so close. And why? Because of some freak rainstorm that chooses just this particular weekend to fuck everything up.

But it wasn't over yet, he thought. Not by a long chalk. Not if he could help it.

The way he saw it, there were two choices open to him. He could either follow the river down to Shinnook and get picked up as a survivor of the flood; some dry clothes, some hot food and a ticket out of there. Or he could head upstream and start looking for the woman.

It didn't take him long to make up his mind. He was heading upstream, and he was gonna start right now. If he didn't find her in the next twelve hours, he'd play survivor, a fisherman caught by the flood – everything swept away. But if he did find her, dead or alive, she was still a valuable commodity. In fact, dead would be better, he decided. He'd bury the body, then reacquaint himself with Mr Zan Pearse a few days down the road. A couple of million dollars and hubby could have her back. Just like he'd planned. Easy as that.

As far as Mort could tell he was a good twenty minutes downstream from the cabin – his sofa ride to Quarry Falls and the log ride after that – which meant at least an hour's climb to get back up there. But he knew he was being optimistic. Hiking up hill, in a forest, in the dark, and barefoot? Make it two hours, maybe more, if nothing else went wrong.

Just so long as he could find her.

Just so long as she hadn't come past him while he'd been stranded on that rock. And gotten out of there.

But first he had to find a way across the river.

Of all the goddam luck his 'island' was on the wrong side of the Hanish and the main torrent here still looked too strong for wading. He'd have to follow the river upstream until he found a way across.

Gritting his teeth, wishing he had a torch, his knife, and something on his feet, Mort set off upstream, trying to make as much ground as he could before darkness closed everything down.

95

When the opening sequence of *Die Another Day* appeared on the lime-washed back wall of Baxter's Mall, the Drive-In audience erupted. Not cheers or whoops, but a volley of tooting car horns and assorted six-note klaxons. It was the third time this movie had featured at the Drive-In since the start of the summer, but the number of cars drawn up rank upon rank in the Mall's back lot was no less than at previous showings. As legendary surfer Laird Hamilton and his accomplices swooped down that rising wall of water, and the familiar James Bond theme filled the interiors of the seventy-odd cars assembled there, the audience went wild. Not even the rain had put them off.

Seven rows from the front, four in from the aisle, in her late husband's old Buick, Shelley Caine wondered for the hundredth time at the suitability of a Bond movie for little Alexa. *Ice Age 3* was showing at the Delmont on Main, but young Finn had swiftly vetoed that option. As he'd pointed out when the three of them had gone through the local paper to see what was showing, Alexa had a habit of falling asleep as soon as the title credits rolled – 'I do not so'; 'Oh yeah you do' – and Finn had prevailed. *Die Another Day* it was.

As soon as Shelley had parked the Buick, and tuned in the dashboard radio to the soundtrack, she had surrendered the front seats to the kids – Finn behind the wheel, of course, and Alexa tucked up in her quilt with her teddy bear, Blister, on the passenger side – and settled herself behind them. Sitting in the back seat did not provide optimum viewing this close to the screen and Shelley's view was limited to the bottom five feet of the action, but with a flask of watered Bourbon in her handbag, she wasn't too bothered.

What did bother her was that she hadn't heard a word from Zan or Mulholland since lunchtime, when Zan had phoned from the house on South Bluff Drive to say that he was heading up to Shinnook with the Chief. They were going to start up some kind of search as soon as the weather cleared, Zan had told her, and he hoped that Shelley wouldn't mind keeping the kids just a little while longer. Now that details of the land deal between the National Parks and Pearse-Caine had been broadcast, he was convinced that Dasha would be found safe and well somewhere around Shinnook. The way he saw it, Zan had told her, these were clearly eco-terrorists, kind of fundamental environmentalists, and not the kind of kidnappers to do his wife, and Shelley's daughter, any harm. Now that they had what they wanted they would let her go. He was certain of it. And he wanted to be there when she was found.

Right through the afternoon, while the children watched TV in her bedroom – the biggest screen in the apartment – Shelley had watched the hourly news broadcasts on her kitchen set. With only a few changes and additions the coverage was much the same on all the channels: shots of her daughter and Zan, the lawyer Tom Gold reading out a statement outside the Seattle offices of Pearse-Caine, followed by a comment from the National Parks Commission – how she loathed that crowing National Parks' spokesman in his four-button jacket and shiny tie; someone oughta shove something large and prickly up his self-satisfied, self-righteous fundament, was Shelley's opinion.

What she couldn't understand was why no mention was made of Dasha's kidnapping, that the land transfer was being forced. She was starting to get cross about it when she realised that it was fortunate nothing had been said. If Finn or Alexa had somehow caught the same news as they surfed the channels in her bedroom, there'd have been some explaining to do.

Within ten minutes of the film starting, just as Finn had predicted, Alexa's eyes had closed and her head had started to nod. Leaning between the seats, Shelley caught hold of the little girl and lifted her into the back seat, settling the sleeping child on her lap and tucking the quilt around them, the flask now neatly concealed.

As she did so, a small tide of water trickled across the concourse, sliding past the Buick's wheels – and every other set of wheels at the Drive-In – as the nearby Susquahanish quietly breached its banks beyond the mall and started to rise.

96

Dasha found the cars easily. Two of them, set broadside against the treeline a hundred feet below the cabin, piled one on top of the other like wrecks in a breaker's yard. Swept there by the flood, one had been flung over on to its roof and pointed left, the other still upright, balanced on top of its companion and pointed to the right. Despite the tangle of branches and cabin planking draped across them, she recognised the vehicle on top immediately, the forestry truck she'd stopped for on the trail. The one squashed below it was unfamiliar, its doors open and its interior choked with broken branches and a muddy mat of undergrowth. Getting down on her hands and knees and pushing aside the strew of branches, Dasha played her torch through the passenger door, hoping to find something useful. There was nothing.

Cursing her handcuffs, she clambered up on to its upturned chassis and worked her way along to the passenger door of the forestry truck, suddenly remembering the tool chest she'd seen, and praying it was still there. The door was jammed tight and wouldn't open. She tugged at it, then froze as the trucks swayed away from the trees then settled back against them. Carefully now, she peered in through the broken window and saw in the torch beam an interior as bare of promise as the car below, covered in a slick of stinking mud.

Climbing down from the trucks, Dasha worked her way along the treeline. As far as she could see there was no sign of the Lexus. Had they left it on the trail? Surely not? And then her foot caught on something and she stumbled forward, only just managing to keep her balance. Turning round to see what had tripped her she saw in the torch beam what looked like a tangled mound of wet laundry. And then the mound took on shape and form. She saw a hand, and the outline of an arm, a leg, two legs, the back of a head, a pale face. She reeled back, heart hammering. Two bodies, one of which she recognised as Elroy, crumpled together at the base of a tree, water licking around the twisted limbs.

For a moment she just stood there, taking deep level breaths, trying to control the impulse to scream, to run, to get away from there. Then, gritting her teeth, she knelt down, put the torch on the ground and pushed the stiffening bodies apart, lining them up side by side as best she could and reaching for their pockets – jeans, jackets, shirts – going through them methodically, searching for anything that might be useful. It wasn't easy pushing handcuffed hands into wet pockets – when she got a grip on a pocket lining she simply pulled the pocket out – but she persevered, ending up with nothing more promising than a handful of coins, a Zippo lighter, a wallet containing a driving licence in the name of Edward Dougan with an address in Astoria, a metal comb, and a sodden packet of cigarettes. She flicked the wheel on the Zippo but there was no spark from the flint, no flame. And not a single shoe or boot between them; she'd have to make do with her two left-feet trainers.

By now it was dark, everything outside the beam of her torch reduced to shades of grey and black, a mono-chrome world of shifting, shadowy shapes and dripping, trickling sounds. And somewhere to her right, the distant soft moan of a river. Turning away from the bodies, Dasha pushed herself to her feet and started along the treeline, focusing on the sound of the river, trying to gauge how far she would have to go before she reached it. Get to that river and follow it down. That was the way she must go, that was the way out of here, she was thinking, when the play of her torch beam flashed off something silvery in the trees. She stopped and swung the beam to her left.

For a moment, she couldn't believe her eyes.

Just inside the treeline. A thin moving slick of water streaming past a pair of fat black tyres.

Front fender tipped up against a tree.

Doors and windows closed.

Her Lexus.

97

'Once upon a time, in a galaxy far, far away, I lived to surf,' said Ty Guthrie, stretched out on a sofa in Fluke's main cabin. 'Now I work to surf. Nothing changes 'cept the time between the waves, you know what I'm sayin'?'

Across a long low coffee table loaded with surf books and the latest surfing magazines, Mungo chuckled. 'Tell me about it,' he said. 'It's why I became a board-shaper in the first place. It made me enough money to get by, but kept me close. Except those times I got the sander on, I can hear the surf – all day long, all night. Right through the year, I'm out there.' Mungo tipped back some beer. 'Can't imagine a life any other way.'

'So how did you start? Shaping the boards, I mean. There's a lot of competition out there.'

Ty had a very direct manner – open and, as far as Mungo could see, straightforward. There appeared to be no edge to him; he was just a nice guy.

Mungo shrugged. 'Guess it's in the blood,' he said. 'My grandfather was a carpenter, came out here from

Scotland after the Great War and built most of the drying sheds back of the beach, as well as a lot of houses in town, when they were made from wood.'

'And your dad?'

'He started out a carpenter, actually built the shed where I live and have the workshop. But the money was better on the whalers.'

'He live around here?' asked Carrie. She'd been chopping vegetables in the galley kitchen, humming along to Jack Johnson on the hi-fi, listening in to the men's talk. She put down the knife and swept the vegetables off the cutting board and into a wok.

Mungo shook his head, took a last pull of his beer. 'Lost at sea. Went down with all hands when I was a boy.'

There was a moment's silence. 'Sorry to hear that,' said Ty at last. 'Here, let me get you another beer.'

Mungo handed over his empty glass and while Ty dealt with the refills he looked around the cabin. It may have felt like a typical surf bum's pad – some boards racked up on the ceiling, a pile of wetsuits dumped in a corner, and a set of Billabong XXL Tournament posters dotted around the walls – but it was altogether more expensively equipped. The native Indian-weave rugs on the blond wood deck were the real thing, the Nakamichi hi-fi was top of the range, and the soft-hide sofas were stylish and deeply comfortable. Whatever Ty Guthrie did back there in Seattle, he was certainly well paid for it.

Mungo had arrived for dinner right on time, a gusting breeze from the ocean tugging at his parka and spattering a mix of rain and sea-spray over his hood as he stepped down on to the tipping inner harbour pontoon and walked along the row of houseboats moored there. Fluke was last in the line, a twin-deck shingle-sided vessel painted a light blue, its cabin lights shining through brass-ringed portholes, an old ship's bell by the front door tarnished with verdigris and rung by means of a frayed surfboard leash from Mungo's own supply shop. There were other houseboats moored along South Bluff Quay where the old lumber yards had stood, and against the outer harbour wall, but Mungo knew that these were the most sought-after, and the priciest to buy.

But for all the money, for all the trappings of a successful career – a Pearse-Caine houseboat, an upcoming trip to Tahiti, a Wave-Walker on order – Ty was still a beat-up surf bum at heart. Mungo hadn't seen him ride a break yet, but over their second beer he could tell the man was a serious player. He was quiet about his waves, respectful, and it took just a few probing questions from Mungo to establish that the man had seen his share of smokers and bombs – big faces and fearsome breaks. After arguing the toss over tow-in versus paddle, he was telling Mungo about a ride out on the Cortes Bank when Carrie called them through to the dining room. They were just taking their places, shadows flickering in the candlelight, the air soft and smoky with incense, when something heavy bumped against Fluke's aluminium hull.

Carrie started nervously.

Mungo frowned.

'Don't worry,' said Ty. 'It's the sharks. They started coming in this afternoon. Just a few of them – baby bulls mostly.'

Another bump sounded on the hull – like a Zephyr nudging up alongside – and Carrie gripped the table.

'It's okay, honey. It's okay. Now where's that shiraz?'

98

The Lexus was unlocked. And dry. And, to Dasha's sudden consternation, filled with something she hadn't expected. A swaddling, wonderfully comforting sense of familiarity. Memories of the real world – her scent, the smell of the children, an oaky whiff of Zan's aftershave. A little piece of home, here in the forest. It took her by surprise. For a moment, after clambering into the back seat – the front doors of the Lexus were too high to reach safely – and closing the door behind her, she just crouched there and breathed it all in, everything she knew and loved, until she felt her lips start to tremble and her throat tighten.

Not now, she thought. Not now . . .

She was still handcuffed. Out in the wilds. And she wasn't home yet.

Snapping to, she pushed aside the false comfort of memories and concentrated on survival. For the moment she was safe, and she had found herself some shelter – pretty luxurious shelter all things considered. All she needed now was something to eat. She was starving.

She knew where to look and, drawing Mort's knife from her belt and pushing its blade between the seats so that only its hilt showed, she started with Alexa's carseat. Jammed beneath it, just as she'd expected, were five sandwich crusts. Finn hated crusts. She couldn't count the times she'd told him not to hide them under the seat. But being Finn he'd paid no attention and done it anyway. And thank the lord for that, even if her heart did skip a beat when she lifted the first crust to her lips, its edges scalloped by the small arch of her son's teeth.

After the crusts Dasha climbed up between the front seats and reached, double-handed, for the glove compartment where she kept emergency rations for the kids, praying that her kidnappers hadn't taken them. And there they were: two apples, two bananas, two Snickers bars, a small pack of biscuits and two small bottles of water. A Snickers went first and quickly, followed by three biscuits, a banana and a slug of water. Screwing the cap back on the bottle Dasha felt suddenly full, and for a moment wondered whether she was going to throw up. The crusts, the candy, the biscuits, the fruit. She'd eaten too much, too fast. Take it easy, take it easy, she thought, suddenly remembering the last thing she'd eaten. A tiramisu, at the Suttons, served by their butler and thrown up in that dark basement. It all seemed a century ago, Courtney bringing her husband, Win, out to Wilderness One for the first time. Dasha wondered how they were, and wondered, too, if the flood that had hit the Hanish – if that's where she was – had also hit the Susqua. Fortunately the Suttons were far enough up the valley to be pretty safe from any real threat of flood, with, Dasha recalled, their very own rescue helicopter if anything ever did go wrong.

Fed and watered, and having established that the ignition keys were missing and nothing seemed to work in the Lexus – radio, lights, heater – Dasha retreated to the back seat, removed Alexa's car-seat to give herself more room – a tricky job in handcuffs – and located their travel rug behind the back seat. Kicking off her odd shoes and her wet trousers, and pulling her T-shirt over her head and down to her wrists, Dasha dried herself as best she could with the blanket and then wrapped it around her. Curling up on the seat, feeling a soft warmth seep back into her after hours of chill shivering, she switched off the torch and settled herself down. She was only a hundred yards from the cabin, but it felt like a mile, and she thought again of Zan and the children, smelled them in the rain-tapping darkness.

The man she loved, the children she adored.

Earlier that day, trapped in the basement, she had wondered if she would ever see them again.

Now she knew that she would.

99

Both Zan and Mulholland breathed a sigh of relief when they saw the streetlight glow of Melville up ahead. It had been a long and difficult ride from just below Drivers' Cut to the outskirts of Melville. A journey that would normally have taken an hour had come in at close to three. After any number of delays along the route – bypassing broken sections of the road where the river had taken a bite out of the black-top, weaving through the wreckage of what two hours earlier had been the Cedar Creek gas station – they had finally overtaken the flood crest on a straight section of road that strayed away from the Susquahanish and rose up through the trees. By the time they got back to the river, they could see that its height and speed had been softened and slowed by the wider plain of the Melville Valley. The problem would come, as both men knew, when the valley started to narrow again before dropping down on to Melville. A couple of miles ahead two spurs of land rose to left and right, reaching up through fir-clad slopes to the headlands of the North and South Bluffs and channelling road and river through another gentle sloping dog-leg. It wasn't as steep or as narrow as Drivers' Cut but both men knew that the approaching flood, forced through that low pass, would pick up some real pace and muscle.

As they closed on Melville, a damaged manifold rattling beneath the Durango like a rock in a watering can, they knew what they had to do. As quickly as he could, Zan was going to find Shelley and the kids at the Drive-In, and get them and everyone else out of their cars and on to the upper level of Baxter's Mall. While he was doing that, Mulholland would head on into town and start moving people off the street and, away from the river, as high up the slopes of South Bluff as he could manage.

'How long do you reckon we have?' asked Zan, as the first streetlights on upper Main flicked past, filling the Durango's interior with a low orange glow.

Mulholland gave it some thought. 'Up by the Drive-In, I'd give it forty . . . forty-five minutes, if you're lucky. Further down, we'll have longer, but it won't take more than an hour tops before that flood reaches the harbour.'

'If Shinnook was anything to go by, it's not gonna be nice,' said Zan, seeing Baxter's Mall up ahead.

'That's why you and me are gonna get as many people off the street as we can,' said Mulholland, pulling into the kerb. 'Here's my badge,' he said, taking a wallet from his jacket and handing it to Zan. 'Flash it around as much as you like. You'd be surprised what it'll do.'

Zan took the wallet and levered himself out of his seat.

'Oh, and I'd like it back after all this is over, you hear?' said Mulholland with a smile.

'You bet,' replied Zan and tipped the older man a salute, feeling a strange sense of loss settle on him as he watched Mulholland drive away. The two of them had been through a lot together in the last few hours, and now they were going to have to do it all again.

On their own this time, without each other.

But there was no time for sentiment. They might have made it back to Melville in one piece, but Zan knew that didn't mean they were out of danger.

Favouring his good leg, he turned and set off down the path towards the mall.

Right behind it was the Drive-In.

And his two children.

The clock was ticking.

100

Officially RubyRay's closed at eight on a Saturday night. Ray had already killed the gas on the griddle and was scraping down the hotplates, and Ruby had started cashing up, keen to shift the last two customers sitting at the counter. But she'd forgotten to flip the OPEN

CLOSED sign on the door which now swung open with a rattle of blinds as two men stumped in from the rain.

'Shoot, but that's wicked out there,' said the first man, his thick plaid jacket soaked through at the shoulders, glistening with raindrops on his sleeves.

'That's the way we like it, hereabouts,' offered one of the old-timers, scooping up the last of his apple pie at the counter.

Ruby's heart sank. She knew Ray – he'd have that griddle fired up in no time. Couldn't never turn a customer away, could Ray. She could have kicked herself for not switching that damn sign.

The two men took their stools – an empty one between them – and elbowed up on to a counter that Ruby had just wiped down, reaching for the menu cards she'd just neatly stowed. Wishing death on the pair of them, she picked up the Cona off a cooling plate, reached for two mugs and walked down the duckboard towards them.

'Thank you, ma'am. That's mighty kind,' said the man in the plaid jacket as she poured his coffee.

'You got any steaks back there, ma'am?' asked his companion.

'Ray,' she called over her shoulder, pouring the second mug. 'You got steaks for these gentlemen?'

It wouldn't have taken much to say 'no'. But not Ray.

'Sure have. Delaney's rib-eyes are fresh out, but we got the New York strips still.'

Ruby heard the gas pop and flames flare up on the griddle.

Whispering a curse under her breath, she turned the

Cona hotplate back on, rigged a new roll in the cash register and went round the counter to switch the door sign. It was going to be another late night.

101

In the minutes after reaching the chicane a mile or so out of Melville, the Susquahanish River did just what Mulholland and Zan had known it would do. With no other way out of Melville Valley, it had pressed between the two ridges leading up to the North and South Bluffs and immediately increased its power and its speed. It also built up a sizeable pressure wave that pushed ahead of it down the slope to Melville. On the outskirts of town, this pressure wave suddenly went underground, whistling through the network of pipes and conduits and drainage systems laid out beneath Melville – water, phone, power-lines and sewage. This narrowing of its field served to accelerate its speed even more, and a rush of stinking, faecal air burst up through the plugholes of kitchen sinks, baths and lavatories in homes and businesses three blocks either side of upper Main Street, rattling manhole covers, and hissing like a sack of snakes from sidewalk drains.

This high-energy blast of reeking air was followed, of course, by the river.

Like the air that had gone before it, the speed of its flow increased dramatically in these confined underground spaces, and this tunnelling bore roared ahead of the wave above ground. The same sinks and baths and lavatories that had blasted out foul rotten air, now became fountains, pipes of water gushing up like the blast from an upturned hose. Around Melville that Saturday night more than twenty people, most of them young children in the warm soapy nests of their bathtime, were killed in their homes before the real flood hit.

Out on the streets, particularly at the upper end of Main, it was just as bad. Four fire hydrants ruptured and pig-iron manhole covers leapt from the roads and sidewalks, hoisted several feet into the air by high-pressure plumes of stinking black water. One man was killed by a flying hydrant plug and three others along upper Main were hit by manhole covers as they clattered back down on to road and sidewalk.

In Melville that Saturday night, they were the first to die, thirty-six in all. And not one of them drowned.

These were isolated incidents, however, and so sudden and swift and private, that they barely registered on the early evening crowd downtown, huddling under umbrellas, heading off to bars and restaurants along Promenade and lower Main at the start of a Saturday night.

By now the river that ran down the middle of Main Street had started to show some muscle. Between the harbour and the outskirts of town there was no more than a twelve foot drop over a mile and a half, but the flood made the most of it. Channelled between stone-walled banks that in normal circumstances showed six clear courses above the level of water, the river had risen nearly two feet in as many hours with only four courses of stonework now showing. Running full and strong most of the day, it had now begun to pick up some bulk and in just a matter of minutes another course of stone was lost.

Of the three bridges that crossed the river along Main Street, the upper pedestrian bridge, ten blocks up from downtown, was proving a popular vantage point from which to view the tumbling water. As early evening traffic headed up and down Main, and in the minutes before the power failed, crowds leaned over the bridge's railings to watch the water race below them, most of them residents rather than out-of-towners. The younger ones shouted and pointed, excited by the high water, while the older ones looked nervously at the rising level and wondered if there was any chance the river might break its banks and cause their homes damage. In thirty years there'd never been a flood in Melville, even the worst rainfall and snow-melt run-offs effectively controlled by the Shinnook barrage. If they'd known the barrage was down, they'd have been off that bridge and back at home, shifting their furniture and their valuables to upper floors.

Standing in the middle of the bridge, a half dozen local kids were using the fast, high water to play a game. On the upper side of the bridge, three kids dropped soda cans and sticks and rolled-up balls of paper into the surging river and, on the other side, their three companions wielded rock-pool nets to scoop them up. When they missed and the can or stick raced away, there were boos from their friends, or triumphant whoops when they got it right.

Their supply of cans was pretty much at an end when one of the kids looked upriver and spotted the first surge, nothing more than a two-foot ripple heading towards them, splashing up and curling against the walled banks, a mat of undulating grass and undergrowth riding along in front of it.

'Wow, awesome. Just look what's coming,' the kid shouted, pointing upstream. Heads turned and looked along the street-lit course of the river. A hundred yards away that two-foot wave didn't look like much, but the closer it came the bigger it got.

The grown-ups didn't like the look of it at all, and after watching for a couple of seconds, they started off the bridge. Whichever end was closest. Two or three of them stayed on, trying to move the kids along, or maybe just their own kids.

'Hey, game's over,' they called. 'Let's get outta here.'

They'd left it too late. Not only was the surge growing taller, it was also starting to pick up speed. As the mat of undergrowth slid beneath the bridge, slickly narrowing between the pilings that supported it, the wave that followed hit those same supports in a blast of white water, shaking the bridge in a screech of wood and metal. From either end of the footbridge it looked as though everyone out on that forty-foot span had been caught in an earthquake, the bridge visibly moving underfoot, the kids and grown-ups staggering about like a bunch of late-night drunks, reaching out for something to hang on to as two inches of water sluiced round their ankles, sprayed up around their knees.

In seconds this racing stream started to pick them off, one by one to begin with, then groups of two and three, and there was nothing anyone watching from the bank could do about it. There wasn't even time to point, or scream. Just wide disbelieving eyes.

The lad who'd spotted the bore went first. Jostled by the chill breeze that rode ahead of the wave, he'd stepped back when he saw what was hurtling towards him. In that instant, he must have known he was in serious trouble. This wasn't 'awesome', it was deadly.

The stepping back, not looking where he was going, did for him, singled him out as the first to go. He tripped, stumbled, and fell backwards. There was no time to get to his feet. Those rushing two inches of water caught him like the soda cans he'd been tossing into the river just minutes earlier and they swept him across the bridge. He hit the railings sideways on, facing downriver, the water piling up against his back.

He didn't drown. He was strangled. In just seconds. As the water flattened him out against the railings and pummelled against his head, his face was forced between two of the railings' metal struts. It was a tight fit, scraping skin from the young man's forehead and chin. But it wasn't the scrapes on his chin or his scalp, or the battering on the back of his head, that killed him. What killed him was the strut that snapped past his chin and hit his throat like a karate chop, flattening his Adam's apple and crushing the hyoid bone in an instant.

The others on the bridge probably didn't know the boy was dead – just trapped, in need of help. But none of them was able to get to him. Nor would they have thought to do so. It was enough trying to look after themselves. And when they saw how easy it was for the water to get them if they fell over, they were all desperate now to stay upright.

That was not to be. Two inches of water racing over the bridge, and the earthquake shuddering set up by the flood, were enough to make walking a tricky proposition. Keeping one foot firmly planted while trying to place the other, and the balance just went. One after another they tumbled over, sucked across the bridge and piled up against the railings. One or two managed to struggle to their feet and started to hand-haul themselves along, making for the banks, but their efforts were doomed. With a creak and a snap that could be heard above the raging water, the railings broke away from their mountings and a section swung out over the river. In one lip-licking swallow the river took everyone with it, leaving just one of the teenagers, a girl in pony-tail and tight jeans, clinging to the rail, climbing up on to it, trying to straddle it. For maybe a minute she hung on, screaming her heart out over the roar of the river raging just inches below her, begging for help, whimpering, weeping.

No-one could get to her. Already the river was over the final course of stone and herding onlookers further and further back. As the last ones turned to make good their escape, the girl simply let go of the railing and was tugged away.

For twenty feet, her head stayed above water, bobbing along.

Then it just disappeared, sucked under.

102

Finn's eyes were wide, and his fists gripped the steering wheel of his grandmother's Buick. The film was even better than he'd dared hope, and even the snores from the back seat didn't bother him. Every time he heard a grunt from behind him or a gust of rain hitting the roof, he'd notch up the volume on the dashboard FM. He also knew how to work the wipers, so if the windscreen got too blurred, he just flicked them on.

Up on screen Bond was sipping a cocktail in a beach-side bar in Cuba when the film seemed to stutter and melt on the back wall of Baxter's Mall and the soundtrack on the Buick's FM broke into a hiss of static.

It took a moment or two for Finn to realise what had happened.

'Oh man,' said the boy, banging the wheel with his fist, just like he'd seen his dad do. 'What's wrong with the . . .'

In the darkness, without the soundtrack, the bump sounded loud and close. It came from behind them, and Finn felt the jolt. He caught a movement in the wing mirror and watched in disbelief as the car behind them swung its back end out and slammed into the car beside it.

'What was that?' asked Shelley, waking with a jerk.

But there was no time to reply. The very next instant Finn felt the Buick pick up and start forward, as though the bump from behind had been a signal.

'You let the brake off,' called Shelley, shifting Alexa off her lap and reaching forward. 'Get the hand brake on. Push the pedal.'

'It's on. I didn't touch it,' Finn began, watching their hood bang into the car in front, feeling their own back end swing round. Another bump and they were now sideways on to the screen.

The Buick wasn't the only car on the move. Through the windscreen Finn could see other cars crunching into each other, a slow rag-tag waltz. Horns sounded and headlights flashed as, one after another, in a denting, crunching scrape of metal, the cars in the Drive-In started moving forwards, pressing up against the back wall of the Mall.

'It's a flood,' cried Finn, looking out of the window and seeing a swirl of fast, dark water splash up between the cars.

'Move across, get in the passenger seat,' cried Shelley, trying to squeeze between the front seats, hauling Finn clear of the wheel, then settling behind it and pulling at the brake. But just as Finn had said, the brake was on; he hadn't touched it.

Not that there was too much time to think about what Finn might or might not have done while she was asleep. By the time Shelley got behind the wheel, water was starting to show against the side windows and splash up over the bonnet. She tried the ignition and her head-lights blared on for a moment then blinked off, the engine just turning with a dud cough. Whatever she tried, there was nothing she could do to stop the car moving, as though it had a will of its own.

Up ahead, the cars in the middle of the rows were beginning to pile up against the wall and each other, bonnets rising above trunks, the bigger cars mounting smaller ones and pushing them down. Those at the end of the rows were sweeping away to the side, spinning on the current like bathtime ducks and heading for the exit lanes either side of the mall. For a moment Shelley wished she'd parked at the edge, so that she wouldn't be where she was now, caught in the main press of cars. But then she spotted one of the cars spinning towards the exit lane suddenly dip down, turn over and start rolling like a log – over and over and over, the people inside just shadows tossed around like clothes in a spindryer.

'Gramma, I'm frightened,' called Alexa, kneeling on the back seat and looking out through the side window. Even in the darkness, the little girl could see that things were happening that shouldn't be happening. There was banging and crashing and cars were moving in odd ways and people were starting to scream.

And then, without warning, the Buick reared up, grinding and jolting over the car in front of it then tipping to the side. A moment later the front passenger door flung open and water cascaded over the seats.

103

The sheriff's office was five blocks back from the harbour, on the corner of Boulevard and Main. Mulholland had already called ahead to let Sergeant Calley know what was coming their way and was pleased to see that a crew of his men were working their way up Main, getting people off the street.

But the boys were doing it on foot, stopping people, talking to them, pointing the way to higher ground. There were no squad cars, no lights, no sirens – no real sense of urgency. Leaving the crumpled Durango in the parking lot out front on Main, Mulholland hurried into the building and up to the Squad Room on the second floor.

'We got any units?' bellowed Mulholland. 'We need cars, lights, sirens, for chrissake. We ain't got time for no chit-chat out there.'

'Only car we got is stuck in a ditch top of North Bluff Road,' said Sergeant Calley, following Mulholland into his office. 'We got another up past Stover Park we can't get through to, and two coming back right now from the Hogsback.'

'What the hell they doin' down there?' asked Mulholland, frowning. 'That's Queets country. Over the county line.'

'Big pile-up. Usual thing,' replied Calley. There was no need to explain. Drivers on the coastal highway taking in the view, and not watching the road. Next thing you know there's a four-car traffic incident, or someone's over the cliff. While Mulholland was trying to break through a fence up in Shinnook, an RV had piled into a Haz Chem lorry and blocked the road. 'Got our fire rigs down there too,' added Calley, before Mulholland had a chance to ask.

'Well, we got to get people moving,' said Mulholland, dropping himself down in his chair to pull off his mud-welted snakeskin boots. He tossed them into a corner then went to his locker and pulled out a pair of rubber galoshes to replace them.

'I've been on to Pringle a couple of times,' Calley offered. 'Said he's trying to sort out some problem down at the pumping station, but he'd try to organise some sandbags for properties most at risk.'

Mulholland looked aghast. Sandbags?

'Get him on the line now,' said Mulholland. 'And get him to fire up the sirens.'

'Ain't that a state order he needs for that?' queried Calley.

'I don't care if he needs a message from God. Get him to flick that switch right now, or I'll be down there to stick this boot up his ass and do it for him. You got that?'

'Loud and clear, Chief.'

104

Zan was hurrying across the mall's front parking lot when he noticed the water. Not rain water, not clear and clean and smacking into the ground, but tiny pulsing ripples of dirty, brackish water that smelled of drains and slid past his heels heading down the slope towards the Melville Court Motel. Strong enough, Zan noticed, and fast enough, to roll a styrofoam coffee beaker ahead of it.

Other people on the lot, pushing trolleys or carrying bags to their cars, didn't pay this tiny tide much attention, more intent on getting their groceries loaded and in out of the rain. But Zan knew what it was, and he peered ahead, across the parking lot, tracking the water back to the Drive-In entrance on the left-hand side of the mall. He could see it curling round the corner of the building, lifting just an inch or two off the ground but already coiling and eddying across the polished concrete entrance to the mall.

Zan increased his pace, as much as his knee would allow, heading towards the Drive-In entrance.

The closer he got, the faster the water flowed, now lapping over the toes of his boots.

That was the moment he started to run, or as close to it as he could get, somewhere between a skip and a kind of hobbling jog.

'Get back into the mall,' he shouted at a couple loading groceries over the tailgate of their car. They looked at him as he went past, startled for a moment. Then they gave each other knowing looks and carried on with the loading.

But Zan kept on shouting, waving his arms as he ran, trying to herd people back into the mall. He must have looked like a madman, he thought, as he jogged on towards the Drive-In, flashing Mulholland's badge. 'Stop them coming out,' he screamed at a security guard. 'I'm a deputy. There's a flood coming. Get everyone up to the gallery.'

When he reached the corner of the mall, he flashed Mulholland's badge at the woman in the Drive-In ticket booth.

'Hey, that's no ticket . . .' she shouted. 'You can't come in here.' But before she could do anything about it, Zan was past her, heading up the entrance lane to the Drive-In, a low bank of fenced shrubbery on his left, the mall's side wall on his right. The water was running faster here, up around his ankles now, and in the dying light from the screen he saw a couple of cars start to move off, as though the film had finished and they were all heading home.

But the film hadn't finished, it had stopped; and the cars weren't just moving, they were floating.

By the time he reached the back of the mall, with the screen above his right shoulder, he could see that it was the cars furthest away, the ones closest to the river, that were beginning to move forward and pile up, crumpling into the rows ahead of them, the sound of scraping metal and the clash of fenders covered by a soundtrack of racing water.

But where was Shelley?

Where in all those cars were his kids and their grand-mother?

Turning to his left Zan waded across the knee-high river, now starting to funnel into the Drive-In entrance, and wincing with every step he climbed up the bank. At the top he turned and looked out over the sea of cars. A few windows had been wound down and he could see people shouting at each other, gesticulating. But not a single person had dared get out of their car. Zan could see why. Get out and you'd likely get crushed. From his vantage point he could make out their desperate shadows inside, faces pressed to windows, wondering what was happening? What to do? For the time being, at least, they were safer staying where they were, to see where they ended up.

And somewhere in that scrum of grinding metal was his son and his daughter.

Somehow Zan had expected to see them right away. Right there. Right in front of him. Finn and Alexa, and Shelley. Sitting there, watching the movie, rapt silvered faces through the windscreen. That's what he'd imag-ined. And in the light from the screen he might well have done so. Made them out quite easily. But not now. Not in that lowering rain-lanced darkness. And so many cars. Far more than he'd expected. Sixty, seventy. Maybe more. And all of them on the move, in a kind of slow-motion, senseless dance.

Overwhelmed by all this, Zan suddenly couldn't remember what make of car Shelley drove.

What to look for? A Chevvie? Volvo? Buick . . . ?

Buick, it was a Buick.

And the colour? He tried to remember . . . Blue, it was light blue.

And as if bidden to appear, there it was, about five cars away, maybe six rows back from the screen. And moving in his direction.

By now Zan knew that the water below him would be too strong to wade through. It would snatch his legs from under him and sweep him away. But how could he get to the Buick, now approaching quite fast, catching up with the car in front and mounting its back end?

And then, as it rose out of the water, through the side window, he caught a glimpse of Alexa's terrified white face framed in a rain-blurred fringe of blonde curls.

That was all it took to get him moving. And if he was behaving like some demented Indiana Jones then so be it. Without a thought he launched himself on to the bonnet of the nearest car, passing right by him, feeling it sink down with his weight, then bob up again. And as it did so, noting astonished faces in the front seat staring out at him, he leapt across on to the trunk of a second car as it spun round towards the Buick, like some log driver dancing over a jam of timber. Five more jumps and he was clawing over the roof of the Buick and reaching for the door. Seconds after that, he had the door open and was squeezing in on top of Shelley.

'Dad!', 'Dadda-dadda!' screamed the children.

'And am I glad to see you,' said Shelley.

105

Dave Pringle was standing thirty feet underground, in the bowels of the Melville pumping station. He was wearing a zip-up plastic coverall, white plastic boots and an air tank, and was badly out of breath after clambering down the circular staircase that led from the control room into the basement pump room. If he'd been in a bad mood getting called out on a Saturday evening to coordinate a possible flood defence programme, right now he was seething fit to bust.

Melville's pumping station was located behind South Bluff Quay, the shell of a quaint Victorian villa artfully concealing the silo-like wet-well tank that stored all of Melville's raw sewage, and the two original Galt and Jefferson motors that pumped this sewage to the settlement and filtration tanks out past Baxter's Mall. Normally, the old pumping station was supervised by George Daintree, who'd taken over when Pringle got himself promoted to Town Hall. But since Daintree was on holiday and since his maintenance boys weren't answering their phones this Saturday evening, Pringle had known that at some point in the evening he'd have to call in at the station himself. With the rain they'd been having and a flood supposedly headed in their direction, they'd need to ensure sewage and waste-water levels were kept stable in the wet-well. And to do that they'd need both pumps working.

It should have been easy. Just the flick of a switch on the main control panel. Nothing more than that. Two minutes in and out. But things never quite work out how they're supposed to.

The moment Pringle snapped down that worn red toggle in the control room, he should have been able to hear the second pump start up in the chamber below him. But he hadn't heard a thing. He'd tried it a couple more times, but there was no response. Like everything else in the old pumping station, time and hard service had taken their toll. Daintree had been complaining about it for weeks, some kind of shorting in the main control system, he'd said in his report – the same report that had itemised rusting pipes, worn gaskets and unreliable level indicators. But Pringle, now comfortably quartered in his Town Hall suite of offices, had let it ride. After all, he wasn't the poor sod who had to climb down into the basement and start the pumps manually. Now, in Daintree's absence, he was having to do just that, and paying the price for his complacency.

Pringle hadn't visited the pumping station since he'd crossed Main Street for the Works and Resources job. But he knew the drill, knew what he had to do. Crossing the pump room he checked the display on the wall-mounted gas monitor. Nothing showing. No indication that any hydrogen sulphide was present, always a risk when a wet-well was buried below sea-level.

So he pulled off his mask, rubbed a hand over his cheeks and, wincing at the rank smell of untreated sewage, he turned his attention to the two 3000-watt pumps bolted to the floor in the middle of the chamber. They looked like giant snail shells, six feet high and six feet apart, steel domed and shiny, a pair of eight-inch feeder pipes from the wet-well wall connected to each of them. On the other side of the pumps a single larger pipe snaked out of each and coiled round into a riveted 'D' bracket junction, the two outflows connecting to an even larger pipe that disappeared through the opposite wall.

As expected the duty pump was singing sweetly, sucking sewage from the wet-well tank, but the stand-by pump was silent. This was the one that Pringle needed to crank up. Checking that the in-flow valves on the stand-by feeder pipes were operating correctly, Pringle reached for the manual starter button on the second pump and pushed it down for a count of five before releasing it. As his thumb came off the button the pump engine caught and a low electric whine started up under its polished steel hump.

Result. Job done. By the time he reached the steps leading up to the control room the chamber was humming with power. In a single hour, working together, those two pumps could easily shift a thousand cubic metres of waste, quite enough to keep the wet-well from overflowing, whatever the flood threw at them.

Pausing at the bottom of the steps Pringle tipped off his boots and struggled out of his coverall and air tank, leaving them on the floor. At least he wouldn't have to struggle up the stairs with that lot weighing him down, the legs and arms of the suit swishing annoyingly with every step, the tank harness pulling on his shoulders. Let Daintree tidy it up when he got back from his damn holidays.

Pringle was about to start climbing when a phone beside the gas monitor began to ring. Clucking his tongue with annoyance, he strode over to it and picked up the receiver.

'Pringle. What?'

'Boss, it's Johnson.' Johnson was his assistant back at Town Hall. 'I got Sergeant Calley here saying Chief Mulholland wants the sirens on.'

'Well, he can't have them,' replied Pringle testily. He was fed up with the police department telling him what to do. And expecting him to jump to it. So far, he'd had to come in on a Saturday evening, tog himself up in those damned coveralls and climb down here into a stinking pump chamber, all thanks to them. So he wasn't in the mood to cooperate any further. He'd done his bit. As for sounding the civil defence siren, well he needed State clearance for that.

'The chief says it's urgent. Got to do it now,' said Johnson.

'Well, the chief just better—' It was as far as he got. From somewhere along the main pipe leading out of the pumping station and up to the filtration plant came a low moan that sounded like distant thunder. In seconds the moan was a booming bass blast that seemed to shudder down through the outflow pipe, shaking the brackets that held it to the floor, popping rivets on the D-shaped junction like the buttons on a stretched shirt, and suddenly rupturing the fourteen-inch steel tube like the barrel of a blocked shotgun.

It was an astonishing sight – a fountain of raw sewage

spraying out of the shattered end of the high-pressure pipe like brown tail flames from a rocket, and gushing in puking pulses from the two severed feeder pipes, splattering across the white tile walls of the chamber. In seconds the floor was ankle deep in swirling sewage and rising fast. Then the lights went out, and in the darkness all Pringle could hear was the deluge of thick, warm sewage showering over him. Seconds later the emergency generator cut in and red warning lights flashed through the pump room.

In that strobing, scarlet light, Pringle dropped the phone and made a dash for the stairs. But the rising slush of sewage tugged at his legs and his socks slithered across the polished concrete floor. Like an ice-skater making a poor landing, his feet shot out from under him and he was up to his shoulders in a surging mass of lumpy, liquid waste, batting away the rising tide as he tried to struggle to his feet.

If he hadn't gone to answer that damned phone he'd have been halfway up the stairs by now and out of danger. But he had answered the phone, and right now the stairs seemed a very long way away. If it had been just the feeder pipes that had ruptured he could have clawed his way back to them, closed the isolator valves and shut down the stream from the wet-well. But there was nothing he could do to stop the flow from the pressurised pipe, not quite two miles of high-pressure waste hurtling back into the pump room. If he didn't make the stairs and get out of there in the next couple of minutes Pringle knew he was a dead man.

By the time he got himself upright, his feet just lifted off the floor and he was out of his depth. Coughing out a mouthful of warm slimy sewage, he struck out for the stairs. But he was swimming against a mighty current. All he could do was keep his head above the churning surface, go with the flow and pray that the whirlpool of bubbling waste would swing him round the room and wash him up against the stairs.

If only he'd kept on his breathing apparatus, if only he hadn't taken it off . . .

It is in the nature of strong water in a confined space that eddies start up. It was into one of these, in a far corner of the chamber, that Pringle was flung. And held. There was no way to break free.

Gasping for breath in that stinking froth of human waste, he began to scream his wife's name. A minute later the rising sewage slapped up against the ceiling, but by then Pringle's body was drifting back down through the thick murky lake to the floor of the chamber.

106

By the time Zan had settled behind the wheel of Shelley's Buick, the car was pitched at a forty-five degree angle towards the passenger side, wedged between the car whose trunk it had just ridden over and slid off, and the tilting bonnet of a Ford Taurus on which it had landed. The Taurus looked new and its young driver looked terrified. The car probably belonged to his father, Zan decided, and the kid was more scared about what the old man was going to say when he got his car back, than anything the flood might do to him. With the weight of the Buick pressing down on it, the water was coming close to the kid's windscreen, swirling over the bonnet, and the girl sitting beside him was as white as a sheet.

What happened next put a chill through Zan. One minute the young man and his date were sitting there in the Taurus, watching the water slide around the wipers and wondering what to do, the next minute the car behind them seemed to rise up and smash down on top of them. The roof held, but the car was pushed down into the flood, water rising fast up the car's windows, sealing the couple in. The last thing Zan saw as the Taurus sank out of sight into the floodwater was the driver trying to wrench open the door and the girl beside him screaming.

Shelley had seen it too.

'We can't stay in the car,' she shouted at Zan. 'We've got to get the kids out of here.'

'You want to get out? In this . . .' Zan shouted back.

'Dadda, Dadda, don't get out, please don't get out,' shrieked Alexa from the back seat, flinging her arms round his neck. Finn just looked at him, as if to say, 'I'll do whatever you want me to, Dad.'

'Baby, please, please,' said Zan, disentangling himself from his daughter's arms. 'Listen, listen to me, now. All of you.' He looked at the three of them, at their scared pale faces as the Buick bucked and writhed in the mess

403

of cars. 'We're not getting out, okay? We're staying right here.'

There was another loud crash from behind them and the Buick swung to the right, pushing against another car. Zan glanced over his shoulder and saw that, because of this sudden shift to the right, they were now closer to the entrance lane than they had been. Turning back to Shelley and the kids, he said, 'We're going to be pushed out into the stream. Any minute now, the current will get a hold of us and start moving us away from here. We just need to hang on tight and see where we end up.'

Shelley was shaking her head. 'Zan, we can't, it's too . . .'

'We can and we will,' he interrupted. 'You saw what happened. We're not going to get stuck in this. So make sure your windows are wound up tight and hold on.'

By now the water was coming into the Drive-In fast and deep. Zan saw a hefty length of tree trunk ride past them on the flood and he held his breath as it reached the entrance lane. He had hoped it would snag and catch there, and that when their turn came to be swept away they'd be held by it, something they could climb up on to to reach the bank. But it slid into the gap lengthways on, touching neither bank nor mall wall, and was gone.

The next instant it was the Buick's turn to hit the stream, just as Zan had said, forced out by the press of cars behind it. With a wrench of metal parting with metal, the Buick tore loose from the Toyota that had slammed down on the Taurus and spun forward.

For a moment they were pointing upriver, like Mulholland's Durango at Drivers' Cut, and Zan could see a huge spray of water blasting up around the projection booth. The booth was built of sheet-board on a wood frame and Zan knew it wouldn't last long with that gush of water hammering into it.

As he watched, the two-storey building suddenly crumpled, staggered forward, and a wave of water surged over the ruins, smashed into the mess of cars and pressed them even more closely together – some cars sinking, others rising high enough to topple over.

Zan was glad to be out of it. But he didn't have time to think about it. Unlike the Durango, sitting on its bridge span, the Buick was lighter and more manoeuvrable and the current swung it round until it was facing forward. It was extraordinary how swiftly they accelerated, how fast they were going, dancing over the water, occasionally, on a dip, scraping over gravel. Instinctively, Zan stepped on the brake but nothing happened. If anything, they seemed to be going faster. Zan wasn't surprised. The entrance lane between the mall and the bank was coming up fast and the water was building up to get through. Twenty feet away, the car in front of them shot forward, was sucked into the gap, and was gone. And then it was their turn, the Buick's bonnet surging up over a swell, then dropping down like a sledge into the gap, coming close enough to the mall wall to snap off a wing-mirror but still steady and facing the right way.

Which meant all four of them could see what was waiting for them up ahead.

107

Three blocks down from Baxter's Mall, on the other side of Main, Ray had finally closed down the griddle and was humping a sack of garbage out back of the diner when he noticed water streaming past the wheels of his van. It was shadowy in the yard and the low cloud cover and rain made it seem darker than it was. But Ray could see that this was a faster flow than they usually saw in a rainstorm.

At first he thought it might be a fractured water main, which would have accounted for the drain in his sink acting up a few minutes earlier. And a fractured mains was certainly what it looked like it was. When he came round the side of his van he could see the water boiling up from an open manhole. But there was water beyond the manhole too, coming down the alley from Upper Main and sluicing over it. In fact, he could only see where the manhole was because of the bulge where the water it was pumping out joined the flood.

Because that's what it was. A flood. Coming right at them across the highway. A hundred feet away, on the other side of Upper Main, a wave was already building up on the corner of the Melville Court Motel and breaking on to the sidewalk, which meant – Ray sniffed the air like he did when the wind was blowing from the north-east – that the primary settlement tank at the sewage treatment works, further up the slope, had to have been breached.

Sure enough, a sinuous coil of rank soiled air slid through the rain and whipped past his nostrils. Dropping the garbage bag where he stood, Ray hurried back to the diner and through the back door into the warm-fry smell of his kitchen.

'We got problems,' he called through to Ruby. 'We got ourselves a flood out there, I'm telling you.'

Everyone in the diner turned to the window, but with the rain slashing against it and the diner's interior reflected against it, it wasn't easy to see what was going on outside. One of the men working on his steak at the counter got off his stool and lumbered over to a booth, leant across it and cupped his hand to the window.

'And ain't that the truth,' he said. 'It's just . . .' Suddenly he leapt back from the window as if he'd just been bitten. 'Whoa,' he cried and pointed at the glass. Outside the water had lapped over the sill and started to surge and slap against the window. A couple more feet and it would be like being at the aquarium.

'Shoot, that's my car,' cried his friend, coming off his stool and pointing into the lot.

Twenty feet away a Toyota flatbed truck had swung round and was bearing down on them.

'Jesus, it's gonna hit,' cried the man in the booth, and he shuffled his way back out of it as the Toyota reared up, smashed through the glass and crashed down against the counter stools.

No-one was hurt by the truck, but all four customers

were picked up by the following wave and flung around the diner, slamming against the Toyota and counter, stools and booths, sliced and slashed by the shards of window spinning through the current.

Acting as a breakwater, the counter gave Ruby and Ray just a few seconds' reprieve. It wasn't enough to make much difference. In a boiling surge the water flowed over the top of the counter and spilled down over the duckboards, pinning Ruby against the cash register before lifting her up over the shelves and then tugging her under.

Ray, wide-eyed in the hatch, was the last to go, the incoming water sending up a billowing cloud of steam from his griddle.

It was the steam, as much as the water, that blinded Ray, and he never saw the 'D' of 'Diner' painted on to a blade of broken glass that surfed through the hatch and sliced off the left side of his head.

108

The tree trunk that Zan had seen race past them while they were still stuck in the press of cars had careered down the entrance lane until a corner of the mall's front awning snagged one of its branches. Caught and held in one of the support struts, the trapped branch had swung the trunk lengthways, its tangle of roots hammering through the ticket booth and ploughing up on to the bank, the floodwater spraying over it and sucked beneath it. Already, two cars had smashed into it and been forced under, blocking the flow even more.

'Hold on,' Zan shouted, and a moment later the Buick smacked into the tree, crumpling the bonnet and sending a web of cracks across the windscreen. For a moment the car stayed where it was, bucking in the current, its occupants badly jolted and dizzy from the impact. Then the flood caught hold of it again, spun it ninety degrees and smashed its passenger side broadside-on against the tree.

'This is where we get off,' shouted Zan, levering himself up from behind the wheel and pounding his fist against the windscreen. If they stayed in the car, or got hit by another one coming up behind them, the chances were they'd be sucked under the tree and trapped. As far as he could see, they had no other choice. He had to get his kids, and Shelley, out of the Buick as quickly as he could.

The windscreen finally gave way, and a mix of rain and spray washed into the Buick's interior, bringing with it a foetid blast of sewage. Wasting not a moment Zan squirmed through the gap and out on to the wave-tossed bonnet. Staying on all fours he slithered along it and reached up for the branch snarled in the awning strut. When he was satisfied with his grip, feet planted on a lower branch, he turned back to the car and stretched out his hand.

'Finn, you first,' he shouted. 'Shelley, get him up on to the hood and as close to me as you can.'

Without any argument, Shelley caught hold of her grandson and helped him through the windscreen. The boy looked terrified, but he held his nerve, reaching out for his father with Shelley hanging on to a leg, just in case.

'Shelley, let him go. He needs to come closer,' screamed Zan over the sluicing roar of the water. 'Finn, you got to get closer.'

With his grandmother reluctantly letting go of his leg, but still a couple of feet from his father's outstretched hand, Finn was on his own, on all fours like his father before him, the Buick bucking beneath him.

'Come on, son. Just slide if you have to. I'm here. I'll catch you.'

And slide the boy did, on all fours, bravely letting go of the car to reach up a hand as he closed on Zan, finally managing to grab a hold of his father's wrist.

'I've got you. I've got you,' panted Zan, hauling the boy up and over his legs and hugging him one-armed against his chest, spray and rain blasting against his face. 'Okay, now. You ready?'

He felt his son's head nod against his chest. 'Now I'm going to hold you as long as I can, but you just gotta climb up over my shoulder and get into the branches. Get as close to the awning as you can and then jump down on to it. You understand? You got that?'

'Got it,' whispered Finn, hardly loud enough to be heard, and started to scrabble up over his father as quickly as he could, desperate to get away from the flood. To get to safety.

In an ideal world, his father would have gone with him, helped him those last few feet. But something told Zan he didn't have the time. The tree was not going to hold for ever. Already the trapped branch was beginning to creak and quietly splinter and Zan could see that the metal awning spar that held it was bending outwards in an alarming fashion. His son would just have to manage without him. The boy had climbed enough trees up at Wilderness One and was probably more at home in them than Zan.

Turning away, praying his son would make it, he looked back to the Buick, grateful to see that Shelley had managed to bundle up a screaming Alexa in her arms and was whispering something in her ear.

'Come on, baby. Come to Dadda,' shouted Zan, fear shooting through his limbs in paralysing bursts.

Down in the Buick, with a final kiss on her grand-daughter's cheek, Shelley managed to push Alexa through the windscreen, backside first, the little girl's arms still tight round her grandmother's neck.

'You gotta let go of Gramma, baby,' shouted Zan. 'You got to come to Dadda, you hear?'

Painfully slowly, Shelley freed herself from Alexa's grasp and pushed her out on to the Buick's bonnet. The little girl screamed even louder and Zan's heart burst with fear for her.

'Come on Alexa. Come on sis. Dad'll get you,' came a voice over Zan's shoulder.

Zan turned and glanced behind him. There, safely on the awning, ten feet away and four feet above him, was Finn, hands around his mouth, yelling encouragement at his little sister.

Down on the bonnet, Alexa was flat on her stomach now, not daring to move, blonde hair plastered over her face, her cheek pressed against the crumpled hood, a shower of spray blasting over her.

'Come on, baby. You gotta come to Dadda,' Zan cried, just loud enough to be heard over the roar of the flood but not loud enough to frighten her even more.

Zan could see what the problem was. Shelley may have got her through the windscreen, but his daughter was facing the wrong way. Before she could reach out for him she'd have to turn herself round, to see where she was going, to see where he was.

Over the roof of the Buick Zan caught a glimpse of another broken length of tree swooping down towards them. It wasn't as long or as large as the tree he was hanging on to but it was heavy enough to hit the side of the Buick with a mighty thump that sent Shelley sprawling back between the two front seats and lifted Alexa clean off the bonnet. She landed on her side and immediately started sliding towards him, scrabbling for a hold on the crumpled panelling rather than reach out for his hand.

'Get her, Dad! Get her, Dad!' screamed Finn from the awning.

But it was impossible, impossible. If she didn't reach up for him right now, Zan knew she'd simply slide off and be sucked under the tree.

She had to turn. She had to reach up.

And then, somehow, she was on her back, legs in the air, hands pressed down against the bonnet trying to brake the slide. A second later she surfed past within inches of him. As close as she was ever going to come. And Zan lunged, stretching down as far as he dared but suddenly latching on to an ankle. His fingers squeezed around it and she swung sideways against the tree, the weight of her nearly ripping Zan from his perch, sending burning flashes of pain through his bandaged knee.

'I've got you. I've got you!' he screamed.

But that's all he could do. Hold her. There was no way he could lift her, no way she could climb up on to him like Finn. All he had done was delay the inevitable – something else smashing against the Buick, or his strength giving out. And then the floodwater would have her.

In that moment of gut-wrenching fear and panic, wondering what on earth he could do to save his daughter, Zan felt fingers slide into the back of his trouser band and get a grip, and he heard a familiar voice calling to him through the rain. 'You can let go. Let go of the branch, Dad. I've got you.'

Glancing round, he saw Finn on the other side of the tree trunk, legs hooked round a branch, belly to the wood, giving a tug on his father's trousers to show him what he meant, that he had him. Somehow the boy had got back down from the awning and scrambled back to lend a hand.

Not daring to think it was possible, but left with no other option, Zan held on to Alexa's ankle with one hand, while loosening his grip on the branch with the other. And felt himself held. Almost weeping with relief, he bent forward, pulling up with one hand, reaching down with the other, a lance of pain shooting through his knee. If his son let go now, he and his daughter were doomed.

'Reach out! Reach out, my darling,' he shouted to her.

And she did. And he had her, blood pumping painfully in his head from the effort, pressing behind his eyes.

With Finn hanging on to his trousers, Zan let go of Alexa's ankle, grabbed her other arm and hauled her up, high enough to get her feet on the bonnet, telling her she needed to push down against it so he could pull her to him.

At first she wouldn't drop her feet into the water now lapping over the hood. But finally, pleading with her, Zan persuaded her to lower them and he felt the weight come off his arms. Getting a better grip under her armpits, he gave her a one, and a two, and a three . . . and heaved her up off the bonnet.

109

It was still early for a Saturday night but Mama Surf was humming. An old sail-making hall put up on Melville's main quay a hundred and fifty years earlier, much of the original building remained – the long room where sheets of canvas had once been laid out for sail-making or repair on the worn wood floors, the high beamed ceilings studded with blackened rigging hooks, and the timbered walls gouged with names and dates – French names predominantly, because Melville had first been settled by French trappers. Here, Georges

Dubois – Juin 1890; Paul Crécy – Octobre 1911; Daniel Jacquot – Mai '06; Les Frères Goujons – 1855–74.

Back then the place had smelled of wet canvas, sour sweat and creosote. Nowadays only the sweat remained, laced with the sweeter notes of perfume, stale beer and the club's mascot tomcat, George Dubya. For more than a century the only sounds here had been the slap of rope and rustle of canvas, the bubbling of tar cauldrons and, years later, the whirr of sewing machines. Now the action was held together by the occasional snick-snick soundtrack of cue stick and ball over on the pool table, a low, thumping sound system and the commentaries from two TV screens bolted either end of the long bar – one dedicated to news, the other to sport, usually a surf competition somewhere.

By the time Jed Roberts arrived, pulling off his dripping trucker's cap and stuffing it in his coat pocket, the bar was already three deep, the music was loud and there appeared to be no sign of Ginny. Pushing through the throng, getting high fives along the way from friends, and the odd glare from anyone he might have dealt with on a professional basis, Jed finally found her in the end booth, sipping a Mojito and looking hot. Her wavy red hair was thick and artfully tossed, her lips a glistening scarlet and her eyes as green as the mint in her cocktail, but turning lazy and disinterested the moment she caught sight of him. She was wearing a white silk blouse sufficiently unbuttoned to reveal the front of a well-filled black bra and her wrists jangled with silvery hoops.

She looked good enough to eat, thought Jed hungrily. But he knew he'd have to watch his step. This one bit. Before he sat down he reached into his pocket for the birthday present he'd bought, at eye-watering expense, from Pierre's, the jewellers, and put it on the table in front of her. As she pulled at the ribbon and loosened the paper, he slid into the booth and watched her lift the silver whale charm from its tissue nest and examine it.

Much to his delight, and relief, the gift seemed to work – 'It's so cute!' she squealed happily – and as she squirrelled it away in her bag he watched her reach down below the table, cheek to the wood, keeping those eyes on him every second. A moment later her warm stockinged foot rubbed up his leg, and then burrowed between his thighs. 'You shouldn't have,' she told him with a sly grin, feeling him start to respond. 'And Pierre's? Why you just gotta be hungry for something, boy.'

Then, primly, job done, the foot was removed, and Ginny sat up and reached for her cocktail, rattling ice in an empty glass. 'So just what exactly does a girl have to do to get herself a drink round here?'

It was in that instant that Ginny's expression changed, from a teasing smile to a questioning frown. Then she jerked in her seat. 'What you . . . ?' she began, indignantly. 'You trod on my toe, goddammit. And hard too.' She leant down to rub her foot, and her green eyes opened wide. She could feel fur sliding past her fingertips and something warm curling round her ankles. 'Jesus, it's that fucking cat . . . I got bitten by that fuckin' George Dubya.'

But it wasn't a cat under the table. George Dubya was nowhere to be seen.

Then, in the next booth along, a woman screamed. And then another. As the jukebox played on, the screams increased in number and volume. Some of the women were climbing up on to their seats and on to the tables, and over by the long bar customers had leapt on to stools, or up on to the bar itself, or had started stamping their feet like maddened flamenco dancers.

Back in their booth, Ginny bent down even further to see what had bitten or scratched her. She had a terrible feeling she knew, but she didn't dare believe it. Thirty seconds before the power died and the lights went out she came face to face with a pair of beady eyes, twitching whiskers and glinting incisors – one of a score or more of rats squirming beneath their table and now streaming out into the bar like a Hamelin plague.

110

Shelley was the last to leave the car.

By now the Buick was starting to sink, or was slowly being sucked under by the current, the foot-wells sloshing with the rain and floodwater lapping in through the broken windscreen. Thrown into the back seat when the log hit, Shelley watched Zan haul his daughter up into the tree, climbing up afterwards to shepherd her and

Finn back to the awning. When he had them safe, he turned back and started crawling along the tree trunk, shouting her name.

She couldn't hear his shouts over the roar of the water but she knew what he was saying, knew that it was now her turn to crawl out on to that bucking bonnet and take her chances. Lying there in the back seat, she reached out a hand to pull herself forward and her fingers touched her flask of bourbon. For a moment she couldn't think what it was. And then, with a gasp of gratitude, she remembered. While Zan struggled along the tree, she unscrewed the cap and tipped the flask back, feeling the spirit push a warm stream down her throat. If she was ever going to squeeze herself out of that windscreen, and then go climbing, she'd need whatever Jim, Jack or Hiram – she couldn't remember which bourbon she'd used – could give her.

Too soon what was left in the flask had gone. But it was enough. By now, she could see that Zan was back in position and calling out to her. Slowly she dragged herself between the front seats and poked her head through the windscreen, the rain and flood-spray batting against her face and streaming into her collar like cold fingers, the stench of sewage stronger now than it had been.

'You gotta get out on the hood,' she heard Zan shout. 'It's the only way I can get to you.'

'Yeah, yeah,' she said, under her breath. 'I hear you.'

Helping Finn and Alexa out had been easy enough, but doing it herself was not so straightforward, no-one behind her to give her a shove. Instead she managed to get the heel of her shoe hooked against the steering wheel and pushed herself forward, out on to the bonnet, scrabbling for a hand-hold as the Buick rocked and bucked.

'Please God, please let me make it,' she cried to herself. 'I swear I'll never touch another drop again. I swear it. Just let me get through this.'

'Look up, look up. I'm right here,' Zan's voice came down to her. He sounded surprisingly close, but she couldn't see him because her cheek was pressed tight against the car's bonnet and her eyes were closed. 'Quick as you like,' he continued, only half joking.

Shelley opened her eyes, lifted her head and tried to raise herself up, wishing she didn't need to. Three feet away, Zan's hand reached down to her, waving her on. Just three feet, that's all it was. Not so far, really. But she could see that it would take her right up to the top of the radiator where the boiling water churned and sucked. That's how far she'd have to go to reach him, that's how close she'd be to the muscling, hungry current.

But there was no choice. She had to do it. For herself, for Dasha, for the kids. And for the man up there, risking his life. So she pushed herself forward, just an inch or two in case she started to slide and couldn't stop herself.

But she didn't slide. She just moved forward a few inches.

So she did it again. And again, getting the rhythm of the bucking Buick and managing to ride it. If not for the appalling danger, she could see it might be fun.

Finally she was where she needed to be, her weight starting to tip the hood down, water swirling up over it with such venomous intent that she edged back to counter the drop.

'Just reach out,' cried Zan. 'Just come this way a little

more and reach up . . . that's it. That's the way,' he told her, reaching down and finally catching hold of her fingers, her hand, and then her wrist. He closed his eyes as he took the weight, then opened them when he realised she wasn't as heavy as he'd anticipated. 'Okay, now, you've just gotta climb up on to that stub of branch there, and haul yourself up. But I got you. It's okay.'

He watched her search for the branch with her free hand, just a nub below the surface. And then she had it and was lifting her leg to fit her foot to it.

Before putting any weight on to it, she looked up and caught his eye.

'If I don't make it,' she called to him, 'if I don't make it, tell her I love her, you hear?'

'Tell her yourself,' he shouted back. 'You're coming with me, or we both go for a swim.'

111

Tod Breamer didn't see the lights go out. He had other things on his mind right then. He had planned a good burst for Rita and the Dodge up the Shinnook road, maybe as far as Drivers' Cut, before heading back down to Melville for some spicy ribs and a pitcher at Arty's Hot-Bones. But Rita had other ideas.

'Why don't we go down to the harbour?' she'd suggested, after she slid herself into the Dodge and made all the appropriate noises, reaching out her fingers and stroking the beading on the back of his seat. As every single guy with a car in Melville knew, this was the kind of suggestion usually made at the end of a date, not before it. There was a quiet section of wharf right at the end of South Bluff Quay, past the old lumber yards, that was a favourite make-out spot. 'I want to see the waves,' she told him. 'And the sharks. You wanna take me there?'

Even on a hot date Melville Harbour wasn't the kind of place Tod liked to park his Dodge. All that salt just whacked out his chrome work and paint-job, and most times he kept the Dodge three blocks clear of the ocean. But one look at Rita and he'd headed straight for that quay. Tod knew it was too dark to see any sharks, but if they couldn't see the waves, they'd sure as hell feel them. Not that Rita had seemed too interested in waves or sharks when he finally parked up on the edge of the Outer Quay breakwater. Five minutes after killing the V-8, his meaty fingers were sliding up under her skirt and her nylon thighs were parting.

He was pressing his tongue into the furthest reaches of her hot, minty mouth when something massive hit the back of his Dodge. In that single split second of impact, Rita's teeth clamped down and severed Tod's tongue at exactly the moment his bony forehead cracked against hers. The two of them were wrenched from their seats, flung into the back of the Dodge and pressed into the rear window ledge as the car leapt forward over the edge of the quay.

Both were dead by the time that old Dodge Charger went airborne, burying its scarlet snout into a tumble of rocks thirty feet below.

112

After the screaming in the booths and the last of the stamping at the bar, there was a strange, whispering kind of silence in the seconds after the lights went out in Mama Surf. Thanks to a few dozen candles set around the old sail-maker's hall – at either end of the bar, on the shelves behind it and in each of the booths – it wasn't so much darkness that descended as a softening of the light, and a sudden hollow emptiness as the music from the sound system died.

And in those seconds of stillness and soft guttering light, in that rustling, muttering silence the rats simply vanished. The sinuous flow of their slick shiny fur, the whipping shiver of their stiff hairless tails and the scurrying scratching of their thousand claws on the bare wood boards suddenly thinned and disappeared, as though they had drained away through some unseen sluice, leaving the floor still and empty.

Jed's phone had started buzzing in his pocket at almost exactly the moment that the lights went out, and had carried on buzzing as the rats passed down the length of the bar. By the time he had helped a screaming Ginny up on to her seat, the buzzing had stopped.

Without thinking, he pulled out his cigarettes and lit up. He noticed he wasn't the only one who was smoking. Even Ginny, who usually only indulged if grass were a part of the mix, reached for his cigarette and took a deep trembling drag. In the candlelight her hair flamed and the shadow in the unbuttoned recess of her blouse swelled and shifted as she inhaled, blew the smoke out.

'Did you see that?' she asked. 'Did you see those fucking rats. I don't believe it.' Her eyes were wide and horrified and the hand that passed the cigarette back to him was still shaking.

Clamping the cigarette between his lips, Jed dug for his phone and flicked to Missed Calls. Sergeant Calley at the Sheriff's Office calling him back in. It wasn't too much of a leap to assume that his Sergeant's call and the appearance of the rats and the power-out were somehow connected.

But before he could phone back, someone shouted, 'Water!', and the word was picked up as other customers looked down at their feet, Jed and Ginny too. Curling into their booth, a ripple of water lapped around the table stand and over the toes of Jed's trainers.

Looking to locate the source of the water, Jed turned and followed the glistening stream back to the pool table at the far end of the bar, set below a line of elk-horn trophies hung on the wood-panelled wall. Below these trophies was a locked door leading to store rooms out back. As his eyes settled on it, Jed frowned. The door appeared to be trembling in its frame, its panels creaking. If it hadn't seemed too fanciful, he could have sworn it bulged.

'What the hell—?' he heard one of the pool players say, but the words that followed – if there were any – were whipped away as the door burst open and a solid wedge of water blasted over the pool table, throwing ahead of it a chill slap of air that stank of drains.

The two men who had been playing there were snatched off their feet and sent flying – under and over the pool table – arms, legs and cue sticks flailing as they were swept down the length of the room, knocking over anyone or anything in their path like a pair of bowling balls taking out skittles. Instinctively Jed leapt up beside Ginny, crouching on her seat as the water surged past, rising fast, whirlpooling into each of the booths and dragging people out, their drinks, their bags, the candles on their tables, picking up stools at the bar, chairs and tables in the centre of the room, flinging everything down to the doors leading out on to Promenade.

Jed and Ginny, in the booth closest to the pool table and the first to be hit by the water, escaped the worst of the snatching whirlpools. Instead the incoming water sprayed up over the top of their booth with a whooshing, rushing sound, chill and reeking, steady and strong, as though there was plenty more to come.

Cowering on the seat, wisps of red hair slickly plastered across her cheeks, her black bra now showing clearly through her blouse, Ginny grabbed at Jed and pulled him close, clung to him.

'It's okay, it's okay,' he shouted over the roar of the

water overhead and the rushing suck of it as it raced past their booth.

'Okay? This isn't okay. It's fucking . . . terrifying. What're we gonna do? What're we gonna do? You gotta get me out of here, Jed. Out of here right now.'

Jed got his arm round her and gave her a hug, looking over her shoulder and wondering just how exactly he was going to manage that little trick. It was abundantly clear to him that the water was running fast and fierce enough to snatch anyone off their feet. Go out in that, and it was a ninety-foot helter-skelter surf to Mama Surf's front door which, in the dim light, he could just make out at the end of the line of booths, already piling up with furniture and customers, like debris caught in a plughole. As far as he could judge, they were better off staying where they were, even though the water was rising steadily in their booth, tugging hungrily at their legs and starting to eddy around the top of the table. Maybe it would stop soon, he thought; there surely couldn't be much more water left after such an explosive dam blast?

But there was no let-up. The water kept coming and its surging level continued to rise, the roof of water combing off the top of their booth like a silvery ceiling.

'Jed, you gotta do something . . . !' screamed Ginny. 'This is not good . . . this is not fucking good . . .'

But she got no further.

Toppled by the flood, the pool table smashed against the back of their booth and, with a splintering crack, one of its carved legs speared through the wood panelling just a few inches from Ginny's shoulder.

113

It was Carrie who appeared to knock over her glass of shiraz. And she really did think she had. But her fingers were still inches away when the glass toppled over as Fluke suddenly rose and tipped. Ty and Mungo's glasses would have toppled, too, if they'd been on the table. But the two men had reached for their wine at exactly the same moment – and laughed about it. Which was when Carrie reached for her glass.

'How silly of me,' she began as the glass broke and wine spilled over the cloth. She was about to push out of her chair when the houseboat rocked again as though some passing boat had thrown out an inconsiderate wash. She reached for the table to steady herself and looked anxiously at the two men.

'It's just . . .' was all Ty was able to say before the houseboat suddenly rose up like an express lift, then crashed back down on the edge of its mooring pontoon. There was a loud grating and splintering sound, the candles on the table toppled over and spluttered out, and the houseboat lurched over at an angle that saw all the dishes slide off the dining-room table, pictures fly from the walls and any furnishings that weren't screwed down roll and tumble across the cabin.

Ty, Mungo and Carrie were tipped from their chairs, and the three of them rolled down the slope of the deck in a tangle of limbs and a shower of shattering glass and china. As far as Mungo could tell something had thrown the houseboat over on its side. Something raw and massive that now hammered insistently on the exposed hull, the drum roll of some powerful elemental force that had ripped the houseboat from its pilings and pushed it across the pontoon, snapping mooring and power lines and wrenching cleats from the deck, pinning it up against the wall of the quay.

It could only be water, some vast surge, a rogue wave, thought Mungo as he scrambled to his feet, standing now on a wall that had once had pictures on it, his back against the ceiling, reaching down in the darkness to help up Ty and Carrie, the three of them grabbing hold of each other in the thundering gloom. Through a porthole on the wall above his head Mungo could see the flashing red beam of the harbour light, and he suddenly realised they were on the wrong side of the quay to be hit by an ocean swell. It would simply have blasted against the stone wall of the quay and exploded over the roof of the houseboat. Whatever had hit them, whatever held them against the quay wall, had come from the land. From the river. But that was surely not possible.

'You okay?' he shouted to Ty and Carrie over the hammering din from the hull, now shielding them from whatever was out there.

'Fine,' replied Ty, wiping a hand across the side of his face. 'Just a cut, I think. Carrie? You okay?'

'A few scratches,' she replied, shakily, as the house-boat started tipping back to the level, crashing back down on to its hull, settling on to a surging swell of water. Once more they were tipped forward, slip sliding down the wall until the deck was back beneath their feet again.

Clambering through to the main cabin, leaving Ty with Carrie, Mungo wrenched open Fluke's bulkhead door and looked out into the sheeting rain. It took him a moment to get his bearings. They were floating again, right side up, but adrift, turning slowly in a raging torrent of water that, as far as he could see, was cascading into the harbour from the town. A river flood. A massive one, thought Mungo. Like nothing he had ever seen before. And as the houseboat carried on turning, he could suddenly see the danger they were in. No longer moored to the pontoon – there was no longer any pontoon to be moored to, just a scattering of match-wood planking – they were drifting out into the middle of the inner harbour, followed by the other houseboats berthed along that stretch of quay and also torn from their moorings. One had turned turtle, just a hull floating low in the water, waves washing over it, but the other four were upright, spinning helplessly in the surge, bucking and pitching, carried along by the wind and the current just like Fluke.

As far as Mungo could see, two of these houseboats appeared to be occupied. Peering through the stinging rain and slapping spray from the ocean, he could make out a dozen or more terrified people clinging to door frames and companion-rails.

'Jesus, we're loose,' came a voice beside him. It was Ty. 'What the hell happened?'

'Flood. A big one. Looks like it's coming right through the town and just pouring into the harbour. We must have been hit by the leading crest. It just dumped us on the pontoon and then wrenched us away. Right now it looks like we're heading towards the outer harbour.'

He was interrupted by a grinding crash. Thirty feet away, two of the houseboats had rocked up against one another. Ty and Mungo turned to see what had happened, but Fluke's spin had taken them out of the line of sight. Coming back round they saw that the bows of a lighter houseboat had risen up over the stern of its larger neighbour. People were shouting and pointing, and there, splashing in the water was a man, clearly flung from the deck in the collision and desperately trying to make it back to safety.

As the two houseboats swung round, still joined stern to bow, Mungo realised what they were all screaming about. Cutting through the swell were three fins, heading straight for the man in the water. With Fluke still turning in the swell, Mungo and Ty clambered around the deck trying to keep him in view. Someone threw a roped lifebelt and the man grabbed hold of it, his friends hauling him in as fast as they could.

But the sharks were faster.

114

Within seconds of the table leg piercing the back of their booth, the watery ceiling above their head was gone, the last of it spattering down on top of Jed and Ginny.

Gently removing Ginny's arms from around his neck, Jed stood up on the seat and peered over the top of the booth. In the dim, shadowy light he could see the same solid plug of water barrelling through the store room door, tearing greedily at the door frame as though trying to make the gap wider. It was clear at once that the flood wasn't going to ease up any time soon, strong enough to have tipped over the pool table and to have shoved it across the floor at a high enough speed for one of the legs to burst through the back of their booth. Jed could also see why the water above their heads had stopped so abruptly. The pool table, wedged against the wall and the back of their booth, had dramatically deflected the flow, the water now beating and pummelling against the angled blue baize top and coursing around it in a vicious twisting torrent. So great was its power that the pool table actually shivered, trembling down through the leg that had speared their booth.

As far as Jed could tell, he and Ginny were the only ones left in the bar – no heads showing above the booths below them, no-one clinging to the bar as the water swept past on its way to the front door.

'Hey! You okay there?'

The voice came from behind him, from the stairs leading to the restrooms on the first landing. Jed turned and saw two men standing there, a couple of steps clear of the flood, and just a few feet beyond the upturned pool table. They were dressed in jeans, smart jackets and open-necked shirts, and had the look of out-of-towners, Jed thought, here for the weekend. A young woman, clutching at her skirt as though to keep it from getting blown up in the blast of cold stinking air, came down the stairs and joined them. As she took in the surging water she wiped her nose with the edge of her hand, tipped back her head and sniffed. In an instant, Jed knew what they'd been doing, up there in the restrooms. Taking time out for a line of coke, they'd missed the party and saved their lives.

But now was not the time to play cop.

'Yeah, fine,' Jed shouted back. 'Just stuck is all.'

Leaning over the back of the booth, he checked out the pool table, the leg that had burst through the booth's panelling and the leg that had not, the leg that angled the pool table out against the water and redirected its ferocious course.

'You can make it,' shouted the man on the stairs. He had seen what Jed was looking at and had reached the same conclusion.

'There's two of us,' Jed shouted back. 'I'll send my friend over first.'

'Better hurry,' said the second man. 'That wall doesn't look like it's going to hold much longer.'

Jed looked over at the back wall and felt a sudden jolt of fear. As well as roaring through the open store room door, the water was now starting to spray out between the wood panelling either side of the door – and above it. Any minute now, it looked like the whole wall would give.

Jed dropped down beside a shivering Ginny. Her wide eyes latched on to his and she reached for his hand.

'We need to get out of here,' he told her, hoping he sounded more confident than he felt.

'You're telling me,' she replied, licking her lips. Seeing her do that made him realise that his mouth was also dry, dry with fear and shock.

'We're going to climb over the booth and get across to the stairs,' he told her.

She didn't say anything. Just looked at him, searching his face to see if he was being straight with her.

'All you got to do is slide along the edge of the pool table,' Jed continued. 'It's jammed the other side of the booth. And there's a guy on the stairs to catch you.'

'Catch me?' she said through chattering teeth.

'The last bit you gotta kinda . . . jump.'

'Jump? How far exactly? Jump how far?'

'A few feet, maybe less. It's easy.'

'I bet,' said Ginny, but she unwound herself and stood up on the seat. She looked over the booth and took it in. 'You are joking, Jed. You are fucking *joking*.'

'If you want I'll go first. So you can see what to do.'

'Hey cop, if anyone's going first, it's me, right?'

Jed smiled. 'If you say so.'

'I say so.'

432

'Okay then,' said Jed, keeping an eye on the far wall and the spray of water squeezing through the panelling. 'Let's just get you up, and' – he bent down and she put her foot into his clasped hands – 'hup we go.'

Ginny was not a large girl, maybe fifty kilos max. And Jed was big, broad-shouldered, strong. It was what she liked about him. Just that expanse. But he didn't know his own strength, and she found herself hoisted well up over the back of the booth.

'Hey, not so fast, okay? Not so fucking fast,' she told him, grabbing the table leg that had not broken through into their booth, swinging her legs down and clamping them round it. Standing in the booth, Jed leaned forward, kept his hands around her waist. 'So just shimmy along, then climb up, okay?'

'Shimmy? Is that what you said? Fucking *shimmy?*'

Over on the stairs, the two men stripped off their jackets, handed them to the woman and came down as far as they dared to the boiling rush of water.

'Come on, Honey. It's fine. We'll get you.'

By now Ginny was past Jed's reach and trying to get herself up on to the side of the table. Just a few inches below the corner ball-pocket the water roared past, spitting and splashing up at her. If she lost her grip here, and fell the wrong side of the table, the water would have her. But she didn't. With a deep breath she clambered up on to the edge of the pool table and slowly raised herself, like a gymnast preparing to work out on a beam, one foot in front of the other, one hand gripping the hem of her skirt, the other reaching out for balance. Then, as Jed watched, she bent her knees and launched herself forward over the torrent.

And the men on the stairs had her, dragging her away from the surge, the three of them sprawling backwards.

She shrugged off their helping hands and turned back to Jed.

'Piece of cake,' she shouted across at him.

'Didn't I tell you?' he shouted back.

'So what are you waiting for, chicken?'

115

It took a while for the sharks to pull the man under. While his friends hurried to reel him in, he clung to the lifebelt with one arm and slapped at the snapping predators with the other, kicking out with his legs in an effort to keep them at bay.

The sharks were small enough to feel a direct hit and back off, but they soon came again, taking nips at his legs and arms when they managed to squirm through the kicking and the slapping, their slanting juvenile jaws not yet wide enough to get a good grip on the man's body. Spitting out mouthfuls of water, registering every tug and bite beneath the water with a panicked, frantic scream, he begged his friends to hurry. But coordinating a rescue attempt on a houseboat spinning in the current was not easy. As the houseboat turned, the three men trying to haul in their friend had to struggle around the deck to stop the rope snagging or being pulled under the hull. And all the time the sharks kept coming in for more.

Watching from Fluke's deck, Mungo saw one of the sharks latch on to the poor man's slapping hand and hold tight, gulping at it to get a firmer grip, its slashed gills rippling with the effort, its pale white throat pulsing. In an instant the two remaining sharks left off his kicking legs and came in for the arm holding the lifebelt. It was as if they'd coordinated their attack, as if they were communicating with one another. I've got one arm, you guys take the other. It was almost like a game, exuberant kids hanging on tight to a favourite uncle, trying to bring him down. But this was no game and kids didn't hang on with razor sharp teeth.

'They're gonna get him,' said Ty. 'And nothing we can do.'

Mungo nodded. 'Not a thing.'

Suddenly Ty pointed at the water. Four more fins were heading towards the man in the water, honing in. They hit him, and the other three sharks, like torpedoes, blasting out of the water, one of the new arrivals biting down on the lifebelt in its haste to get a mouthful of something.

Over the wind and the rain and the thundering surf out in the bay, the man's cries grew weaker. With at least seven sharks hanging off him, tugging hungrily at his limbs, he was finally torn from the lifebelt and pulled beneath the surface.

116

Heart pumping fit to bust, rain smacking against his face, bare feet bloodied and torn, Mort climbed on between darkened treeline and racing stream, wondering just how much goddam further he'd have to go before he found somewhere to cross the Hanish.

For more than two hours now, Mort had followed the river, staying as close as possible to its raging course but often forced into the woods when some obstruction barred the way. Quarry Falls, where he and his sofa had parted company, had been a real problem. Rather than try and climb the sheer, streaming face of stone, he'd had to branch off into the forest until he could work his way up and around it – a half-hour detour that had him spitting with fury.

Given the circumstances – no shoes, the pitch-black night, the relentless struggle uphill – he was making good time, anger pulsing like a super-fuel through his limbs, always urging him on. But he still hadn't found a crossing. Twenty minutes earlier, he'd stumbled across the fire-break track that led off the main Hanish trail to the cabin and felt a surge of hope. The last time he'd been there, the river hadn't reached higher than his hub-caps, an easy crossing. But now, as far as he could make out, the river was twice as wide and a whole lot deeper and faster. Which meant he'd been forced to go higher still to find a way across.

More pain. More delay. More distance to cover . . .

Pausing now for breath, letting it stream out through gritted teeth, dragging it back in, Mort rested his shoulder against a tree trunk and dropped his head to his heaving, thumping chest.

If he couldn't find her when he got back to the cabin . . .

If she'd gotten out of there somehow . . .

If she'd passed him on the other side of the stream without him seeing her . . .

For a moment, doubt shivered through him like an icy blade. A doubt for every breath he took.

The uselessness of what he was doing . . .

This endless, crucifying climb to God knew where . . .

The goddam fucking unfairness of it all . . .

But then the anger surged back, that old friend, scorching through his limbs, scouring out the doubt, filling him instead with a raging goddam desire to kill, to maim, to do goddam damage . . . to win, to turn the tables, to make good every rotten goddam lousy throw of the dice, to settle every goddam score outstanding, beginning with that fucking Pearse woman, that smug, self-satisfied, greedy bitch just the other side of that fucking forty-foot span of water. In that instant he felt like raising his face to the rain and screaming out curses into the night. Screaming out every fucking obscenity an unfair, unjust world had taught him . . .

And then, up ahead, a sound broke through the smack

of rain, the roar of the river and the teeth-clenched heaving of his breath. A great thundering roll of stone and rock close enough to send a tremble through the bleeding soles of his feet. Four, five, six seconds – no more than that – and then the thunder settled and the tremor faded.

For a moment, it was as if nothing had happened. Just the rain, and the river, and the blood pumping through his head.

But Mort knew that something had happened – something significant – and he knew what it was.

He could suddenly smell the rich clean stench of freshly turned earth coming down to him on the breeze.

A rockfall. Just up ahead.

That close.

Pushing away from the tree, he stumbled on through the darkness, squinting ahead with his one eye, searching for the line between bank and stream, just as he'd done for the last two hours, and holding to it.

He heard it first. A hissing spray that whistled past his head.

And then he saw it. Right there in front of him. A long low fall of rock and earth and boulder blocking the bank ahead, but reaching out into the stream, high enough and strong enough to hold back the water.

How long the dam would last before the weight of the water building up behind it brought it crashing down, Mort couldn't say.

But right now it was there.

All he had to do was wade out into the slower stream, climb up on to the rockfall and somehow clamber across . . .

117

For a time, after the sharks pulled the man under, Mungo and Ty and the people on the other houseboat stared at the water, as though none of them could believe what they had just witnessed. But a minute or two was all they had.

Still spinning, slow and jerky like ballerinas on the mirrored floor of a child's music box, the five houseboats that had been moored to the inner quay were now working their way into the middle of Melville's inner harbour. With nothing to anchor them, they were drifting helplessly, at the mercy of the current, a great bulging muscle of water pouring down from the mouth of the Susquahanish, curling with vicious eddies at its edges and heading out to sea. Across the harbour, all the lights had gone in town and torch beams lanced through the darkness along Promenade. From somewhere behind its black shadowy wall of buildings came the rising wail of a siren starting up, only to falter and fail before it had reached its optimum level.

Suddenly, Ty's houseboat was caught by this fast-moving pelt of water and the spinning stopped, the houseboat stabilised by the current. But if the spinning had stopped, its speed now increased.

'It's pulling us into the outer harbour,' said Mungo, watching the water slap against their hull, as though spurring them on. He could feel its turbulence and power, coming up through the redwood decking, rippling into the soles of his bare feet. And, somehow, its threatening intent. It was as if the water was a living thing, planning their destruction, leading them to their fate. For a moment he saw Miche's face and he prayed she was okay. He knew where this flood had come from and he knew that Miche would have been right in its path, up there in the Susqua hills, canyoning the Cougar. But something told him she'd have sensed what was coming and gotten her party clear of it. She knew those hills too well; she'd never have gotten herself into trouble.

Off their port side, the two houseboats that had collided and locked together had also reached the river road and with a tearing screech of metal on wood they now parted company. For a moment or two they bobbed and curtsied to each other, but then the water caught them and straightened them out, all five houseboats now pointing towards the outer harbour, a small flotilla bow to stern, twenty feet apart. And not an engine or an oar between them. Only the overturned houseboat remained in their corner of the harbour, caught in an eddy, moving slowly, round and round, water splashing over its raised twin brass screws. Of the six houseboats moored to the inner quay, it was the only one with an engine.

'You got rope?' asked Mungo, turning to Ty.

'Under the kitchen floor. A ton of it.'

440

'Let's get it,' said Mungo, and the two men went back into the salon where Carrie, pale faced, was trying to sort out the mess – housework as a kind of therapy.

'We're moving, aren't we?' she asked, as Ty disappeared into the galley kitchen.

'Yes, we are,' replied Mungo. Without breaking stride he raised his leg and punched out his foot like a kung-fu fighter, kicking down the metal chimney that connected with Fluke's wood-burning stove. It took two kicks, and a couple of hefty tugs to free the stove completely but it was done. All Mungo could think was, thank God it hadn't been lit.

'And what do you plan doing with that?' asked Ty, coming out of the kitchen with a length of rope over each shoulder and a coil of it in his hand.

'You'll see,' replied Mungo, rocking the stove off its stand. 'Here, help me shift it, out on deck.'

While Carrie watched, the two men dragged and hauled the stove across the cabin, heaving and cursing.

'Jesus, it weighs a ton.'

'Exactly,' replied Mungo with a brief smile.

Suddenly the younger man understood. 'The rope. We're gonna make an anchor.'

Mungo grunted something as they hefted it over the door lip and manoeuvred it out on to deck. The slanting rain hit them like cold tracer fire.

'Will it hold us?'

Mungo shot him a look. 'Holding would be good. I'm just hoping it'll slow us down.'

Ten minutes later, they'd dragged the stove to Fluke's stern, roped it up and secured one end to the main support beam for the roof.

'You ready?' asked Mungo, squatting down to get his fingers under it.

Ty did the same, found a grip. 'Ready.'

With a grunt, they lifted the stove off the deck and tipped it up against the rail.

Checking their feet were clear of the rope coils, they gave one final heave and the stove was over. It didn't make much of a splash in the turbulent water and it sank very fast, whipping away the rope on deck until the last ten feet of it snapped taught against the support beam, angling out into their wake. The houseboat juddered for a moment and a following stern wave swamped over the deck.

Mungo looked out at the water, watched the way it streamed past them.

Overtaking them.

The flood was now going faster than they were.

118

Mulholland couldn't believe the water surging down Main Street. Even after hightailing it down the Shinnook road, trying to keep ahead of it, the flood hadn't seemed quite as bad as this. Already the Durango he'd parked outside on the street, the same Durango that had survived so much on their way back from Shinnook, had been swept away, pushed over on to its side by the first flow spreading out from the river, then pushed over again and again until the water and momentum had enough power and purchase to roll it down Main Street.

He'd watched from his office window, knowing there wasn't a whole heap he could do about it. Already the river had broken its banks, streaming out across North and South Main, sweeping all before it, and the last time he'd looked it was three feet deep and rising down on the ground floor.

Since he'd gotten back to the office, the calls had been coming in as thick and as fast as the water surging across their forecourt, starting with the sewage treatment plant up at the top of Main where the settlement tanks had been breached, and the Melville Court Motel where the flood had brought down one entire wing, most of it ending up in the courtyard swimming pool. Down the length of Main, shop windows had been smashed either by the pressure of the flood water or whatever object the current carried, and burglar alarms were whooping; along Promenade a lot of the bars and clubs were having serious problems with clapboard walls down and people swept away; and up at Baxter's Mall fifty or so shoppers were holding out on the gallery level because the ground-floor shops were under water, which made Mulholland wonder whether Zan had found his kids and got them to safety. He certainly hoped so, suddenly missing the man's company, his quiet determination. Those few hours heading up together to Shinnook and racing back down to Melville by road and river had been a hell of a ride. Looking around the office, Mulholland decided he could sure do with a few more like Zan around the place. All he had was old Calley, Tabs Wain and a couple of the night boys. They'd put calls out for the standbys – Roberts, Henderson and Gilles – but, pretty much cut off by the flood, there seemed little likelihood of anyone getting through. Which wasn't a bad thing, Mulholland decided, half listening to Tabs Wain on her radio, promising the Harbour Master that they'd sure try to organise some help for the dozen or so houseboats floating around the harbour. If the standbys had their cells or radios to hand, they could maintain a police presence round town and help coordinate some of the rescue work, zero in on the most urgent calls.

Because it sure didn't look like they could rely on any outside help.

Right at the start, the moment Mulholland had gotten back to the Department, he'd had Tabs put in a call down to Emergency Services in Olympia. Tabs was a good choice. Wasn't no-one in the whole wide world'd get Officer Tabs Wain out of their face if she had a mind to get something done. He might duck whenever she caught his eye, but Mulholland had to concede she was one hell of a deputy. But not even Deputy Tabs Wain was winning this one. Requests for helicopter assistance – Air Sea Rescue, National Guard, whatever the hell had rotors and an aircrew – was coming up blank. Right now, it seemed, it was everyone for themselves.

'Still no choppers, Chief,' said Sergeant Calley, poking his head round the door. 'An hour earliest is the best we got, from Portland. Said they have us on their list, but they're not making any promises. Got floods all the way through to Aberdeen, a mudslide down Queets County that's taken a half dozen cars off 101, but the real ringer is a liner bound for the Juneau Passage. Gone aground off Croom Shoal with eight hundred passengers aboard, and getting all the attention. Looks like we're joining the queue.'

Mulholland grunted. Just what he'd expected. There were bigger towns down the coast, more people to rescue, and those places would always be the first in line. Little old Melville was just going to have to watch out for itself. New Orleans and Katrina all over again. If it could happen there, he supposed he shouldn't be too surprised it should happen right here in Melville County.

'How many men we got on?' asked Mulholland.

'Just you, me and the night crew,' replied Calley. 'Five in all. Out on the street, maybe another four, but so far they haven't called back. Then there's the guys coming back from Queets.' Both men knew it would be hours before they got back in any kind of shape.

'Well, I'll tell you what I want,' said Mulholland, turning from the window. 'We leave one of the boys here to man the radio and keep communications open, and the rest of us get up on the roof and see how far we can get, roof to roof. Up and down the street. Help out where we can. With the stream running the way it is, it's pretty much all we can do right now.'

Calley nodded. 'Also, your wife called. Just to let you know she's fine. Said the water's got into the basement but hasn't risen any further.'

Mulholland nodded. Apart from his garden tools and the boiler there wasn't much down there worth worrying about. What did worry him was that the water could have reached so high up the side of South Bluff where their house was, and so quickly. They were just two blocks back from Lower Main but it was a fair old hike uphill to get there. If the water was swilling round their basement, there'd be a good few premises below them that would be up to their gutters in it.

A little too late to be of any use, a low wail started up from the Town Hall. At least Pringle was being helpful, thought Mulholland. He'd known the man long enough to know that even the simplest request often took a while to implement. And as if to underline that, the siren promptly failed. Mulholland wondered if the man had switched it off himself, or the system had simply given up.

Knowing Pringle, he favoured the former.

119

Clasping Ginny to him, it astonished Jed just how swiftly they'd exchanged their precarious possession of the booth for the safer shores of the stairs. And all thanks to an overturned pool table. He felt a burst of disbelieving exhilaration. They had survived. They had made it.

But sitting there on the stairs, he also knew that a lot of other people hadn't been so fortunate. How many had there been in that ground-floor bar, Jed wondered? Eighty? A hundred? The place had been packed when he arrived; he'd had to push his way through. People he knew and people he didn't. And out of that number, as far as he could tell, he and Ginny and the three cokers were the only survivors, the only ones not to have been plucked from their booths, their tables, their stools and sent hurtling down to the entrance and through it to Promenade beyond. How many had survived that fearsome rush? How many had managed to squeeze through that narrow space without serious injury?

'You were lucky,' said one of the men, wiping the back of his hand across his nose.

'You too,' replied Jed, looking up and smiling.

The man sniffed and swallowed. 'Never say no to a line, I guess. Name's Bart, by the way, and this here's Pea and Mikele.'

'Jed and Ginny,' said Jed. There were nods and smiles.

'So anyone else up here?' asked Jed, getting to his feet, peering up at the washroom landing a few steps above them. Beside him, still crouched on the stair, Ginny reached out and took a hold of his leg, as though she didn't want him going anywhere. He rather enjoyed the sensation. He was a cop; he was going to take control.

'Just us three, and you guys,' replied Bart.

'You think we're okay here?' asked the girl, Pea. It wasn't clear which of them she was speaking to.

'Not if that wall goes,' replied Mikele, nodding back at the blast of water coming through the store room door. 'You ask me, I say we head for the roof and see if there's some way out of here.'

'Well, let's go take a look,' said Jed, helping Ginny to her feet. 'You okay, honey?'

'I've had better birthdays, big boy.'

'Hey,' said Bart. 'It's your birthday? Well, many happy

447

returns. Guess it'll be one you won't forget in a hurry,' he added, his eyes straying to the front of Ginny's wet blouse. Jed caught the look but couldn't blame him – she might have been soaked through, but his girl still looked hot enough to sear steaks.

'You can say that again,' she replied, pulling her blouse into place and taking Jed's arm.

Up on the roof, the rain was pelting down, coming at them from almost every direction, the clouds low and the town around them dark and shadowy. Normally, there'd have been the sound of traffic cruising Prom and coming down Main, the bass throb of car stereos played too loud, the occasional whoop from passers-by and the toot of horns on a Saturday night. But the only sound that Jed could hear was the pounding rush of water gushing down side streets and cascading across the quay into Melville harbour, a distant roar of surf, and crackling claps of thunder that sounded like they were bursting through the heavens right above their heads.

Leaving Ginny and Pea in the raised doorway, the three men hurried across the flat roof to the front balustrade overlooking Promenade.

When Jed had arrived at Mama Surf there'd been cars lined along both sides of the quay. Now the only ones left were those parked on the town side of the harbour, just half a dozen along the four blocks of Promenade, parked in the lee of the buildings and, so far, beyond the reach of the water that poured between the buildings in a powerful rush. Every other car had gone, presumably swept into the harbour by the torrent blasting across the road.

Out in the harbour Jed could make out a wide flow of turbulent water streaming out towards the sea, carrying rafts of debris and tugging a line of houseboats along with it. Leaning out over the balustrade and looking down, the only people he could see were huddled in shadowy groups in doorways and on the sidewalk, just a few steps back from the raging flood. Some of them had torches whose beams flicked out over the raging flood-water. On their tiny sidewalk islands, they were as isolated as Jed and Ginny and the rest of them up there on Mama Surf's roof.

Jed could see at once that there was no way to get off the roof. Mama Surf stood alone, a narrow block in its own right, with just three fire escapes – at the back of the building and on either side – all of whose lower sections disappeared into a stew of racing water. Unless they could rig up some kind of bridge to get across to neighbouring, and maybe stronger, buildings, they were stranded.

Jed pulled out his phone, dialled Calley.

'Sarge, it's Roberts. I'm stuck on the roof of Mama Surf. Any chance you can send someone down from the station to help out?' There was a pause, Jed pressing the phone against his ear. 'I got that. I'll try.'

'You a cop?' asked Bart, looking nervous.

Jed, pocketing his cell, nodded, then smiled. 'Am now, but wasn't back there, okay?'

'So what do you want us to do?' asked Mikele.

'Like the sarge said, there's not much we can do right now. Just sit it out.'

But there was no chance of that. Down in the bar, the piling water finally broke through the back wall and the entire building sagged backwards. Up on the roof, Jed and his companions tensed at the movement, reached out for something to hold on to.

'Shit, what was that?' shouted Bart.

Jed felt the roof begin to shake under his feet. He knew

in an instant what was happening. He turned away from the balustrade and began to make his way back to Ginny. But the tremor from below was increasing and it was harder to walk. Suddenly the roof tilted back towards the harbour and both Ginny and Pea were running down the slope towards him. He reached out a hand but before there was any chance to grab either of them he was off his feet and rolling backwards. With a mighty juddering screech the whole building crumpled forward and crashed down over Promenade in a blast of shrieking timber and shattering glass.

The next moment, Jed was in the air and falling.

120

The makeshift anchor that Mungo and Ty had dumped overboard was definitely slowing them down. There was a slim chance it might even catch hold somewhere, down there in the murky swirling depths, before they were swept out to sea.

The people on the houseboat next in line, the one that had already lost a guest, had seen what they'd done and were even now manhandling their own stove on to deck. As they closed on Fluke, one of them leaned over the rail and shouted out to them, wanting to know if they had any rope.

Houseboat sailors, thought Mungo. At least Ty had some sense.

'Have we got enough to spare?' asked Mungo, as he cupped a hand to his ear, pretending he hadn't heard what the man was saying.

'Two coils. Good length,' replied Ty.

'So go ahead. Throw one over to them. The shorter of the two.'

As the two houseboats passed, with maybe twenty feet between them, Ty aimed the rope and tossed it over, keeping hold of one end in case he had to throw again. But the man caught the coil first time and, while Ty and Mungo watched, they tied up the stove in a bundle of knots and secured the other end to a support beam.

'If we'd just had the one coil of rope, what would you have done?' asked Ty.

'Exactly the same as I hope you would have done,' replied Mungo, with a philosophic shrug. 'Sometimes a hearing problem can be a useful thing.'

By now the second houseboat was drawing ahead of them and Ty and Mungo moved to Fluke's bows to watch the desperate efforts on board as their neighbours neared the end of the quay. Once past that flashing red light they would move into the outer harbour, with nothing between them and a thundering ocean save a hundred metres of open water and one final breakwater. Held by the stream, it was just a matter of time before they were pulled from the safe shelter of the harbour into the raging seas of Melville Bay.

Like Mungo and Ty, the men on the leading house-boat wrestled their stove on to the end railing and, with one final shove, they heaved it over the side. For one of those men, their desperate attempt to create a drag anchor was a death sentence. Unlike Mungo and Ty they didn't check the rope coils on deck. Seconds after the stove plunged to the depths, a loop of rope snapped around the ankle of one of them and snatched him into the air. He was gone so quickly he had no time to cry out. That was left to the woman who'd been watching the men at work. After a moment's stunned silence, her terrible scream rang over the turbid, boiling waters of Melville harbour. The man's wife, wondered Mungo? His daughter? His mother? His sister?

And then the rope that had taken the man – whoever it was – went slack. Either the stove had hit bottom and had yet to take in the spare rope, or the knots had failed, or the rope had split. It didn't take long to discover which. Seconds later, the end of the rope rose to the surface, twisting and trailing out in the houseboat's wake.

121

Jed came spluttering to the surface, gasping for air, spinning round in the ice-cold water as if caught in the wash of a giant propeller. There was nothing he could do to stop the spin – pushing back his hair and wiping the water from his eyes he watched the town, the slipway, the quays swirl past him, dark shapes cut with torchlight and slashed by a silvery rain.

He couldn't remember hitting the water. Maybe he'd been knocked unconscious? Maybe the freezing water had brought him to his senses? As far as he could see, three of the old wood buildings along Promenade had followed Mama Surf's example, tumbling down on to the road, across the quay, and sliding into the harbour. He knew, too, that if they hadn't been up on the roof they'd have been crushed by the collapsing building, and he cast around the choppy black swell for Ginny. She'd been sheltering in the doorway with that girl Pea, the coker, at the back of the roof, when the building started to go, and the last time he'd seen her was when she came tottering towards him, reaching out for him but missing. If he had ended up in the harbour, it stood to reason that she had too.

But there was no sign of her. He called her name and tried to push himself up in the swell so that he could get a better look. But there was nothing, just a turning raft of wreckage – timbers and shingle and broken furniture.

He was maybe fifty feet from the quay, trying to push through the debris – none of it sturdy enough to provide any real support, but plentiful enough to make progress slow – when he spotted what looked like a riderless jet-ski coming in his direction, caught by the current, turning front and back end on, rocking on the swell like some giant water beetle. It was one of the many jet-skis moored by the slipway, the same jet-skis that surfers used for towing when the breaks were too high for a normal paddle approach. Jed knew that there'd be no way to start it up – no-one ever left a key in a jet-ski's ignition – but at least, if he could get to it, he'd be out of the freezing water.

Slowly, tantalising, the jet-ski drew nearer, caught by the current as much as he was, and by the chill wind that pressed against its raised flanks. Like Jed it was being pushed out into the harbour, heading, as far as he could tell, in the same direction as him, towards South Bluff Quay. Which made sense if they were being carried along in the flood. There was nowhere else for the river to go but the open sea, out there beyond the breakwater, the sound of the ocean's booming surf growing stronger now as he moved further away from Promenade.

With the wind and the current playing in the jet-ski's favour, Jed could see it was catching him up, now no more than twelve, fifteen feet away. Pushing past broken planks, thrashing out with his legs because his hands were too busy clearing himself a path, he tried to cover the water between them, close the gap, cursing his tight jeans with every desperate kick. They clung to him, weighed him down and he wondered if he shouldn't just try to pull them off. It would sure be easier pulling himself up on that jet-ski if he didn't have them on.

Closing now on the jet-ski, Jed stopped pushing his way through the floating debris and started unbuckling his belt and working down the zip. Taking a breath he ducked under and got a grip on the waistband, pushing the jeans down over his thighs. He came up for air, gasping in a stinging lungful of salt-shit air, then ducked down again, and managed to push the material past his knees. He'd already kicked off his trainers, but the jeans now snagged around his ankles, greatly restricting the power of his kicks. Up he came for another gasp of air, turning his head to keep the jet-ski in view, then down again to work on his jeans. A trouser leg came free and he started on the other. But he needed more air. This time it seemed he had further to go to reach the surface, just a black ceiling somewhere above him, no light to indicate where it was or how far away. Finally he broke through and blinked his eyes, wiped a hand across them, searching for the jet-ski, paddling fast to swing round, locate it.

And there it was, riding up above him, and crunching down on the mess of debris. Within easy reach. With his free leg he kicked out and stretched forward, feeling the drag of his jeans holding him back.

The first time he lunged, he came up short and the jet-ski started to turn beam end on. In another ten seconds it would be side on and he'd surely get it then. Rather than work off the last remaining leg of his jeans and risk missing his opportunity, Jed got himself into position for the turning jet-ski, gauging the moment, the angle.

Slowly, slowly it swung round to him, in minute degrees, beginning to present him with an increasingly easy target. Taking a deep breath, and kicking out with his good leg, he lunged again for the jet-ski and his hand caught hold of the edge of its right foot-well. Shaking the water out of his eyes, he hauled himself up to it, clamping both elbows into it, making himself secure. All he had to do now was strip off that last leg of his jeans and climb up unencumbered into the saddle.

122

Through slanting rain and stinging horizontal pellets of ocean spray, Mungo, Ty and Carrie watched the remaining houseboats slide past them, thirty feet off their port side. The first to pass them was deserted, no-one at home, no lights showing. The other had five people aboard, all of them out on deck, arguing about what to do next. Even over the sloshing and slapping of the water against their hull, the drumming rain and the distant roar of the ocean their voices carried across to Fluke, a dim murmur of fear and uncertainty and disagreement.

'Why don't we throw them a rope?' suggested Carrie. 'I mean, if we tie up together, won't that slow us down?' She looked at Ty and then Mungo, the two men standing either side of her, watching with a kind of stunned helplessness as they finally passed the inner harbour wall and followed their four neighbours into the wider outer harbour.

'Right now, I'd say we're safer by ourselves,' replied Mungo, and Ty nodded his agreement. 'Too much weight on our anchor line could snap the rope or shatter the support beam. It's best we stay separate.'

By now they were out in the main stream of the flood, a roaring black cascade still pummelling across Promenade and into the harbour. They were also having to contend with a choppy swell from an incoming tide, its storm waves riding into Melville Bay and detonating not half a mile away on the beach. With the South Bluff breakwater only covering half the harbour entrance the water was growing rougher by the minute. If it hadn't been for the drag on their improvised anchor, they'd have been leading their flotilla of houseboats out into open water.

'You got any life jackets on board?' asked Mungo.

'Down below, where I got the ropes.'

'Can you fetch them? We should get ourselves prepared,' said Mungo.

'You think we're gonna sink?' asked Carrie quietly, as Ty bolted back into the cabin.

'If we do, at least we'll have something to keep our heads above water.'

'But there are sharks . . .'

'And there's a lot of people to go round,' said Mungo. 'Don't worry, we'll be fine.'

He hoped his optimism was convincing. The truth was he had no idea what to do; how to stop their slow but steady course towards open water. As soon as they'd passed their own quay and swung out into the outer harbour, he'd seen what the flood had done. Along South Bluff Quay, where a dozen houseboats had been moored stern to jetty with a pontoon between each mooring, the river flood had ripped into the line and sunk, smashed or overturned all but one of them, now drifting free. It was the same story along the break-water. Of the ten houseboats usually berthed there, four had disappeared completely, presumably sunk, another three had been pitched one above the other and a fourth lay broken and battered across the top of the breakwater, just lifted out of the water by the flood and stranded there. As far as Mungo could see just two breakwater houseboats had survived, torn from their moorings and drifting clear of the quay, the water between them littered with pontoon planking and flower tubs and furniture. Eight houseboats, counting those from his own quay, spinning and drifting with the current, bumping into one another like slow-motion dodgem cars at the fairground. And all of them borne along by the flood current, heading for the harbour entrance and the incoming waves.

'It's getting pretty crowded out here,' said Ty, returning with the life jackets. Dropping his own on deck, he passed one to Mungo then helped Carrie into hers, before reaching for his own. 'You got any ideas?'

Mungo looked across the water, felt their anchor line tremble as the stove they'd shoved overboard slalomed across the bottom of the harbour forty feet below.

'I think we should start getting rid of some weight,' he said. 'If you don't mind losing it?'

123

Taking a breather on the corner parapet of Duvall and Main, Mulholland gazed at the floodwaters and shook his head in disbelief. All he could see was one big river, a sliding, rolling body of angry water hurtling through the middle of town and headed down towards the harbour. It was no longer possible to make out the original course of the river, nor indeed any road surface or sidewalk, just the tops of two or three streetlights slicing through the current like submarine periscopes and a great wall of spray arching up off Pointers Bridge three blocks down. Playing the beam of his Hi-Lite torch across Main, on to the rising slope of South Bluff, he could just about make out the far edge of the water reaching at least a block back. Behind him, his side of Main, the flood stretched four blocks back, almost to the edge of town and the terraces of North Bluff. In all his years he'd never seen anything like it.

Leaning over the parapet, Mulholland looked down at the black water raging past. He could feel its power driving up through his feet, and the roaring fury of it was terrifying. As well as snatching up everything in its path, it seemed intent on shaking the town apart. Somehow it seemed worse than anything he and Zan Pearse had seen on the road to Shinnook, stronger, faster, far more aggressive now, and he tried not to think what they'd find when the flood was over.

Unlike Mama Surf down on the quay, the sheriff's office occupied the corner site of a terraced block, fifteen other properties drawn together in a tight square and, to a certain extent, protected by those blocks further up the slope. Three sides of this block were taken up by a number of commercial enterprises: a surf accessories store, a bookshop and a corner coffee-house sharing frontage with the sheriff's department on Main; a line of fashion outlets on Boulevard; and the food shops along Duvall – a baker, a butcher, and a speciality cheese shop, a wine store and a grocery. Every Saturday there was a street market on Duvall – the food from the shops, local produce, crafts, antiques, all set out under striped awnings along the narrow thoroughfare. These stalls had come down early because of the rain and now, except for the police department and Arty's Hot-Bones halfway along Boulevard, all the stores were closed, the bookshop last to lock its doors and turn down the lights at just before seven.

But that didn't mean the buildings were empty. At least a dozen of these shops had apartments on their first and second floors – owned and lived in by the various proprietors or rented out – and it was these that Mulholland and his crew had gone to in the absence of anything more practical to do, working their way from rooftop to rooftop along Main and Boulevard, Duvall and Scout Street which ran parallel to Main.

Breaking open stairwell doors or clambering down fire escapes to warn residents, Mulholland and his crew made sure everyone knew what was going on – if any needed telling – assuring residents that it was better to stay where they were; they'd be safer in their homes than anywhere else. If the situation got any worse, Mulholland assured one old couple on Scout Street where the flood had ripped away two of the six raised porches, they'd have helicopters come right in to take them off. Not to worry, everything was gonna be just fine. Some flood though, wasn't it? His assurances might have calmed the couple but Mulholland knew he was lying through his teeth. If he saw a helicopter come in over Melville any time before daybreak he'd eat his galoshes. The town was on its own and everyone who lived there had better get used to it.

Mulholland glanced at his watch. Two hours since the flood had come down on them, and a few more still to go before they could start organising any kind of effective rescue operation. Until then it was everyone looking out for themselves, and God help them all.

Pulling a Whale-Watcher from his pocket and popping it into his mouth, Mulholland wondered again how Zan Pearse was doing, whether he'd found his kids and Dasha's mother up at the Drive-In. By his reckoning, there'd have been easily enough time to get them out – and everyone else there – and safely into Baxter's Mall. Probably doing exactly what he was doing right now – waiting it out, sitting up there on the mall's first-floor gallery until it was safe to come down.

What he didn't feel so confident about was the man's wife, Dasha Pearse. If she really was up in those hills above Shinnook, he hoped she wasn't anywhere near a river. After seeing that flood come roaring through the old logging town, breaking through the barrage and flooding down the valley, she'd need to be somewhere up on high ground to be safe.

He prayed she was.

124

While Carrie huddled down in the bow, out of the way, Mungo and Ty hurried to and from Fluke's interior carrying sofas, four gas cylinders, the dining-room table and chairs and, from the main bedroom, a bed, mattress, bedside tables and a fine old club armchair, all of them despatched over the side without a second glance. Ty could have been emptying someone else's house for all the concern he showed. Mungo was impressed. He even unplugged the stereo and tossed that overboard, along with a Sony HD, a fridge freezer, and his glass-topped designer-driftwood coffee table. Once in the water, they either sank to the bottom of the harbour, or the current caught them and snatched them away.

Mungo knew it was a risky bet chucking everything overboard. Lightening up Fluke made the houseboat more vulnerable, less stable, and gave the floodwaters greater purchase. But it also meant that they stood a better chance of getting their stove anchor to dig in and hold. And that's what Mungo was banking on.

'Insurance sure is a wonderful thing,' said Ty, when the houseboat had been cleared, watching his driftwood coffee table sink slowly beneath the surface.

'Let's hope you get to make the claim,' said Mungo softly, with a pinch of anxiety. 'Because I'm telling you this does not look good.'

As far as he could see the only vessels in the harbour with engines were a pair of crabbing trawlers moored up by the Quays' slipway. But with no crew on board and no way to get to them, they were useless in terms of rescue. As for the jet-skis used for towing surfers out into the bigger waves, and now floating loose, Mungo knew there'd be no key to start them, and that without power they'd prove more a liability than anything.

Up ahead, the two men watched as the other houseboat owners tried to do whatever they could to keep themselves from reaching open water, fashioning lassoos and casting for any piling or mooring buoy they passed, or trying to steer with plank paddles or improvised rudders rigged up on their sterns. It didn't need much imagination from anyone to work out what would happen to a powerless, rudderless houseboat when it left the relative safety of the harbour and got in the way of a big wave.

Suddenly they felt a terrific tug from behind them and the two of them had to reach for each other to keep from bowling overboard. Somewhere far below them their stove anchor had finally caught on something, and with the lighter load to bear it had dug in.

On the edge of the main stream which had caught all the other houseboats, Fluke now held against the current, a spray of slopping waves breaking over the stern and sweeping across the deck.

'Hey, we did it!' shouted Ty, his face breaking into a great big grin. He reached for Mungo's hand and shook it, clapped him on the back. 'Way to go, man. Way to go.'

125

Jed was reaching down from the jet-ski to pull his foot free from his jeans, thinking he'd better find himself a good plank of wood to paddle with, when he felt the current tug at his leg, or rather at the inside-out pair of jeans that now trailed away from his foot. It was a strong enough pull for him to feel the hem of his jeans actually tighten around his ankle, as though the water was trying to help him get them off, and for a terrifying second or two he wondered if the jeans had snagged on something, that they would somehow contrive to hold him back, or stop him from getting aboard the jet-ski.

But it wasn't the current, or some underwater obstruction, that tugged at his jeans. It was a metre-long bull shark that had been stroked down its baby flanks by the buckle on Jed's belt. In the swirling, muddy darkness the shark had turned to make another pass and snapped blindly when the buckle rasped against its snout. The shark missed the buckle but its teeth caught in the opened zip. It chomped down on the empty jeans and then jerked backwards, chewing free of the cloth. But as it did so, the creature sensed something, something heavy, something attached to whatever was hanging there. So it rose, slowly and silently, to investigate.

Jed was hanging on to the jet-ski with one hand and busily working the jeans over his heel with the other, when he felt something brush against his waist and slide past his thighs.

At first he thought nothing of it – just another piece of debris drifting below the surface. Maybe plastic sheeting, or a length of sea kelp torn away from the bottom of the harbour. But moments later the brush became a bump, and he felt something press against his buttocks and push past the backs of his legs.

And he knew at once it wasn't kelp or plastic sheeting.

There was movement there. And life. And intent.

Sharks.

In an instant he remembered the previous evening, out in the bay when he'd surfed back in with Mungo. Hundreds of them, sharks, patrolling the breaks. Small, but still sharks. And now they were here, in the harbour.

Suddenly he knew what had been tugging at the end of his jeans. And he wondered if it was alone, or if there were others down there, circling him in the dark water.

It was enough for him to forget his jeans and lunge out of the water for the jet-ski. He got his palms on to the edge of its foot-well, pressed down hard and locked his elbows straight, bringing up his knee to hoist himself aboard.

But suddenly he was tugged backwards.

In a second he was off the jet-ski and under the water. And being pulled down. In jerks and spasms. The shark had his jeans and was trying to swim off with them. With him in tow.

Kicking out against the drag he felt the hem of his jeans tighten again around his ankle. Scrabbling against the tow, desperate to get back to the surface, he stopped kicking and felt the hem ease. Then he pointed his foot and started kicking again, slipping free of the hem. The jeans were off him. Tipping his head back he lunged out for the surface, hoping he hadn't been taken too far from the jet-ski, that he could reach it before any shark reached him.

As he broke surface, heart and lungs bursting, the first thing Jed saw was the jet-ski, just a few feet from him, mired in a raft of tangled debris. But that same raft of debris also kept them apart. He couldn't swim through it, he had to clear a way forward with his hands, kicking out with his legs to keep himself afloat, thanking God every time he managed a kick without feeling a shark brush past, or getting bitten.

How big was it, he wondered?

How hungry? How aggressive? How dangerous?

And was there more than one? he thought, as he

kicked out again, and again, three times, four times, pushing through the debris until the jet-ski was looming above him, inches from his fingertips . . .

One final kick . . .

That's all it would take . . .

Four sharks – all of them baby bulls – attacked Jed just about simultaneously. The first hit him in the small of the back and, as he arched forward from the blow, he felt something grab his left foot and slam into his right thigh. The fourth shark took his right lower leg and the first shark that had hit him came back in, and caught hold of his arm, spinning him around.

He knew at once they weren't big fish. He could feel it in the body length of them and their weight and in the feverish shivering of their excitement. But that didn't make him any less frightened and he kicked out with his legs as much as he could, feeling as he did so tiny teeth slicing into ankle, leg and thigh, all the while trying to shake off the shark crunching down on his forearm, its tail thrashing through the debris to get a better grip.

As he struggled with them there in the water – a kind of lancing white pain reaching up to him – Jed knew for a certainty that he could beat them off, that he could get himself up on to the jet-ski. Through the rain, through the splashing water, he could see its looming hull just a few feet away. The sharks were going to take some meat off him, that was for sure, but he knew he'd live to tell the tale. They'd hurt him some, but they wouldn't kill him. He was beginning to think he was winning the battle, inching his way up on to a now badly bucking jet-ski when he heard a voice.

'Jed! Jed! You out there? Jed?'

It was Ginny, close enough now for him to hear her spit out a mouthful of water, maybe just the other side of the jet-ski.

'Ginny?' he shouted back, feeling the shark latched on to his thigh let go and back off, and his friend let go of his foot. 'Where are you?' he cried out.

'Over here!' she screamed back. 'But you gotta watch out. I think there's fuckin' sharks out here. There's a jet-ski up ahead. I'm nearly there . . .'

They were the last words Jed heard. The two sharks that had released him now came in again, getting a firmer purchase on his legs, and four more sharks, attracted by the commotion, streaked in and latched on to various parts of his body with vicious snapping jaws. When he opened his mouth to scream out, he was under the water and being dragged down.

By the time they'd finished with him the sharks were a dozen strong, circling, bumping into each other in the darkness, snapping at anything in a frenzy of bloodlust. But amid all their whipping and snapping there was another movement they could sense. Like the last one, up there on the surface, close by and in distress.

In threes and fours they peeled away from the ragged, bleeding stump of Jed Roberts and rose through the black swirling water to take a closer look at his girl-friend, Ginny Farrell.

126

Thanks to their anchor catching something below, Mungo and Ty had stopped Fluke moving forward. But the full stream of the flood still raced past, splashing up over their stern and sluicing down its sides, swinging them from port to starboard like the arm on a metronome. Up at the bow Mungo, Ty and Carrie watched the other four houseboats from their quay ride on ahead of them, joining up with the South Bluff and breakwater houseboats, sorting themselves out in a jostling line for the right-hand swing towards the harbour entrance.

'You got any binoculars?' asked Mungo. 'Or did we throw them overboard?'

Ty frowned, trying to remember.

'In the knife drawer,' Carrie answered. 'I put them there this evening, before I started prepping supper.'

A minute later Ty was back, pulling a pair of pocket Leicas from their case. Standing in the bow, he scanned the fleet of houseboats ahead of them, then handed the glasses to Mungo.

'They're going faster than if they had engines,' Ty said quietly.

'Looks like a couple of them have tied up together, and they're going quicker than the rest. They should cut loose,' said Mungo. And then he had an idea. 'You got a cell phone?' he asked. 'Any numbers for your neighbours? We could call them, warn them.'

'Left it in the car,' said Ty. 'As for any numbers . . .'

At exactly that moment something carried along in the stream came up behind them and crashed into their stern, sending them sprawling on to the deck. Fluke's prow reared upwards, and whatever it was that had hit them now started to scrape along beneath their hull with a screeching, agonised cry that sounded through every timber, rocking the houseboat from side to side as though it was trying to push it out of the way to reach the surface. Getting to his feet, Mungo raced back to the stern to see their anchor rope angling straight down. He knew at once what had happened, and what would happen next.

Whatever had hit them had snagged on their anchor line and was pulling it under the boat, like a canny game fish fighting a hook and reel, dragging their stern lower and lower. With no power to counter the move, Mungo knew there was nothing he could do. Any moment now the rope or the support beam it was tied to would give way. As Ty joined him, the rope squeaked once, then snapped with a twang and whipped up into the air. The screeching below their hull ceased and the houseboat surged forward, no longer held by their anchor.

After just a few minutes' reprieve they were back in the stream, one of eight houseboats at the mercy of the current.

127

Mort came down through the trees and stepped out on to the sloping front yard of the cabin. It had taken longer than he'd anticipated to cross the Hanish and get here, but he felt a great warmth and sense of exultation that he'd achieved what he'd set out to do. Against all the odds, he'd worked his way back upstream, got across the river, and made it back to the cabin.

Now all he had to do was find the woman.

Slowly, quietly, he made his way across the clearing, keeping low, his eye casting around him, searching for any movement, any flicker of light, listening out for any sound. But there was nothing beyond the whisper and brush of a softening rain, and the distant hum of the river.

The closer he got, the easier it was to make out the cabin. Or what was left of it. As far as he could see, the porch that he and Gene and Eddie had been sitting on just that morning had disappeared completely, along with one whole side of the building. The roof had also collapsed and a long slanting section of it now rested across the ground floor.

Without the porch steps in place, Mort had to hoist

himself up into the cabin. He did so quietly, wincing as the wood took his weight and creaked. For all he knew, the woman had managed to get out of the basement and at that very moment might be sheltering, even sleeping, beneath the slant of roof.

Slowly, like a snake, he squirmed up on to the floor and slid across it – 'walking' with elbows and knees, bare toes pressing down for momentum. Ten feet in, he paused and peered ahead, under the cover of the roof. Nothing. Just the tap of raindrops on the wood floor. Cautiously, he levered himself into a crouch and then slowly straightened up, casting around the ruin of the cabin's sitting room. He remembered the last time he'd seen it, with the flood streaming through it, the chimney crashing down, the sofa.

Turning round he went back to where the front door had been, just a small section of wall still standing, and the gaping hole of a window. He went to this opening and ran his hand around its frame. Twelve hours earlier, he'd plunged his knife into this wall, dragging himself out of the flood. And that's where he and his knife had parted company, stabbed too tightly into the frame for that final lunge through the window, refusing to come free of the wood and slipping from his grip as he dived through the window for the passing sofa.

No knife. Nothing.

Either the blade had worked itself loose after the roof fell in, and been lost in the flood . . .

Or the woman had it.

No longer bothered by any noise he might make, Mort strode across to the trapdoor and examined the bolt and padlock he'd snapped into place after telling Mrs Pearse to get back in the basement. It was just as he had left it. And the key, miraculously, was still in his pocket, a small splinter of metal that had pressed against his thigh every step of the climb back up here.

Opening the trapdoor, he looked down into the basement. He'd expected it to be darker than it was, but he had no difficulty seeing that the place was empty. One of the stone walls had been brought down in the flood and it was clear that this was how the woman had made her escape.

Or been swept away.

Letting the trapdoor fall back, Mort made a quick search of the cabin.

No knife, and nothing much of any use.

Then he looked through the gap in the wall where the kitchen had been.

And he remembered . . .

Somewhere down there, caught in the treeline, were the trucks he'd sailed past in the sofa.

And the Lexus.

128

It was Carrie who saw the first bodies, sliding alongside them in the flood. At first, in the darkness, she'd thought they were logs, pieces of timber, and she simply registered them as that. There was so much out there in the water, so much debris carried along with the current. Just another log. More trees, she thought, brought down with the flood.

When she saw the sharks start snapping at them she suddenly realised what they were. An arm, not a root. A leg, not a branch. The bodies rolling and bucking in the water as the sharks bore in, fighting for a hold, a mouthful.

In the darkness, out there in the wind-whipped harbour, the action beyond Fluke's rails had a kind of compulsive fascination. It was difficult to look away because it was difficult to make out what was happening. Mungo and Ty watched too, all three of them trying to make morbid sense out of the shapes and the splashes, the grunts, snapping and thuds.

Then the rain stopped – stopped dead, just like that – and a bright full moon slid like a round white plate through the clouds, tattered now, silvered at their edges, racing past as if in a mighty rush to get someplace else.

But that bright white moon, still and serene above the black humped slopes of North Bluff, brought no relief. As well as illuminating more graphically the sharks at work – their white rolling bellies, their glinting teeth, their glistening fins slicing through the choppy swell – the moonlight also showed the three of them exactly what else lay in store.

Having passed the end of the inner quay, and now cut free from its anchor line, Fluke had started to swing right on the current, out towards the harbour entrance, last in a line of eight bobbing, powerless houseboats drawn along on the flood. And beyond the harbour, out in the moonlit bay, it was easy to see the white crests of the waves rolling in and pounding down on to Melville beach just a deadly half-mile away.

It was then, in the moonlight, that Carrie spotted something ahead. 'There's someone climbing up on the side,' she cried out, pointing at the lead houseboat. 'It looks like he's going to jump.'

Mungo reached for the binoculars and trained them on the man. With the slanting curtain of rain whipped away and the moon shining down, he could see that the man had stripped down to his shorts, and that a rope was belted round his waist. Balancing on the handrail, clinging to a roof strut, he seemed to pause for a moment, looking out over the churning water at a flight of stone steps leading down the inside wall of the breakwater.

Mungo knew those steps well. Back when he was a kid, he'd sat on them a thousand times, fishing for bass, for mackerel, catching them too, hauling them up on to seaweed-slippery stone that smelt of the cold sea. As far as he could estimate, the lead houseboat was now about forty feet from those steps, mid-channel, the black water splashing and slapping over them in bursts of moonlit quicksilver. In the next couple of minutes that lead houseboat was going to get as close as it was ever going to get, as close as any of the houseboats had come, to dry land and safety after being torn from their moorings. And the people on that lead houseboat were going to do something about it.

As he watched the man prepare for the dive, waiting for that optimum moment, Mungo wondered whether the boat owners up ahead had been in touch with one another over their cell phones, whether they'd planned it. He guessed they had – the approaching steps, the lead houseboat making the first attempt, the man in his shorts with the rope round his waist, his companions keeping a hold of one end. This hadn't been cobbled together on the spur of the moment. They must have planned it, and he could see people on the following houseboats watching, pointing, preparing – waiting their own turn. As though they had known this was going to happen.

All of them holding their breath, fingers crossed.

As though this man – and what he was about to do – might save all their hides.

A good dive, thought Mungo with a quickening pulse of excitement, just a few strong strokes, and he'd make it.

But boy, that water was going to be cold. That water was gonna chill his bones to the marrow. With no wetsuit, the breath would be wrenched from his lungs, muscles stiffening from the first stroke. But once he reached that quay, he could run up those steps and tie off the house-boat to the end bollard. With luck the next manned houseboat along could pass a rope to the secured house-boat and be pulled in too, with the others following suit. Fluke too.

From somewhere on board, near the man's legs, torch beams suddenly swept out over the water, flicking to left and right. And Mungo realised what they were doing. Checking for floating debris, looking for a safe spot for the man to dive, a path through the water.

And fins. They'd be looking out for fins too.

For a moment Mungo had forgotten the sharks.

Then the man bent his knees and was off the rail, a long, reaching dive to cover as much distance as possible before hitting a small patch of clear water.

When he did, he hardly dropped below the surface, his arms flailing out in a frenzy of strokes, the torch beams circling his head, his shoulders, his windmilling arms, the harbour light flashing out its desperate winking red signal.

The next instant, not quite midway between the houseboat and the steps, the man was gone, pulled under.

Then he was up and turning in the water, striking out frantically for the houseboat, still closer than the quay, his friends winding in the rope as fast as they could.

If he hadn't been tied he'd never have made it back.

The sharks would have had him.

Arms still flailing, but slapping at himself not swimming, he screamed as his friends leant down and hauled him aboard, bringing with him one threshing, twisting shark, determined not to let go, its jaws locked hard on to his upper leg.

129

Mort found the two trucks quickly, following the staggered ploughline they'd gouged down the slope when the flood took them. They were just as he remembered them, racked up against the treeline. It didn't take him long, however, to discover that there was nothing of any use to be found in either vehicle. It was as though the flood had washed them clean, then covered them in a stinking mess of mud and debris. As if this was not enough to fuel his annoyance, he cut the side of his hand on a jag of metal as he climbed up on to the belly of the Mitsubishi, and gave himself a fright when he tried to tug open the door of the Toyota, the two trucks swaying dangerously.

Jumping down to the ground, Mort proceeded to follow the treeline to the right, looking for the Lexus which, he recalled, had been swept further towards the river than the two trucks, and pushed deeper between the trees. Then, as an owl hooted in the forest, he took a tumble, thirty or so steps from the trucks. His foot caught on something and he fell forward with a grunt and a curse.

In daylight, he'd have seen the bodies from the trucks. But it was dark, and it wasn't until he stepped on Elroy's arm and lost his footing, that he realised what had tripped him up. Two bodies. Elroy and Eddie. He remembered them pressed against a tree trunk by the force of the water. Now that the flood had all but passed, no longer held in place by the water, they'd fallen to the ground.

But not in a tangle, not in the lovers' embrace that Mort had seen.

Now they lay side by side. Arms out. Both on their backs.

Mort frowned, but it wasn't until he started searching them, looking for something that might come in useful, that he discovered that some of the pockets had been pulled inside out.

Someone else had frisked them.
Someone else had been here before him.
It could only be the woman.

130

Eventually the screaming on the lead houseboat stopped. But the pull of the water did not, carrying the craft out to sea. A moonlit shadow, it slipped past the end of the breakwater and, for a moment, in the harbour mouth, it caught in an unseen whirlpool where the rising tide sliding away from Melville beach met the floodwater streaming out of the harbour.

Once, twice, three times the houseboat spun round, as though unable to make up its mind whether to stay or to go. It was a South Quay houseboat, longer than Fluke and many times heavier, with higher sides and a larger main superstructure. Raised at bow and stern, it had the look and form, broadside on in the moonlight, of some drifting Noah's Ark, with the breakers out in the bay beyond rising higher than its topmost deck.

One by one the other houseboats started to catch up with it, almost queuing up behind it as it spun.

And then suddenly it lurched away, finding that narrow fast-flowing passage of current where sea and river twisted off together along South Bluff and headed out to the ocean. In an instant it was lost to sight behind the breakwater.

Watching from Fluke, Mungo knew what would happen. On a low tide, with its deeper draught, the houseboat might have come up short on the rocks along South Bluff, but this tide was high and the rip was strong, which meant that it would drift out into the bay, gradually straying into the path of the breakers rolling in, much the same route that surfers took to catch their waves. Right now Fluke might have been last in line but in the next ten minutes, maybe sooner, it, too, would find itself caught in that teasing whirlpool and be sent spinning out to sea.

Mungo took a breath, turned away, looked at his two companions.

'I'm beginning to feel guilty that I invited you to dinner,' said Ty with a rueful grin.

'And I'm beginning to wish I'd never accepted,' replied Mungo, feeling comfort in his companion's calm. This man was a surfer, all right. This was a man who could take on Teahupo'o.

The two men smiled at each other.

'Isn't there anything we can do?' asked Carrie quietly, hopefully, the moon lighting her pale face, gathering in the whites of her eyes.

Ty sighed, wrapped an arm round her and pulled her to him. But he didn't say anything.

It was Mungo who answered: 'Well, we've seen what happens if you try to swim for it. Just like everyone else out here. And I don't see any of them volunteering to

480

give it another go.' As if to underline the point a couple of bumps sounded from below, the moon-glittering surface scythed by a fin. 'Which means, I guess, that we stay right here, take our chances.'

'I'm beginning to think we shouldn't have unloaded all that kit,' said Ty, hugging Carrie tight. 'A bit of weight might have come in handy right now.'

Mungo shrugged, spread his hands.

'You think there's a chance we could get pulled out into the breaks?' Carrie persisted, the breeze flicking at her curls.

If Mungo hadn't known it already, he'd have known then that Carrie surfed. Only a Melville Bay surfer would know that tug on the board as you paddled out past the breaking line.

'Maybe, it's possible,' he replied. 'But maybe, past the breakwater, there'll be some opportunity to get off more safely. Maybe we'll even go aground.' He knew it was a lie, but somehow it helped. 'And maybe all the sharks are here, in the harbour. Where it's a whole lot calmer. So we could try swimming again.'

'You think?'

Again Mungo shrugged helplessly, looked out over her shoulder. Up ahead, the second houseboat had slipped into the whirlpool. Lighter than the one that had gone before, it spun even faster, the other houseboats lining up for their turn, some of their owners now desperately casting noosed ropes at that tantalising bollard at the end of the breakwater. None of them caught, of course. They all fell short, coiling silvery snakes of rope slapping against the stones and falling back to the water, reeled back in, cast again. It was like a game-show stunt on TV, thought Mungo. Lassoo that bollard in the next sixty seconds or you lose the game. Or, in this case, your life.

He turned back to Carrie, smiled. For the first time he noticed now that both of them were looking at him – Ty as well. Waiting for him to come up with something.

'One thing's for sure,' he said, and he could see the two of them tense. 'It won't be as bad out there as Teahupo'o.'

131

The silence woke Dasha. It was deep, solid.

Stillness. No rain. No drumbeat tattoo on the roof of the Lexus that she had gone to sleep with. Just an occasional raindrop tap on the roof from the branches overhead. For a moment she lay in the warm folds of her rug, on the back seat of the Lexus, and listened to the soft brush of branches.

Somewhere close by an owl hooted, which startled, and then soothed her.

But then, in the soft echo of the owl's call, she heard another sound that brought her awake instantly.

A grunt, which could have been animal.

And then a curse – what sounded like 'fuck' and 'shit' – which clearly wasn't animal.

Her heart leapt in her chest and an icy fear gripped her insides.

There was someone out there.

Close by.

She didn't need to hear anything else. It could only be one of her kidnappers returning to the cabin. Not swept away by the flood. Not drowned. But coming back to look for her. And, by the sound of it, no more than a few yards away, close enough for her to hear that muttered curse.

Pushing aside the rug and reaching for the knife, Dasha shuffled up in the back seat and peeped out of the side window.

A thin, misty outlook.

Condensation.

She wiped the glass and looked out again. Clearer now, but still too dark to see more than inky outlines. She wondered what the time was. Before midnight? After midnight?

But whatever the time, she knew she was no longer safe.

Someone was out there. And sooner or later they would find the Lexus. And her.

Senses keening she watched and listened for something more.

There was nothing.

But it didn't matter. She'd heard enough, and she knew she would have to leave the Lexus, try to slip away. There was nothing else for it.

132

It was like stepping on to a carousel ride when the houseboat Fluke finally reached the mouth of the harbour, slid across the whorls of sucking jacuzzi current and started its slow spin in the centre of the tidal whirlpool. And just like a carousel their pace increased, the closer slopes of South Bluff and the more distant North Bluff, the stone buttresses of the two quays, the pounding waves, all sliding past in a moonlit cyclorama. And every full turn Mungo, Ty and Carrie could clearly see the seven houseboats that had gone ahead of them, a straggling line drawn by the current out to sea.

In the time it took Fluke to break free from its ride on the whirlpool, the lead houseboat was a clear two hundred metres ahead of them, still holding its treacherous course between a thundering surf in the bay and the tumbled, rocky shores of South Bluff.

Squinting hard, trying to estimate its exact position, it seemed to Mungo that the lead houseboat had drifted further than he'd have expected. On a board, paddling out, you'd have felt the pull from the waves a lot sooner. And waves this big . . .

Mungo felt an unexpected squeeze of hope. If the streaming current that held them was strong enough, it might just carry them past the rocky headland of South Bluff, beyond the line of swells and out into the open ocean, the same course the old whaling ships had taken when the waves were high. Sure it was rough out there, beyond the swells, in open sea, but anything was better than being hit by some breaking monster wave.

Mungo wished he could see more clearly. Then he remembered Ty's glasses, jammed them into his eyes, and focused on the lead boat. There was no question now that it was holding its course, the current strong enough, the houseboat's forward momentum weighty enough, to draw it past those devastating swells rising and breaking not thirty metres off its starboard side.

He dropped the glasses down the line of houseboats following. Not a single one had strayed more than a few feet either side of the lead boat's course.

'Hold your breath. I think we might make it,' he said, handing the glasses to Ty. 'Take a look. See that first houseboat? See how far it's gotten?'

Ty trained the glasses on the line of boats. 'You're right. He's gone a long way.'

'Is that good?' asked Carrie, looking from Ty to Mungo.

'If he passes the headland, and gets clear of those first rising swells coming into the bay,' said Mungo, 'there's a good chance he'll just drift out to sea. And us too.'

Carrie glanced at the bay, out past the incoming swells, then turned back. 'It's still pretty rough out there.'

Mungo shrugged.

'Can I look?' she asked, reaching for the glasses.

Ty handed them over. She adjusted the fit and screwed them into her eyes.

For a moment no-one spoke, just the full detonating blast of the waves on their right and the sharp salty scent of the sea borne on a night-chill breeze. Even this far away the waves were monumental, the rolling swells building into towering faces that seemed to grow and grow and grow until finally the crest broke, and the wall of water collapsed, hiding itself behind a bulging, racing hump of silvery-green phosphorescence.

Off the scale, thought Mungo. Big, lumpy swells rising up into four-storey walls. Maybe higher. The kind of smokers you towed into. Paddling, you'd never get the speed up. It was the biggest surf he'd seen in the bay all year. Correction. The biggest he'd seen in a decade.

'Is it meant to turn?' asked Carrie at last.

Ty straightened, peered ahead.

Mungo reached for the glasses.

'She's right,' said Ty. 'It's turning.'

Through the Leicas, Mungo fastened on the lead houseboat, trying to get the focus right. But he didn't need a sharp image to see what was happening up ahead. Carrie and Ty were right. The houseboat had suddenly started to drift off course. Its bow may still have been pointing out to sea but it was slowly being drawn to starboard, suddenly out of line.

Mungo realised at once what was happening. So far from the harbour mouth, the floodstream was slowing and the greater power of the sea was taking over. As if to confirm this, to put it beyond any doubt, he saw the houseboat's bow start to shift around. From viewing it end to end, stern to bow, he could now see the houseboat coming broadside on to the column. There was no question about it. The houseboat may have passed the breaking zone but it had turned towards the swells coming up behind, was being drawn into them.

Through the glasses Mungo could also see the people on board. There was no sign of the man in the swimsuit – probably inside having his leg treated – but Mungo counted five figures on deck, all of them gathering in the bows, all of them looking at the rising swells they were now heading into. Aware of what was now sure to happen.

At this distance Mungo couldn't see faces, couldn't make out expressions, but he had a fair idea what they'd be thinking. After getting so far along the South Bluff shoreline, so close to open water, here they were being pulled back into the maelstrom that they'd hoped and prayed they'd miss. They'd be scared all over again. Terrified. Desperate.

And there was nothing any of them could do about it.

Or so he thought.

Suddenly one of the five figures separated from the group and came hurrying down the starboard side. In the stern he started pulling off his clothes. He was going to swim for it, Mungo realised. Two or three minutes earlier, he'd have had just a hundred yards to cover before reaching the South Bluff shoreline. Now he had double that distance. Or maybe he wanted to swim to the next houseboat, still heading out to sea, thinking it might stay on course.

Then a second figure appeared in the stern, tried to

hold the man back. Mungo guessed it was a woman, before he caught her long hair whipping around her head in the moonlit breeze. There was something imploring in her body language, the way she crouched, tried to tug him back with both hands gripping his arm. But the man wasn't listening, wasn't having any of it. Pulling free, he was up on the railing and over the side.

The woman must have screamed. The three others up in the bows came racing back, a torch beam jerking along the length of the starboard side. In the stern, one of the figures grabbed the woman, while the one with the torch swung it to and fro in their wake.

Suddenly, caught in its wavering beam, Mungo saw the man swimming away from the boat, arms snatching at the water, legs thrashing – breast stroke, then crawl, then breast stroke again, a desperate freestyle that moved him only marginally faster than the current he swam against.

'Go on, go on,' whispered Mungo.

'Did someone dive off?' asked Carrie.

Ty nodded. 'Just one. Looked like a man.'

Mungo didn't offer the glasses. He kept them fastened on the swimmer, fixed in the pool of light from the torch.

This jerking beam provided a wavering tear-shaped oval of light maybe ten feet wide and twice as long, the swimmer held just about in its centre. The water around him looked choppy and wild and Mungo could make out moonlit spray flung up from his arms.

Up on the stern, one of the figures suddenly pointed ahead, beyond the light, and Mungo tipped his glasses in that direction. Outside the beam of light, the moonlit water was darker, harder to focus on. It was only when a fin sliced out of that darkness and broke into the pool of light that Mungo knew what they'd seen. A shark, clearly larger than the sharks in the harbour, and bowling straight for the swimmer.

That was the last thing Mungo saw. By now, the second houseboat in line had also started to veer off course and its bows cut across his line of vision like a moving wall. The man and the shark were gone, hidden beyond it. But there was no doubt in Mungo's mind what would happen. He dropped the glasses and watched the distant torch beam flick out from the lead houseboat's stern like a silvery pencil, no longer able to see the scene being played out in its oval spotlight.

'Did he make it?' asked Ty.

'Hard to tell,' Mungo replied. 'That second house-boat's got in the way so it's . . .'

The scream was distant but unmistakable. A shrill, piercing shriek that rose above the sound of the waves, caught against the soundboard of South Bluff's slopes and echoed down the line of houseboats.

'Guess he didn't make it,' said Ty, his voice flat, dead.

'Guess he didn't,' replied Mungo.

Between them Carrie shook her head, took a breath, steadied herself.

'We are not going to die,' she whispered. 'We're just so not.'

'Attagirl,' said Ty. 'Course we're not.'

Mungo grunted. He hoped they were right.

133

Crouched between the two bodies, Mort froze. Only his eye moved, flicking to left and right, taking in the immediate vicinity: the bodies, the nearest trees, the shadows beyond. And he listened intently for any sound that shouldn't be there, something out of place. Like he'd been taught to do.

When had she been here? How long ago?

Was she close? Close enough to see him? Close enough to hear him?

Or had she left the area?

He let out his breath slowly and sank back on his haunches, extending his line of vision. Cautiously, by minute degrees, he moved his head from side to side, looked to the right and the left, then, just as cautiously, he stood and turned from the waist, checking the slope behind him.

Nothing. He could see and hear nothing. Nothing save the sound of trickling water and his own heartbeat.

Think like your enemy. Think like your enemy. That's what they'd taught him.

What would she have done when she got out of the

basement? Mort would have searched the cabin – he had no doubt that she would have done the same. Would it have been daylight, or night-time? he wondered. And what might she have found in the cabin, what had been left there after the flood?

He also knew what she'd have done next. The same as him. She'd have left the cabin with whatever she'd managed to find and come down to the cars, probably searched them, like him, and then found the bodies. Straightened them out. Gone through their pockets.

But where was she now?

Close, he thought. She was close.

He breathed in deeply through his nose, as though trying to catch her scent.

She hadn't gone back to the cabin, he knew that. She'd have been scared someone might come back. But she wouldn't have headed off into the forest either. All that time coming up the Hanish, watching out for her from the other bank – she wouldn't have done it. He knew that now, and in the darkness he smiled.

She'd have holed up somewhere until daybreak.

Somewhere safe.

Somewhere she thought was safe.

The Lexus.

134

By now the lead houseboat was starting to rock from side to side as each incoming swell rolled under its hull, broadside on, lifting the boat and settling it, moving it slowly forward into the following trough.

Mungo raised his glasses. On deck the remaining figures had moved away from the stern, but only two of them were visible up in the bow. Man or woman he couldn't tell. There was no sign of their companions. It seemed likely they had gone inside.

'Off they go,' said Ty. 'No turning back now.' Like Mungo he knew that point of no return, when a surfer commits to the swell, spots a wave and paddles out to it, manoeuvres into position. Up ahead, away to starboard, the lead houseboat did just that. Lost for a moment in a trough, hidden by the last rising breaker to pass it, the next time they saw it the houseboat had turned stern on to the following swell and was caught by it, starting to pick up speed, sliding down the rising wall but finally tipped back as it was overtaken. Two more swells followed, catching the houseboat, tipping it forward but racing on ahead, leaving it floundering in their wake. And with each

swell that passed, building up for the break line, the houseboat slipped further into the bowl where the big waves
broke.

There seemed a lull then, a sudden change in the
rhythm of the waves. Up on Fluke's bows, the three of
them peered ahead, out into the moonlit bay, waiting
for the next set of swells to rise up out of the ocean
and roll in.

But for close on a minute nothing stirred, just chips
of moonlight glittering on the chop.

And then . . .

'Whoa,' whispered Ty. 'Here it comes . . .'

And far out in the bay Mungo saw a long low ripple
slide beneath the moonlit chips on the surface, lift them,
scatter them, then gather them together as it rose up
into a massive swell. Up and up it went, moonlight
dancing across its curving face, feathery white manes
leaping and streaming off its rising crest.

Thirty feet, thought Mungo. Thirty-five feet and still
building. Forty feet now.

Though the wave made no sound yet, it seemed to
groan with the weight massing up behind it, sucking
the water towards it. Up and up it went, its lowest
slope now reaching forward and rising under the keel
of the lead houseboat, catching hold of it, lifting it up
and tipping it forward. In an instant the houseboat was
surfing, nose to the trough, the play of the water
racing up behind it, drawn to that mounting, menacing
crest.

For a moment the wave seemed to stand still, the
crest so teeteringly high and massively heavy that it
seemed to stall, to stop, to cease forward motion. Only
the houseboat moved, skittering down that great

moonlight-marbled face, a bow wave spraying up as it raced ahead of the black wall towering above it, desperate now to escape its fate.

For breathless, aching seconds it seemed to Mungo that the houseboat would survive, and that the accumulated mass of the wave, now so preposterously large and high, would somehow work against it, that it would fall back on itself, and be gone.

But as soon as he thought it, Mungo knew it would never happen like that. It never did. He might not be able to see it but he knew in his bones that the wave was still moving forward, still growing, gathering itself higher and higher above the houseboat. And he knew there was nowhere the houseboat could hide.

If there had been a slim hope that the houseboat might ride that wave, be taken up by it, be swept to the beach and cast ashore – Mungo had no doubt that everyone else watching from the houseboats ahead was thinking the same thing – that hope was swiftly and summarily dashed.

'She's gonna go,' whispered Ty.

And go she did, finally toppling over from the stern, rising above the bow, in a huge engulfing maw that simply swallowed the houseboat whole. One minute it was there, rising up the face of the wave, the next it was gone, obliterated in a rage of booming, thundering surf.

As the wave roared past them, heading for the beach, Mungo saw a twenty-foot length of planking shoot up into the moonlight, tombstoning, spinning like a surfboard flung free of its rider, and drop back down to the surf. That was all that was left in the following trough, that single spar, the frothing white water bubbling and hissing around it.

'Is it over?' asked Carrie quietly, her face pressed against Ty's chest.

No, it's not over, thought Mungo. *It's just beginning.*

135

Creeping through the trees, a single stand back from the treeline to limit his profile, Mort suddenly spotted the Lexus up ahead. If he hadn't known where to look, it would have taken him much longer to find. But there it was, just thirty feet away, right where he remembered it, front wheels up off the ground, fender resting against a tree trunk, a silvery wraith in the shadows.

He wondered how long it had taken the woman to find it. In daylight it wouldn't have been too difficult, but at night it would have been a different matter. She'd certainly have come looking for it, hoping it hadn't been left over on the Susqua Trail where they'd picked her up. She wouldn't have known she'd been bundled up in its back seat and driven here, and she wouldn't have seen it in the front yard with the two trucks, but she might have guessed it was there. And if the two trucks had been washed down to the treeline, it made sense that the Lexus would have come in the same direction.

For a moment or two Mort stayed where he was, watching for movement, the flicker of a light, a muffled cough maybe, some sign of life. There was nothing. So he set off to the left, cutting deeper into the trees, circling the Lexus, keeping low and watching where he put his feet. It didn't take long to note the misted windows – thanks to a dark smeared band where a hand had cleared the condensation from the silvery glass – and his heart beat faster.

She was there, he knew it.

But a few minutes later, he came round on the far side of the Lexus, still some distance away, and he knew that she wasn't. She had gone. Even on the tilt, the Lexus's back door hung open. And you didn't bunk down in the back seat of a car and leave a door open.

Mort hurried forward, no longer worried at any noise he might make. Reaching the door, he wrenched it open and looked inside.

It was still warm.

He reached out a hand and felt the seat. Warm too.

And the kiddie's seat had been moved to make room, tossed into the back.

And up front he could see that the glove compartment was open. He remembered candy there and biscuits and fruit. He'd been going to take it into the cabin, but forgot all about it. Reaching between the seats, he felt around inside. Nothing. She'd been here, found the food, slept in the back seat.

And in the last few minutes she'd heard him, and slipped away into the forest.

She was close.

Very close.

136

The sudden and shocking fate of the lead houseboat, and the people aboard, had a galvanising effect on the three manned houseboats ahead of Fluke. One of them still held the line, but Mungo could see that the other two, further on, had started to stray from the shore on the weakening current. Through the binoculars, he watched the people in all three houseboats moving around on deck as if there was something they could do to avoid catastrophe. But there was nothing to do. No place to go. They were caught and, for all their hurrying and bustling, deep down inside they must have known it.

Mungo lowered the glasses and turned to Carrie.

'You okay?'

She smiled, not happily but bravely. 'I've been to better parties,' she said.

Mungo nodded. It was exactly what he'd expected to hear. That's all he needed to know.

He turned to Ty. 'You got any suits?' he asked. 'That's cold water out there.'

'You gonna take us surfing?' said Ty.

'Best be prepared,' he replied.

Ty grinned in the moonlight. It made his tan look deeper. 'You know what? That's just what Carrie told me on our first date,' he said, and took off for the cabin.

Carrie gave him a dig in the ribs as he passed. She used an Indian word Mungo recognised, and he thought of Miche. Where was she? How was she? Somehow, he knew she was fine. She was Miche. She could handle it. He just had to make sure he was there when she came back from the canyons.

'It's gonna be a tight fit,' said Ty, coming back a few minutes later with an armful of wetsuits. 'Carrie and me are okay, but you're gonna stretch the spare.'

Ty wasn't wrong. Mungo was a good four inches taller than his host and he had to stretch and wrestle the neoprene wetsuit into place. It felt like his shoulders were being pulled forward, and every time he tried to square them his crotch squeezed tight.

'That was a five-mil suit,' said Ty, turning for Carrie to zip him up while Mungo squirmed. 'Probably all of three now.'

'Well, thanks for that,' said Mungo. 'I'll keep this suit after we're done, and see you try it on a few years down the road.'

'I'll be there,' said Ty, pulling up Carrie's zip.

'Me too,' added Carrie.

'Only if you put your life jackets back on,' said Mungo, nodding at the waistcoat vests they'd discarded. 'And while you're at it, you can help me with mine,' he added, trying to flex his arms like a performing seal who couldn't quite clap.

For just a few minutes, the three of them had turned away from what lay ahead, put it out of mind, filling the time with chat and chuckles. Now, suited up, they snapped to. Up ahead the second houseboat, unmanned, empty, was heading into the line of swells about a hundred yards behind the breaking line.

Bound into his wetsuit Mungo raised the Leicas against the pull of the neoprene and took a look. The wave that had hit the first houseboat had been the first of a set. Three more had already passed since then and Mungo could make out what looked like another five swells rising out of the ocean. A nine set, possibly a ten-set sequence of big, fearsome faces. It was like Maverick's, Teahupo'o and Pe'ahi rolled into one. He handed over the glasses so Ty could take a look.

Like the first houseboat, the second in line was soon broadside on and drifting through a bubbling silvery surf towards North Bluff, rocking as a fifth, sixth and seventh swell pulsed under it. Each rising wave pushed the house-boat closer to the breaking zone, lifting it higher and higher, each swell just a little bit larger and gnarlier than the one before it.

By the time the eighth swell came in, the second houseboat had turned to face the beach, like a surfer paddling for the wave. In the moonlight, drifting unmanned amid the wild surf, it looked like a ghost ship heading for port, something spectral and hazy about it through the moonlit spray, as though it wasn't really there.

But it was there, and in a kind of hesitant slow motion it rose up the incoming face, near vertical, until a gust of offshore breeze flipped it back over the peak.

'That's sixty foot if it's an inch,' said Ty, handing back the Leicas as the wave rolled past them.

Mungo nodded, clamping the glasses to his eyes. 'And the next one looks even bigger.'

Wallowing in the trough, the unmanned houseboat bobbed around uncertainly, something boisterous and jolly in its careless abandon, as though it didn't care what was coming up fast behind it, what was about to happen to it.

Ten seconds later the ninth, and final swell came in fast, a rolling monster that reared up as ugly and beautiful as they come and hung teasingly above the unsuspecting houseboat. Mungo watched every second, trying to fit wave and houseboat in the same field of view. But the rising wave was so monstrous, it wasn't easy to do. At least this time the destruction was easier to watch. There was no-one aboard. Whatever happened, they would share in no-one's terror. No lives would be lost.

It was just spectacle. A breather.

'He's further along than the first houseboat,' said Ty, taking back the glasses and adjusting the focus, trying for a sharper image in the drifting moonlit spray. 'The wave'll break this side of him, then catch him up and wipe him out in the pocket.'

Mungo had heard the same kind of speculation on beaches and look-out points at pretty much every place he'd ever surfed. It's what you did when you weren't in the water, watching the other chargers out there – pouncing on faults, applauding the drops and the cuts. Ty must have done a fair bit of it himself because he'd read the wave just right. That last crest gathered and broke in a curling left-hander that dragged down the snarling lip of the wall yard by feathering yard. For a moment the second houseboat, already powering down the barrelling face, was lost behind a thundering explosion of spray and surf. Three seconds later it reared up like a dog in the bath shaking off a shampoo. It stayed in the moonlight maybe a second or two more, but finally it toppled forward and was dragged under.

They watched the wave roar on past but there was no sign of the houseboat.

It was gone.

137

The moon took Dasha by surprise. One minute she was moving through the trees with her cuffed hands held out in front of her to feel the way forward, to protect herself from snatching, scratching branches, the next a soft grey light flooded through the forest. Suddenly she could see the way ahead, the dark shadows of the trees standing out against a silvery backdrop.

The first thing she did was crouch down and look behind her, a squelching wetness underfoot, the night drenched with the scent of resin. If she could see, she could also be seen. Senses keening she scanned the forest, but there was no sign nor sound of anyone following her. Whoever it was – and something told her it was Mort – he'd surely have found the Lexus by now, and would have known immediately that she had been there. The warmth, the rug, the food, the condensation on the windows. Maybe even the smell of her.

And even if she couldn't see anything, or hear anything, she knew that he would be coming after her. Somewhere out there in the trees.

But which way would he have gone? she wondered. Which way would he have decided she had gone?

She knew the answer. If he couldn't see her, or hear her, if she had gotten far enough ahead, he would have opted for the river. Just as she had done, homing in on the distant murmur of the water.

Gripping the knife in both hands, keeping the links of the handcuffs tight so they didn't clink and jangle, she rose carefully to her feet. With one final glance behind her she turned to her left now and, keeping low, headed away from the river, down the slope and deeper into the forest.

Every twenty steps, she paused by a tree and looked back, listened out, then set off again. Twenty steps, and another twenty steps, and another twenty steps, until she began to feel her confidence rise. No sound from behind her. No moving shadow in the moonlight.

Stopping once more to catch her breath and check behind her, she was about to head off again when she froze.

A cough, a grunt, not quite a bark.

Somewhere ahead of her.

Peering round the tree, knife up, ready to defend herself, she saw, coming up the slope towards her, what looked at first like a dog.

But it didn't take more than a moment to realise her mistake. It wasn't a dog, it was a small bear. A cub. Just a cub. Its head hung low and its snout swinging from side to side as though following a scent, its silvery brown fur slick with water as though it had just had a swim.

But where there was a cub, Dasha knew, there'd likely be a mother close by.

And there she was, lumbering up behind the cub, rising mightily on hind legs to look ahead, sniff the air.

Close enough for Dasha to smell them now – oaky and feral.

Which meant she was downwind.

They hadn't caught her scent yet, and they still hadn't seen her or heard her.

But before she could think what to do, an arm reached around her waist and a hand clamped across her mouth and she felt a great weight pull her down behind the tree, push her between two moss-covered root limbs.

And lips press against her ear.

And a voice. A whisper. Soft and calm.

'Sssshhhh now, my lovely . . . Not a word. And don't you go moving a muscle, y'hear . . .'

138

It took another five sets before Fluke started drifting to starboard. Maybe a half-hour tossing about on the harbour current, fifty metres clear of the South Bluff shoreline, hungry sharks bumping up against their hull as though trying to keep them in line, herding them along. And in those thirty minutes the houseboats ahead of them were drawn one by one into the swells and lethally played with, finally picked up and then dashed down with a terrifying merciless vigour. And with each kill, the waves just seemed to grow stronger and higher and more fearsome as though the houseboats were somehow feeding the swells, pumping them up.

The first of these houseboats had been empty and swiftly despatched, but the two that followed it were manned, the two that had roped up back in the harbour. As the first of these manned houseboats swung into the troughs, Mungo could see that the line between them had been cut. Someone on board one of those boats had decided it was better to go it alone. It was also the moment that Carrie excused herself and went inside.

Mungo and Ty stayed on deck and watched as, one after another, the two manned houseboats lined up for the ultimate, final break. Maybe one of them would make it, maybe one of them would ride it out. But neither of them did.

On the first, as the killing wave rose above it, Mungo spotted some of the people jumping from the rails before the wave hit, thinking they might be better off in the water than on board. He imagined it was a difficult call, and wondered what he'd do.

'I think I'd stay on board,' said Ty, as though reading Mungo's thoughts. 'Maybe tie myself down, take my chances.'

The houseboat was now passing them, just a hundred feet away, beginning to tip over, caught in that closing hollow below the crest. There was no way it was going to get over the wave and drop back in the trough.

'That's because you're a surfer. And they're not,' said Mungo. 'You know, they don't.'

Their conversation somehow softened the action, quietened the horror as a preliminary fist of seawater sprayed out over the houseboat. Mungo thought he saw another body pitch over the stern, but he couldn't be sure.

'You'd think with the tide up like this, we wouldn't get such high water,' observed Ty, just loud enough to be heard over the thundering surf.

'My dad used to call them cloud-breakers,' said Mungo. 'Even the whalers stayed in when it got this lumpy.'

And as he spoke, the houseboat finally flipped over, started to cartwheel down the face, and in a detonating blast was lost to view as the wave smashed around it in a grinding explosion of wild surf.

Five minutes later the second manned houseboat picked up another smoker, but this time Fluke was too far beyond the breaking zone to see exactly how the wave took it, just its stern showing over the crest of the wave in the seconds before it began its slide.

'So,' said Ty, taking a breath and blowing it out, watching their bow swing round to the swell, just two more unmanned houseboats ahead of them. 'Looks like it's our turn. You got any ideas?'

'How many surfboards you got inside?'

Ty frowned, shaking his head in disbelief. 'I thought you were kidding,' he said, reaching for the rail as they rode over the first following swell, feeling the pull to the beach that came with it.

'Why not?' asked Mungo.

'You're telling me you think we can catch one of these waves?'

'You're the one wants to go surf Teahupo'o. We've even got the tow boat,' he said, tapping his foot against the deck. 'Just think of it as a practice session.'

'What about sharks, all that debris out there?'

'You remember those new boys out on Steamer Lane?' asked Mungo with a wry smile. 'They'll get in your way just like hot-doggers always do, but you learn to avoid them. You got eyes. You got moonlight.'

'And you are insane,' said Ty, with a rolling chuckle. 'Insane, man.'

'He's what,' said Carrie, joining them in the bows. She'd felt the first swell lifting them and come back out on deck.

Ty pulled her to him. 'Our dinner guest wants to know how many boards we have.'

After a brief moment, Carrie nodded. 'Makes sense,' she said.

'Don't tell me you agree with him?'

'Well, I don't reckon our chances staying on board, do you? Seriously? We'll get pulped.'

Another swell lifted Fluke and settled it into the following trough. It was like driving over a bridge sideways, and just a spit too fast.

Mungo steadied himself and peered out to sea, trying to see what was coming.

'You've got maybe three more swells to make up your mind,' he said, turning back to his companions.

'Board,' said Carrie without a moment's hesitation.

'That's two of us,' said Mungo.

They turned towards Ty.

The younger man had an excited cast to his eyes, as

though he was about to be introduced to the biggest wave-set known to man. Cold fear and cool courage jostling for pole position. A coiled tension in his limbs.

Show me. I'm your man, his eyes said. Whether he meant it or not.

'Hey, sounds good,' said Ty. 'Count me in.'

139

Mort kept his hand across the woman's mouth, his arm around her waist, and he listened to the bears rooting around, just a few feet away.

At least she hadn't tried to fight him off. They'd both have been dead if she'd done that. All she did was stiffen in his arms for a moment, then sink down beneath him and lie absolutely still. Just like he'd told her.

He'd spotted her as soon as the moon slid from the cloud-cover and washed over the forest. She was twenty metres ahead and she'd crouched down as soon as the moonlight spilled over her. He'd stopped too, between two trees, and he watched as she turned her head to see what was behind her. And though she must have looked right at him she had failed to see him. Which had pleased him.

This, he knew, would be the moment she'd change her plans. With moonlight, it was a different game. Instead of heading for the river – which he'd guessed she'd do after leaving the Lexus – she now turned to the left, heading down the slope rather than across it, taking the unlikely route, away from the river and deeper into the forest where the trees were thicker.

Gradually cutting down the distance between them, Mort was no more than three trees away from the woman when she made that final stop, casting back behind her.

He'd known she was going to do it. That was the pattern. Every twenty or so steps, she'd stop suddenly and turn. She'd almost caught him the first time, but from then on he'd gone more carefully, and counted.

He was close enough now to see a smear of dirt on her cheek, when her head snapped forward and she peered down the slope. She'd heard something. He'd missed the sound himself and he squinted past her to see if he could make out what was down there, what had caught her attention.

That's when he saw the bear cub, maybe thirty feet below the woman, and bounding up the slope towards her. For a moment it looked like the cub had seen her, and was on its way to investigate. But then it sank its nose into the undergrowth and started rooting around for something.

Mort knew it wasn't over. He didn't know much about bears, but this little fella looked young enough to have a mama. And there she was, suddenly, rising up out of the undergrowth and into the soft, silvery cast of the moonlight, rearing up behind her cub and swinging her head round, snout in the air.

Jesus, thought Mort, *she's gotta be ten feet if she's a fuckin' inch*.

He heard her, too. A low suspicious growl, and then a grunt.

And then he smelled her. A deep, woody stink, warm and foetid. Light at this distance, but unmistakable. Which meant he and the woman were downwind of them, off their radar.

With nothing to alert her, the mother bear now dropped down beside her cub and started to help with the dig, coming round from above and showing them her moon-silvery rump.

That was the moment and Mort grabbed it.

Of course, he could have left the woman, seen whether the bears found her, had some fun.

But he didn't. If anything was going to happen to that goddam woman, it was him who was gonna do it. He owed it to himself. And so did she.

And the anger welled up, fresh and hot and irresistible.

He wanted, he wanted, he wanted . . . oh, he just really wanted to . . .

Silently, just four dancing barefoot steps and Mort was behind the woman.

An arm round her waist, his hand over her mouth, pulling her down.

And now he had her.

Lying there beneath him.

He pressed his cheek to her neck and he breathed her in. A warm, loamy smell traced with a sweeter citrus scent.

She was his. At last.

And after the bears had gone he was gonna have her.

509

140

There were four surfboards in the main cabin. Held in secure ceiling racks, they'd stayed in place when the flood had wrenched Fluke from its mooring and smashed it against the quay. They were all in the seven-foot range. Single-, double-, and triple-finned. And good brands, Mungo noticed. Two Top-Deckers, a Blondie and a Todos Crester. They hauled three of them out on deck, leaving behind one of the Top-Deckers, and Mungo led the way to the stern as another swell lifted them and they felt the bow pull around as Fluke took a bead on the beach. Somewhere in the moonlight they heard a splintering crash as the last of the two unmanned houseboats ahead of them exploded on the reef.

'Time to take our places,' shouted Mungo over the roar of the approaching breaking zone. 'Ty, Carrie, you two take the port side, and go left with the wave. I'll stay to starboard and come round after you. And no fancy cuts, you hear? With no foot straps we'll have to keep it shallow and steady. Chances are the houseboats ahead of us will have pitched back to the harbour, but the more distance we can put between us and them, the clearer the water'll be. So keep your eyes open.'

Carrie leaned up and kissed Mungo. 'See you on the beach,' she said, then turned and hugged Ty. 'You too, surf boy.'

'We'll be waiting,' Ty told her.

'Oh yeah?' she grinned. 'And what makes you so sure you're gonna get there before me?'

As they got themselves ready, another swell rolled up behind them, the stern lifted and they started to pick up speed down the building face of the wave.

A heavier boat would have never made it but the lighter Fluke somehow seesawed back up over the incoming crest, and the breaking wave spat angrily across the deck and sprayed their heads and shoulders with salt-water bullets. For a moment, before they tipped back into the following trough, they could see right down the wall of the wave. Forty-five, maybe fifty feet, thought Mungo. Another ten on top of that before it hit the breaking zone.

He turned to look at the swell even now building up behind them, the last of the set. And the biggest.

'Here she comes,' shouted Ty, resting his board on the topmost rail a few feet behind Carrie, pointing it out to the left as Mungo had instructed.

Once again the houseboat started to rise, stern first into the wave. As far as Mungo could see there was no debris on the glittering moonlit face below them, but that didn't mean there wouldn't be significant amounts ahead of them, where the other houseboats had been crushed against the reef or torn apart by the surf.

Up, up, up, went Fluke, the three of them leaning back into the slope, bracing themselves against it, a chill breeze from the crest whispering around their shoulders, licking hungrily across their cheeks.

'Any time now,' called Mungo. 'Whenever you're ready . . .'

From over his right shoulder there came a rustling sound, a feathering, tickling ripple of spray plucked out of the crest by an inshore breeze. Fluke was almost vertical now, trying to race down the wall of water but being drawn inexorably upwards as the wave came in beneath it.

And then came that moment of stillness, that moment when movement ceased, when Fluke's upward drift was slowed and stopped, countermanded by an increasingly urgent downward imperative.

And in that still space of time, Mungo saw Ty and Carrie launch themselves off the houseboat's rail and drop away from the port side, Carrie first, then Ty, clean drops, boards clamped to their bodies. He waited a second or two longer, until Fluke's stern had risen past the lip of the wave, then he, too, leapt away from the starboard rail and out on to the crest.

For a second there was nothing beneath his board, and he felt as though he was balanced on a wing fluttering through the air. He felt a surge of anxiety, an icy shiver of fear. Had he got his timing wrong, miscalculated his drop? Then the board slapped into the wave and tipped down.

In an instant Mungo was up and into a crouch and powering across that silvery shifting slope of water, feet spread apart, arms out, the fingertips of his left hand streaming through the moonlit face as he sliced beneath a cartwheeling Fluke.

141

Dasha kept her breathing steady, nostrils flaring over the edge of his hand, and felt the weight of him on her. And the smell of him. Dark and rich and wet. And the bristles on his jaw as he pressed his mouth to her ear and whispered his instructions.

It had all been so quick. So sudden. One minute the bears coming up towards her, and then that hand clamping over her mouth, being dragged to the ground.

But I shall do as he says, Dasha told herself, eyes squeezed shut. *I shall do as he says, until the bears are gone.*

And down the slope she heard their grunts as they finished with their digging, and the sound of them bounding upwards again, just the other side of the tree, undergrowth pushed aside, branches snapping.

The smell was stronger now – fishy and rank. And they were close enough for Dasha to hear the whumphing-whumphing breaths of the beasts as they lumbered past.

She opened her eyes, looked into the silvery leaf litter pressed against her cheek, then glanced to her right. Ten feet away, the mother bear had risen to her full height and for a moment Dasha was certain they'd been seen, and that the grizzly was about to fall on them, dig them out of their shallow, rooty hiding place and tear them to shreds.

But she didn't. Instead she backed up against a tree and started rubbing her shoulders and neck against the rough bark, grunting with a huffing, puffing satisfaction, her silvery wet pelt quivering in the moonlight.

And as she did so, her cub continued to sniff around, coming slowly closer, head swinging from side to side, snout snuffling though the mossy pine-needle floor of the slope.

Dasha held her breath.

Closer and closer, the cub came. Just six or seven feet.

Would it find them? Would the little one be the one to root them out, Dasha wondered?

But the mother was done with her rubbing. With a final pleasurable growl she stepped away from the tree and dropped down behind her cub. A cuff and a swipe, and they were off again, headed up the slope.

For a minute more Dasha lay there, breathing again, waiting for the weight on her to move, to shift, so that she would know it was over, that they were safe from the bears, and that the time had come to defend herself against yet another predator.

The arm round her waist moved first, and she felt the hand slide over her stomach and pass over her ribs to grasp her breast, squeezing it hard, then palming it roughly.

She hadn't expected that, not at all, and she tried to squirm away from under him, feeling as she did so a sudden hardness pressing against her thigh.

But there was nothing she could do. He had her tight, his legs pinning her down, his hand now burrowing up beneath her T-shirt, scrabbling against the lace cup of her bra and pushing it off her.

Dasha would have screamed if she'd dared. Or been able to. With his hand still clamped round her mouth all she could really manage was a panting grunt of indignation, trying to bare her lips so she could sink her teeth into his hand.

But then she calmed, stopped struggling and gently pressed her backside up against him, made as if to turn, as if to make it easier for him.

Or so Mort thought . . .

Just as she'd anticipated, just as she'd hoped, the hand came off her mouth and his weight eased off her, as though to accommodate this move, long enough for her to turn on to her back and bring up her cuffed hands, the long damascened blade sliding deep and easily into his belly and slicing upwards till the point of the sternum brought the hilt up short.

She'd closed her eyes when the blade went in, surprised how easy it had been to pierce clothing, skin and muscle, but she opened them now, as his warm blood washed down over her arms. She felt his body stiffen and she watched as his mouth and single eye opened wide in shock – the mouth a shadowy cave, the eye a silvery disc of moonlight above her.

'Holy sh—' he managed to gargle, struggling away from her, sitting back on her legs to survey the damage, before tipping back his head and toppling gently sideways.

142

It was the longest and the loneliest ride of Mungo's life.

Once, many years before, he had surfed under a full moon. Just fifteen-foot swells right here in Melville Bay. Cutting and swooping until he'd ridden the last wave to its gentle curving end, paddling in ahead of a hissing ripple, sliding from his board in water that came to his waist, just a few steps from a moonlight-white beach.

But this wave was different. It wasn't just longer, higher, faster. It was somehow more violent, more conspicuously malicious. After it had flipped Fluke over like a raffia table-mat, crushing its shingle sides and deck planking and aluminium hull beneath thousands of tons of pummelling, driving water, it actually seemed to turn on him, furious that he had escaped at the very last moment.

As he streaked along that rising, deepening concave wall, Mungo could feel the wave coming in for the kill, snapping at his heels as though it really did want to catch him, kill him, swallow him up; a wave that wanted to obliterate him, not just wipe him out; a wave that was even now drawing up the hem of its skirts to reveal the reef beneath, this last monstrous, murderous wave of the set sucking up the water in front of it until there was no more to suck up, leaving just thin puddles of moonlit water coursing through the reef's rocky crevices like quicksilver streams.

If he had lost the wave then . . .

But he didn't lose it.

He didn't fall.

Once, twice, three times, he cut up from that rocky lacework at the bottom of the barrel, always watching the way ahead, sensing as much as seeing the chasing wave hood and cowl and hollow behind him, feeling the chill, snatching fingers of a hungry tube gale rush out and slide around his neck and shoulders and waist, just longing to catch a proper hold.

But still he pulled clear, sidestepped the traps set for him, reading the wave and the tricks up its sleeve, his board chattering and clattering over the puckering curve of water, knees bent to accommodate the compression, arms spread. And after the first ten, maybe fifteen seconds of the ride Mungo felt an ascendancy, a rising confidence that he had the wave's measure, that he could ride the brute out. He knew the wave had other ideas, but he sensed now that he could get away from it.

Yet as soon as that thought settled into his consciousness, Mungo knew that he was doomed; knew then that the wave would win. That it couldn't be beaten.

He saw Ty and Carrie just the once – Ty climbing above him then streaking down in his wake, Carrie coming up from below and passing thirty feet ahead of him, the two of them scissoring his course.

But seeing them gave him no comfort.

He knew the wave wanted them too.

And the wave took them.

Carrie went first, seconds later, cutting too high up ahead of him and coming off the board, arms outstretched, legs splayed. Her board disappeared, sucked into the foaming crest, and for a moment or two she hung in the air like a starfish. Then her hand was in the wave, and the wave grabbed it and flung her down, missing Mungo by just a couple of feet. Glancing to his right he saw her spin down to the reef, hitting the ledge of rinsing stone where the water started to rise up, nothing more than ankle-deep cover to cushion the impact.

Ty must have seen her lose her board as he turned up at the bottom of the barrel. By the time he streaked past Mungo, he was looking over his shoulder, searching for her. And that was his mistake. He cut down too swiftly, picked up too much speed and there was no correcting that headlong course.

The wave had him too.

Mungo did not look back, just held his steady, balanced crouch across the face of the wave. But it did him no good. High above, he watched the breaking moonlit lip slide past him, reaching ahead as though to cut him off. He tipped his board to the right to pick up some speed, cut back across the face and levelled out for a sprint. But there was too much water to cover, the lip now breaking above him and along a line that stretched more than fifty yards ahead.

And he knew then that he could never make it out of there.

He felt the tube gale spit out again from the racing tunnel and reach for him, heard the tumbling roll of the surf closing behind him, above him, ahead of him, crouching lower and lower on the board as his head-room diminished.

And that was it.

He had time to gulp a mouthful of air and then he was swept off his board and buried in the wave.

He spun, he rolled, he cartwheeled through the water. It roared in his ears and flooded into his nose, snatched at his hair and pelted his face with a gritty spray of stony shrapnel.

He tried to reach his knees to hug them to him, tried to curl his head into his chest. But the wave would not let him. It just pressed him down, churning him over the rock, drumming him against the sharp, slippery stone before pulling him up, shaking him by the shoulders, then sending him down again.

And lifting him up again.

And pushing him down.

Are you dead yet? the wave thundered in his head.

Are you dead yet? Are you dead yet?

Well, let's just make sure, shall we?

And then, somewhere in the glittering, bubbling, moonlit darkness – somewhere above him, now some-where below him – he felt the velocity of the wave slacken, felt the octopus arms of the whirlpool spirals cast out from the back of the wave start to tug at his limbs. Soon, he knew now, the drag would ease and he would be tossed to the surface and could grab more air.

The wave had passed and he was alive.

Alive. He could still win.

But the surface took a long time coming, and when at last it did he wasn't ready for it, took a lungful of ocean instead of air, and felt his chest explode and his brain hammer with panic as he was hauled back down.

So this was it, he thought to himself, tumbling through the bubbling surf, the roar of the wave riding on ahead of him. This was what it was like . . .

And, suddenly, he didn't mind any more.

Suddenly the roaring, the thundering seemed to drop to a whisper, seemed to grow quiet and warm.

Because he knew the wave didn't hate him any more. Caressing now, not battering.

The rolls more gentle. The tumbling and pounding softer.

Everything around him so . . . distant.

Out of reach.

It was over.

So there we are, thought Mungo. This was what it was like.

Way to go . . .

143

The greedy floodwaters that had poured down from the ridge line of the Silver Hills had emptied into an angry ocean, and the hungry tide that had reached up over the beach had slowly seeped away along the shores of Melville Bay. The town itself was broken, battered, barely habitable. At a little before six on that blue sky Sunday morning there was a deep silence in the town, just the sound of trickling water, mud bubbles breaking with a slimy pop.

Sunday mornings were always quiet in Melville. Not too many people stirred from their beds that early, and the summoning ring of church bells came later. But the silence that had settled on the town was another silence altogether, cold and empty, somehow amplified by the scenes of devastation – the grinding, heaving rush of violence of a few hours earlier freeze-framed in a great knotted tangle of destruction: splintered telegraph posts poking from the cloaked mud like tilting black straws; cars sprawled across Main Street on their sides, on their roofs, the right way up, some with price tickets on the windscreen, snatched from Mel's Best Choice Autos lot on Upper Main; the pink plaster legs of a display mannequin from Mode Melville pointing up at the sky; a phone booth hammocked on a section of awning that had survived the flood; a lady's dressing table, mirror-frames empty, drawers snatched away, wedged in the broken front window of the town library.

If there was no real sound to accompany the scene, there was the smell. It was almost orchestral in its density, unmoved by any whisper of breeze. And like the silence it was everywhere, invisible, creeping over Melville and swaddling it in a warm, rank, suffocating blanket. Raw sewage, of course, but so much more, all whisked up into a slick slimy tiramisu of mud that covered the central section of town, all the way down Main Street, into the side streets, coating the houses that still stood with a brown tidemark that in places reached as high as the guttering.

Where RubyRay's Diner had stood nothing remained above its stone foundations, the lot out front strewn with rocks carried down from upriver, just a taunting trickle of muddy water, slithering between them. The sandbags that had been so hastily placed around the Town Hall had also been carried away, and its century-old spruce-floored entrance hall had been swept through by the stinking floodwater. Down on Promenade, great gaps showed along the line of buildings that fronted Melville's harbour, not just Mama Surf, but the Harbour Master's Office and Breakers Five-Oh and Pierre's – just empty spaces now.

But the worst destruction – the most haunted, the most savage – seemed to be on Melville beach. Along its entire length, bracketed by North and South Bluffs, lay the splintered tangled wreckage of the town – gingerbread awnings, verandah rails, shop signs, doors, deck and pontoon planking, tumbled jet-skis, the crumpled skeleton of a bus shelter, mattresses, bicycles, waste bins . . . everything that had been snatched up and swept away from the town, from the countryside, tossed back on to the sand, left high and dry by the retreating tide.

There were bodies too, everywhere, caught in the mud, floating in the harbour, washed into heaving corners like discarded flotsam, bloated limbs stiffening, snagged in the debris. Animal. Human. Sometimes it was hard to tell. In the hours to come their remains would be gathered up and taken to makeshift holding areas by incoming emergency services, even now approaching Melville by helicopter, clattering up the coast from Astoria and Aberdeen, and coming in over the low passes from Seattle, landing out beyond Baxter's Mall and in the parking lot behind the sea wall.

But for now, in the stinking early morning silence of Sunday morning, the bodies stayed where they were, naked, in tattered clothes, just sad lonely bundles lapped by the water, trapped by the mud, going nowhere.

There were survivors too, of course, wading through the mess, looking to retrieve possessions, trying to recall the layout of the town, stopping sometimes to look around and wonder where they were, where they were going, and just how exactly they planned on getting there. Most just had a dazed, blank look, arms hanging by their sides, or maybe a hand scratching a head, a handkerchief held to a face.

Up on the roof of St Francis Episcopalian, a dog stood peering down at the street. Hours earlier he'd been swept up against its guttering and in the darkness scrambled up on to the shingles. Now he stood there, thirty feet above the sidewalk, wet, bedraggled, wondering how to get down, wondering when someone would notice him. He started barking and for the first time the silence was broken. Some bell, that Sunday morning.

Out of town, above the North Bluff belvedere and orientation table on Totem Hill, Old Jimmy Looking Eyes sat on his blanket and looked out to sea, humming the long, low jilting cadences of a mourning song. Not for any whale, as they did in the old hunting days, and not for the spirits, lost and lonely, who wandered the streets below him. He knew they would find their own way; others would guide them. Their own families, their own gods. Sooner or later they would reach where they needed to be. They didn't need his help.

It was for one of his own that Old Jimmy chanted in this high place. For one of his own. No one needed to tell him that she was lost. He had felt the blow.

He knew. Now he needed to find her and guide her to the spirit world of her forefathers.

Outside the chain-link fence that surrounded the totem, Old Jimmy's family had gathered about him, his many grandchildren, his sons and daughters, their wives and husbands. And as he hummed and chanted the old words, they stood in groups, or sat on blankets, hugging their arms round their chests in the chill morning air.

In that whole clan gathered there on Totem Hill only one person was missing, one member not present, and in his humming spirit trance Old Jimmy Looking Eyes searched for his granddaughter so that he could point the way to the land of their fathers.

144

Win Sutton woke up on the sofa in the main unit, and knew immediately where he was. He was a little cramped and stiff, his right hip ached where he'd slept on it, but otherwise he felt bright and recharged, and he smiled.

It was twenty hours since Court had been swept away, and he'd gone over the unfolding of that terrible loss so many times that he could run it straight through in his head from start to finish – every second, every step of the way: from the moment she crossed over to the bedroom for a shower; the tilting of the tree and the snapping of the walkway; watching her stagger sideways and fall to the floor; and the rescue attempt – that rope ladder, swinging it to her, managing to secure it and then, goddammit, she'd gone back inside to get a change of clothes – typical. Just typical.

It was then that the unit finally collapsed and he was left there, alone, looking down at the crumpled, splintered mess of timber and seeing that flash of white towelling gown snatched away by the water, borne off into the forest.

Court. Gone.

For a while he'd just sat on the top step of the entrance walkway, searching through the trees, calling her name through cupped hands, over the raucous laughter of the water splashing over the Buren steps below him, hoping to see her, to hear her voice shouting back that she was okay, she'd climbed a tree, she was safe.

And then, against all expectation, against all odds, he had heard her voice. Out there in the trees, while he slept. And he had seen her, holding the collar of her towelling gown with one hand and waving to him with the other, just a few trees back from the river. And somehow he had gotten to her, somehow he had rescued her and brought her back to the treehouse, warmed her, soothed her, hugged her tight. Got her back.

And, for a moment, after Win Sutton woke on that sofa, he knew that she was there. Up already, in the kitchen, perking some coffee, getting them some juice, toasting that high-grain nutty bread she loved, bread that actually didn't brown that well and that they always argued about.

He liked white.

She told him it was bad for his cholesterol.

He said he didn't care about his cholesterol.

She said she did.

The usual Court thing.

Swinging his cramped legs off the sofa Win staggered to his feet, reaching to the table for support, turning to the kitchen, expecting to see her.

But the kitchen was empty.

There was no smell of coffee, of toasting bread, no scream from the juicer.

Nothing. She wasn't there.

For a moment he couldn't quite get a grip on it. Something was wrong. And then he understood. She really had been swept away, and his dream had been just that. A cold, cruel deception.

That was when he realised the rain had stopped. And the trembling of the timbers had eased, he was sure of it. With a hollow feeling in the pit of his stomach, an ache of loss, he snatched at that distraction, went out to the terrace and looked below him. Yes, he was certain the water had receded.

To make absolutely sure he went to the entrance walkway and looked down at the steps. There they were, like up-turned logs, the water sluicing around the stem of the lowest when before it had surged over the highest. Indeed, the rage of the water had subsided so much he could hear the sound of rainwater dripping from the branches of the trees around him, tapping on to the plank steps where he stood.

And in that dripping, trickling stillness, he heard another sound, a low thumping drone from somewhere downriver. In just seconds, before that drone had turned into a steady rising beat that came clattering overhead,

Win had known what it was. A helicopter, a rescue party, and he wondered whether they'd know he was there, or whether he should try to make some sign, something to attract their attention, so that they didn't miss him.

Hurrying back to the terrace, he pulled off his sweater, raised it above his head and started waving it, backwards and forwards. And through the branches of the trees he could see now the chopper's flickering black shape and the blur of its blades, registered the urgent closeness of its rotors, and recognised the change in pitch that indicated they were coming in to hover above the treehouse.

They had seen him. They had come for him.

And as he ran to gather his things, Win Sutton knew he'd be coming back to the Susqua Hills, because that's where Court was . . .

Where Court would always be . . .

And Court would have wanted him to, anyway . . .

145

Mungo didn't know the time, didn't care. It was light, that's all he knew. Another day.

He came from the town, still swaddled in a blanket someone had wrapped around him, padding barefoot past the shattered, windowless shell of The Quays, along the sandy cobbles above the slipway, heading for the sea wall. The ocean was quiet now, three- to five-footers, green as glass, breaking straight and polite in the bay, spent surf spilling up the beach, shifting through the wrack and debris as though trying to get a feel for the new beachscape, before racing back to the ocean, glistening and bubbling over the sand.

Climbing the steps, looking out to sea and remembering his friends, Mungo followed the path to his workshop, two floors of weathered wood planking set on a low rise of dune now surrounded by a shallow pool whose surface rippled in the breeze. The water in the pool was already warm from the sun and he sloshed through it, feeling the sand and the mud sluice between his toes. A minute later he stood in his doorway and looked inside. Although the rain had stopped he could still hear dripping from the eaves above his head, tiny drops of water splashing into a puddle somewhere, tapping lightly on wood.

At first he couldn't decide if it had been waves breaching the sea wall or the river flooding through town that had done the damage to his home. Then, in a matter of seconds, he saw a rooting tangle of kelp by the overturned worktable and detected a sharp salty smell. The sea had done this, he realised, waves crashing over the sea wall and blasting through his home. It seemed appropriate somehow. Account settled.

Looking past the door, hanging from a single hinge, Mungo could see that the workshop had been pretty much trashed. He had never been the tidiest man in the world – as Miche had constantly reminded him – but this was way beyond what he was used to. His eighteen-foot work table with its bench clamps and band-saw had been over-turned and pushed up against the staircase that led to his mezzanine living area; his panel of tools (many of them belonging to his father and grandfather) had been ripped from the wall; and his shelf of shells, picked up off the beach, pocketed, polished and varnished, were gone.

The last time he'd been here, locking up on his way out to dinner with Ty and Carrie, the sawdust that covered the workshop floor had felt soft and warm underfoot. Now it was just a wet sludge that pressed between his toes with every step he took, littered with the masks and goggles he wore when he sanded down his boards, a single work-glove, a toppled, broken saw-horse, maps and charts and a dozen scattered, sodden *Surf* magazines. All three windows – looking over the dunes towards North Bluff, out to sea, and back to town – had been blown out, and the rack of boards he'd been working on had disappeared – a half dozen Wave-Walkers just gone. Three had been ready for pick-up, and three just weeks away from completion. Thousands of hours of work lost. Thousands of dollars worth of business. He hoped his insurance was up to date, and then wondered if some technicality might be brought into play – something from the small print that excluded cover when the sea came calling. It wouldn't have surprised him. Nothing would have surprised him now.

Stepping carefully around the room, aware there might be glass bedded down in the sludge underfoot, Mungo tried to recall what had been where, nodding his head when he remembered, shaking his head when he couldn't, as though silently compiling an inventory of damage and loss. Then he pushed through into the shop, putting his shoulder to the door to open it, and coming in behind the counter, or where the counter had once stood. Now there was nothing, just a great sweep of piled sand and a tangle of beach rubbish – old rope, blue plastic bags, styrofoam beakers, driftwood. He could see at once that all the gear had gone – Indian weave leashes, tins of wax, surf shorts, sunglasses, watches, postcards, tide timetables, books, magazines – every single item of stock stripped from the racks, the shelves, the baskets, the trays, the ceiling, the shop window. Even the sheet of glass had disappeared, not a splinter standing in the frame. For an idle moment Mungo wondered where everything had gone.

Into town, buried somewhere in the mud?

Or out at sea, to be lost forever?

Or one day, maybe, to be swept back in with the tide?

Rubbing the tiredness from his eyes, Mungo crossed the shop floor and stepped out on to what was left of the verandah. High above, gulls swirled and swooped through the sky, their cries carried on an inshore breeze, a taunting, gleeful screech as though the town and everyone in it had finally gotten what they deserved.

Sitting on a corner of the verandah, pulling the blanket around him, he clasped his hands and gazed across the shivering pond that surrounded his home, looking east over the rooftops of Melville to the distant Silver Hills still hidden that Sunday morning behind a line of low grey cloud.

Of all the things he'd lost that night, there was only one in that gutted building that he missed, one thing he mourned for. Not his father's collection of crosscut and back saws, or his grandfather's bulky planers and braces, or the old valve radio that had belonged to his mother and had stood within reach of the work table.

Something much more valuable than any of those.

Something he could never replace.

He knew that she was gone. Knew it for certain. He'd read the names on a report sheet at the Sheriff's Office in town. He'd gone there as soon as he could, to see if they had any information about Charlie Gimball's Wild Water party. It was Sergeant Calley who had broken the news, or rather, handed him a flight report from a Forestry pilot out of Shinnook.

Two vans and ten bodies below Cougar Canyon, spotted along a half-mile stretch of the Susqua Stream between Fiddler's Chute and the Tall Trees campsite, eight of the victims in wetsuits.

It was all he needed to know.

Lowering his head, Mungo hunched his shoulders and wept, mourning for the girl he had loved, and lost.

146

In their bedrooms on South Bluff Drive, Alexa and Finn slept soundly in their beds.

They'd arrived at the house an hour earlier, after being brought down from the awning on Baxter's Mall and taken to Melville Hospital for a check-up.

'Not you again,' the doctor had remarked as he bound

up Zan's knee and administered another cortisone injection. 'And this time, please try to keep it rested.'

Without bothering to undress his daughter, Zan had laid a sleeping Alexa on her bed, tucked her in, and then gone to Finn's room where the boy was already stretched out, eyes closed, mouth open, a soft whisper on his lips.

An hour later, two floors below, Zan sat forward watching the news broadcasts, flicking from station to station. All they had was cell-phone footage from the night before as the Susquahanish swept into Melville – various and unsteady scenes of the water breaking over the banks of the river, swamping the shops, growing in strength and starting to pick stuff up, roll it along. And now, with blue skies above, there were news helicopters buzzing around, filming the devastation, the occasional rescue – someone brought out from the tumbled ruin of their home, stretchers amongst the mud and the rubble, hard hats and reflective yellow jackets.

If there was one thing Zan wanted to do, it was sleep. His knee might have calmed down some, but the rest of his body ached with fatigue. Yet sleep wouldn't come. Switching off the TV he went upstairs, stripped off his clothes and showered. Back in the bedroom towelling himself dry he slid open the terrace door and stepped out on to the deck. Down in the bay the sea was striped with tidy white combers, the sky high and clear, the fog lifted away. Knotting the towel round his waist he leaned his elbows on the rail and looked out at the ocean, searching for that distant line where sea becomes sky. Wherever it was, it was so far away the two became one.

Then, from inside, he heard the bedside phone start to bleat.

It was Mulholland. 'So how's it goin' with that knee?'

'I'll live. Any news?'

'Nothing so far, I'm afraid. But it's early days, you know? She could turn up any time.'

Zan could see the older man rubbing his hand through that big grey walrus moustache, wishing the news was better.

But then, as Mulholland started asking about the kids, he suddenly stopped short and said: 'Hang on there, Zan. Just give me a minute, willya?'

There was a moment's pause, a hand held over the receiver at Mulholland's end, just a low murmur of voices. Zan thought he could make out a 'Yeah? What you got for me?', but he couldn't be certain.

For some unaccountable reason Zan felt a chill shiver of premonitory grief slide through him. And in that moment he knew that what he had feared most had happened. That his wife had been found and the news was not good. He took a breath, tried to steady himself, tried to find some shred of strength to prepare himself. He wondered how Mulholland would break it to him. After all they'd been through together. What words would he use? How would he say it? Straight, or roundabout?

Pressing the phone to his ear, Zan tried to make out the muffled conversation at the other end of the line. Then there was a deep, black silence, as though the connection had been cut.

'Hello? Is anyone there? Chief? You there?'

There was a scratch of static on the line.

Then another dull, dead signal.

He was about to break the connection himself and redial when the line came alive again.

And he heard a voice.

Distant, cold, exhausted. 'Zan? Zan, is that you?'

The breath caught in his throat. 'Dasha? Dasha?'

'I'm here. I'm here. It's okay. I'm okay.'

They brought her back later that day. Zan was waiting for her, expecting an ambulance, wondering how long it would take them to make the trip from Shinnook where she was being treated. He was sitting on the rise of meadow above the front door, clasping his knees and looking out to sea. It was calm, its surface glittering in the afternoon sunshine, just some low swells rolling in, a few scattered pieces of wreckage rising over them, drifting slowly north on a long tongue of brown water that licked out from the river. Twenty yards away, along the slope, Finn and Alexa were playing in their treehouse, a prototype child-sized model of the first Pearse-Caine Wilderness retreat. When he heard the helicopter he paid no attention. Just another TV chopper filming the wreckage and the ruin of Melville, sweeping round South Bluff for a new angle or maybe heading home.

It was Finn who pointed up at it as it came clattering over the slope and seemed to hang there, its blurred rotors flattening the grass around him.

'Someone's waving,' the boy cried, climbing down from the treehouse and running along the ridge with Alexa close behind him. 'It's Momma! Look, look! Momma!'

Scooping up the kids, Zan watched the helicopter come in to a hover twenty feet above the driveway. It seemed to take an age to settle, whipping up a dusty blast of bark chip. But the rotors didn't slow, the helicopter skids finally just brushing the ground. Zan saw a side-door slide open and the big rolling bulk of Chief Mulholland climb down, then reach up for someone. It was Dasha, wrapped in a blue blanket, just bare head and bare feet showing. Finn and

Alexa had seen her too and Zan felt them squirm in his arms, wanting to run to her, but he kept them clasped tight.

And then Mulholland was climbing back into the chopper, leaving Dasha there, like he was some big old cheery Father Christmas delivering a parcel. When he'd got back into his seat, someone pulled the door into place, the engine pitch changed and the helicopter lifted away. Looking up, Zan glimpsed Mulholland behind the glass window as the bird turned towards the ocean. The older man tipped him a salute and Zan raised an arm and waved.

It was raising that arm that did it. No longer in their father's firm grip, the two kids now broke free and ran towards their mother. She went down on her knees and they tumbled into her arms, holding her as tight as they could.

As Zan limped after them, Dasha looked over their shoulders and he could see there were tears streaming down her cheeks.

'Some lunch date,' he managed, when he got close enough, then clamped his jaw tight and swallowed to keep his own tears away.

'Some fishing trip,' she replied, getting to her feet and pulling the blanket back around her shoulders. They stepped towards each other, into each other's arms, and held on tight. Dasha sobbed. Zan swallowed hard.

'I thought . . .' she began.

'Me too,' he replied.

Beside them, Alexa tugged at the blanket and looked up at Dasha with a serious expression.

'Gramma's gone to heaven, Momma. Did you know? She and Blister, they went to heaven. And I saw them go.'

Dasha nodded at her daughter, smiled through her tears, laid a hand on her head, smoothed her hair.

'I'm so sorry,' said Zan, taking a deep breath to steady his voice. 'There was nothing I could do. One minute I had her, the next . . .'

'I know,' she said. 'I know. They told me. It's all right.'

For a moment he wanted to tell her in his own words what had happened. And what Shelley had said, seconds before he'd seen that overturned Chevrolet spin round the corner of the mall and bear down on them. But the moment wasn't right. He'd leave it for later.

Over a drink, maybe. Shelley would appreciate that.

And anyway, he thought, putting an arm round his wife's shoulder and leading her to the house, Dasha would have known what her mother's last words would have been.

147

With only two real time-outs – their sushi lunch the previous day in Melville, and their hour or so in bed at the Saw Mill Lodge – Jenna and Pico had been on the go-get for more than twenty-four hours. They were as wasted as their power packs. Earlier that morning Pico had been halfway through a shot of Jenna to camera, with the first rescue helicopter coming in to land in the lodge parking lot, when their last pack gave out and he knew it was over.

The filming and them.

And when she saw him heft that camera off his shoulder, the words died in her throat and Jenna just hung her head as though a puppeteer's strings had been cut, let her shoulders droop. She knew it was over too. Then she stepped forward into Pico's arms and clung to him, suddenly weeping, then trembling with the shock.

'I thought we were going to die,' she whispered into his damp sweatshirt. 'I never thought we were going to get out of this.'

'You and me both,' replied Pico, hugging her tight.

'You wanna go home?' she asked.

Though she couldn't see it, she felt the nod.

'Yeah. I wanna go home,' she heard him say.

They got out of Shinnook on a medi-vac flight bringing in emergency supplies and taking out the injured. It cost Jenna her Rolex, and provided only a cramped space back in the tail of the bird. It was a bumpy stomach-churning flight, particularly when they swooped around the ridge line of the Silver Hills and dropped back down towards Tacoma.

But their film made it to the CTACtv studio.

Sitting together in a darkened viewing room an engineer ran the hard disc footage for Gerry Coons, who'd sent them to cover sharks and ended up with a three-hour-seventeen-minute playback of death and destruction in a town called Shinnook, courtesy of Mother Nature.

As the footage rolled, word got round the newsroom and by the closing sequence, with Jenna fading from view as the first rescue helicopter came clattering in, a ton of people had crowded into the viewing room. Five rows of six seats taken and two narrow side aisles packed, standing room only.

At the end, after that closing sequence, there was a kind of stunned silence. No-one moved, no-one's eyes left the blank flickering screen, as if waiting for more, wanting more.

There were tears too. Tears and snuffling in that warm, dark silence.

Then someone started clapping. Others followed. Someone whooped, someone whistled. Others stamped their feet on the carpet. You didn't hear that kind of thing from newsroom hacks. In seconds the small viewing room was thunderous with applause.

Gerry turned to Jenna.

'So the baby lived?'

'You saw it. The buggy got caught in that tree. The baby was strapped in.'

'But the mother died?'

'It was just too much for her, I guess. She was devastated, you know? Just broken. We finished filming, and one of the men she was with tried to coax her inside, out of the rain, away from the flood. Away from the memory, I guess. And right there, right then, like I said in the voice-over, she just tugged free of him, pushed the other man off and leapt into the stream. And she was gone, just like that . . .'

Gerry turned down his mouth, considering what she'd told him, and what he'd seen.

'It was a long way to go for a "could-be",' he said at last.

'You don't go, you never know,' Jenna replied.

He gave her a crooked kind of look, held it for a moment, then grunted and shook his head. 'You did good, kiddo. I mean, really, really good. The both of you,' he added, glancing across at Pico.

Then he turned to his engineer. Back to business.

'Fred, I want an edited thirty-minute highlights slot to follow the Six. This evening. Full titling. You've got till then to do the best job you know how. Also, get copies handed round and have your boys edit down the footage to all categories – twenty-second to four-minute sections – anything we can syndicate. Also, I reckon we got enough for a two-hour Newsline special, Monday prime-time, cut with these two heroes' – thumbing over his shoulder at Jenna and Pico – 'talking to camera, eye-witness kinda thing . . . And, Lynn,' he called out, waving to a woman he'd spotted in the aisle, 'get Marketing in for ad rates and promo. Okay,' he said, pausing for breath, looking round the room, from face to face, trying to work out if he'd covered all the bases. He had.

'So . . . Let's get to it, people.'

148

There were four bodies in the sloping meadow below Fiddler's Chute and Cougar Canyon on the Susqua Stream. Three of them were spread around the tideline of debris from the swollen river, still full but now drop-ping back towards its original course. From a distance, in their neoprene wetsuits, they looked like so many black bin liners tossed up on the shore, still and crumpled.

The fourth body was not on the ground. It was caught in a tree nearly ten feet up, supported by the length of a branch. If the body had been placed there deliberately, it couldn't have been more delicately or artfully composed. The bare head rested on an elbow, the other arm hung down. The legs were crossed, left ankle behind right knee. If the other bodies looked like discarded bin liners, this body looked like a black panther asleep on a branch.

There were no fins and no neoprene socks on the body, no helmet and no rubber hood. These had been torn off in the raging torrent of the Cougar Canyon. So the head and feet and hands were the only parts of the body exposed.

The black hair was wet, matted with twigs and leaves and strands of moss, and it clung in licks across a pale cheek. The feet were small and delicate, and you didn't need to see the red nail varnish to know that they belonged to a woman. And the hands were no different, small, finely boned, the fingers long and slim.

Signs of damage to the body were the next thing an observer would have noted. Unlike the bodies on the ground, grotesquely twisted and bent, the limbs of the woman in the tree seemed straight and natural. Closer inspection, however, would have revealed an ugly black bruise on the inside of the left ankle starting to yellow out at the edges, a bloody, swollen wound across the right temple, and numerous tears in the skin of the neoprene suit, on arms, legs and body, stretched and taut like the opening wounds a flensing blade makes on the hide of a whale, ready to peel open with only the merest encouragement. Through some of these tears it was possible to see skin beneath, marked with a scarlet cross-hatching of cuts and scrapes.

These four bodies – and others like them – had been spotted by a rescue helicopter working its way up the Susqua Stream. Unable to land, it had radioed in the location – three hundred yards below Fiddler's, north bank, three on the ground, one in a tree – and a rescue team had driven up the trail and come down through the woods to bag and tag them.

But there seemed to be a problem. The Forestry pilot had reported four bodies, yet the ground crew could find only three. Apparently there had been a body in a tree, caught in a branch the pilot and his spotter had said. But whichever tree it had been in, it wasn't there now. The rescue team had walked along the stream, checking the treeline, looking up through the drooping branches, three or four trees back into the forest.

If there had been a body there, they would have found it.

But there was nothing.

It was only later, after they'd carried the three body bags up to their vehicle, and turned back down the trail for Shinnook, that they found that missing fourth body.

But it wasn't a body.

Coming round a bend in the trail the driver saw a figure hobbling along ahead of them, dressed in a tight black skin, hair still wet, feet bare. As they drew closer, the figure turned and raised a weak arm, as though there might have been a possibility the rescuers would drive right past on this lonely, narrow, rutted trail, without seeing her.

At first it was hard to tell if it was a man or a woman, but as they pulled to a stop they could see it was a woman. Her eyes were wide, her lips a pale, ghostly grey, and her teeth clenched to control the shivering. Having waved them down, she tucked her hand back into her armpit and hugged her trembling body, almost bent over with the wracking chill.

As the rescue team jumped from the car with their medi-pacs and blankets, the woman just seemed to collapse in a heap, right there beside the trail, as though she couldn't take another step, couldn't stand another moment.

In a second they were beside her, wrapping her shaking body in the insulating rug, rubbing warmth and circulation back into her limbs, pushing the hair from her face.

'What's your name, honey?' asked one of the medics, while his two colleagues worked on her.

At first she didn't respond, as though her clenched teeth made speech impossible. She just looked at him, head nodding, as if she could hear the question but didn't know how to answer.

'You got a name, sweetie?' the rescuer asked again, picking some twigs from her hair, smiling at her gently, his eyes filled with concern.

The woman swallowed, tried to get a grip on her voice. She sniffed once, twice – big sniffs, tipping back her head to accommodate them – her chest heaving as if she needed a good lungful of air before she could speak. The word, when it came, was a whisper.

'Say again, darlin'. I didn't catch that,' said the rescuer gently.

Her lips pursed and she nodded again, to let him

know that she understood, that she was trying, that she really was trying to speak. Then her voice caught and tears spilled from her eyes.

'Miche,' she said. 'I'm Miche.'

And her face just melted, and she surrendered to her tears, gave in to the grief.

149

Melville and Los Angeles
Twelve months later

'Good evening, Ladies and Gentlemen, and welcome back to the Academy of Television Arts and Sciences' sixty-first Emmy Awards ceremony, here at the Nokia Theater in downtown Los Angeles.'

Up on stage, the show's host quietened his audience and started into a riff about TV ad breaks and all the things you could get up to and . . .

'Have I missed anything?' asked Dasha, hurrying back into the living room. She was carrying a bag of taco chips to fill up the bowl on the coffee table, two cans of Grolsch and had a bottle of Californian merlot under her arm.

'Just back on. Grab a seat,' said Zan, thumping the cushion beside him, and reaching for the beers.

Apart from the children, now asleep upstairs, there were four of them there at the house on South Bluff Drive – Zan and Dasha, and the Mulhollands, Bill and his wife, Julie. They'd had dinner together on the terrace, watching the sun slide away into the ocean and the sets roll in to Melville Bay, and after the two children had been seen off to bed they'd settled in front of their TV screen, like most of the residents of Melville and Shinnook, to watch the awards show.

After the wine glasses were replenished, and cans of beer popped, Dasha curled up on the sofa beside her husband, and watched as the compere warmed up his audience for the next presenter.

'. . . Another good reason to have ad breaks,' the host explained, 'is so our guest presenters can spend just a few more minutes talking to their agents and publicists, renegotiating gross points for their next movies, and asking for a last-minute rewrite from a gag-writer who's already spent a year honing down their twenty-second intro speech. Not that our next presenter is guilty of any of that. He probably renegotiated his points a long time ago and, really, he doesn't need an agent, a publicist or a gag-writer. Ladies and gentlemen, will you please welcome . . . Mr . . . George . . . Clooney.'

'Now that's what I call a good-looking man,' said Julie Mulholland as a spotlight picked up George Clooney coming out on stage and strolling over to the glass lectern.

'You already got a good-looking guy,' said Mulholland,

with a deliberate burp from his beer. 'What you want another one for?'

On screen the applause died down and George Clooney began to speak.

'Television is a good place to be,' he began, 'and I should know.' Clooney stood back from the lectern as a surge of delighted applause and a few hoots of laughter rose up from the audience.

'At its very best, television tells us about ourselves, and the world we live in,' Clooney continued as the applause subsided. 'A small screen, maybe, but a very big picture. And this next category, ladies and gentlemen, is about the very best there is – the best television-reporting from the front line, whether that front line is in a war zone overseas or a disaster zone here at home, or out in the wilds where exploration is rapidly turning into exploitation. These are brave, inspired stories that tell us what's happening in our world, stories that pull no punches, stories we should never forget, will never forget. And they're made by people who care enough to do it, by people who sometimes put their own lives at risk to go out there and bring it back for us.'

There was a murmur of approving applause from the audience.

'This year,' Clooney continued, 'the nominees for Best Factual Television Reportage are . . .

'*Lost Landscape – The Northern Prairies*. NBC. Mike Lowe, Adam Edwards, Martin Riley. Producer, Bob Ashley.

'*A Long Way Back – A Veteran's Tale*. Foxhill Productions for ABC. Hamish and Tara Van Gruisen. Producer, Mike Mitchell.

'*Shinnook — When the Waters Came*. CTACtv. Jenna Blake and Pico Ramirez. Producer, Gerry Coons.

'*Sands of Time — The Greening of a Desert*. Zander Productions. Sharon Walker and Clare Musgrave. Producer, Hugo Evans.

'So why don't we all just sit back and take a look,' said Clooney, when the applause died down, 'so we can see for ourselves what "Best" really means.'

The lights in the auditorium dimmed and a giant screen behind Mr Clooney flickered into life . . .

Mungo McKay sat at the bar in Mama Surf and watched the lights go down and the first footage flicker up on to the screen way down the coast in Los Angeles. There was quite a crowd at Mama Surf that night, only the third since Lindie Cass reopened her old tavern on Promenade. It had taken time and money and endless delays but the rebuild was pretty near done, the place laid out exactly how it always had been – the booths, the long bar, the pool table. In the weeks that followed the storm, much of the original wall panelling had been salvaged from the harbour and the beach, brought in with the tides, and on one of these planks, set on the wall above the booths, Lindie Cass had cut a line which marked out the height of the flood that had swept through her tavern that terrible September night.

Mungo had come to Mama Surf alone. He could have watched the programme at home, up in their sail-loft bedroom, but he knew it would have driven Miche from the house. A year on from Cougar Canyon she was still given to occasional tears and sudden shaking, and he didn't want to make it any worse. He'd simply left her a note and come out alone. As soon as the awards were done with, he'd head back and maybe they'd take a cool walk out along the sea wall together. It would do them both good. It always did. Remembering the kids that had been lost and the two new friends that Mungo had made that distant day and would never see again. Right now though, he tipped back his beer and watched the screen with everyone else at the bar.

Gerry Coons didn't do black tie. He didn't do chicken dinners and four sets of cutlery. He didn't do small talk and normally he'd have paid good money not to be sitting where he was. At least, that's what he'd always thought.

But tonight, here in Los Angeles, sitting in the darkness and waiting for the clip of news footage his team had brought in and which he had produced . . . well, tonight had been different. For the first time in his career he was at an awards ceremony, as a nominee, had walked a strip of red carpet in a state of stunned disbelief, and in the last four hours had shaken the hands of men and women he'd grown up watching on the small screen.

Whatever happened in the next few minutes, Gerry Coons was happy to be there, and whatever the result he was proud of his two young reporters and what they'd done. He glanced at them across the table, Jenna Blake and Pico Ramirez. His team. His kids. Just dark profiles in the flickering shadows.

He didn't need to ask how they were feeling – all he had to do was check his own pulse.

Jenna Blake sat as tight as a wound spring. She looked at the tablecloth, she looked at her empty glass, she felt sweat dampen her hot palms and she thanked the sweet lord for darkness. She'd practised her loser's smile so many times that her face ached. She hoped that when the winners' names were announced the smile would just slide into place and she'd applaud Sharon Walker (somehow) or whoever else got to go up on that stage and receive the award from George Clooney – (George Clooney, for God's sake!). Or at least she prayed it would.

But right now, in the warm, lonely darkness, there was no smile. Just a cold shiver of anxiety and dread. Already she could see the TV floor crews closing on the nominees' various tables – including her own. She knew if she looked up now, she'd see a camera jack setting up beside Gerry Coons's chair, waiting for the clips to end and the lights to come up and the winners to be announced – to capture that stricken rictus of defeat on three sets of faces and delirious disbelief on the fourth.

Her heart hammered and her dress pinched and Jenna knew she'd never been so terrified in her life. If she could have directed the action, she'd have made this moment stretch out for ever so that she'd never have to hear the result and deal with the consequences and flash that loser's smile. Or maybe fast-forward a few years so that all this hoopla, all this icy, trembling terror would be just a dim memory.

Beneath the table, pushing aside the starched folds of the linen tablecloth, she felt her husband's hand slide on to her knee. She could feel its heat through the sequins on her dress and she knew that Pico was just as scared and nervous and terrified as she was.

And just when she thought it couldn't get any worse, from every speaker in the house, in front of all these people, Jenna suddenly heard a familiar voice filling the auditorium.

Her voice.

'*The waters have gone now, and a town called Shinnook has gone too. In just a few terrifying hours we watched it die when a raw, merciless Mother Nature came calling. But we survived, and so did many brave, resourceful people. And you know what? So will a town called Shinnook.*'

And then the lights came up, applause swept over their table, and George Clooney stepped forward and opened the envelope.

'These guys sure know how to play it out,' said Mulholland.

'Quiet, Bill,' shushed his wife.

'I can't watch,' said Dasha, covering her eyes. 'I so want them to win . . .'

'Everyone does. And they will, you'll see,' said Zan, and he remembered for the first time in months the sad smile that Shelley Caine had given him in the seconds before she was swept away.

Up on stage, George Clooney slid out a stiff card from the envelope, turned it the right way up, read the words to himself and nodded.

'Well, it's sure the one I'd have gone for,' he quipped. 'And the winner of Best Factual Television Reportage is . . .'

Hushed silence. Time frozen. Just hearts hammering in the darkness.

Mungo felt a hand slide around his waist, saw the ring on her finger, and felt Miche's lips whispering at his ear.

'Have they won? Please tell me they have,' she said.

A big smile broke across Mungo's face and the scars and the creases cut deep paths in his stubble.

'Any second now,' Mungo whispered back, kissing the top of her head. 'Any second now. And I'm glad you made it.'

'So am I,' replied Miche, and her eyes turned to the screen above the bar at exactly the moment that George Clooney leant forward to the microphone . . .

'And the winner is: *Shinnook – When the Waters Came*. Jenna Blake and Pico Ramirez. Producer, Gerry Coons, for CTACtv . . .'

. . . And the Nokia Theater and Mama Surf and every house in Melville and Shinnook exploded with whoops and whistles and applause and cheers . . .

. . . And hot tears spilled for those who weren't there to see it.